for cinzia...
     who connects my dots and makes me whole

Messiah ... Money & Mayhem

DAVID MARCUS GILBERT

is a former chef / restaurateur / hotelier, consultant and food blogger. He has worked in nineteen (19) countries on four continents. Before entering the hospitality industry he was a technology broker dealing, mostly by choice ... on the dark side. His combined careers give him a unique insight and greatly influence his writing. He lives in Italy and continues to travel the world.

Messiah ... Money & Mayhem

2017

1994

Mitchell Krinsky eased the shell white Volvo 240DL wagon into an empty space in the small parking lot that fronted D'Aiuto's Discount Wines & Spirits. His new employer was expecting them for dinner. Karly, Mitch's second wife, had just reminded him again, on his new cellular phone, that they needed to show up with a decent bottle of wine. After the last fiasco, when Mitch had insisted on bringing a royal blue tin of Danish butter cookies, his wife had grabbed the reins. That would not happen again.

" Get a nice bottle. Something expensive. And they always cook Italian."

Karly Krinsky was determined to make Mitchell the Head of Division, a position which had recently been created. This dinner party would be an important opportunity to show his boss that he was ready.

D'Aiuto's was on Route 17, just a few minutes from their house. The illuminated sign out front wished Mike and Diane a

HAP Y 10TH ANNI ERSARY

Even though Frankie Aiello took out half page ads in the Bergen Record it still remained a mostly local shop.

He locked the car, set the alarm and jogged the ten yards across the lot. It was already a quarter of seven, and they were expected no later than eight. The automatic door was still not working after half a dozen repairs. A hand written sign, taped to the glass, apologized for the inconvenience. Mitch pushed his way in and searched for a clerk. He knew nothing at all about wine. Karly'd cautioned him to get some advice.

2

"Excuse me," he said to a guy with a pipe stuck in his mouth, " I can use some help picking out a wine."

" I'm sure you can," he replied. "Why don't you ask someone who works here."

Krinsky shook his head in a sort of semi-apology and spotted a heavyset guy wearing a badge that identified him as " ART - ASK ME!"

" O.K. Art. I need your advice."

" Talk to me."

" Italian, white, not too expensive."

The sales clerk shook his head, knowingly, then turned and headed towards a wall of bottles under a neon ITALY, buzzing in red, white and green.

" Dry or sweet?

" It's for a dinner."

" Dry. How much you wanna spend?"

" That's no problem. I mean, not a hundred bucks. Like fifteen, twenty?"

" Cortese. Same grape as Gavi. A terrific wine. Good as Gavi for a lot less. Let's see."

While the clerk looked for the wine, Krinsky eyed the cashier. He saw the white plastic VISA, like a dashboard Jesus, atop the register. 'Thank you god.' Mitch never had enough cash.

" This is a good one. Conte-Candoli. Goes with everything."

" Fine. I'll take it."

He grabbed the bottle and took his place on line behind the pipe smoker, who was reaching for his wallet. The jerk pulled on the unlit pipe and waited for the cashier to applaud his selection.

" Young lady, I'd suggest you try this Brouilly with a classic ragout of lamb!"

" Ten-oh-eight with the tax."

" Note of vanilla on the finish. That's how you tell the good ones."

" Who's next?"

Mitchell paid for the wine, signed the charge slip and bolted out of the store. It was already five after seven. At this rate he'd have to skip the shower.

" Aw fuck," he groaned. His horn was blasting on and off. That's when he spotted the broken taillight. Somebody had smacked him while he was in the shop. Shards of red plastic covered the ground just to the left of his rear bumper. "Fuck!" he shouted as he slammed the driver's door, killed the alarm and headed home.

Ten minutes later he was in their bedroom, changing his shirt. Karly was pacing the floor.

" I cannot believe this, Mitchell. Sometimes you really piss me off!"

" Hey, it's not my fault that the fucking bridge was backed up. Don't worry. The old man'll be late too."

" It's his goddamn house! He can do whatever the fuck he wants."

" O.K. I'll be ready in two minutes. How's this tie?"

" Awful. Can we please get out of here?"

Nicolas Drago lived in an overstated mock Tudor home. The fourteen room mini-mansion was set back from the road in a stand of Norfolk Pines. Nicky, as he preferred to be called, was a self made man. His business, started from nothing, had grown into the metropolitan area's largest independent shoe chain. With sixty-three stores in three states, he was riding high.

HOMEBOYZ SNEAKER CRIB was a huge success. Other firms had entered the fray, but nobody out-played Nico. He purposely opened his stores in the metropolitan area's most impoverished sections. Drago had once been invited to a New York Knicks dinner and had sat next to the legendary Bernard King. At the time, Bernard was 'The Man' to most inner-city kids. They imitated his moves on the basketball court and whatever B.K. wore, they wore.

"Hey. You that shoe store dude. I recognize you from the commercials." He smiled at Nicolas. "Why don't me and you open some places where kids can buy my kicks?"

" Interesting idea. Let me think on it."

Drago thought on it for the rest of the evening and the following day took Bernard's advice. He began to plan a series of stores selling what the star had suggested. Of course, he never bothered to thank Bernard for giving him the idea and compensation was out of the question. 'Fuck him,' thought Nicky. 'Shoes are my game. Niggers, they got their own.' Ten years later, Nicolas Drago (born Nicola Braggi) was a very rich man with some very ambitious ideas for the future. That's where Mitchell fit in. The shoe king knew little or nothing about sweatshirts or gym shorts but was smart enough to hire some experts. This "garmento" Krinsky was just who Nicky was looking for. He was young, but not too young, and had a good record on Seventh Ave.

"Tina!" No answer. "Tina, goddamn it! Where the hell are you?" Nicolas Drago had treated his wife like shit for the past twenty-nine years. That she stayed with him said more about her than him. "You're a doormat," her brother Vincent told her over and over. Her response was always the same. What was she supposed to do? They had children and good Catholics stayed married, no matter what. That was the way she was raised. Didn't her mother suffer the same way? She put up with him because that's how it is.

" I'm here. You don't have to scream."

" You know how important this dinner is. I got a feeling this kid's gettin' ready to bolt on me. I need him to stay put. What I don't want is he should hold me up. Capish?"

" Whatever it is you want from him, Nicolas, I'm sure you'll get it."

" Just don't open a mouth to him - like the last time. So he brought some kind'a shitty fuckin' cookies. 'Mr. Drago only eats Italian cookies.' He mimicked her New Haven accent. "You made the fuckin' kid turn purple! Just smile and say 'thank you' if he brings 'em again. Whadda' we gonna' eat?"

" Linguine red clams and brajole RED SAUCE. Everything red. What a surprise."

" Hey, I happen to like it. So what's so terrible? I know it ain't fancy enough for your company. They gotta have filet fuckin' mignon. Sue me if I wanna eat like a fuckin' wop, Mrs. French Fuckin' Gourmet. Too goddamn bad. It was good enough for my mother, may she rest in peace. Besides, this is a fuckin' jewboy from Queens. It'll be a treat for him. Like goin' to fuckin' Little Italy for San Gennaro!" She gasped and crossed herself. "Except here we dish it up on china plates."

The doorbell rang, or, more correctly, it chimed. Caterina Drago loved that door chime.

" Leave Maria answer the door," he bellowed from the stairs on his way up to the second floor bedroom. Their dinner guests would be impressed by a maid in uniform. She sighed as their new housekeeper came out from the kitchen to open the heavy stained glass front door.

" How very nice of you to come this evening." Tina, as everyone called her, forced a smile and shook hands with Mitchell and Karly Krinsky. Maria led them into the den.

" Some white wine for dinner, Mrs. Drago." He handed her the bottle.

" That's very thoughtful, Mitchell. I'll just save it for another occasion. We're drinking red with dinner this evening."

Krinsky's chin dropped in the general direction of the marble tiled floor.

" I think my husband meant that we hope you'll enjoy the wine some time - when it's appropriate."

" Yes, I'm sure he did, Mrs. Krinsky. Excuse me just a moment. I need a quick word with the cook."

" The guy at D'Auito's said it went with everything," he whispered to Karly, after their hostess had left the room.

" Mitchell, why can't you just keep your mouth shut? You could have just handed her the bottle, for Christ's sake." They spotted the ornate plaster crucifix at the very same moment. Despite their sniping at each other they both had to laugh.

" Working for goyim. My old man would've shit."

" Shut up Mitchell, here comes Nicky."

Their host bounded into the room dressed in a grey and fuchsia jogging outfit that Krinsky had designed.

" Mitchell! Karly! Glad you could make it."

" A pleasure, Nicky. We've been looking forward to this all week." Mitchell shot her a glance. She'd always called him Mr. Drago.

" Great. Hey, you didn't happen to bring anymore of those cookies, did you? They were pretty tasty. We really loved 'em!"

" But I thought...," started Mitchell. Karly cut him off.

" Mitchell brought a nice Italian wine. Please enjoy it when it's appropriate to what you're having."

" What's wrong with now? I'll go open it up." He left the room, turning back for a second. "You like linguine, right?" Nicky Drago didn't wait for answers.

" **No.** I'm sure he said Jackie Baker. I heard it in the car. Sugar Simms played like twenty minutes of it."

" Sorry, but it's not ringing any bells. Is it old?"

" I don't think so."

" Then I'm double sure I don't have it."

" Anybody else in town, you think?"

" If I don't have it, boss, you're not gonna find it anyplace."

" Maybe I should call the station."

" You do that. Just get me some more information."

" Cool. Thanks, brother man."

' Dickhead,' thought old Lawrence Mack, as the well dressed black man buttoned his Burberry trench coat and left. If there was one thing he had no patience for, it was a stuck-up *nigger* trying to be somethin' he wasn't. 'Brother man' my ass. Oreo piece a shit!"

Axle Green stepped out into the cold Chicago night. His grandfather used to refer to the ferocious wind as "the hawk." He loved that expression. It was so... righteous. Ax was making money. Real money. He was, at age forty, the youngest vice-president at First Illinois Bank. His family finally had someone to be proud of. He'd known, since the first time he'd gone into a bank with his dad, who'd bolted together G.M. chassis for thirty-two years, that this was the job he wanted. His friends had all laughed. Well, they weren't laughing anymore. His income had steadily climbed since joining the bank. Last year he'd pulled in two hundred plus. Axle checked his Rolex Submariner. Right on time. He walked along West Madison, turned right on Michigan Avenue, then crossed the street to the headquarters of First Illinois. He'd jump in his bright red 300ZX and be at Ambrosia by eight. The attendant gave him a wave as he wheeled out from the parking garage under the bank. 'Yes indeed, I love that space with my name on it.' Out on Lake Shore Drive he watched the shivering masses, at war with the brutal cold. 'Frozen mother fuckers,' he laughed, as he tweaked the digital climate control. The traffic was heavier than he'd expected. Joanna would just have to wait. Ah! Joanna. The final frontier. Joanna Van Dorn, as in Benton & Van Dorn, the largest discount brokerage in the United States. There was even talk that they were about to take over a major New York bank. 'Why not make it Benton-Van Dorn & Green.' It wasn't so farfetched. She was crazy about him and her father was so far gone that he couldn't even put on his pants. Their majordomo, Nelson, had assumed that unpleasant chore after Van Dorn's wife had disappeared. Joanna's mother's mysterious departure was something they never discussed. Ax had heard that it had something to do with Scientology. So there it was. Right there before him. Marry the daughter and bingo. She didn't seem to care that he was "a negro" as her mother had referred to him, before she split for England. Or was it Florida at the moment? No matter. Tonight he'd sort of hint at what he knew she wanted. Mrs. Axle Green had a nice ring to it, he thought.

Ambrosia was the best restaurant in Chicago. The owner was an old friend of the Van Dorns and Ax loved the fuss that they made. He pulled the slick sports car up to the entrance and waited for his door to be opened.

" Treat her gentle, my man," he said to the valet, slipping him some skin.

" Sure enough, Mr. G. I'll put her right there," pointing to the most prestigious place. There were customers' BMW's and Jags parked further down the street. But this spot was deliberately left for him. Axle had his secretary drop by at lunch and deliver the man a crisp new fifty.

" Good evening Mr. Green. Nice to see you again." forced the bronzed Maitre'd.

" Good evening Dario. Miss Van Dorn here yet?" Darijo Jervic could barely produce a smile.

" Yes, sir. She's with Mr. Mancini in the bar. They asked that you join them."

" Thank you. I believe I know the way."

" I'm sure you do sir," replied the Serb.

The small space was dominated by an enormous pasta sculpture, framed in gold and hung on the wall behind the bar. Perhaps someday the banker would understand its appeal.

" Axle, darling."

" Mr. Green. Buona sera"

" Good evening Gino." The two men shook hands. Joanna tilted her mouth up and accepted his kiss.

" And how is ChiTown's most eligible and more importantly, most gorgeous bachelorette?"

" Divine, my sweet."

The reality was that Axle was half right. She was certainly the most eligible, if money was the measure. As for gorgeous. Well. Whoever first said that beauty was in the eye of the beholder deserved the Nobel prize for good manners. The nicest thing that you could say about Joanna Van Dorn's appearance was that there was never a hair out of place. Three hundred bucks a pop got you a really terrific haircut. Her hairdresser, Eduardo, whom some snidely referred to as *Mr. Ed*, arrived at her home each morning. Her clothes were bespoke from the best ateliers in Paris. For a hundred and eighty five pounder, this was often quite an adventure.

" Axle, I'm famished. I think we'll just skip the cocktails tonight, Gino."

" Whatever you like, my sweet. I'm actually hungry, myself. We're ready, Gino."

" I'll have Darijo seat you. Buon appetito, ragazzi."

" Grazie, Gino. Molto gentile." Joanna had spent a semester studying Renaissance portraits at the British Institute in Florence. They were escorted into the rococo dining room and seated at a large corner booth. The room was what a certain kind of twit would call "a riot of white and gold." It reminded Axle of some movie he'd once seen, something about a French king, played by what's his name, Rob Steiger.

" Buona sera," smiled a smarmy captain in a Today's Man dinner jacket, appearing from behind a potted plant.

" Buona sera, Carlo. Come va?"

" Benissimo, signorina. Grazie. Hai fame?"

" Sempre, Carlo."

They laughed. Axle might have been just another vase of flowers to them. 'Bitch,' he thought. 'I'll make her beg me for it later.'

" Tonight, as antipasto, we have a lovely mousse di salmone affumicato. Molto delicato. Very delicious. We have a tartare of Sicilian tuna, served with a light, light mint maionese...and an insalata di mare, fresh-fresh. Very nice tonight with red shrimps from Spain."

" Ooh, Axle! They all sound yummy. Let's have one of each. Shall we share?"

" Joanna, order whatever you like." He was still fuming.

" Signorina. For the vino, this evening?" A nice dry white with the antipasti, no?"

" Fine," shot Axle, not giving his companion a chance to reply.

The captain immediately picked up on the vibe. He'd put this clown in his place. After all, the Van Dorns, not this *mulignan*, were his bread and butter.

" Do you have a white you prefer, Signore Green?"

" What do you suggest, Carlo?" Joanna made a noble attempt to save face for Axle.

" Perhaps the gentleman should like to try an Arneis. It would be an interesting choice."

" Fine," growled Axle as the captain turned and left.

" Oh. Poor baby have his feelings hurt?" Joanna grabbed him under the table. In spite of his anger, he immediately hardened.

" Fuck you, Joanna!" She glared at him. He smiled to break the tension, leaned over and planted a kiss on her lips. Not too passionate. But not too perfunctory either. The focus of his thoughts, as always, remained on the corner office at Benton, Van Dorn & Green.

Sometimes shit just happens. Take for example the case of Juan Maria Guizado Barbosa, scion of one of Argentina's oldest and wealthiest families. Juan Maria enjoyed the life of a playboy. He drove a Ferrari Testarossa, had apartments in Caracas, Miami, and in New York's Trump Tower. He'd studied law when he was at school in Spain and considered himself an expert in the Catalan Modernism of Gaudi and all facets of romance. The enormous holdings of his family allowed him to live well without the need to work. On this rainy day he was sitting in the breakfast room of his mother's country home, a few hours outside of Mendoza. The maid had just brought him the latest La Prensa, trucked in from Buenos Aires. He immediately turned to the sports pages for news of his latest polo performance. He scoffed as he read about Raphael Rodriguez and that transplanted Nazi, Karl Gabler. But no news at all of himself. His team was suffering a terrible dry spell. It had been days since he'd made the big city papers. He sipped his feca and picked up another section of the enormous Sunday paper. There on the front of the travel section was a picture that really ticked him off.

12

His cousin Paulino stared up from the page. He was shaking hands with the great El Dulce, Spain's #1 matador. In the photo, "The sweet one" had his left arm around Felipe Gonzalez, the popular Prime Minister.

" That maricon Niño is probably sucking Felipe's fat cock right now," he grunted angrily.

" Dispénseme, Juano?"

" Nada, mama. I was just talking to myself. I'm thinking about going to Spain today."

" Spain, mi cordero?"

" I need a change of scenery."

" You can go to B.A. for that. Why all the way to Madrid?"

" Not Madrid, mama. I need to go to Sevilla."

Once more, he glared at the newspaper. The King, Juan Carlos, who was adored by Argentines of Spanish descent, would be spending a month in the old southern city. He was determined to have his photo taken embracing his majesty. Juan Maria would show everyone which Barbosa had the real status.

" But Juano, I never get to see you. And you promised to stay here all week. You've only just arrived, and now you're off to Sevilla."

" Then why don't you come with me? It will be good for you. That's it! I've made up my mind. You'll come to Sevilla today.

" But Juano..."

" No mama. My mind is made up. Go tell Estella to pack your bags. I'll call for the tickets right now."

She laughed. This crazy son could make her do wild things. He jumped up from the table and crossed the kitchen to the telephone. Juan Maria looked up the number and quickly dialed the phone. He tried Aerolineas first. Their Madrid flight was full. The next call was to Iberia. They had no departures until the next evening. However, if he must go today, they could get him to Rome on Alitalia with a good connection to Sevilla. And yes, first class was available all the way through.

" Bueno. Alitalia esta noche a través de Roma. Si, dos. Si, si, muchas gracias!"

" Mama! It's set. We leave this evening."

Two hours later they were on their way to Buenos Aires. There was plenty of time to make their flight, so Juan Maria let up a bit on the pedal. Their luggage had been sent on ahead, so that they could ride in the small Ferrari in comfort. Mama was never quite comfortable in the close confines of the bright yellow Testarosa, but she loved to drive with her son. They arrived in the city, entrusted the car to one of their housemen and were driven to Ezeiza by Alvino, their city chauffeur, dressed in his crisp grey, black and white livery.

The Alitalia flight left Buenos Aires half an hour late. By the time mama felt properly settled in her seat it was nearly time for dinner. The balding Senior Cabin Manager proffered them menus as well as a glass of spumante. The Ca' del Bosco Brut was flowing freely in the front cabin of the 747. Doña Melina had been sipping champagne since just after nine that morning and was starting to feel the effects. They studied the menu together.

" You must admit, Mama, the Italians do have a way with food."

Juan Maria nibbled on a small mountain of icy orange crab claws.

" Yes, I suppose they do. It's just so....I mean, look at this menu. To serve us turkey at the prices they charge for this ticket. And this one. Stoccafisso accommodato! It says it's "stockfish." Never! I don't feed this to my workers. Call the steward. I'm sorry. This is not acceptable."

14

" It's bacalao, mama. Perhaps they have something else.
Let's find out."

Juan Maria punched the call button. The elegant Cabin Manager
reappeared almost immediately.

" Signore. How may I help you?"

" My mother is unhappy with your dinner selections."

" Young man," snapped the Doña, even though the chief
steward was probably close to sixty. "The idea of serving turkey in
the first class is appalling. Don't you have anything else?"

" Signora, this is not simply turkey. This is cotoletta di
tacchino alla bolognese. One of the most celebrated of all the
dishes from the most splendid city in Italy for dining. Bologna, La
Grassa, signora. Bologna-the fat, as they call it"

" Very well. How is it prepared?"

" Signora this is a dish that is only attempted when the fresh
truffles from Alba are in season. Perhaps we will only be able to
offer this for two or three weeks this year. Truly something to be
savored. The prosciutto ham from Parma, the parmigiano cheese,
the Marsala wine. And the tacchino, signora. I assure you, the
beast is of the very best quality."

" Please. Enough selling. Just bring it and make sure the
meat is well cooked. It's such a filthy bird to begin with. We would
never serve it at home."

" As you wish, signora. And you signore. The same?"

" How is the fish? Is it very dry?"

" Ah! I understand now the problem. The English translation
is somehow not very, how shall I say, appetizing. This is
stoccafisso alla Genovese. A much honored meal in Genova.
Believe me, it is also among the most important regional dishes of
Italy. In fact, this month we honor a different city for each of our
second plates."

" Then I accept. Bring us a good wine with the dinner. My mother cannot take red wine. This evening we shall drink a blanco, something Argentine."

" I'm very sorry, signore. We carry only Italian wines on board. I'm sure that we can satisfy the lady. I'll have my colleague bring the cart to you straight away."

Rémy Limon reached for his cigarettes. "Merde." The pack was empty. He looked at his watch. " Mon dieu." It was past three in the morning. He'd been at these figures all night. The more he looked the worse it became. Sales were dreadful. It wasn't just the weak dollar that was killing his business, it was also the competition. Chile, Australia, even South Africa was getting into the act. Never mind the Italians, with their pis d'caval. They were suffering as much as he was. The very idea that anyone would prefer another wine over his beloved Muscadet was unthinkable. But there it was, in black and white. Sales were down another 9% on top of last year's disastrous slide. What was happening to this world? Ah well, things would be better next year. The head of his coopérative had assured the members, only last week, that something was being done. It had even been on the television. Well, it better be true. There was little time remaining for Rémy. Another year like this and he'd be finished. After five generations there would be no more summer fetes, no more harvest dinners, no more Chateau Gros Limon.

" **Eccola!** Arneis from Cornegliano."
The tuxedoed captain poured a bit of the wine into Axle Green's glass.

" It's fine." The banker nodded his approval after a clumsy swirl and a sniff.

' Like this scimmia might know the difference,' thought Carlo, to himself. He poured them each a half-glass. A waiter appeared with their antipasti and served a bit of each to the couple.

" Buon appetito."

" Grazie, Carlo," replied the lady, as she swallowed a forkful of tuna.

" Mmm. Ax, you have to try this." She pointed at the tuna with her fork.

" Are you sure it's cooked enough? It looks raw to me"

" It's tartare, silly. It is raw."

" Oh," was his feeble response, as she reached for the wine, emptying the glass with one swallow.

" Salute, darling," she laughed.

Joanna was polishing off the remains from Axle's plate when Carlo made his return.

" Buona?"

" Buonissima, grazie."

" Primo tonight, signorina?"

" Si. Axle, feel like some pasta, baby?"

" Whatever you like, Jo. But no more fish."

" Isn't he adorable, Carlo?" She reached out and stroked her companion's cheek.

" Pappardelle, sugo di lepre? Do you fancy lepre, signore?" The captain just couldn't resist.

" Perhaps the gentleman would care for something else...less adventurous." Joanna, again, to the rescue.

" Bring us two," shot Axle, purple with rage.

" Bravo, Signore. The wild hare is very tasty today. Flown in fresh, from Italy" he lied, while pouring the remains of the white wine into Joanna's glass. "Another bottle? "

" No. I'm thinking rosso with the lepre."

" Brava, signorina. Barolo?"

" Don't you think?"

" Ottima scelta. Mascarello '82? Remember? You enjoyed it so much the last time."

" Va bene, Carlo. Grazie."

When the captain left, Axle exploded.

" He's fuckin' with me. He doesn't have to talk down to me like that!"

" Axle, he's doing his job."

" Insulting me is not his fucking job!"

" I think you're just the teensiest bit too sensitive."

" I'm sorry, Joanna. That kind of shit pisses me off."

A strange, far away look in her eyes made him suddenly uneasy.

" Sick," she whispered. "I'm going to be ssss..." Joanna Van Doren collapsed, face down, into the last of the pale pink mousse.

The Air France flight from Paris touched down at twenty minutes to nine in the morning. It was already hot and humid. Léon Drei watched the first of the passengers come through the security doors. After a few minutes he spotted his brother, Henri, looking no different than the dozens of other arriving passengers. This was good. There had been no trouble with immigration or customs. The younger man glanced at him and headed in Léon's direction.

" The car is outside. Everything all right?" They embraced.

" No trouble at all. I have everything with me."

" Excellent."

18

" How was Paris?"

" Meh."

The two men walked, stride for stride through the sliding glass doors, across the walkway, past the uniformed taxi dispatcher and down a short flight of stairs. It was Sunday morning and the airport was surprisingly quiet. They entered the parking garage through an open gate, walked down a line of cars, finally stopping at a black Crown Vic that had seen better days.

" Are we staying in town, or going straight there?"

" Straight there. No surprises, Henri. You know how he gets."

" Right. You'd think, after all these years, that he'd learn to just take it easy. Relax a little. No?"

" Our work's only just beginning. I find it hard to believe that you don't you realize that."

" I only meant..."

" It doesn't matter what you meant. You don't get it, do you? You and me, we don't count. We're worker bees. Don't ever lose sight of that. Look, Henri, I'm not criticizing. You're a good boy. But this is war. You see how he is. He knows. It wouldn't hurt to act like him. Be pious, but be strong! "

" You're right Léon. You're always right. That's why I love you. You and the others. Since the very beginning."

" We're going to succeed, Henri. Then you get your reward. Like it's supposed to be. So, tell me. Was it hard in Paris? They treated you well?"

" They don't seem so serious."

" It will be easier for all of them. Once he's here. When the Moshiach..."

" How long do you think before...?"

" Soon, Henri. Very soon."

Giusy Brunetta glanced in the mirror then dropped the Dior compact back in her purse. She put the bag, an old Valentino, from when he was still doing designs for the airline, into the storage bin under the galley sink. She undid the wheel brake on the first class cart and pushed it into the aisle. Were these getting heavier, or was she getting older? Ten years ago it wasn't such a struggle. That was how long she'd been walking these aisles. How many kilometers did they say they walked on the South American routes? Ten? Lately it had felt like a hundred. She'd taken this job to land a rich husband but so far she'd only been promised. "I promise to call you," and "I promise, I'm not married." Each time she felt it was going to be different. That 'this one is really sincere.' But in the end they were all alike. Just like the one in 3B. The purser had asked her to give special attention to Sig. Barbosa, who'd been VIP'd by the Milano operations desk. Guisy shoved the drink cart past two aging Cardinals, seated in 2A and B.

" Signore, Signora, some wine with your dinner?" She flashed the smile that had won her Miss Vibo Valentia 1981.

Juan Maria looked up, shot her some cuff, exposing an overstated Hublot gold and diamond watch.

" Si, cariña. Por favor. Mama, some wine?"

" Whatever you like, Juano. These airliner wines all taste the same to me."

" Tell me, linda, what do you like?" He leered, as if he already knew the answer. She looked back at him, as if she'd never heard it before.

" It's what you like, signore, that's important to me."

" Very well then, something with a nice long finish."

" That excites the back of the throat. I have just what you're looking for."

Giusy reached for the Villa Valente Gavi and poured a taste for Don Juano. He sampled it slowly. His eyes never left the woman.

" As delicious as you are beautiful."

" Si, squisito da vero, signore."

She filled their glasses, turned away and offered her wines to the priests. Juan Maria did not merely undress her with his dark beady eyes. This kind of man prefers the tongue. Like a lizard eating an insect. That was how Barbosa enjoyed devouring his women.

The Cabin Manager delivered each of them a small garlicky bagna caöda.

" And this is what?" She pointed to a crisp piece of cardoon on her plate.

" This is cardo from the Monferrato. An essential part of the dish, signora."

" Take it away now. It looks rotten!"

" As you like, signora."

" Don't you have caviar? Or is that not Italian enough?"

" Let me have a look."

" Dios mio, Juano."

" What is it, mama?"

" As I said before. This was a mistake. I should never have allowed you to talk me into this trip. A vegetable like this...served in the first class. This would not happen on Aerolineas. Italians! How did they ever conquer the world?"

The steward returned with a tin of osetra caviar that the crew had put aside for themselves.

" Signora. I hope that this will be more to your liking." He presented her with a generous portion.

" That's much better. And another glass of wine for my son. If it's not too much trouble."

21

" Subito, signora. I'll be back in a just a moment."
Suddenly, the Argentine's eyes widened for the last time in his life.
He turned towards his mother. At that same moment, Piero
Selvatico, Alitalia's most senior flight attendant, was looking stage
left towards Giusy Brunetta as Don Juano took his final bow.

At the Centers for Disease Control, Keshore Patel returned the
letter he'd just received to its envelope. His uncle certainly had a
gift. He could write like the great Vishnu poets. And such joyous
news! Keshore's nephew had been appointed as an Associate
Professor in the chemistry department at the University of The
Punjab, in Lahore. And at age twenty-five! So wonderful was this
news, that he decided to take the letter with him to lunch and read it
over again. Keshore opened his desk drawer and took out the foil
package his wife had carefully wrapped. Curry egg was his favorite
treat. Everyone in the staff cafeteria knew when she prepared it. He
got up from his chair, turned off the desk lamp and walked across
the room.
 " Ready, Luis? It's already past twelve."
 " One more minute. I'm just finishing up this report."
 Keshore paused for a moment and gazed out the window at the
broad expanse of lawn. The winters in Atlanta were milder than any
he'd seen in the six years he'd spent in New York. It was already
November, but the grass still remained a luxuriant green. His friend,
Luis Vega-Llosa, who'd gotten him this post, missed his old
hometown. Brooklyn had been a frightening place for Keshore
Patel, but to Vega-Llosa it was heaven on earth. The two men
strolled the length of the hallway, their arms linked loosely together.
They stopped at the elevator and waited patiently. It was rush hour.

" Keshore! Just a second. There's a phone call for you." The voice belonged to one of the woman who covered the lunch hour switchboard.

" Thank you." He picked up a desk phone, and tapped the blinking button.

" Dr. Patel here...Yes, I'll hold...Tommy, what a nice surprise! How's everything in Chicago? Breezy, as ever? Ha! Ha!...I see...I understand...Yes, of course...Send me a fax as soon as your tests are complete...The sooner the better...You too...Regards to your lovely bride...cheers."

" Leong?"

" Yes. It seems that a young woman died last evening. In some fancy restaurant. They suspect it may be MITH."

" Anyone else affected?"

" No. That's the strange part. She wasn't drinking alone."

" Not so strange. I've seen cases where you have a single *vic* and everyone else is O.K."

" Not much consolation for the d.b. I'm anxious to see the tests. I'll bet five dollars they were drinking an Italian wine."

" You'd think those people would have learned a lesson."

" No bet, Doctor?"

" No way, Jose."

Nicky Drago grabbed a handful of shucked littlenecks, opened his mouth and tossed them in. He raised his eyebrows and smiled.

" Hey, I just opened those clams. Lay off Mr. D! That's for your dinner."

" Sorry, Paulie. I couldn't resist." Maria's husband, who did the cooking and drove the Drago's Mercedes, smiled and shook his head. He loved the job, loved the boss and if he wanted the clams, hey - no big deal.

" Tina, whaddya' do with the kid's wine?"

" It's in the icebox. Why?"

" I just thought since he brought it, it would be nice if we opened it up."

" With this dinner?"

" Hey, ask me if I give a flyin' fuck. They brought it. We should at least drink it. Maria bring a tray wit' some glasses. Tina get your ass out there and be nice."

" What ever happened to please? Maria, we need four glasses - in the den, *please*."

Nicky opened the fridge, grabbed the bottle and headed back to the Krinskys. Mrs. Drago followed him out.

" Here we go! How's about a nice icy-cold glass'a wine?"

" Sure, Mr. Drago."

" Hey, how come Karly calls me Nicky an' you're still with the Mister Drago?"

" O.K. Nicky, it is. Whatever you say, Mr. Drago."

" Just gimme a second here. Friggin' corks. Easier puttin' it in than takin' it out. Eh, Karly?"

" For god sake, Nicolas. Can't you be civilized for once in your life?"

" Just jokin' Tina. No harm, no foul...eh, honey?" He squeezed the arm of his guest just a little bit too long.

" It's fine, Mrs. Drago. I'm used to it, living with Mitchell."

" Got it!" Nicky uncorked the wine and poured each of them a glass. He looked at the label. "Corteeze. Didn't he discover Miami?" Tina just winced.

" Nicolas, I think it's pronounced core-tay-zee."

" O.K. Mrs. Knows Everything. Why don't you just cor-taste it for us."

" Whatever, Nicky." Tina sipped and then swallowed. Her face contorted as if there was something rancid in her mouth.

" Is there something wrong with the wine, Mrs. Drago?" Karly sounded panicky.

" It's fine, doll. My wife was just makin' a joke. Right babe?" Mitchell turned around just in time to see Tina hit the floor.

" Oh my god! Mrs. Drago! Somebody call 911."

Luis Vega-Llosa tore off the fax, ripping it almost in half.

" Jesus. This thing can print a picture from halfway around the world. So why can't it cut the paper straight? Patel! You got another poisoning!"

" What's that? Luis, bring it here, please."

" It's confirmed. MITH again. This time in Jersey."

" Same as yesterday? Italian white wine. Same brand? How many...? "

" Hold on. Let me read. What was the one in Chicago?"

" Luis, just give me the fax."

" Just the fax, ma'am," imitating Sgt. Joe Friday, which he thought was very funny. "This is the city, Los Angeles, California. I carry a badge." Keshore quickly scanned the report while his colleague cracked up laughing.

" Not the same wine, according to this. But definitely chemical poisoning. Very fast acting. This time in a private house. Four people. Only one *vic*. The others never even got the chance to taste it."

" Something's wrong here, Patel. Don't you think this is odd?"

" How so?"

" Two confirmed deaths in two days, one in Chicago, one in New Jersey. Two different kinds of wines. Something's screwy here. Looks to me like tampering, not contamination."

" Unless the same company makes them both. But I agree. The T.V. is already screaming for recalls and..."

" They're right. We've got to get this stuff off the shelves."

" So only these brands?"

" I see what you're saying. What about the police? Anything from them?"

" The usual. It's under investigation."

" So what do we do? Just wait? You can bet the Director will be on the phone asap."

" I say we do nothing for the moment. We can't just pull everything off the shelves."

" Patel. There's going to be shit storm. A big shit storm. The media is going to have us for breakfast. Two dead white women. Poisoned. We need to do something fast."

" O.K. You're right. Let's recommend a recall on both brands. That will at least buy us some time."

" I'll get started on the paperwork."

The sun was setting on Léon Drei as he put down the International Herald Tribune. There it was on the top of page five. **NEW TROUBLES FOR ITALIAN WINE**. He smiled. This time they wouldn't be able to cover it up. The American buyers would run like rabbits.

" Henri. Come here and look what we've accomplished."

The young man sat down, perused the story, his face breaking into a grin.

" I don't believe it. This is better than we hoped for. They're taking it right off the store shelves. God Bless America."

26

" It's just the beginning."
" Has The Rebbe seen it?"
" I'm sure. He looks at all the papers."
" How does he have time?"
" It makes you feel proud, no?"
" What a stupid question. Of course it does."
" The Moshiach, Henri. He's coming."

   The Italian Trade Commission occupies space on New York's most prestigious thoroughfare. The commissioner, Giangiacomo Rossetti, surveyed Manhattan from his sixteenth floor window. This morning, he'd gotten word that this little nothing recall was causing panic at home. Orders had been canceled, not only from the U.S. but from all around the world. 'Porca miseria! It doesn't make sense. These two small producers make wonderful wines. There is no reason for them to play games. Those stronzi back in the 80's - they were making shit, so they tried to put one over. But Villa Valente and the other? They had such good reputations. Their market was completely secure. They didn't! They wouldn't!' Something was wrong here. He'd spoken to both producers himself. Each one assured him that the wines had been tainted after they'd reached the U.S. Rossetti believed them. He'd said as much yesterday evening, on Nightline. But it hadn't made a difference. In the eyes of the American consumer, Italian wines were no longer safe to drink. This time it would be hell to smooth things over. At any moment they'd be calling from Roma. His ass was hanging out on the laundry line. He might as well pack his bags. The phone on his desk rang once.
       " Roma's on the line for you." He reluctantly reached for the phone.
       " Pronto."

" Rossetti?"

" Si."

" My name is Baglione. I'm an investigator in Roma."

" What can I do for you, Commissario?"

" Ah. But it's what I can do for you."

" Please don't tell me. My son is in trouble again."

" I'm not that kind of policeman. I work in agriculture."

" Excuse me, but today I don't need any eggplants. I have other things on my mind."

" Yes some unpleasant business."

" You know something about this?"

" It's my job, after all."

" Please Baglione. Don't torture me. I'm being recalled, too. Like the wines. That's what you've rung up to tell me."

" Relax. I have good news for you. There's been another poisoning."

" Dio cantante!"

" Rossetti. Are you still there?"

" I'm here. I'm here."

" Yes? Good. Now, about this poisoning. This time on Alitalia."

Gegè, as everyone called him, groaned and reached into the top drawer of his desk for the Maalox.

" And why, please tell me, is this good news?"

" I'm getting to that. The latest case took place on a flight that terminated here. In Roma. We had the body within a matter of hours. The stomach works quickly, but our forensic experts were able to examine the contents. Your poison was not the dreaded MITH that everyone is convinced of. Rather, it is a similar chemical, used in the manufacture of certain fertilizers."

" I'm still waiting, Baglione. What is this good news?"

" This particular product is not used in Italy. In fact it's not permitted."

" And..."

" Aren't you curious as to where it is made?"

" Please, I beg you. Don't drag this out."

" What would you say if I told you it's only manufactured in one factory - in Lyon."

" You mean this poison is French?"

" Precisely. And very tightly controlled."

" Grazie, dio!"

" Oh, but there's more."

" Go on."

" The company that makes it uses most of the product for its own internal consumption. That is, in the further manufacture of other products. Only a very small amount is sold outside the firm."

" And you've found out where it went?"

" Very good, signore. You'd make a good detective. I mean, not to say that your present position is in danger. I don't pretend to know everything. Anyway, getting back to my point. The small amount of this chemical that does not go into this internal production was shipped to only one small user in France." He paused.

" Yes! Yes!"

" How is your French? Never mind. This one's easy to understand. The customer's name is like this. Please forgive my deplorable French pronunciation.

" Go on."

" The customer's name is Union Cooperative de Viticulteurs Muscadet."

" Mamma mia."

" It gets better. One week ago, in a speech broadcast all over his district, the head of the co-op announced to his people that the white wines of France would soon be making a comeback in the market. That better days were ahead, and soon. He did not go into any more detail. So what do you think about that, eh? Rossetti. Are you there?"

The collection of weary travelers, sitting in the USAir lounge had little to do but watch TV and drink their gin tonics. As usual, air traffic was awful at this hour of the day. Why anyone flew in or out of LaGuardia in mid-afternoon was a mystery. The CNN news endlessly repeated the top stories. A laundry worker at a Houston hospital had opened fire on his fellow employees, killing three and injuring sixteen. A congressman from Washington State had drowned in a rafting accident on the Snake River. Citrus growers were marching in D.C. protesting a hike in rail prices. October unemployment was up.

The bartender handed over another tepid can of Miller Lite and the mixed nuts were still soggy. Just another rainy, New York Friday.

Two men in hats sat at a table nervously eyeing the clock. Their flight to St. Louis was delayed by an hour. At this rate they'd get there in darkness. The larger of the two men tipped the last of the sparkling water into his glass. He'd be glad to get back home. One more Marriott was just about all he could handle. Tomorrow they'd fly back to Europe.

" Léon, this rash is driving me crazy." He drank the remains of his water.

" Cheer up. We did really important research in Florida. Better even than they hoped. Maybe it's just a sunburn?"

" Do I look like a beach boy to you?" said the other man, glumly.

" I beg your pardon. Standing in a field with a Tupperware full of flies is not exactly a week at The Fontainebleau. But we weren't there for vacation, boychik. Right? Henri, look. It's all just a means to the end. What do the Americans say? Don't worry. Be happy. It's good advice. You should take it."

" Do you think they'll cave in on the prices?"

" Deigeh nisht! - Don't worry! Katz says that we're good with that committee. Better than good. Six years, it's taken. But there's no longer any doubt. It's a cinch."

" I hope you're right. If it works."

In his dream, a large creature was astride him, head back, snorting and panting wildly.

" No. Please. I give up. No more. You're hurting me," he murmured, the sleepy mumble of an overworked policeman.

" Eh, Corrado, you used to like it like this. What's happened to you?"

The detective opened his eyes and looked up at his wife's flabby chin. She rolled off him, sweating, and sponged herself dry with the sheet.

" What time is it?"

" Time you acted like a real man." She pulled at him, trying to get him to enter her again. He looked at the clock.

" Porca! I'm late! The train leaves at nine. I'll never get there on time."

" Relax. So what if you get there late."

" Someone from the embassy is meeting my train. Do you know what will happen to me if I'm not on it. They all have sticks up their ass. Besides, I don't know how to get around that blasted city.

By the time I found my own way, it would be after they all went home."

" Why are they sending you to Parigi?"

" It's that business with the wine. I'm supposed to clean up the mess."

" Why should you have to fix it?"

" Rosalba, it's my job. They shit, I wipe."

" You deserve better, Corrado. Twenty one years you're a policeman. When will they ever promote you?"

" Please. Not that old song again."

" You want to know when? Never. And I'll tell you why. You have no balls. You lost them years ago."

" Basta! O.K!" He jumped out of bed, whacking his toe on the frame.

"Porco zio!" Baglione grabbed his foot and hobbled into the bathroom, slamming the door behind him. He held his head over the tub, grabbed the hose and turned on the water. Nothing happened. Not a trickle, not a noise. For the second time that week there was no water. He cursed Rutelli, the new mayor, and walked back into the bedroom.

" No shower again, huh? Poor old policeman. Has to go off to Parigi all sticky."

" Vaffanculo." He put on his uniform for the trip to Paris and checked his appearance in the full length mirrored doors of the mid-century, plastic veneered guardaroba. 'Not bad,' he thought, for a middle-aged cop from a poor Salernese family. He was still lean, unlike many of his colleagues. His wife wasn't much of a cook even though her mother had labored in the kitchen of a white tablecloth ristorante in Naples for much of Rosalba's childhood. The only decent meals these two ate at home were cooked by the detective, who fancied himself a "buongustaio." She was a looker when they'd first met. It wasn't until they were married that he understood she was no Artusi in the kitchen. Baglione, dark skinned, neat moustache, with a proud aquiline nose and full head of chestnut brown hair had resembled the leading men in popular Italian films. Films that they often went to see while they were dating. Women still gave the policeman more than a second look. Corrado quickly packed a small suitcase and left their third floor walk-up, slamming the heavy wooden door behind him. The early morning smog was already choking the city. His junior was waiting in the bar downstairs.

" Buongiorno, capo."

" Buongiorno, Pippo. Up early this morning, eh?"

" Si, capo. You haven't got much time. The train waits for no one. Isn't that what they say?"

" Let's go then. You can jerk off after I leave."

" How long will you be gone?"

" No more than two days. Speriamo. You know how those French can be."

" I've never been to France. In fact, I've never been anywhere. Not like you."

" Tell it to my wife."

" And how is the signora this morning?"

" Grassata e arrapata. Fat and horny. Just the way you like 'em. Eh, Pippo?"

" It's true what you say. But don't worry. Your wife is safe with me."

" Why don't you go back and give her a toss after you drop me at the station?"

" Give you the horns, capo. Never!" A smile crossed his face. It was just what he had in mind. They pulled up to the station with plenty of time to spare. Corrado stepped out of the car, grabbed his suitcase and walked up the stairs. His second in command saluted and then drove off. The investigator glanced up at the board and laughed. The 09:05 train to Parigi was two hours and ten minutes 'in ritardo.' However, he could board the 06:30 train which was still waiting in the station. Baglione swung himself up into the first class carriage.

" Biglietto, signore. All seats are reserved," smiled the grey jacketed head conductor.

" Here you go."

" Ah, I see that you are early and, as happens sometimes, we are late."

" Good for me. But not so good for you. Eh, capotreno."

" I must disagree, signore. This is my train, early or late. I'm afraid that for you, the news is not so good. Your seat is on the following train. So please be so kind. We must get under way at this moment."

" But surely you can take me. I have a ticket. You have a train. We are both heading in the same direction."

" Yes, but this train is an Intercity. You must pre-book or you cannot ride, Signore. Mi dispiace."

" Capo," smiled Corrado, "perhaps you can somehow bend this rule for an officer of the government who is travelling, in uniform, on official business." He showed the man his I.D. and smiled.

" Commissario, it is my pleasure to make your acquaintance. Now if you will just remove yourself from my train, we can proceed."

" Surely you can agree that I am the one who is on time. I have to be in Parigi by six this evening."

" Then I suggest you take a plane. Now get off!" The trainman was about to lose his temper.

" Hey, fratello. No need to get so excited. Why don't you call for a policeman? I think I can help you there."

" Vabbè. We go with you, under my protest! Don't think you're getting away with this. I have your name!"

Corrado was staring at the large vein in the man's forehead. He had never in his life seen one so ready to burst.

" Cretino," muttered the conductor." Thinks he can walk over me. We'll see about that!"

Commissario Corrado Baglione, the Senior Investigator assigned to the Agricultural Ministry, fighting for a train seat. Maybe his wife was right. After twenty one years of dedicated service, he still hadn't gone very far. Top man in a department of two. Not even really a department. Just two cops permanently assigned to ICRF, a subdivision of a subdivision of the Ministero delle Risorse Agricole, Alimentari e Forestali, to be used as the bosses desired. In Italy, the government changes almost with the seasons. But the civil servants, lolling about in the trenches,
they're in it forever.

" **Bonsoir,** monsieur. Paris-Lyons. Monsieur, Paris, Gare de Lyons."

Corrado opened his eyes and looked out. The train had come to a stop. He stood up and almost fell to the floor. His left leg had fallen asleep. He fumbled around above the seat for his suitcase and cap, which he took great care positioning just so. He was not an elegant man but he imagined himself as having a bit of panache.

" Commissario?"

" Si."

" Claudio di Pisa. From the embassy."

" Piacere."

" Piacere." They shook hands and walked towards an exit.

" And Pisa, it's also your birthplace?"

" Si, signore. I come from the family that ruled the city."

" Quattrocento, if I remember my history from school. I'm honored. Royalty is usually met. Very rarely does it do the meeting."

' Terrone for sure.' Lazy and full of himself and most definitely from the south, thought Claudio of Pisa. The embassy car was parked right in front of the station. Driver at the ready. The two men climbed into the back seat of the blue Citroen XM.

" How do you like this car, di Pisa? I'm thinking of getting one, myself."

" I wouldn't know. It's my first time in this one. Usually I drive myself in a Panda. But you must be important. We got a message that a *vip* was arriving from Roma today. So here we are, you and me, with the big car and the flag."

Corrado concealed his smile. He'd sent the dispatch himself. If only Rosalba could see this, maybe she'd get off his back.

" As requested, we've booked you into the George Cinq. Must be nice to have privileges, eh Signore."

" Grazie, Claudio. Yes, I've always enjoyed that hotel." Several years before, he'd taken a coffee in its airy garden cafe.

" I'm afraid that the Ambassador has gone home for the day. He'll see you first thing in the morning. And now, if there's nothing else, I'll say good-bye."

" Just one more thing. Does the Embassy maintain an account here?"

" Of course. Your bill will be seen to. By the way, if you're going to eat in the hotel, I'd recommend their poulet de Bresse."

The customs agent opened the suitcase, grimaced at the dirty clothes and waved the Orthodox Jew, with his long payess and beaver hat, through without speaking a word.

" I told you Ruud, they think we're animals. Did you see how he looked at the valise? I'm telling you, if the drug smugglers were smart they'd hire *us*." He laughed and slapped his companion's back.

" I hope our little friends are still alive,"

" Ruud, you're a worrier. Just like your mother."

" She worries about you too, Mr. Wandering Jew."

" Hey. A few more days and we'll be home. Now let's go wake up these tiny fellows. They have a lot of work to do."

" Do you think it will go ok? Will they do the trick?"

" Don't k'vetsh so much. They'll do it. Now let's go."

" There he is. There's Ruben."

A tall, thin man stood next to a cream colored '72 Grand Safari. The fake wood panels had mostly peeled away from the doors. They shook hands and got in. The driver started the engine and gunned the big Pontiac out of the lot.

" Would you like some air-conditioning?"

" Terrific," replied his passengers, in unison.

" Who wouldn't. Unfortunately it doesn't work. Like everything else in this farkakte country."

" Let's go right away. Out to the melons. I want to get rid of these flies."

" Ruud, we just got here. Can't we stop for a bite?"

" Our friend has packed us some food. Didn't you, Ruben?"

" Look behind the back seat."

" You see, everything has been planned. How's your brother?"

" Léon is Léon. How far do we have to go?"

" Just a few hours. We take the road up the coast."
Everywhere they looked there were cherry trees in bloom.

" What's in the basket for us, Ruben?"

" Take a look. I'm not sure."

" Henri, only a Frenchman would think of his stomach at a time like this."

" I can't help it. I haven't eaten since New York."

The flight to Santiago had been a long one and LAN CHILE was not renowned for their food.

" Look at those shacks. How can people live like that?

" They're like your schvartzes in America, Ruud. They have no choice."

" Mine? I don't think so," he chuckled. " I might live in Brooklyn but I'm Dutch, remember? Dutch, as in Holland."

" You call this lunch?" Henri was examining the contents of the basket.

" It's not so easy to keep kosher here."

" I'll be so glad to get home. Ruben, can we make it there and back today?"

" I think so."

" So we can leave tonight, Ruud?"

" Our tickets are for tomorrow. On the KLM."

" Ruben, is there a plane tonight?"

" There's always LAN to New York."

" That would be so much better," Henri replied. "We can change planes easier at JFK."

" Henri, eat some fruit and relax."

Two hours later they were surrounded by vast fields bursting with melons.

" Pull up there, Ruben. We can make like we're stretching our legs."

The driver did as he was told. He eased the big station wagon off the road. Henri opened the suitcase that customs had been loathe to touch and extracted two flat, square Tupperware containers. They had been modified slightly, to keep the contents alive.

" Everything alright?"

" Yes Ruud. It all seems to be ok."

" Good. Open them up."

Henri walked a few steps, removed the lids and shook out the flies. They quickly disappeared into the fields.

" Let's get out of here. Ruben start the car. Henri, get in. We can't afford to be seen here. In a few weeks time, the USDA will be all over these fields. And the Canadians and the French. Everybody. They won't be able to give these melons away. O.K., Ruben. Give it some gas!"

Baglione walked deliberately along the Rue Lauriston. He crossed the Avenue Victor Hugo looking for Osteria Nardini. He spotted the sign and walked in.

" Bonsoir, monsieur."

" Buonasera. Nardini, si?" The maitre d' smiled and pointed to a second door. " Mi scusa. I thought this was..."

" Bon appetit, monsieur.

He ducked out of Bistrot l'Etoile and into the connecting doorway.

" Bonsoir."

" Buonasera. Sono Baglione."

" Oui. You are expected."

Strange, thought Corrado as he looked around. There must have been a hundred straw covered Chianti bottles lining the walls. There were the requisite red and white checked linens and across the back wall a mural depicting a faded Grotta Azzurra. He wondered why di Pisa had sent him here. The waiter nodded and he was seated.

" Francais, Anglais. No Italiene."

" Va bene. I'll take a Punt e Mes, no ice and a piece of orange."

" No Punt e Mes, Campari. Same thing"

" Fine, but I assure you, they are not the same."

" Only Campari."

" Ok. Campari con tonica. You have tonica, si?"
The waiter shook his head and dropped a menu on the table. Corrado was thinking of when and how he would strangle that asshole di Pisa. He glanced down at the cover of the menu. Mustachioed chef, twirling a pizza. The choices consisted entirely of what the French perceive to be Italian food. His waiter returned with the drink.

" Ready to order?"

" I take the hearts of artichoke wrapped in Italian ham with olives and carrot stick," he laughed, reading straight from the menu.

" Anything else?"

" The spaghetti 'bolognese style' served with grated parmesan cheese."

" Anything else?"

" The veal cutlet marsala served with fried potatoes."

" Chianti, half bottle?"

" Splendid."
Baglione looked around the room. An idea popped into his head. He got up and walked towards a sign pointing down to the toilet. Just next to it was the door he'd come in through and beyond that l'Etoile. Without glancing back he left fake Italy and returned to real France.

" Monsieur, it's nice to see you again."

40

" Grazie. You knew I'd be back?"

" It has happened before."

" I have just tonight in your city. Can you make it memorable?"

" Avec plaisir. Please follow me."

He showed the policeman to a choice table and offered some suggestions.

" If I had but one meal to eat, monsieur, this is what I would do." He suggested a soup made with green lentils from Puy which was delicious. It was followed by a pot au feu trois viandes that reminded Baglione of a good bollito misto. A bit of two year old Comté Fort Saint-Antoine from the Jura, served with a dish of toasted walnuts, then a spectacular tarte aux pommes to end the meal. He enjoyed the last sips of a lovely '88 Boutignane Corbières. Well fed and pleasantly drunk, Baglione insisting on personally thanking the chef. These French, thought Corrado, are not so bad after all.

The car stopped a few hundred meters up the road from the farmhouse. Two men, dressed in black, opened the car doors as quietly as they needed to, then slowly approached the house from the side.

" What kind of farm is this? No barking dog..."

" Léon took care of that yesterday."

Indeed he had. The big blond Labrador had been fed a handful of contaminated sausages by a substitute postman. Not lethal, but just enough to land the dog in clinic.

Fernand Huber had been a farmer all his life. His family had grown grapes in the region for generations. They made no wine, except a little for themselves, selling most of their fruit to the local coopérative. In fact, Fernand had recently been elected head of the growers' organization. As the vines on his farm began to wither and die, Huber became increasingly desperate. His entire life's savings were invested in these vineyards. Without a decent crop he was sunk. A month or so back, a man had appeared on Fernand's doorstep. He needed some help and was willing to pay. If it were possible for the co-op to sell him a small amount of Dizactin, a chemical they used for research, the man would be happy to help Fernand with his problem.

" No, no, monsieur. It's not allowed," he'd told the stranger. "To obtain this...it's not easy. It would be impossible to divert even a small amount." After hearing how much the man was willing to pay, Huber changed his tune. "Perhaps just this once I can find a way."

Dizactin is a quirky substance. Used properly, it can increase the yield in dozens of crops. It had but one nasty side effect. Some plants, mostly grapes, could occasionally concentrate the chemical in one or two clumps on the vine. If you ate them or drank them you would feel the effects almost immediately. Strange effects. It could be nothing more than a mild stimulant to some and immediately fatal to others. For this reason, it was strictly controlled and had been banned in almost every developed country. France, being France, refused to go along with its neighbors. The authorities maintained that it had great promise and gave beneficial results when used in a proper manner.

Huber's cooperative, the only "test" customer, was required by law to account for every gram and to keep a government chemist in house. With all these precautions, how was Fernand to deliver? It took some planning but he eventually figured it out. He solved his problem in a low tech, old-fashioned way. He stole it. Or actually, he made it look like it had been stolen. Everyone was shocked and distressed to learn that the stuff had been filched. For weeks the authorities had questioned everyone in the co-op, especially Huber,

42

without concrete results. Just when things seemed to be turning back in the farmer's favor someone had poisoned his dog.

As he lay there in bed, he dreamed of his favorite French actress, Simone Signoret.

" Ready, amigo?" The tall Salvadoran, a professional killer now living in Galicia, had been hired through a series of intermediaries. He nodded to his partner and carefully tested the window at the back of the house. It was not locked. They'd been told that Fernand lived alone.

" Let's do it." The second man, a Frenchman, ex-militaire of Moroccan descent, steadied a packing crate as the paid assassin eased himself into the bedroom. The accomplice passed a wooden club up and through the window and in an instant, the killer landed a blow on the sleeping farmer's temple. Then two more blows! The life went out of Huber. After taking a few minutes to ransack the house, to make it look like a robbery, the two men were back in the car and on their way to Paris.

At the embassy, Baglione was accorded all the honors due his rank. The Ambassador had another engagement and could not see him. His deputy was also unavailable. Even di Pisa had pressing business and regretfully would not be able to brief him. He did leave a thin file folder with some sketchy information about the movement of the chemical, Dizactin, and instructions with the garage to provide the inspector a car.

Half an hour later Corrado was on his way to the town of Chasseloir. He studied the road map and shook his head. It didn't look possible to drive there, nose around and return to Paris that evening. He would have to re-think his plans. Midway there, near Le Mans, he stopped for lunch.

The sign on the highway offered gas, food and rooms. Baglione parked the embassy's Clio next to a large black motorcycle. He admired the big Harley-Davidson as he walked toward the restaurant entrance. There were several other similar machines lined up along the front. Probably some kind of club. He stepped through the doorway and into 1950's America. The music assaulted him first, the greasy food patiently waited its turn. The Italian took a seat at the stainless steel counter. Baglione, on the thin side at five feet seven and graying at the temples in brown slacks, white shirt, and olive silk sport coat did not look like a French biker.

Everyone at the counter was eating, smoking, or both. Corrado smiled when the gum cracking waitress dragged herself off her stool to find out what he wanted. He pointed to a chalkboard behind the bar.

" Cali-burger. Bon." He pointed to a bottle of beer sitting in front of a very young blond at the end of the counter.

" Puis-je vous acheter une bière, mon oncle?" laughed the girl's ponytailed companion.

" Pardon. Non parlez Francais."

The man from Rome knew enough French to understand the general tone of the curse that someone mumbled behind him. He heard a bottle break. Baglione got up slowly, turned, then made a run for the door. He blasted through it without once looking back until he'd locked the doors of the white Renault and driven off. He was sure that he was about to be a dead man. When Corrado realized that no one had followed him out, he began to think that maybe he'd over-reacted. That the broken glass was an accident, not a threat. Now he felt totally ridiculous. And hungry.

At a quarter past five, he reached the offices of the Union Caves Cooperative de Viticulteurs Muscadet.

" Bonjour, madame," he said to the high mileage redhead at the reception.

" It's mademoiselle. And it's bonsoir. Do you prefer French or English? I'm afraid I speak no Italian."

" English, then. And how did you know I was Italian?" The woman offered her 'what else could you possibly be?' expression.

" How can I help you?"

" I'm Baglione. I believe that the embassy made an appointment for me with your boss."

" But Monsieur. You did not receive our message? Our poor Fernand was killed two days ago by robbers. In his house. We've been closed here since it happened. I've just now re-opened the office." She wiped her eyes with a lavender scented handkerchief. Baglione thought they might be lover's tears.

" Oh. Mi dispiace. I'm sorry. I didn't know. I received no message. If I had known I wouldn't have come all this way. I mean, I wouldn't have troubled you so, so soon after the..."

" It's alright. I could use some company right now."

" You two were close, then?"

" Like peas in the pod, monsieur."

" Perhaps you would like to close up early and join me for a bite of supper. It will take your mind off him, off...things I mean."

" That's very kind of you, detective. I'll just get my coat."

   Forty minutes later they were in bed. Her soft, fluffy, down filled, wrought-iron bed.

" Mademoiselle, that was delicious."

" We French are known for our cuisine."

" Your cuisine is magnifique." He kissed a flabby breast. " And your wine cellar," as he felt for her under the duvet. "And your..."

" Stop! I have no more rooms. This inn, monsieur, is totally full."

" Speaking of which, I must find some accommodation for this evening. I'm afraid that I am required to speak to you, on an official basis, tomorrow."

" Why not stay here, cheri? This evening, you can interrogate me as you like."

" Mademoiselle. The Italian taxpayer thanks you and I accept your gracious offer. On one condition."

" Which is?"

" You must allow me to treat you to the most splendid dinner in the Loire. How does that sound?"

" Delightful. I know the place."

And she did. They ate oysters. First, a dozen Quiberons, while knocking back a Muscadet Sur Lie. Then a dozen Cancales, just so Corrado could try them. They shared a chateaubriand and drank a local red called Pineau d'Aunis that was made by one of the lady's friends and very delicious. For dessert, a caramelized apple souffle with a dollop of calvados creme.

The following morning, they dressed quickly and quietly.

" Tell me about Monsieur Huber."

" What is there to tell? He was a nice man. And then some bastard killed him."

" Was he acting strangely before he..."

" ...was murdered. The answer is this. Fernand always acted strangely. If people only knew."

" Strange behavior in the office?"

" No, no. In the office he was a perfect gentleman. Always it was about the business. No, cheri. It was in the bedroom..."

" I don't think I need to hear about this. I'm interested only in the affairs of the co-op. What do you know about this chemical, Dizactin, that you use for testing.

" That again. We've already told the police and the persons from the dangerous...something bureau. I forget the real name - everything that we know."

" Why are the police asking questions?"

" The robbery, cheri. I thought ..."

" What robbery."

" Someone broke into our laboratoire and stole this… this Dizactin. One week, no ten days ago."

" What do the police have to say?"

" They have no answers. It's a mystery."

" And now, Huber, the head of the co-op, is murdered. Does anyone, besides me, think this is strange?"

" But his house, it was robbed. There was no reason to suspect..."

" No reason! What kind of police do you have here?"

" We are a small village. There is only one..."

" I must go at once to his house."

" Fernand's house?"

" Si, Fernand's house! There's got to be a connection between the two cases. It's too much coincidence. A good detective does not believe, never believes, in coincidence. Come. We'll go now. I'm sure you have a key to the house?"

" Of course I do."

" Yes, you would."

" What does that mean?"

" Please. Take your coat and let's go."

" Oui, mon capitaine!" She jumped to her feet, clicked her heels and saluted.

The drive to the house was a short one. The poor woman was distraught. Here she was, three days after the murder of her lover, two days after his funeral, walking into his house with a man she'd known for less than twenty-four hours. A man who had already shared her bed. It was really too much for her.

" What's wrong, cara?

" What's wrong? Are you serious?"

" I only meant..."

" Huber is dead, murdered in his sleep and here I am, before his poor body is even cold, using my own key to his house to show it to a man I've already made love to, who still doesn't have the good manners even to ask me my name. And you ask me what's wrong?"

" Liliane. Your name is Liliane Portier. It was right there on your desk."

" You're a liar. There's no sign on my desk."

" I read it off a paper."

" Upside down! You were reading my personal papers? How dare you do such a thing!" She stomped off in the direction of the house. Baglione followed her. There was some yellow tape and a sign, handwritten, on the door informing all that this was a crime scene and no one was allowed inside. She'd just put the key in the door to open it when Corrado realized what she was about to see. He tried to stop her. But it was too late. There was blood everywhere. And the place was a mess. It looked like a robbery-murder. No doubt about that. All the evidence pointed to that. Everything, thought the inspector, except the nagging coincidence of the theft at the co-op. Something was wrong here.

" Liliane, I'm so sorry. I shouldn't have brought you here."

" Oui," she said dazedly, "you shouldn't have."

He took her outside. She took several deep breaths of air on the porch.

" Sit down over here." He took her arm and led her to a faded plastic lawn chair. She sat and stared out at the yard.

" I wonder what's happened to Jules? I hope someone remembered him."

" Jules?"

" His dog. Fernand's dog. It was poisoned a few days before...before..."

" It's still alive?"

" Yes. Taken to the clinic. Poor thing ..."Her voice trailed off. Liliane was really shaken by what she'd just seen. 'Now this...this is a woman,' thought Corrado. Not like his own wife, the conniving bitch.

Arthur Morrison couldn't bring himself to call them peep shows. They were his "diversions." Something to take his mind off the increasing pressures of his position as head of the United States trade delegation at the GAAT meetings in Geneva. The stubbornness of the bureaucrats in Brussels, who wouldn't bend on farm subsidies, had endangered the whole accord. There were some in Washington who were screaming for sanctions against the Europeans. The new administration did not show any signs of backing away from the threat of a major trade war. He'd better be tough if he wanted to keep his job. Fucking French. They were the cause of the problem. The luxury tax had softened them up by devastating their perfume sales. But it had not been enough. He needed a knock-out punch.

The Ambassador dropped a token into the slot. The metal shade jerked and rose slowly, revealing a sleazy sexual tableau. A slightly overweight teenage girl with pimples on her chest was reclining on a pink pleather couch. A towel under her ass kept her from sticking to the plastic. She rolled her tongue from side to side and stroked her crotch with a detached up and down motion. Occasionally she inserted a chipped red nail that was glued to the end of her right index finger. Morrison reached for the phone. He put the handset to his mouth, waited for the girl to pick up and then whispered.

" I miss you, sweetheart."

" School will be over soon, daddy." She knew the drill. Arthur was one of her regulars.

" What shall we do when you come home for the summer?"

" Whatever you want me to do."

" Will you suck my cock?"

" But daddy, it's so big."

" You'll do what I say. Or I'll.."

" Spank me. Ooh. Not that. It hurts when you do that."

" But you like it. Don't you?"

" Well. It does make me wet. What else will you do to me, daddy?"

" I..." The metal shade dropped and she was gone. He fumbled in his pocket for another five dollar token. The curtain rose once more.

In a van parked across Eighth Avenue, two men sat and listened. The bug was working beautifully.

" That's revolting. Disgusting."

" Yes, but the quality of the recording is outstanding. No?"

The tape would be played for Arthur Morrison and certain demands would be made. Custom duties on wines from Europe were about to double, putting increased pressure on the better producers.

Baglione ordered a croque monsieur, surprised at how good his French was becoming. He sipped his wine and looked around the café. It was a typical workingman's place, the kind that was disappearing at an alarming rate in France. Too bad, he thought. This was the soul of a country. The door opened and a uniformed man appeared.

" Uff. The postman returns. Michel, where in hell have you been?"

" Flat in my bed."

" What happened to you?" asked the barman.

" Something I ate."

" Your relief man told us you were sick."

" Damn American food. Last week, along my route, a truck was parked in the road giving free samples. Some kind of promotion for the 'real Coney Island hot dog.' I ate two of the little bastards. That afternoon, mon dieu, I was dying. Food poisoning, the doctor told me. Out of work for a week. I tell you, I've learned a lesson."

Corrado sat at his table and listened.

" Excusez-moi," he asked, in passable French.

" Oui, monsieur."

" By chance, is the Huber farm on your route?"

" Oui. A terrible loss, his death. I saw it on the television."

" Yes. Murdered in his bed. A terrible way to die."

" Strange, monsieur, how anyone could get in that house. His dog is a terror. I leave his mail outside the fence. No one can enter that yard."

" Yes," said Corrado. "A strange coincidence."

" Monsieur?"

" First you are poisoned by someone you don't know. Then the following day, Huber's dog. And finally, the man is murdered in his bed, with no dog to protect him. Thank you, monsieur. You've been most helpful."

" Not at all."

" Oh, by the way, monsieur postman. Your replacement. Do you know him personally?"

" No. A new man. Sent from Nantes. Never seen him before."

The figures were encouraging. Domestic market share for the fledgling kibbutz, turned winery, had gone from less than three percent to almost fifteen in just over two years. But their main competitors still easily dominated the Israeli wine business. Carmel had been around since 1882, when Baron Edmond de Rothschild founded the winery as an opportunity for Jews escaping the pogroms in Russia. To its credit, Carmel had begun to change with the times. Their traditional sweet kosher wines were gradually being replaced by the dry table wines the market now favored.

Kibbutz Shofar Vineyards owned a good chunk of land on Mount Hermon, in the occupied Golan Heights. It was a well established fact that the area was suited to growing wine grapes and it was fast becoming a center of attention. At elevations around two thousand feet, emigres from California had planted thousands of acres. Moshe Segall, a UC-Davis trained winemaker was in charge of Shofar's production. His Sauvignon Blanc and Chardonnay were considered among the country's finest. But the domestic market was small. The kibbutz soon realized, as Carmel had learned early on, that the U.S. was where they needed to sell. Of course, there were other places where Jews demanded their meshuval treated wines. For a wine to be considered 'kashrut' it must be handled according to the code recorded by a sixteenth-century scholar. These laws, called the Shulkhan Arukh, require that wines must be produced and even opened and poured by observant Jews. Meshuval process wines are a modern, rabbinically engineered compromise. Through a high temperature pasteurization process the final product can be handled by anyone, allowing the kosher producers to sell to a much wider market. Carmel had pioneered a new technique for making drinkable meshuval wines. The trick was to modify the heating process which normally damaged the freshness and flavor. Shofar merely ~~copied~~ emulated the industry leader. Now they were poised to enter the volatile international market.

Across the world, in places like Australia and South Africa, other producers had much the same idea. The wine wars were heating up. To the Israelis at Shofar it was war like any other. The stakes were high and whatever it took to come out on top...

The drive back to Paris was uneventful. He'd amused himself with a bit of food shopping along the way. As Baglione pulled into the embassy garage his mind was racing. He now knew for sure that something wasn't right. But what had he really learned? Someone wanted the wine drinking world to believe that the Italians were up to their old tricks, spiking their wines with MITH. The culprit was, in fact, a distant relative of the chemical - used only in France. A small quantity was unaccounted for, stolen from a winemaking cooperative whose director had been murdered. Someone had set out to sabotage the Italian wines. Someone clever. Make it look obvious and then not so obvious. He was really no closer to the truth than when he'd first been assigned the case. Di Pisa was waiting for him in his office.

" Baglione. Please sit down."

" What have you learned?"

" Always cover your ass." The young attache snickered in the detective's direction. "I checked with the postal authorities in Nantes. Just as you asked. The replacement for the sick mailman was a local. A permanent temporary worker. So French. Don't you think?"

" Too bad for us, eh Di Pisa."

" Maybe not. The substitute left his job right after Huber was killed. No good-bye and no trace."

" The civil service must keep records. Surely..."

" Of course. His name is Herbert Blomstedt. Age thirty-one. Six years on the job. No trouble. Kept to himself. He was sent to replace the regular postman by the supervisor in Nantes."

" Have you interviewed this boss?"

" I tried."

" Let me guess. He's also disappeared."

" Retired."

" To where?"

" No one knows."

" That's impossible. If he's retired he's sure to get a pension. Find out where the checks are to be sent."

" I'm ahead of you there, capo," smirked the aristocratic Tuscan. "A postal box, here in Paris."

" Find that man. He's our only lead at this point..."

" D'accordo. I agree. It's all we have."

Sirens wailed outside the General Motors building in Manhattan. Hardly anyone paid attention to this urban soundtrack. Each man entered the room and drew a breath, as if entering a holy place, then found a seat at the old oak library table. They could easily have passed for scholars. Although all were in their thirties and forties, to a man they looked much older. These seven men. There was no conversation among them. No handshakes. No simple greetings. No exchange of pleasantries. They sat and waited in silence.

The door opened again. A tall man with a neatly trimmed salt and pepper beard, dressed in brown slacks and cream colored sweater quietly entered the room. He took his seat at the head of the table.

" Good day to all of you. Reports, please " he said in a low unaccented voice. "Let's begin with Florida."

A heavyset man with old fashioned glasses and an unruly gray mustache cleared his throat and began.

" Everything is going as we planned. Our man on the railroad commission pushed through the rate increases you asked for. The price of oranges in the northeast will rise very quickly."

" Rise enough that we can be competitive?"

" I believe so. Yes."

" Would you briefly explain this to everyone."

" As you all probably know our product can now enter the U.S. duty-free. The waiver was granted in exchange for our government making certain "concessions" regarding our Lebanese neighbors. Our votes in the Knesset were crucial to the Americans' peace plan. We gave them willingly...after the trade agreement was signed."

" Won't the Florida growers smell a rat?" asked the man at the head of the table.

" Good question. The provisions of the new pact were far reaching. Our waiver was just a pimple. The numbers involved are of little importance to anyone but ourselves."

" So how do we benefit?"

" Over the long term. We take one small step at a time. You'll see. It will work in our favor. I know my business."

" This commissioner who fixed the freight rates, what about him?"

" He'll retire. For health reasons."

" And then?" asked the man in the cream colored sweater.

" His family will bury him and collect a substantial inheritance."

" I see. Now, Italy. Tell us what's happening."

" It's as we expected," replied a second man, similar in appearance, dressed in a grey chalk-stripe suit.

" Their sales were hurt by the publicity surrounding the tainted wines. Now with the imposition of the new import duties they will really start to feel it."

" Let's not get ahead of ourselves." The man known to them as "*The Builder*" rubbed his eyes and wrote himself a note. "How about the acquisitions?"

" In the works. When the big producers begin to feel the squeeze, we'll step in and offer them a very fair price for their holdings. In my estimation we can control five to ten percent of the Italian industry within five years. Their government is so focused on their own corruption and hanky-panky, they won't act to stop us."

" The same will be true in France," interjected a third man. "The new tax will kill their exports. And...we already own most of their paper." Banc Lucien Battenburg, privately owned by the Milstein family, had lent aggressively in the past ten years and now dominated a sector previously controlled by Credit Agricole.

" Ruud. What about Chile?"

" The flies have reproduced at a rate even we couldn't imagine. They must like the climate. Our lady friend in the USDA, says they'll move this week to ban the fruit entirely. Their season will be a disaster. We can raise our prices on the melons we already produce and then offer to buy their existing fields - for a song."

" What about the Chilean government? Those Chicago boys are not stupid."

The Builder was referring to the disciples of Milton Friedman's Chicago School of Economics, many of whom had returned to Chile to join the new administration's team.

" They are anxious to buy our technology. We can help them with the approvals. Believe me, they won't rock the boat."

" How about New York, Mr. City Councilman?"
The son and grandson of orthodox rabbis tipped back his grey fedora, fixed his gaze on the men at the table and spoke slowly with a thick accent that belied his history. Born into a rabbinical family, Dov Tolchin had lived his whole life in Borough Park, Brooklyn. The folksy Jewish lilt to his speech was no more genuine than his Pierre Cardin necktie.

" Gentlemen..." He paused, like the seasoned public speaker that he was. "Our illustrious mayor will serve only one term in office. His distinguished career will end with the next election. After the riots start up again, he'll be lucky to get a forty share of the vote."

" I'm impressed, Dov. You handled it well. Have we taken care of the other one, what's his name?"

" The schvartze from Inwood. It's a done deal. We're giving him City Council President."

" Is that such a good idea?"

" Don't worry. It's pretty much a ceremonial job."

" And the Italian?"

" He'll withdraw. I can promise you that. Our man's as good as..."

" ...good as...or?"

" I give all the credit to his father."

" Sol Baum doesn't do anything for just credit."

" How soon after the son's in office can we expect to see results?"

" A year. Maybe two at most. He's a loose cannon, the son. We need to watch him very carefully. At this point all anyone talks about is that ridiculous hair comb of his."

The Builder was silent. Everyone at the table sat motionless. He finally raised his head and spoke.

" Next year, after things have settled, we'll move into Spain and California. You've all done well. The Rebbe's very pleased. In fact, I have personal messages for each of you. Pick them up from Sylvia on your way out. Gentleman, we meet again in four weeks time."

On the journey back to Roma, Baglione began to sort out what was happening. He needed a lot more information. Perhaps the post office thing was a start. But that was in France. And he could only push so hard there. He'd have to find a link. Some common thread. Ah well. For now he was content to ride this train and think. Alone and in peace.

The detective was a train lover. He took them everywhere. In a train a man could do some serious thinking. He extracted a plastic sign from his briefcase which he'd had made up years ago. In three languages, like all good railway signs, it said:

IN QUARANTENA - QUARANTINE - QUARANTAINE

The sign looked very official. Even the French train staff were reluctant to enter. Corrado hung the plaque on the door and stretched out. He'd passed up a trip on the TGV for this slower regional train. Nice was still six hours away. He'd change at the border, in Ventimiglia, for the train to Genova and then on to Roma.

As the countryside rolled past his window, Baglione unpacked his **alpitour** tote bag and spread out a picnic lunch. That morning he'd stopped at a farmer's market in Chartres on the road from Nantes to Paris. The four hundred kilometer drive was perfumed by the various treats that he'd shoved into his overnight bag. Now Baglione was ready to begin the feast. He unwrapped a pair of small goat cheeses, a Crottin de Chavignol and a Sainte-Maure de Touraine. Next came a good chunk of saucisson and some thin slices of air cured ham. When the train stopped in Lyon, he'd raced off to buy freshly baked bread and a small jar of rillettes in the station. Lilianne had presented him with a nice Muscadet. He'd had it chilled and opened by the train's voiture-restaurant barman who'd delivered it (and a proper glass) just minutes before. The policeman poured the wine, a Louis Métaireau '91 Sèvre-et-Maine, swirled then sniffed. The aromas put a smile on his face. Usually these French whites smelled strongly of hay and horse piss. He tasted. Creamy, dry, a bit of salt on the finish and really delicious. Baglione would have to reconsider his opinion of French wines. Perhaps there were one or two decent ones, at that. He wondered how much the wine had cost. Probably too much for Mlle. Portier.

The Chavignol had ripened a bit on the trip to Paris. It choked the Métaireau. A choice had to be made. Corrado thought for a moment and flipped the cheese out the window, right above the warning sign about not doing just what he'd done. He settled back and finished the bottle of wine. 12% wines rarely made him tipsy. Well, maybe a little.

Baglione found himself staring at the discarded cork. That's it! Somehow, they'd managed to compromise a cork. This is how he'd find those bastards. Find out who'd tampered with the wines and he'd have his answer. Quickly he pulled out his rail map and studied the route of the train. Nice to Ventimiglia, then Genova to

Roma. The inspector made his decision. He'd get off in Genova, rent a car and drive up into Piemonte. The three tainted bottles had all been produced there. On the map, the town of Gavi was not so far from the coastline. He'd go there first. Then on to the tiny frazione of San Lorenzo. A check of his notes showed him that the Roero Arneis, the one that had killed the woman in Detroit, came from a village near of the town of Alba. That would be his third stop.

Wizman, *"The Builder,"* reached for his pipe, an old Ben Wade meerschaum, and his tobacco. He tamped the Davidoff Black Cavendish blend into the bowl and lit it. Claude Roland Wizman had spent his childhood in an orthodox Canadian family. His father was a strict follower of a very narrow doctrine. Young Claude had a rebellious streak, not enough to move outside his religion, but enough for a few small deviations. His mentor was from a radical group with an intriguing view of the future. They followed a man whom they believed to be a savior. The Messiah. After earning his MBA in Economics from HEC, Montréal, Wizman left Canada for New York City, where he met the *chosen one* in person. After their first meeting he'd made a decision. He would devote his life to that man. Claude had the mind of a chess player, someone who could think through several problems at once and devise an equal number of viable solutions. His ability to retain whatever he read used to be called *photographic* but was now labeled *eidetic*. The young man got things done. He learned early on not to reveal his nastier side and, although it was never said, the elders preferred to remain in the dark. This suited Claude. He realized that if they knew too much, they'd never approve of his methods.

He stood up and stretched. *The Builder* had been in the chair for hours, going over every detail in his mind. Other groups around the world, like the various Islamic Jihads, concentrated on acts of terror to accomplish their goals. Wizman's plans were always founded on sound economics and, more importantly, his organization had the necessary financial resources. He dismissed other movements but confessed to a grudging respect for the new generation of Italian mafiosi. They understood that legitimate business interests, combined with political clout, made formidable enterprises, with the use of violence only considered as a last resort. And of course, Claude's movement had The Rebbe. Their secret weapon, the one who legitimized their activity, was none other than God himself. Or at least his representative here on earth.

Wizman opened his closet and ran his fingertips over the perfectly folded stacks of sweaters - cotton, wool, cashmere, silk, nearly all with Bergdorf Goodman labels. They were arranged by fabric and then by color. After careful consideration he selected a beige cotton v-neck from the hundreds laid out on their custom built shelves.

Claude *The Builder* was an enormously complex man. Relaxed and refreshed by his meditation among the sweaters, he returned to his agenda. The culmination of twenty-five years of thought. When the Messiah returned… they would be ready.

The sun was rising as the train approached Genova. The Stazione Principe is of indeterminate age. The tracks and platforms are shabby but clean, the signage - late twentieth century. Baglione took down his quarantine sign and carefully stowed it away. He gave the remains of the roast chicken he'd purchased in Nice to a disheveled man on the platform.

The detective descended the stairs and walked through an underground passage. He emerged in the main station hall. Looking around, he spotted the string of car rental booths.

Bypassing Avis and Europcar he stopped at the window of LiguriaAutoRent. Just the kind of place he was seeking.

" Buongiorno," he said loudly. The girl in the booth had her eyes closed. Her headphones bounced to a beat. She did not acknowledge his jaunty good morning. Baglione reached over and switched off her Walkman.

" Ma va'! What's this?" she demanded.

" I need a car. You rent cars. So here we are...together."

" You want a car from me?" The girl was used to watching everyone queue up at her better known neighbors.

" Si."

" For how many days?"

" Let's say two, maybe three."

" Seventy-five thousand per day. That's twenty-five thousand less than the others."

" Charge me an even one hundred thousand per day " said Corrado, pulling a government charge card from his wallet.

" What! Are you crazy? You want to pay more than I ask?"

" I think you know just what I'm saying. Don't act so surprised. Put it in for three hundred and we split the difference. Capisci?"

The girl smiled. She wasn't so naive. This was standard procedure with these low level government types. She did such a deal at least once or twice a month. In her estimation, no one got hurt. The taxes in Italy bled everyone dry. This was just a way to get something back. A tax return, if you like. She looked at the Ministry of Agriculture credit card and laughed.

" At first, I thought you were Fiamme Gialle. You look like one, you know." The financial police often patrolled the station.

" Guardia. Me? That's a good one." Baglione chuckled and pocketed his thirty seven thousand five hundred. He'd treat himself to a decent spumante before leaving the station. He signed the credit slip then returned his license and charge card to a battered leather billfold. She handed him the keys.

" It's the white Panda just across the road. The one with the broken window. Fucking football 'ooligans, here from England for the partita. Where's the vigili when you need them?"

" Grazie, signorina." He scooped up the keys and headed for the nearby station bar for his spumantino. He hoped it wasn't one of those new style places with no character and high prices. It unfortunately was. Baglione entered and ordered a glass of sparkling wine.

" Senti. This is the best you have?"
The barman looked up with tired eyes.

" Belin. This is Stazione Principe, not the fucking Via Veneto."

" It tastes like last night's puttana."

" Mine or yours?" laughed the man returning to his pale pink *Gazzetta dello Sport*.

" Grazie per niente."

" Niente, grazie."

The policeman stopped briefly on his way to Gavi for a few bites of farinata, a local favorite and something he'd only ever read about. The flat pancake is made from chickpea flour, oil and water and is Genova's second most beloved snack(after focaccia). Baglione watched with great enjoyment as the cook removed the day's first enormous copper pan from an ancient wood fired oven. After eating he returned to the car and sped off. After a few confusing turns he joined the motorway near Sampierdarena. The oil left on his hands coated the steering wheel, making a general mess of the thing. He muttered to himself and pulled off at the first rest area he came to on the autostrada. He wiped the wheel with a piece of paper which did no good at all. Finally, in desperation, Corrado pulled out his shirt tail and did the job properly. At Busalla, he exited the A7 and followed the signs. The road to Gavi twisted through the hills that extended up from the sea. It was a beautiful drive which he enjoyed immensely. From the pretty town of Voltaggio, Baglione called Villa Valente, one of the poisoned wines' unlucky producers. They would see him after lunch. Since no invitation was extended, he asked for a recommendation. Perhaps there was a nice homey trattoria near-by? They, instead, directed him to a proper ristorante called La Filanda. A San Carlo potato chips driver pointed him in the right direction.

" Buongiorno."

" Buongiorno. Posso mangiare?" The waiter nodded and showed him to a table.

" Today we have a funghi salad. Porcini and ovoli nostrani."

" Per me è buona."

" Poi?" asked the waiter, sensing an eater.

" Primo?"

" Ravioli, u tuccu. Fatto in casa." It was a statement, not a question. "Acqua?"

" Gas. Vino bianco...Gavi Villa Valente. C'è?"

" Certo." The man sang his approval.

He returned immediately with the wine and poured Baglione a glass. In this part of Italy there was no ritual opening. All wine was good or it wouldn't be offered. An off bottle was very rare. Baglione took his first sip.

" Buono."

" Si, ottima scelta, signore. You made a good choice."

" Too bad about the publicity, eh?"

" Peccato. A shame for such a good maker. Signore Mario, himself, eats here quite often."

" How does such a thing happen?"

" Good question. How? It's simple. Someone doesn't like him."

" Why do you say that?"

" He's rich. The wine is his hobby. He doesn't do it for the money."

" So others resent him."

" Perhaps, signore. It's happened before."

" Tell me about it."

" I only mean that such things could happen. Please excuse me."

Another waiter brought the policeman his funghi. Baglione turned his attention to the mushrooms. They were delicious. The two different varieties, foraged that morning, were drizzled with a delicate Ligurian oil from Balestrino. He wondered if they'd sell him a few liters to take back to Roma. The first waiter returned with his pasta, but didn't utter a word. To Baglione, he now seemed very wary. Maybe he'd asked too many questions and his accent was not from here. As befitting the dish in its birthplace, the ravioli was exquisite, filled with lean pork, beef and sausage and a hint of borage and marjoram. U tuccu, the Genovese style meat sauce, was perfect. Baglione ate every bite and then wiped the remaining sauce with a piece of crappy local bread. He picked up the wine bottle and examined the remains of the capsula, the part that covered the cork. He remembered hearing, from a winemaker friend in Lazio, that lead was now out of favor. Too unhealthy. He looked closely. No identifying marks on the dark green plastic. Very easy to duplicate. It would not take much to remove the covering, inject the Dizactin right through the cork and seal it again. In fact, it could probably be done without having to remove the capsula at all. The question then became where and when was it done, and by whom? He hoped that Villa Valente could shed some light. But, truth be told, he had no real expectations. This was going to take some work. Baglione swallowed another mouthful. The wine was wonderful. He examined it more closely. The color was like straw, the perfume, like wild flowers. He sipped. The taste was fresh and long lasting. The finish was soft. There was no sweetness at all, just a hint of apricot that he found very pleasant. Baglione closed his eyes and enjoyed it.

" Signore." The waiter had returned. Corrado opened his eyes.

" Sorry. I was enjoying the wine."

" I could see that." He laughed. This guy wasn't so bad after all.

" Secondo, signore."

" What do you think?"

" Faraona with carrots from our orto."

" Fiducio. I trust you."

The plump guinea hen was spectacular. Baglione left only the bones. Then it was on to dessert. Torta di nocciole. Hazelnut cake, dry as dust, followed by a coffee. The waiter also brought him a pale gold barrel-aged grappa, made from moscato, in a town called Silvano d'Orba.

" Do you like the grappa, signore?"

" It's excellent. Can I buy it from you?"

" Why not! We're lucky to have two great distilleries so close by. I'm sure that we can sell you a bottle."

" So who's in the kitchen?"

" My brother. He cooked your lunch today."

" You own this place?"

" The two of us. With help from our mama."

" Complimenti."

66

" Grazie. Molto gentile, signore. Un altro?"
" No, no. Basta. I still have to drive."
Baglione paid his bill, shook hands with the man, and left. A bottle
of grappa and a bottle of olive oil in hand. Now back to work.

In another dining room, in Atlanta, Georgia, Dr. Keshore Patel
finished his vegetable soup. He studied the lab report. The results
were conclusive. The remains of the wine, sent from New Jersey,
had not been tainted with MITH, as the preliminary findings had
hinted. No further incidents had been reported. The Italian analysis
had been right about the Alitalia death. It was definitely a poisoning.
Caused by a substance they identified as Dizactin.

Baglione drove from Voltaggio to Gavi, missing the turn-off to
Monterotondo for Villa Valente. He asked for directions at a bar and
after a quick caffè he was back on the right road. The winding lane
was flanked on both sides by vineyards. This was some of the best
grape growing land in Italy. The white Cortese grape had been
planted in the area hundreds of years before, but only in the past
twenty years had the name Gavi joined the ranks of the finest white
wines in the world. Just when the policeman thought he'd missed it
again, he saw a sign for Villa Valente. Baglione pulled up in front of
a set of massive wooden gates. He spoke into the intercom,
identified himself, and the doors slowly opened to reveal a
magnificent villa and gardens. To the right was the winery,
separated by stables from the imposing, cornmeal colored main
house. He remained in the car until someone appeared and
showed him where to park. A young woman, the daughter of the
owner, shook hands and asked him to follow. As they entered the
old stone building, Baglione noticed two things. The familiar strong
scent of grape juice immediately piqued his senses. The gentle

swing of the daughter's behind (lato or side B to Italians) also caught the inspector's attention.

" Stefania." They shook hands.

" Piacere. Corrado."

" My father is expecting you. He is very sorry that he could not invite you for lunch. There were clients here from America."

" That's quite ok. I had a delicious meal at the place he recommended."

" Cantine del Gavi?"

" No. Filanda, if I remember. Does that sound right?"

" Si, si. It belongs to our cousins. Did you have the ravioli?"

" Si. Strepitoso. And a bottle of your wine."

" It will please my papá."

" He must be quite upset about the poisoning?"

" Certo. The Americans who were here today are his importers from New York. I think they brought him bad news. I skipped lunch at the table. I didn't want to be there."

" It's certainly a shame. Do you suppose it could have been done by someone who disliked your father.?"

" It's true that some of the local people are jealous of us. You know that we are relatively new to this area. My father was born in Rossiglione, still in the province of Genova. But for some of these locals it might as well be the moon."

" Can you think of anyone who would intentionally set out to ruin your father?"

" Perhaps I can answer that better." Mario Parodi stood in his office doorway, smiled and extended his hand.

" Mario."

" Baglione...Corrado." Stefania quickly disappeared.

" Commissario, please come in."

68

" Your estate is quite magnificent. As is your charming daughter."

Sig. Mario did not acknowledge the comment. So Baglione left it alone.

" Would you care for something to drink? Perhaps a glass of wine?"

" I've just had a fantastic bottle of yours at lunch. Complimenti. I enjoyed it very much."

The wealthy winemaker smiled.

" And what did you drink?"

" La Villa. A most extraordinary wine."

" Molto gentile, Corrado. Grazie. Then I insist you take home a gift. I'll have a carton put into your car." Mario knew how to play the game.

" I regret the circumstances of my visit. Did the Americans give you some bad news?"

" You don't waste words, do you Inspector?"

" So what did they tell you? That our beautiful Italian wines are no longer so beautiful?"

" Perhaps...for the moment. But as soon as the public understands that the wines were not tainted for business reasons, that this was an isolated instance, a terrorist act..."

" That's interesting. Why do you call it terrorism?"

" Isn't it obvious? Someone is trying to ruin the reputation of our wines. All of our wines, not just my own. If that is not terrorism, I don't know what else to call it."

" Any ideas about who it might be?"

" Many. But first let's have a drink of something new. I'm interested to hear your opinion."

" I'm flattered. And I'm ready."

Parodi picked up the telephone and asked for a bottle and glasses. After a few minutes a man appeared. He was introduced to Baglione as Villa Valente's enologo.

" Giovanni Buonanno, Commissario Corrado Baglione. The detective is here to talk to us about...well you know what it's about."

" Si. An unpleasant occurrence for Signore Mario. Unpleasant for all of us."

" Of course. Your reputation, as the winemaker, most certainly could be damaged."

" One hopes not. Those who know understand that we are also the victims."

" Have you thought about how it could have been done?"

" I have thought of little else. Since it was only one bottle. We hope it was only one. The poisoning, it could have happened anywhere. The Alitalia hostess, even she could have done it."

" Perhaps. However, that doesn't really make sense, in light of the fact that there were three separate incidents. Three different wines. Conspiracy is a rather strong word. Nevertheless, I rather discount the idea of anyone at the scene of the crime being responsible."

" So," added Sig. Mario, "the wine must have been tampered with somewhere in the line of distribution. We sent 360 bottles by truck to their catering at Fiumicino. That means it could have been the driver or an employee at Alitalia."

" Or someone here." Baglione was looked for a reaction, however tiny it might be. An acknowledgement that perhaps he'd hit a nerve. As an investigator he liked to allow the conversation to run its course. Sometimes he learned more from what they didn't say. Italians were famous throughout Europe for their body language.

" Surely you don't think anyone at..."

" Gio, the Inspector is simply making a point."

70

" That one of us... but why? For what reason?"

" Enologo, who had access to the wine here? During and after bottling?"

" Not so many people. Maybe we should have a tour. So you get a better picture."

" I was just going to suggest that. By the way, this wine is very interesting? What is it?"

" Do you like it?" asked Giovanni.

" Well..."

" Be honest," laughed Sig. Mario.

" It's different. But, really, I'm sorry to say that I don't like it."

" Bravo," said the two wine men in unison.

" It's chardonnay from California. We like to play this little joke sometimes. Congratulations, you have a good Italian palate. Now let's go look for the bad guys."

They descended a narrow set of stone steps to a cantina under the main building.

" Here is where we do tastings and entertain."

The large room, with brick walls and vaulted ceilings, was charming. A fireplace and a wood oven dominated one end of the rectangular chamber. They walked through it and down another three steps to an open door which led to the bottling room. Giovanni Buonanno began the narration.

" Here is where the wine, when I, we, feel it is ready, is sent to this machine. The bottles are here in this track. They stop under this tube, are filled by hand, then travel to here. We insert the cork at this stage and the bottle then becomes easier to move. In the case of the whites, which are ready to drink immediately, the bottle then drops, very gently, down here. This is the machine which attaches the capsula to the bottle. For the past few years we are using a plastic that tightens with the heat. So you see that there is no chance that one bottle could be poisoned without stopping the line. We have two men involved in this operation. Surely one of them would have seen something funny. No? If the tampering took place somewhere, it was after it left here."

" How strong is the plastic. Could a syringe, perhaps, penetrate it...and also, the cork."

" See for yourself, Inspector." Buonanno reached for an unmounted capsule and handed it to Baglione. The policeman looked at it and placed it in his pocket.

" May I?"

" By all means, take whatever you need."

" Grazie. Gentleman, I think I've seen enough."

" What about the list of my enemies, Baglione? Don't you want to interrogate them?" Parodi seemed disappointed that the interview was over.

" Signore Mario, I don't think that it was the work of anyone you know. The fact that you were not the only one to be targeted leads me to think these unfortunate incidents were probably directed from outside the region. Perhaps from outside the country."

Claude Wizman sat at his computer. He'd just acquired the latest model from the Compaq company in Texas. Its 66mhz processor almost had the speed to keep up with *the Builder's* own brain. The spreadsheet that he looked at kept him up to date on a number of fronts. The most encouraging figures related to the sale of Jaffa oranges in the United States. Before the freight rates from Florida were raised, it was not cost effective for the Israeli growers to sell into the big East Coast markets. But after his man on the railroad commission had finessed the increases through, and the U.S. Commerce Department had given the Shamouti oranges, which were marketed as *Jaffa*, a duty free waiver, sales had increased fivefold. The customs exemption was buried in a trade agreement that had been signed just two months before. 'Pull back from Lebanese territory and name your price.' That was the gist of the deal the Israeli government agreed to on behalf of the growers.

Wizman studied the computer projections. He memorized the pertinent facts, deleted the file, then used a little known utility called INFOWIPE to obliterate the data, like some high tech paper shredder. He then re-read an eMail.

LDV CONTAINER MO9856 317798:

TERRAFIRMA LTDA. PORTO LISBOA.

VERIFICATION - MANIFEST READS COMPLETE

AND ACCURATE. RGDS.

The railroad Commissioner, vacationing at his birthplace in Portugal, had suffered a fatal heart attack. The body was quickly cremated. His family was left alone, in Portugal, to grieve.

When he'd first received the message, Claude Wizman had uttered a short prayer for the dead. Although he had ordered the man's death, respect must still be shown. The next item to be considered was the upcoming New York mayoral election. After years of laying the groundwork, this particular piece of the puzzle was about to fall into place. Imagine having the mayor of the most influential city in the world accountable to him. This was not yet a certainty. In an election, anything was possible. But Wizman was a firm believer in eliminating as many variables as possible. The current field of candidates had been skillfully manipulated, stretching back to the last election, an election that had put the first black man in the office. This mayor was not for sale but he might just blunder himself out of office. It would take minimal orchestration by Claude Wizman to see him go down in defeat. The winner, already preordained, was not even aware of what was planned for him. He would win the upcoming election by default.

The riots that followed an 'unfortunate traffic accident' had been manipulated by Wizman's people. Claude's provocateurs worked both sides of the conflict. *The Builder's* ability to predict behavior was chillingly accurate. One act begot another, as each group was savaged. A knifing here, a beating there. It didn't take much more than that. The racial tensions had simmered for quite a long time. It would be easy to bring Crown Heights to a boil. Another summer of bloody riots would force out the incumbent mayor. Solomon Baum, the real estate baron, and his idiot son, the next mayor of New York, would forever be entwined with Wizman.

Baglione consulted his map. He would stay in nearby Ovada that evening and see the Cortese producer first thing on Wednesday morning. Wednesday afternoon he would drive up to Alba for his last interview before returning to Roma on the late evening train. He sat parked in the AGIP petrol station in Gavi and attempted to refold his map.

" Ma, porca," he muttered after another unsuccessful try. It still would not fold properly. Finally he just tossed it on the passenger seat, started the Panda and drove off. As soon as he left Gavi, Corrado reached a fork in the road. San Cristoforo or Novi Ligure were his choices.

"Boh'," said the policeman to himself. He had no idea which road to take. He shook his head and aimed his Fiat north, towards Novi. After a short while, he spotted a sign for Ovada that sent him back to the south and west. Baglione drove for another half hour. He finally found the medieval town which announced itself a *citta*. A sign pointed in the direction of Albergo Italia. 'Clever name, very original,' he thought. After turning into the centro storico, the historic center of town, Corrado searched for the hotel. He found it, facing a piazza with a church. After parking the Fiat, he crossed a small street and attempted to enter. The door was locked. A notice read

CHIUSO MARTEDÍ/TUESDAY CLOSE

" Dio cane. Ma non e possibile. A hotel cannot be closed on Tuesday." The shoemaker, from across the narrow street heard Baglione curse.

" Signore. Not to worry, they open again at six."
Corrado looked at his watch. Ten minutes to five.

" Where can I have a coffee?"

" Just in the next piazza." The man gestured with his head. The policeman, out of uniform, walked along the cobblestone street. He noticed a statue of some holy person. It was strange. The eyes seemed to be following him. Baglione stopped and read. This was San Paolo della Croce, the patron saint of the town. The building behind the statue was his birthplace. He continued along the Via San Paolo, past a tabaccaio, and was almost hit by an ancient wheeled bakery cart, which emerged from a scruffy courtyard. He then strolled into a fine old piazza. A massive church dominated the space, its plain exterior typical of the region. Inside, he imagined, would be grand. Corrado looked at the other buildings that flanked the piazza. In true Genovese style, the facades were all painted with trompe-l'oeil designs. On his left was the Caffe' della Posta. On his right was Bar Claudio. Posta was also closed on Tuesday, so he crossed over to Claudio. It was actually a pasticceria, a pastry shop and bar. He ordered a spumante. This was wine country. He would not be disappointed - unlike at the stazione back in Genova. The barman, smartly dressed in white shirt and purple bowtie, poured him a frosty tulip. Baglione smiled.

" It's delicious. May I see the bottle?"

" Prego, signore." It was from Gancia, Cuvée del Fondatore. A legendary wine. "I've read about this one, but never had the pleasure to try it."

" To be honest, signore, I opened it for myself. It's expensive, in fact, too expensive for the Ovadese. Braccia corte, if you know what I mean."

Baglione wondered how much it cost and if he should have a second glass.

" I hope it's not too expensive for a lowly Chief of Detectives."

" Don't worry about it, signore." Message delivered. Message received.

" In that case, I'll have another. Will you join me."

" Grazie, Signore...?"

" Baglione. Corrado if you like."

" Piacere." The two shook hands. "Here on vacation?

" Business, I'm afraid. But I don't like to deprive myself of life's small pleasures." Corrado pointed to his spumante. Both men laughed. "I'm here to investigate this unfortunate business with the wines. Have you heard about the trouble?"

" Si. Conte-Candoli."

" And Villa Valente."

" Si. None of us believes that they did it."

" That who did it? Did what?"

" The produttori. Nobody thinks they did it."

" Piano." Slow down. "Signore....?"

" Scusa. Sono Fulvio."

" Dimmi, Fulvio. Who do you think did fuck with the wines?" He had little patience for these country people. In Roma, one asked a question and expected an answer. The policeman look directly into the barman's eyes.

" I, I only meant that no one from around here would do such a thing."

" You're speaking about Conte-Candoli? They're not from around here, eh?

" Si. It's owned by...stranieri."

" So one of these 'foreigners' could have done it?"

Fulvio look away, sheepishly guilty of betraying a trust.

" No. I don't mean to say that. They're decent people, Conte-Candoli. Even if they aren't Ovadese.

" Now Grasso," he whispered. "That's another story. I suggest you talk to him."

" Grasso. Why?"

" It's...He dresses crazy. They say he's a gay. I don't know anything else. I'm only a barman. I hear things. Please. I'm busy. I have to get back to work. The spumante is on me. Excuse me, I'm needed in the kitchen."

The detective understood that the interview was over. It was also obvious to Baglione that this Grasso fellow was not guilty of anything. Well, at least the wine was no charge. He checked his watch. It was almost six. He started back towards the hotel. This time the door was unlocked.

" Buonasera, signore," said the desk clerk. The policeman pegged him as North African. Tunisian or maybe Moroccan. He spoke good enough Italian.

" I need a room, just for one night." Corrado flashed his credentials. The deskman took note.

" Of course, signore. It would be no problem. I have a room available. Would you like to see it? Do you have any luggage?"

" If you say it's alright, then I take it. My bag is out in the car."

" Give me your key. I'll fetch the bag and move your car to our parcheggio. You cannot leave it in the piazza. They'll remove it and give you a fine. Tomorrow is market day and those police here don't give a..."

" Here are the keys. I certainly don't want a multa," laughed the policeman from Roma. "But I do want a good dinner. Can I walk to someplace from here?"

" Let me think. Pignatta is closed on Tuesday. As we are, here in the hotel." He paused for a moment. "Napoli is open. In the Corso Saracco. It's a bit of a walk from here. Just out of the centro."

" Not to worry. The night is beautiful. A good passeggiata always makes me hungry. All roads lead to Napoli, no?"

The clerk didn't laugh at his joke. Perhaps his Italian wasn't so good after all.

At a catering hall near Köln, Ottmar(Maxi) Fleischig began his speech with a story. He related an incident that had happened to him in the final days of the war. His audience was attentive. Several guests at the head table had fought along side him at the end. The speaker told of the courage of a handful of SS troops, stranded in Italy as the Germans began to retreat. It seems that these soldiers had occupied a small town near Courmayeur, in the region of Val D'Aosta. When the order to evacuate finally came through, the town was hopelessly buried in snow. By the time the roads cleared it was already too late to withdraw. The Allies were closing in. The Germans panicked, fearing capture or even worse. Their leader, a crafty lieutenant proposed a plan to his comrades. If the enemy entered the village, they would pose as Italian peasants. As long as they kept their mouths shut, it would be possible for them to survive. The locals were Aryan looking, not at all like the southern Italians. They spoke a dialect that sounded vaguely German. As expected, one frigid afternoon, at a little past noon, the American forces swept into town. The Colonel in charge immediately made for the one small hotel in the village. The German soldiers had commandeered it when they'd arrived almost three years before. The management was now German, a corporal and four or five privates. The cook was a soldier, as were the barman and waiter. The American officer and his two younger aides sat down and asked for some lunch. One of the aides was an Italian-American from Brooklyn named Beppe Olivieri. Beppe did all of the talking. He announced that the town was now "officially liberated." The Allies would eat and be out of there by that evening.

" No sweat," thought the German officer. "We feed them and then they'll be gone. No one in town will dare to give us away." The lieutenant had taken a few of the locals hostage. Anyone with loose lips would be held responsible for their deaths.

" Make some noodles with rabbit. Tell them it's chicken. The Americans won't even notice that the cook is Bavarian."

" Yes sir, but what do we give them for wine? They already asked." The German soldiers always drank beer. There was no wine, except for a cheap aromatic Muscat called Petit Grain.

" So give them some wine. Those uncultured morons will lap it up like puppies." The corporal laughed and followed his orders. He served the rabbit along with two liters of the chilled Moscato. After the meal, the American officers thanked them heartily, tossed them a few coins, wished them well and drove out of the town with their troops. The American officers were eventually reprimanded when their superiors discovered the ruse.

Everyone at the banquet laughed at the speaker's story. Maxi Fleischig picked up his glass and proposed a toast.

" Gentleman, to that glorious day, the day that we saved our little village. The officers raised their glasses of Muscat Lo Triolet.

"To the stupidity of the American army. If only they had been the slightest bit smarter - we would all now be dead."

The speaker and his mates downed their glasses of wine. Suddenly Fleischig's eyes widened. His face turned red as he began to gasp for air. Three others, seated on the dais, dropped along with him. At the back of the room a waiter slowly turned and walked away.

Corrado took a stroll through Ovada. The *newest* buildings in the old city center were several hundred years old. One, he read, was built in the late 7th century. He walked along the Via Cairoli, past an odd assortment of shops. Baglione paused in front of a pasticceria called B&C to admire the local pastries. He made a mental note to try some on his way out of town in the morning. The polenta cake looked especially delicious. He'd eat some for breakfast in the car.

When he finally spotted the place that the desk man had sent him, he wasn't all that impressed. The nondescript 60's facade was anything but inviting. But there were lots of cars and lots of people near the entrance. He walked inside, past a small bar and immediately changed his opinion. It smelled wonderful. There was a wood burning oven out of which emerged a spectacular looking...something? The proprietor, a large doughy man with a baby face, welcomed him with a nod. Baglione was led to a table in the cozy front room with a view of the pizzaiolo.

" Fame?" asked the man.

" Not hungry. Starving."

" Bravo. Here's the menu. We also have a few specials tonight. Bere?"

" Vino."

" Bianco o nero?"

" Bianco. Something local."

" Of course."

The wine arrived in a half-liter carafe along with a puffed up pizza-like bread that Nino, the owner, called focaccino. It was piping hot and charred on the bottom, topped with meltingly thin slices of lardo from Biella. When the bread was cut, the escaping air released a smoky aroma. The wine was delivered and poured for Baglione. He sipped and nibbled and sipped some more.

" Gran bel culo, eh?" Although the proprietor spoke to Baglione, their eyes followed the great ass on the blonde walking by.

" Porca." Baglione was really liking this place.

" And how are you liking my wine?"

" It's delicious. Gavi?"

" Cortese. Same grape. Same soil. I grow it in Tagliolo. Unfortunately for me, I'm just outside the "sacred" zone. Those stuck-up Gaviese are a bunch of bastards. My wine is just as good as theirs. Better even. But I can't call it Gavi so I can't charge their prices. It's you who get the benefits, not me. Ah well. That's life, eh? So where are you from? You sound like you're from the south."

" I live in Roma, yes. But I was born in Salerno."

" No! I'm from Sorrento."

" Practically neighbors. But why do you call this place Napoli?"

" Every town has to have a Pizzeria Napoli and a Hotel Italia. Si o no?"

" Si. Vero. I was just thinking the same thing." Baglione laughed.

" Antipasto, primo? Whatever you like."

" What do you suggest?"

" Primo. Tonight we have pansotti, sugo di noce. Fatto in casa. Agnolotti col vino - very local. Tagliolini, sugo di funghi."

" Funghi freschi?"

" Certo."

" O.K. If the funghi are really fresh."

Nino flagged down a passing waiter. "Tagliolini funghi e portami un bicchiere. May I join you?"

The large man sat down at the table with Corrado. The waiter, an Egyptian, quickly returned with an empty glass. Baglione poured him some wine.

" So what brings you to Ovada?"

" I'm here about the unfortunate business at Conte-Candoli."

" So you're a policeman. I could tell. As soon as you came in."

" Poliziotto? Really. I'm curious. What does a policeman look like?"

" Like you." Both men laughed. "I suppose you want to ask me some questions. I warn you. I'm very, very close mouthed. Where I'm from, you learn that early. But I don't have to tell you that. Eh....?"

" Sorry. I should introduce myself. I'm Baglione. Special Branch." He liked the sound of that. In fact, he'd just made it up. 'Special Branch.' It sounded like Interpol or Scotland Yard. Perhaps he'd have some cards made up when he returned to Roma.

" I'd like to ask you a few questions."

" What would this 'Special Branch' need to know from me?"

" Who's playing games with the wines?"

" Can't help you. Next question."

" What do you think of the people at Conti-Candoli?"

" He seems nice enough. What else?"

" How I can make some fast money in the borsa? Where can I get laid? These are all things I would like to know." The proprietor

82

shook his head. The policeman raised his eyebrows. The pasta
arrived with the Egyptian.

" Buon appetito." Nino got up from the table. Corrado gave
him a half-smile. He'd get no information from this guy.

" **He** did what?...Oy a veytik chaz meir! The fool!... Quiet...Just
shut up!...Let me think for a minute."

Claude Wizman understood immediately. He had a problem. A big
problem. This idiot, this *Johnnie* person was supposed to follow
orders. Pick an ordinary place somewhere in Germany, get a
waiter's job and, just like that - another death attributed to Italian
wine. Germany. The second largest market for Italian wines in the
world. That was the plan. But this, this kuppe drek, this piece of shit
with his rat poison had done something so colossally stupid that
Wizman's entire machiavellian scheme, twenty-five years in the
making, was now in danger of total collapse.

" What was his reason? What did he say?...Payback! What
does he mean 'payback'? Payback for whom? For what
purpose?...Honestly, I don't give a good goddamn about his
reasons! What I do know is that he cannot be tied to us. This is
going to put us all under a fucking microscope or worse. I want him
removed now...No trace...Eliminate this moron. Vishtayz?"

Anamaria Conte was a second generation winemaker. Her farm,
Azienda Agricola Conte-Candoli, in San Lorenzo (outside Ovada)
was planted with just three grapes. Cortese, not her favorite, but
which was now causing her such problems, Barbera, Piemonte's
original red wine, and Dolcetto, her particular pride and joy. When a
small band of Cortese producers had decided to compete
vigorously with Gavi, Anamaria's husband, Vincenzo, decided that
they should take it more seriously. In fact, she didn't like or even

drink white wine. She sold some locally, mostly in the neighboring towns, but so did two or three dozen others. It wasn't until the Gavi prices went through the roof that customers started turning to Cortese. Not to take anything away from La Scolca, Moccagatta, Broglio and the others. Their wines were quite good. But to charge more, just for the name, was difficult for the local producers to swallow. Smart consumers were turning to makers like Conte-Candoli who made credible wines for half of what the Gavi producers were charging. As her sales increased, Anamaria began to pay attention. Just when things were starting to go well this *disastro* had to happen.

Corrado sat on the crest of a hill overlooking the vines. Vineyard after vineyard. His eyes wandered and then fixed on the remote hill town of Carpeneto and its castle. As Baglione unwrapped a pastry he looked at his watch. It was nearly ten o'clock. He would have just a small piece of this marvelous torta and keep the rest for later. After all, he didn't want to ruin his appetite for lunch. The policeman had been invited to eat with the owners at Conte-Candoli. But this *Polenta di Ovada* was delicious. The chocolate cream filling reminded him of Nutella, only better. The blend of hazelnut and cocoa had always been one of his passions. Perhaps just one more small piece. He re-wrapped the cake and got back into the Panda.

The little Fiat took him up the steep winding road to San Lorenzo. Since leaving the center of Ovada he'd driven completely surrounded by vines. In fact the road was called the "Strada dei Vini." San Lorenzo, the town, was easy to find. Conte-Candoli, the winery, not quite so easy. Baglione eventually did see a sign that pointed him in the right direction. A small stone house with a winery connected to it appeared down a long unpaved driveway. There were vineyards stretched out in every direction. Corrado felt as if he were afloat in a sea of grapes. He aimed the car at the house and threaded his way down the vibrant green track. The career civil servant fantasized about owning even a modest house like this one. But on a policeman's salary it would never be more than a dream. He pulled up in front. Anamaria Conte-Candoli was waiting below a wisteria covered pergola that ran from the house to the parking area. The titolare was a short, stocky woman with close cropped red hair. She wore a pair of khaki shorts, white shirt and white sneakers. Her sunglasses matched the ebony cigarette holder that she held between thin colorless lips. As Baglione approached, the woman barely nodded her head. When the detective got out of the car he realized that the signora was blind.

" Baglione, I presume."

" Si. Signora Conte?"

" In the flesh, as the Americans like to say." Corrado thought that a strange remark. The woman extended her hand. Her grip was strong. The policeman wondered if she was making a point. For some reason blind people always made him nervous.

" Thank you for seeing me," he stupidly remarked.

" I'm sorry, I meant that..."

" Detective, please save your...By the way, how do you like the Panda?"

" It's...How did you know?"

" I can tell by the sound the door made when you closed it."

" Remarkable. I never thought..."

" I'm just having fun with you, Inspector." The woman laughed. "My tuttofare told me you were coming down the driveway. Sightless people make you uncomfortable, Baglione? You can be honest. I'm really very used to it."

" To be perfectly frank, Signora, that's true. I'll try not to show it."

" Are you a fan of chocolate, Commissario? I detect a bit of something sweet on your breathe."

" Your man was spying on me again?"

" No, no. My sense of smell is very good. Helps me in my work."

" Can we talk about that a bit, Signora?"

" Anamaria. And the answer is no. No business until after lunch."

" Va bene. That's something I need no help with. And it's Corrado."

" Very well, Corrado. Let's eat."

The woman had no trouble negotiating the complicated route to her dining room. Baglione followed closely, barely keeping up on the steep wooden stairs that led to the house. They ended at the entrance to a simple whitewashed room, lit with an ancient gas chandelier. The table had been set for two. An elegant man, in a cerulean blue dress shirt and blue-gray ascot appeared from another room.

" All ready, cara."

" Enzo is a wonderful cook. What will you surprise us with today. Eh?"

" Some small fishes to start. Gnocchi made as we both like it, then one of our nice plump rabbits. We raise them here. Just where you turned, at the bottom of the drive."

" Splendid, Vincenzo. Baglione, shall we sit?"

" Of course."

" Please." The husband gestured towards the table. Corrado could hardly move the massive walnut chair out far enough to sit down. Anamaria crossed the room stopping at an old breadmaking table which had been converted into a serving bar. On top was a selection of her wines. Whether it was by location or shape of the bottles, the proprietor seemed to easily distinguish one from the next. She picked up a Cortese, deftly removed the capsula and uncorked the bottle.

" Let's start with the one that has caused us such problems. Without it, you wouldn't be here. Isn't that right, Inspector?"

" I'd be delighted to try it."

Anamaria Conte-Candoli approached the table, bringing the bottle with her.

" Would you pour for us Corrado? I'm afraid that I'm not much of a sommelier."

" Certo."

" Just a drop for me. I hate vino bianco." Baglione poured her a bit and then filled his own glass.

" Cin Cin," she said, raising her glass.

" Salud." They drank.

" Ma, Signora, it's delicious."

" It's my answer to the Gavi growers who sneer at our efforts. They all know we can produce a wine that's every bit as good as their own. Same grape, you know."

" Si. But grown under different conditions."

" Umm. I'm not sure I agree with that. Certainly they have slightly different soil and the clima is not precisely ours. But the fruit is identical. I do harvest a bit later than the others. If it was labeled as Gavi, which, by the way, has been known to happen, you couldn't tell any difference."

" Really?"

" The public, in general, is ignorant. Facts are unimportant to them. We started a real marketing effort for this Cortese and the results have been surprising. It may have something to do with the times. Our wine costs far less than Gavi. Even imbeciles understand that. Thankfully, the days of trying to impress with just a label are over. Well, maybe not over, but certainly it's quality that counts more now."

" As a wine drinker myself, I can certainly agree with you, Signora."

" Ah, here comes our lunch."

A young woman, dressed in baggy jeans and a faded white **Edil-M** t-shirt (advertising a local business) entered the room carrying two plates of tiny fried fish.

" Your husband's not joining us?"

" Enzo's busy in the kitchen. Deliziosi, these acciughe. Don't you agree?"

" Delicato and very fresh, Signora. Complimenti."

" You're an eater, mister policeman. That's one point in your favor."

" So I'm being rated now?" he laughed. "May I remind you that I'm here on official business."

" So you are, Detective."

" However, a good lunch is a good lunch, especially for someone far from home."

They finished the fish in silence. Romina, the housekeeper, re-entered at their last bite of anchovy, as if she'd been watching the room.

" The gnocchi is ready," she said dryly, clearing the plates.

Anamaria returned to the bar.

" For the pasta you should try our other Cortese. It's from a single vineyard, here - close to the house. It was the first wine I made when we bought this place. We used to make it only for ourselves. It's my husband's favorite. Still the best...in his opinion." She uncorked the wine and another unlabeled bottle of red and carried them back to the table. Once again Baglione did the pouring.

" I'll drink Dolcetto if you don't mind. But please, try this bianco. I'm curious to know what you think of our oldest child?"

The policeman tasted the wine.

" It's fabulous. You should be very proud of this one. Your husband is right."

" Please tell him that. Vincenzo's still busy in the kitchen."

" Now that's a good husband."

They laughed as Romina came in with two plates.

" These are so good. This gnocchi is one of his best dishes. He uses a bit of smoked salmon to make the pasta and a bit more in the sauce. It goes nicely with our wine. Don't you think?"

" Squisito. I'm enjoying this immensely."

For the next course, Signora Conte shared the open red with her guest.

" My husband's way of cooking the rabbit is fantastic. It's very nice with the Dolcetto, I think."

" It's marvelous. My mother often made this dish, but not nearly so well. God rest her soul." Baglione savored every bite. This third bottle of wine was starting to play with his brain. After a last long swallow, he attempted to push back from the table. The chair wouldn't budge. He tried again. This time harder. The table suddenly slid forward, hitting the signora just under her rib cage.

" Ughh," exclaimed the woman, "are you trying to kill me? I'll confess. Just don't hit me again." They laughed loudly together.

" Perhaps I should start my interrogation now."

" But we haven't had dessert yet!"

The housekeeper collected their plates and looked fiercely at Corrado. She apparently disapproved of him. Vincenzo came in and sat with them at the table. He brought a fresh white cheese and an open bottle of wine.

" I'll only stay for a moment. Furmagetta from a friend. Ottimo with this passito, signore. A fine way to end your meal." Indulging him, seemed to Corrado, to be the correct thing to do. So he sighed and followed instructions.

" Take a small bit of cheese and some of the honey that my stepson makes on the property. Then a nice long sip of the wine. You'll see why I'm so insistent. The cheese is especially good today. Don't you think?"

Corrado nodded. They'd succeeded in getting him drunk. 'Damn,' he thought, 'I hate when I can't feel the floor.'

" Perhaps a short nap, Commissario? We can talk later."

It was dreary in London that morning. The cloud cover was worse than usual. Without a clock it would have been hard to tell it was morning. The soft glow of a computer screen provided all the illumination. A few quick strokes, a macro he'd set-up when he purchased the program, got Claude Wizman the eMail he was anxiously awaiting.

LDV CONTAINER RO5226 853882:
TERRAFIRMA GMBH. BREMEN
VERIFICATION - MANIFEST READS COMPLETE AND
ACCURATE. RGDS

Johnnie Olivieri was dead. An accidental drowning. The poor man had fallen off a ferry, just as it was docking. *The Builder* would have to clean up the mess Olivieri had made in Köln. How had he let that happen? The German 'initiative' was supposed to look like another random poisoning, another blow to the Italian wine producers. But this idiot Olivieri had to make it into a vendetta, to avenge his father's disgraceful demotion after he'd failed to identify the SS troops way back in '45. Many G.I.'s had lost their lives as a result of his old man's blunder. Murdering Fleischig and the others may have satisfied Olivieri, but it put the entire operation at risk. A link had been made...to Claude Wizman. Johnnie paid the ultimate price but the problem still existed.

Wizman absent-mindedly stroked the sleeve of his pale green Loro Piana sweater as he recited Kaddish, the Jewish prayer for the dead. He was reaching for his pipe when the first pain shot up his left arm. It jolted him back in the chair. Then nothing. No pain. He examined his arm. No blood - so he hadn't been shot. Wizman carefully ran his hand up and down the arm. The fabric hadn't been penetrated. That ruled out darts from a blow gun or a syringe that had been set as a trap. Except for some shortness of breath, which he attributed to nerves, *Claude the Builder* was unharmed. A few moments later he returned to his work.

Wizman picked up the phone and punched in a number. It rang twice.

" Ja."

" It's me. I'll be there tonight."

Baglione's eyes opened. He blinked, remembered where he was, and got up. The room was pure white, with one enormous piece of polished mahogany furniture, set in the corner. He found a light switch and pressed it. A dim gauzy glow illuminated the room. The hanging lamp was swathed in ivory silk. Corrado now realized that he was in his undershirt and shorts. His clothes had been hung neatly inside the massive guardaroba. The policeman strained to read his watch. The effects of the alcohol had not completely worn off. It was fifteen minutes to midnight. He quickly dressed, after rinsing his face in a washbowl that had been left for him. From its temperature, he surmised that it had recently been set in the room. Fragrant white jasmine floated in the delicate china bowl. Baglione opened the door and found himself in a darkened hallway. He felt his way to a staircase that led him to the floor below. The house was extremely quiet. The Inspector spotted an envelope, propped up on a small marble table. His name was handwritten on the front. Corrado opened it and read from a stiff white card.

Egregio Commissario, Anamaria apologizes. She has retired for the evening. If it is not an imposition, she asks that you spend the night. If you would be so kind as to take breakfast with her tomorrow, she will answer any questions that you might have.

grazie e cari saluti, enzo

Baglione was starving. He decided to look for the kitchen. After a few missteps, he found the proper door. Seated at an old wooden table was the housekeeper, Romina. She had on a red flannel bathrobe and fuzzy, fake fur slippers. She turned to him slowly.

" Are you hungry?"

" Uh, no. No, no grazie. I was, uh, actually looking for...for the toilet."

A messianic fervor had begun to spread throughout Brooklyn, more specifically, through the substantial Orthodox Jewish community living in Borough Park. The faithful firmly believed in the imminent appearance of *the Moshiach*. There were signs in the shops and newspaper stories. Even bumper stickers heralding his arrival. Fueled by their particular interpretation of the Talmud, the followers believed that in every century there was one who existed, whose mystical powers and pious devotion signaled a possible savior. The Boravitchers of Borough Park, Brooklyn believed that they had such a figure in their Grand Rebbe Moshe Buchsbaum. Their conviction was based on two assumptions. The first was that the end of the world was at hand. The war in the Gulf and the outbreak of fighting in Europe were genuine signs that the end was approaching. Some said that these were the conflicts alluded to in the Scriptures. True or not, the followers of Rebbe Buchsbaum believed it. That the Rebbe was childless only further stirred things up. With no clear successor (bloodlines being the rule) it was time for the Rabbi to reveal himself as the *Anointed Redeemer*. His health had been failing, so what better time could there be than this. The Old Testament clearly spelled it out.

Claude Wizman really was a believer. He believed in his Rebbe, he believed in the Boravitchers and most importantly he believed that it was his duty to prove to the world that the 'new' order had hopelessly failed. Through his efforts, this orthodox sect would save what was left of mankind. The Rebbe would look after the spiritual end, and he, *Claude the Builder*, would tinker and tweak on the rest.

Baglione woke again at half past seven in the morning. He dressed quickly and joined Anamaria for breakfast. The glassed in terrace afforded breathtaking views of the rolling, vine covered hillsides. The terrace itself was lovely. The green iron frame was the color of young grape leaves, vibrant through the clear glass panes. The furniture was heavy wood, 1930's. The cobalt blue upholstery had a deco pattern woven into it. The white tile floor was studded with matching blue diamonds. Delicate white lamps and shades were scattered among the objects d'art that graced each piece of furniture. In one corner there was an artist's easel supporting an unfinished painting. Someone in the house was a very talented painter.

Anamaria took a bite of brioche, more like a croissant, filled with apricot marmellata.

" Did you sleep well?"

" Like a baby, signora. The lunch was magnificent. I woke only for a minute. It seems that I was tired. More than I realized, actually."

" Have been working hard to solve this problem of ours?"

" Si. I've been traveling quite a bit."

" So what have you discovered?"

Corrado sipped his caffé (macchiato, just as he liked it). He bit into what Romina, the housekeeper, called a cannolo. It bore no resemblance to the kind he grew up eating in the south. This one had a flaky crust with a luxurious pastry cream filling. The thin paper liner identified the bakery.

Pasticceria Zoccola Alessandria

" I'm sorry to tell you that at this moment we know very little. I was hoping that you could throw some light onto this."

" How can I help?"

" Have you any enemies, anyone you think is capable of something like this?"

" Perhaps. But the fact is, I'm not the only victim. Maybe you should be looking for someone or some group that has it in for us all."

" Brava. It's certainly a possibility, Signora. One which, I assure you, we are examining closely. I ask this question only to determine if there have been any specific threats directed towards you. Have there been any?"

" Nothing direct. I have heard that a few of the Gavi growers are quite upset with me. The success we are having with the Cortese makes them nervous."

" Yes, but there was also a tainted Gavi. On Alitalia."

" I heard that. Killed a Spaniard didn't it?"

94

" Argentinian."

" Whatever."

" The third death came from an Arneis."

" A delicious grape, Baglione. I wish I could grow it. Killed an American, si?"

" Yes, in Chicago."

" So perhaps our enemy is trying to make it hard for Italians to sell our wines abroad."

" It would seem so, Signora. Any thoughts on who it might be?"

" Shouldn't I be asking that question of you, Investigatore?"

" You'd be surprised," laughed Baglione, "at how much I learn from the victims."

" Vincenzo has also made some inquiries. He has many friends in Roma. Seems that you're known as quite the bulldog. Very tenacious once you've gotten your teeth into something. I respect that. In a way, I'm like that myself."

" Then you'll keep me informed, as well. In the event that you hear something, Signora."

" Of course. I'd like to see this resolved as soon as possible. By the way, I asked my husband to put some of our wines in your car."

" Si?" Baglione's eyes lit up. "Ma, molto gentile, signora. Grazie. Grazie mille. That's very kind of you."

" Figurati. Think nothing of it, Inspector. It's a just a small thank you."

" Well," said the policeman looking at his watch, "I must be going. I have one more stop before catching the train back to Roma."

" Give my regards to Vanessa. That's who you're going to see now, isn't it?"

" Good-bye signora. Thank you for your help and for your hospitality. And please thank your husband for everything."

" I'll give Enzo your regards. Poverino. He's always so busy in the kitchen."

Claude Wizman checked into Das kleine Stapelhäuschen under the name Serge Souverein. The passport was one of a dozen, manufactured for him in Asuncion, Paraguay by Artur Bubin, one of the world's best document forgers. 'Serge' was in Köln for an opening at the Ludwig Museum. Modern art was another of Wizman's passions. However, the real purpose of the trip was to sanitize the awful blunder committed by the late Johnnie Olivieri. Claude was joined in Köln by Léon and Henri Drei. They felt that it was prudent to meet somewhere other than the Stapelhäuschen.

It was well past midnight when they met up at the Hotel Chelsea. The bar there reminded *The Builder* of the bohemian hangouts back home in Montreal. There was no such thing as a non-smoking section at the Café Centrale. Claude ordered a cognac, Delamain Tres Venerable. Difficult to find and very expensive. The two brothers shared a bottle of mineral water.

" The ferry accident. Can it be traced to us?"

" Of course not," answered Henri.

" You're sure?"

" It was professionally done. A Salvadoran with impeccable credentials. We've used him before. Jörg Bissel made the arrangements. It wasn't cheap, but worth every penny. I assure you."

" Yes. Jörg Bissel."

" He's completely dedicated to The Rebbe - and he admires you so much. Embedding him in the Köln police turned out to be a stroke of luck, Claude."

" Bissel was about your age when I first found him in Odense. But enough of this talk. What about the body?"

" Mangled."

" Unidentifiable, Léon?"

" His teeth were broken before the 'accident'. Fingertips torn off as well. After he was crushed by the dock, we had a diver run him through the propeller. Believe me, this time there were no screw-ups."

Wizman nodded his approval. He had spotted these boys when they were ten and twelve years old. They'd been removed from their parents' house when the mother and father divorced. The Orthodox rabbi who'd re-located the children to a camp in upstate New York had been briefly detained by child welfare authorities, but Claude managed to smooth it over. For the past thirteen years the brothers Drei had received a very special education. If *The Builder* had had children of his own, he would have raised them the very same way.

" I'm very concerned about the link between Olivieri and what was his name, the Nazi?"

" Fleischig. SS Lieutenant Ottmar Fleischig. Better known as Maxi." Henri was always good at names.

" Can Olivieri be placed at the hall?"

" Honestly Claude, we just don't have enough information yet," said Léon. "He was a temporary worker. Was he in that room? Probably. I can't say it's 100% sure without raising suspicion."

" Why don't we just let it die?"

" Henri, I wish it was that easy. If he was spotted at that dinner it could lead back to us. What about the local police?"

" They're puzzled by the deaths. Bissel says that they've contacted the Italian authorities," added Léon.

" So by now they know it was murder." Wizman finished his cognac. "The Italians are bound to send someone here. Find out who's close to the investigation? Do we even have someone in Rome?"

" You mean in the Italian government?"

" Exactly, Henri. Let's find out what's going through their minds. I leave it up to you. Can you access their computers?"

" The Italians," sniffed Henri. "It's not so difficult. You'll have your answer tonight."

" Léon. Take a photo of this Olivieri fellow to the catering hall. Find some excuse to show it around. If any of the employees identify him, we'll know better what's got to be done."

" Sure thing."

" All right then. We meet at the Ludwig Museum at six. Here are your invitations. So, my young friends, I'll see you tomorrow."

With a few exceptions, the route from San Lorenzo in the direction of Alba was pleasant. Baglione loved driving these roads that cut through the vineyards, punctuated by the occasional hilltop castle. This was the Alto Monferrato, known for its dozens of medieval castles. It seemed that every town had its own. He drove through Nizza towards Alba, took a wrong turn and found himself hopelessly lost. Corrado noticed a sign for the enoteca regionale at Grinzane Cavour. He arrived just in time for a tasting. A chalkboard informed him that the afternoon session was about to begin.

He parked the Panda in a gravel courtyard. The old castle was ivy covered and dark. Baglione followed the arrows through a doorway and down a flight of ancient stone block steps. He entered a large vaulted room, really a series of rooms, and walked until he heard some conversation. A warm "buongiorno" acknowledged his arrival, followed by a "grazie" after he paid the five thousand lire.

" Signore, come in. We're about to begin."

A short, bearded man was pouring wine into a dozen nicely polished glasses. The participants were a mixed lot. One couple was almost certainly English, with bright pink faces and National Health eyeglasses. There were a few young Asians. Their well dressed escort translated for them. Baglione guessed they were Japanese, or maybe Korean. A few locals and a blond guy in a red and white Ajax shirt rounded out the group of tasters. The speaker was saying something about French barrels. Everyone tasted. The Englishman rolled the wine around in his mouth then spit into a small silver bucket. The speaker continued.

" The next is Gattinara. The same Nebbiolo grape, slightly different terroir. Please rinse your glasses."

The enoteca had provided the bucket and pitchers of water so that each wine could be properly judged. This was to be an informative look at the various Nebbiolo wines produced in the region. There was a Barolo, two Barbaresco and one each of Gattinara, Ghemme, Bramaterra and Carema. It was interesting to Baglione that one single grape could make so many different wines. The demonstration was informative. Deliciously so. The policeman thanked his guide and climbed back up the gravel path to his Fiat Panda. In twenty five minutes time he arrived at Tenuta Rambaudi.

The modest winery shared a hillside with the owner's villa. The house and gardens overlooked the Tanaro river. They produced one Nebbiolo here, designated Roero in this particular zone, one Barbera, one blend of Nebbiolo and Barbera, and one Arneis. Each was well made and highly respected by a small number of cognoscenti. The Roero are the hills which flank the western side of the river. Arneis, their white, is the name of the grape but colloquially also means "little rascal" (or little fucker depending on who you ask to render an opinion). So named due to its unpredictable behavior. Although its origin can be traced to the fifteenth century, it remains almost unknown outside of Piemonte. Judging from the size of the property, Baglione surmised that Vanessa Rambaudi would never get rich from this venture. Apparently she had other means of surviving. When he wasn't banging Baglione's wife and actually engaged in some detective work, Pippo D'Orazio wasn't a bad cop. He'd discovered that the lady was a well known professional thief. Never in Italy - but pity the French Riviera. Vanessa fished from Menton to Marseille trolling for cash and jewelry.

She was waiting for him at the impressive wrought iron gates of the Tenuta Rambaudi. When he pulled up, Baglione saw an elegant woman, early-fifties, slender, tan and smiling. She reminded him of the actress, Monica Vitti. The policeman got out of his white Panda with the broken window and introduced himself.

" Signora Rambaudi? I am Baglione. We spoke on the telephone."

" Inspector. Benvenuto. Welcome to my home. How are you today?"

" Molto bene, Signora. Grazie."

" Would you mind, terribly, if we took dinner out? I'm afraid my house is a bit of a shambles. I've just returned from a trip. The staff, unfortunately, is no longer with me. There's dust everywhere. I still have a cook but she..."

" Please Signora. No need to apologize. Can we have a quick look at the winery? It would help me. Then we go. Va bene?"

" Of course."

She led him through the small facility. The other producers he had visited were small but not this small. Baglione guessed the volume of production to be very limited. Enough to be noticed, but not enough to make a living, or float this estate. He knew how she earned her money. Pippo had checked into the backgrounds of all the owners. Villa Valente and Conte-Candoli were old money. Vanessa Rambaudi was a whole other story. She was an American by birth, Italian by marriage to a Lorenzo Rambaudi, scion of a well-to-do family. For Vanessa Terry, born August 16,1942 in Battle Creek, Michigan, it was a storybook marriage. She'd been introduced to her handsome husband by a mutual friend in New York. The dashing young Italian got her attention, big time. They'd married almost immediately. She quit her job as an illustrator at a department store chain and, for family reasons(his), they relocated to northern Italy.

" How large is your Arneis production?"

" Perhaps a few thousand liters. Enough to drink here at the house, with a little bit left over to sell."

" It must be excellent...for such a high class ristorante in Chicago to serve it."

" I'll let you be the judge, after you've had a taste."

She laughed. A bit of a tease, this one, and just his type. 'Steady Corrado,' he thought to himself. 'This lady is nothing but trouble.' But she was ravishing at fifty-two, and far more interesting than any woman that he knew and, after all, she was only a *few* years older than he. Baglione was 46 and no longer counting.

" May I, instead, invite you to dinner? Or more honestly, may the Italian government invite you to dinner. And please call me Corrado."

" Un grande piacere. Corrado. Shall we go?"

Vanessa looked at his car and suggested they take hers. The Signora led him around to the back of the house. She took a small remote from her purse and aimed it at the garage. The heavily varnished wooden door slid smartly to the right, revealing an elegant dark grey Rolls-Royce. She proudly identified it as a 1959

Silver Cloud, James Young Style, SC20 convertible. One of only two ever constructed. The woman obviously knew her automobiles and really loved this car.

" Will you drive?" she asked, tossing him the keys. He ran around to her side of the car and opened the door. Or tried to. Baglione pulled but nothing happened. She laughed again, and showed him how to unlock the doors. Vanessa then pointed to the ignition switch and smiled. The detective eased himself into the most comfortable seat he'd ever encountered in an automobile. The red leather Connolly hides were slightly worn but still beautiful. He managed to get the Rolls started. Once in reverse, he maneuvered the car out of the garage. Baglione, unused to the enormous machine, stalled the engine. He restarted it, jerked ten feet forward and killed it again. His face turning a shade similar to the fine scandinavian leather interior. They both had to laugh.

" Darling, let's put the top down. What do you think?"

' What do I think,' he thought to himself. 'I think she just called me *darling*.'

" The switch is just to your right."

He had no trouble getting the soft roof to retract. Now the policeman had the feel of the car and he confidently steered towards the gate. She touched another button on the dash and the massive iron doors swung open to let them out. Once on the highway, Corrado began to whistle. This was a long way away from Roma and a long way from Rosalba. He hadn't thought much about her for the past several days. Pippo was probably banging her at this very minute. Well, he thought, good luck to them both.

It was a little past six when they turned to the west. The sun was beginning to set behind the hills, their vines arranged in orderly rows.

102

" Is it allowed? A policeman flirting with the victim of a crime?"

" I didn't realize that I was flirting."

" And I think you know just what you're doing." He loved the way she laughed.

" You're very sure of yourself, signora."

" No, Inspector, I'm very sure of you."

" Where shall we go for dinner? Do you have a favorite place?"

  She looked at him, tapping a red painted nail on her lips.

" I'll bet anything that you're a gastrofighetto. Am I right Corrado?"

" Brava. That's an interesting word. I've not heard that before. A nice compliment, I think? Gastrofighetto. I do enjoy a good meal. In fact, I enjoy everything in life, Signora."

" Look out!" she screamed. Baglione turned his eyes just in time to see an old three wheeled Ape pulling out onto the road from a muddy path. The mustard yellow scooter was loaded with empty damigiane, the huge, round wine bottles that seem to live permanently in the back of these barely motorized contraptions. Corrado spun the wheel and hit the brakes, throwing the large heavy car into a slide. Too late. It brushed the front of the Ape, just enough to send it spinning into a mound of wet sand. The empty bottles slid out the back with a thunderous shatter of glass. Baglione recovered and slowed the car to a stop. He took a few deep breaths and sank back into the seat. The contadino in the Ape was shaking his fist in the air. Corrado looked over at Vanessa Rambaudi.

" Are you hurt?" She did not reply.

" Are we there yet?" she asked with a smile. He stared at her in disbelief, got out of the car and walked back towards the farmer.

The man was screaming something about Corrado and his ancestors. The policeman showed the man his identification and was promptly told to stick the credentials up his ass. After a few minutes the driver calmed down and Baglione returned.

" He's o.k. The bottles were empty. Most of them survived. Why are you laughing? Is there something funny?"

" No, no. It's just that..." she was trying not to break up.

" ...that I'm an imbecile. That I have no business driving a car like this!"

He was frustrated and getting a little angry. She leaned over and kissed him passionately on the mouth. The contadino, seeing this, unleashed a string of invectives that would have embarrassed a kitchen full of cooks. They ignored him and continued to kiss. First quietly. Then...not so much. She laughed and began to unbutton his shirt. The farmer went wild. Baglione lost control, as well. Nothing like this had ever happened to him. He tried to climb on her in the massive front seat of the car. She helped him to unzip his pants. Vanessa's skirt inched up nearer to her waist. The poor man with the broken bottles had never seen such a thing. He shoved his Ape out of the sandpile, invoking the name of some long suffering saint.

The Ludwig Museum had mounted a show of modern paintings on loan from the Barnes Foundation in Philadelphia. There were Matisses, Rousseaus, Renoirs and many others of equal importance. The centerpiece was Cezanne's turn of the century masterpiece, The Card Players. Sharing the spotlight was Picasso's Acrobat and Young Harlequin, which hadn't been seen in Europe in years. Claude Wizman was also a collector. Nothing of this quality, he wasn't one of the super rich, but his tastes were nonetheless refined. He was looking forward to the exhibition. The brothers Drei couldn't have cared less. They feigned interest only so that attention would not be drawn to them. Claude accepted a glass of Peter Lauer sekt from a passing waiter and looked across the large main room toward the Dreis. He nodded toward the crowded end of the space, where the Cezanne was on display. Slowly each of them crossed, in turn, to the gold-framed painting. Wizman studied the work, three men at table, two others observing the game. It was magnificent. Léon and Henri looked at *The Builder*. He was a strange, remarkable man. Every Boravitcher knew of Claude Wizman. His notoriety had grown after the assassination of Meir Kahane in 1990. Many thought that he was responsible for the radical rabbi's death. It wasn't true, but Claude was amused by the speculation. Whoever was behind it had earned *The Builder's* respect. It was a brilliant piece of work. The killing was relatively unimportant. But the fallout. That was extraordinary! He agreed with his admirers. It smacked of his kind of scheming. His mind drifted, momentarily, towards the coming New York election. Selecting his own candidate for the mayoral race, and getting him elected would be a stunning achievement for Claude and the movement. After that, who knows? Putting this in motion had been easier than he'd expected. With his man in place the stage was almost set. The Mayor of New York influences many other races. A Senator, maybe even a President. But that would come later on. For now, he was content to see this bit of his plan reach fruition. The Boravitchers were about to become a very potent force, not only in the U.S. but also in all of the world's major markets. Within a dozen years they would, conceivably, control much of the planet's food supply. Fruits and vegetables now, meats and grains in the future. The wine, the oranges, the melons were only to test the waters. Their people would be placed on commissions and advisory boards from Sacramento to Singapore. The world would be made aware of the Messiach's impending arrival. Governments would be given no choice but to cooperate. Food was all. If you controlled that, you controlled… everything. Claude eased over towards the brothers. He spoke to them in French.

" Are you enjoying the exhibit?" he asked.

" Yes of course," answered Léon. "It's marvelous."

" Cezanne, he was a genius. Eh?"

" Yes. Yes he was," replied Henri.

" Have you seen the Matisse downstairs? The Red Madras Headdress. They say that the subject was Madame Matisse."

" I'd very much like to see it," said Léon." Perhaps you can show us the way."

" Avec plaisir. It's just at the foot of those stairs."

The three men walked slowly towards the staircase, talking about nothing specific, the kind of small talk that is normal at these events. The conversation shifted when they were out of earshot of the other invited guests.

" Have you been to the catering hall?" asked *The Builder.*

" I went this afternoon."

" And?"

" The police had been there all day. Apparently no one's identified Olivieri as the odd man out," Léon answered.

" We're damned lucky if that's true. How about his contacts here? Who knew Olivieri was in Köln?"

" Just the three of us. At least we think so." Léon seemed convinced.

" What have you learned about the Italians?"

" Our man in Rome sent something this morning."

" Tell me, Henri."

" Their investigation is small scale. They've sent a nobody from the Agricultural...oh what's it called? The Political Ministry of Agri..something, something affairs. A corruption scandal has got

everyone's attention. The cabinet may have to resign. This is low
on the totem pole."

" Good. Who's the nobody?"

" Carabinieri, apparently on lifetime loan to the Ministry of
Agriculture."

" I wonder what he did to deserve that?" mused *The Builder*.

" Our man says that he's got a reputation as a bungler. Not
stupid, but can't keep his fly shut. He's solved a few unimportant
cases but they don't give him much help or pay him much attention.
One assistant, also Carabinieri."

" Where is this guy now, Henri?"

" Someplace between Paris and Rome. He has no secretary
and the assistant's been out of the office."

" Names."

" The one in charge is called Baglione. I'm not sure how to
pronounce it? The other is called Pippo D'Orazio. He's the one
back in Rome."

" Excellent, Henri. What about the Germans? Have they put
two and two together yet?"

" Yes. This morning," replied Léon. "The police, here, are
convinced the catering hall deaths were no accident. It's all
explained in an Interpol bulletin. The Italians have been notified."

" So this Bag fellow knows that?"

" Our man doesn't think so. He's apparently traveling. He
hasn't checked in and his man hasn't been able to find him."

" That won't last forever. He's got to get in touch with Rome
eventually."

" Do you think he'll show up here?"

" Do cantors sing in the shower?"

Dinner was delicious. After they'd cooled down from their quickie in the Rolls, Baglione and Vanessa drove aimlessly through the countryside, enjoying the breeze. They ended up in the little town of Albaretto della Torre. She knew a restaurant where the food was sublime. The proprietors, Cesare and Silvana, were old friends of Vanessa. The evening's menu was discussed in great detail. Carpaccio di spada to start their meal.

" Buon idea," said Baglione enthusiastically. They drank an Arneis from Tenuta Rambaudi. "The wine is delicious, just like you cara."

" Dai, Corrado," she laughed. "Give it up. You're not capable of making me blush."

For primo they ate tagliarini with a roasted cherry tomato sauce.

" Piace?" asked Silvana, the owner.

" Strepitoso," smiled Baglione, wiping his chin.

" Tomatoes from the garden. We eat them like candy.

" Delizioso davvero."

" Grazie. Now we talk about secondo. Contrafiletto di fassona - from Chieri. Cesare gives it a drizzle of olio and, literally, throws a big handful of wild rucola on it. Like a crazy person!"

" Brava, signora And with it, we should we drink a Barolo, no?"

" Leave it to me." She returned with bottle in hand. " Just taste. Don't look." She hid the label from him, and poured each of them a glass. Vanessa smiled. She was enjoying this policeman's company. Corrado picked up his glass, swirled then sniffed, looked and then tasted.

" It's wonderful. What is it?"

" What do you think it is?" laughed Silvana.

" Barolo? Seriously, what is it? Don't torture me."

" The grape is Nebbiolo, same as Barolo. It's Ghemme from near Novara." Baglione examined the label.

" Collis Breclamæ. It's Latin, no?" He looked at the back label. "From vineyards that once were Caesar's. Interesting. More important still, it's delicious."

" Vanessa, hold on to this man. I like him."

" Don't you worry. I think I'll keep him in my cellar. For the winter. When it's cold."

The two women laughed. Silvana excused herself.

" Are you serious? About keeping me for the winter."

" Oh Corrado. If it was just that simple. If we could just do whatever we wanted. Life would be so much better. But... we, I, live in the real world. I don't believe in fairy tales."

" I'm sorry. What an idiot, I am. I mean we just met. We hardly..."

" Baglione. I have something to tell you. You're not going to like it."

" I'm a lousy lover. I know. But have patience, my sweet."

" It's not that," she laughed but only for a moment. "I'm not what you think."

" You mean you're not a beautiful, intelligent woman. You're really a horrible criminal. A thief. Give me some credit, please. I knew who you were before I set eyes on you. Now ask me if I give a damn."

" Do you Corrado?" She looked straight into his eyes. " I'm fifty-two years old. I've supported myself for years, by stealing from people I don't know and don't care about. If this fucking incubo with the poisoned wine wrecks my business I'll have to start again. Just when the winery was starting to work. I can't stand to think I'll have to go back to that life."

She began to cry. Baglione wanted to believe that the tears were for real. He wanted badly to believe her.

" I have a confession of my own. I'm a married man."

" Like all the good ones."

" But I'm miserable. She's a cow. I don't even like her anymore. And she..." He paused.

" Yes. Tell me."

" She thinks I'm a failure," he said quietly.

" I don't believe that's possible." She touched his cheek with her hand.

" You don't know me, Signora. We met, what, ten minutes ago?"

" I'm a very good judge of character."

" Let me tell you something about my character. I'm Carabinieri for twenty-one years. A couple of lousy promotions, based only on my time. Banished to a ministry that makes me count cow turds. And...in spite of all that, I like my job. How about that for character?"

" We are a pair, aren't we?"

" So what would make you happy, Vanessa Terry from Bottle Creek, Michigan?"

" Battle Creek."

" Whatever."

" It's the cereal capital of the world."

" Scusami."

" Battle Creek. It's where all the breakfast cereal comes from. Kellogg's Corn Flakes. Post Toasties."

" I think you're making fun of me. I'm trying to be serious."

" I know you are. I apologize. Corrado?"

" Yes."

" Will you help me? Will you straighten out this mess? Help me to clear my name. Let me have my little wine business back. I don't want to go to prison. But it will happen. I can't do the things I used to. Do you know that I once jumped from a hotel room balcony, right into the sea, when the people I was robbing came in the door? Can you picture me doing that now? No, Corrado, I can't face it. I'm tired. I'm getting older. I want to stay home and have my garden. Grow my eggplants and my zucchini. Have lots of dogs and cats."

" Vanessa, I want that too. Believe me I do." He stopped for a moment. "Look this is crazy. Let me do my job. Let me get to the bottom of this. O.K.?"

" O.K. You're a sweet man. A no bullshit man."

" You think?"

Silvana came to the table with two plates neatly arranged with slices of beef under a mountain of the bitter fresh greens.

" Sorry. I didn't mean to interrupt."

" Non è un problema. Baglione lives for his stomach. Eh, caro?"

CHILEAN APPLE EXPORTS SUSPENDED

SANTIAGO (REUTERS) - Exports of Chilean apples to Mexico were suspended on Friday after Mexican health authorities discovered larvae in a container shipment, said official sources.

The Chilean Ministry of Agriculture announced that the sale of 25,000 tonnes of apples has been suspended in Mexico, where 75,000 tonnes have already been delivered. Chile, to resolve the problem, has invited a team of Mexican health experts to Santiago. They are due at the end of the month. The insects in the apple shipment destroy fruit and belong to a variety of flies not found in Mexico, according to a report from officials in Mexico City.

The suspension of apple imports hit hard. Chilean exporters report sales of apples to the European Community have dropped this year to 203,000 tonnes from 268,000 tonnes in 1992.

Claude Wizman put down the International Herald Tribune, turned to his notebook computer, hit a series of keys and then waited. And waited. This kind of thing took forever. He missed the new desktop model that sat in his New York office. It was time to step up from this portable. He made a mental note to do something about it when he returned. Retail electronics was one of the core businesses of the Boravitcher movement. Wizman had gotten them into it back in the early nineteen-seventies. Now they controlled 70% of the retail and mail order business in the tri-state area. Recently the operation had expanded into California, Florida, Texas and Illinois.

He entered the figures from the newspaper and watched as his spreadsheet adjusted to the new information. The flies had been introduced in the Chilean apple fields ten months before. They'd obviously liked the climate. *The Builder* returned to PROGMAN and pulled up WinFax Pro. He composed a short buy order for his real estate man in Santiago. The instructions were quite simple. Buy all available orchards. They already owned large pieces of the business in the U.S. and France. Next year they'd ease the prices up slightly. He sent the fax directly from the ZDS notebook. Not a bad machine, just too slow for his needs. Wizman would pass it along to Henri.

The phone rang. It was Léon.

" The Italian just called in. They told him about Köln."

" Is he coming here?"

" They didn't know."

" Where is he now?"

" In Italy. A town called Cornegliano. I looked it up. It's near Turin."

" Connections?"

" By train it's twelve hours. By plane it's a few hours less. The connections are awful."

" What time did he talk to his office?"

" Around ten this morning. If he left right away, he'll be here tonight."

" Find out and call me back."

Baglione walked back into the just cleaned and scrubbed kitchen at Tenuta Rambaudi.

" Did you get through to your office?"

" Si. There's been another poisoning. In Germany. Four dead."

" Oh no! Not my wine?"

" No. No. A moscato from Val D'Aosta."

" Thank god. I mean, I'm sorry that it's happened again. But better someone else. No. What am I saying? It's terrible. It's bad for us all. Corrado you've got to stop them."

" I'm going there right away."

" To Val D'Aosta?"

" No. To Köln. Maybe someone's gotten stupid. It seems the victims were all old SS. Toasting to the past. Disgusting, if you ask me."

" That's bizarre. In Germany? In this day and age. Isn't it against the law?"

" Unfortunately, it seems that it isn't. How do you get from here to Köln?"

" I'm not sure. Where is Köln?"

" Near Frankfurt I think. Do you have a map?"

Vanessa got up from the table and walked down the hall to her study. She came back with an atlas of Europe.

" It's nearer to Bonn, than to Frankfurt." Signora Rambaudi had on a pair of reading glasses. Something that Baglione had not seen before. "I think you can take the train from Milano. I'll call."

" Isn't Torino closer?"

" Not to worry. I'll drive you to Milano. Unless you'd like some company in Köln."

He thought for a moment and was about to answer when the phone rang.

" Pronto...Ezio! How are you darling?...And Carlo?"

'So I'm not the only one she calls darling,' thought Baglione

" When?...For the weekend. It sounds positively wicked...Hold on a second." Corrado was shaking his head no. She covered the phone with her hand.

" No, I shouldn't go Corrado - or no, you're not taking me with you?"

" You want to come to Köln? Come to Köln. I certainly can't stop you."

" How romantic." She got back on the phone.

"Ezio, I'm afraid that I can't make it. Perhaps some other time." She smiled and looked at Corrado. "But thank you. Big kiss… Caio...Ciao Ciao...Ciao."

" Who was that?"

" A friend. Baglione, you're not jealous are you? We've only just met."

" But what about, about...us? What you said."

" Us. 'Us' just met yesterday afternoon. There is no 'us'. At least, not yet."

The policeman, deflated, said nothing.

" Oh dear, I've hurt your feelings. Corrado listen to me. Neither one of us is a kid. You're a married man..."

" I told you..."

" Let me finish. Before yesterday, you didn't even know me. Today you're leaving for Germany. Who knows if I'll ever see you again. Last night was fun..."

" Fun?"

" Maybe it could turn into something more. Or maybe not. I'm a practical girl, Baglione."

" Come with me to Köln."

" And?"

" We take it slowly. What do you think about that?"

" I'm just not...I mean, I...O.K. I'll pack a bag and meet you outside. Yours is by the door."

" I'll call and make us a reservation. What do you think about flying?"

" Absolutely not.. I hate making love in those toilets." She laughed and ran up the stairs.

" **He's** arriving tonight, just after nine - on the train."

" Henri I want you to go to the station. Meet his train. I want to know what this Baglione is doing. Find out his hotel, if he's renting a car, if the Italian consulate is involved. I don't have to tell you, you know what to do."

" He's not traveling alone. The reservation was made for two."

" Who's the other person?"

" I don't know. We just have to wait and see. I can tell you it isn't his man from Rome."

" Where is Léon?"

" At the catering hall. The police have finally cleared out of there. He's trying to find out if anyone singled out Olivieri."

" I trust he's being extra careful. We don't want to call attention to anything. You understand what I'm saying."

" Of course. Léon's good. Maybe even better than me," laughed his brother.

" It's difficult for you both, isn't it Henri?"

" In what way?"

" This business. This living in a world you don't belong in. I know it's hard. Having to eat trayf, to sit on the bus next to women. Or is it, Henri? Maybe, down deep, you enjoy the forbidden fruit? Eh, what do you say, my young friend?"

" It's my job."

" That's it? 'It's my job'."

" What do you want me to say? That I enjoy eating food that's not kosher. That I dream of seducing women. I don't like it. I just do it. I do it for him. Just like Léon. Like you do."

" Damn it, Henri! Enough already. It's working. Everything's going as planned. When *The Moshiach* comes, we'll be ready."

" Do you really believe he's coming soon? He'll tell us. Won't he? I know it's him, Claude. It has to be him."

The door to the hallway had an old fashioned bell and string. Pull the string from outside and it rang a bell in the room.

" That must be Léon. I'll go let him in...And stop with the whining."

Claude realized he was speaking a bit too harshly to his young protégé and tried to moderate his tone.

" Please be careful."

" Isn't Jörg downstairs?"

" Just be careful, Henri."

He crossed the room, walked to the door and opened it slowly. Léon was standing outside with a smile on his face.

" Hello, hello. How is everyone today?"

" What did you learn?" snapped Wizman, clearly still on edge.

" Relax, Claude. Remember me? We're on the same side."

" I'm sorry, Léon. This is very serious. You realize that, don't you? It could be the end of us if we're not careful. I have a bad feeling."

" I understand. But not to worry. I spoke with a few of the waiters. Even the one who poured the wine. They saw no one. Nothing out of place. There is no link to Olivieri - so there is no link to us."

" Alright then. But let's not take any unnecessary chances. Henri is going to the train station. The Italian's arriving tonight. I want to know his every move. When everything's safe and secure, we'll leave Köln. O.K?"

" Not a minute too soon for me. Germans make me nervous," said Léon without a trace of humor.

The EuroCity train from Milano, with a connection in Zurich, stopped at Basel, Mannheim and Bonn. At Basel, Corrado and Vanessa briefly had the compartment to themselves. The two American backpackers they'd shared the space with collected their possessions, smiled a good-bye smile and departed. Baglione dove into his suitcase and took out the **IN QUARANTENA** sign.

" I don't believe you," laughed Vanessa, as he fastened it to the door.

" Don't you want a little privacy?"

" Baglione, God help me, I think I'm falling for you."

" That's a change from this morning. Remember when you said 'Corrado, there is no us'."

" A woman can change her mind. Katherine Hepburn did it a million times in the movies."

" Who?

" Catarina Ep-boorn – la conosci?"

" Kath-er-een Epp-urn. You see I can say it too. Kath-er-een Epp..."

" O.K. I believe you. Remember in WOMAN OF THE YEAR, she told Clark Gable one thing when she really meant just the opposite."

" It was in IT HAPPENED ONE NIGHT and it wasn't Kath-er-een Epp-burn. It was Claudia Colbert."

" And who," asked the conductor, "is responsible for this ridiculous charade?" Corrado looked up. The large Swiss woman, in her smart blue uniform, removed the **IN QUARANTENA** sign from the glass window in the sliding door to the compartment. Two nuns squeezed past her and took their seats opposite the lovers.

" May I have a word with you outside," Baglione said to the conductor. They stepped into the narrow corridor.

" I am Dott. Baglione, Medico Neurologo, travelling to Köln for a health emergency. The lady is my patient."

" And I'm the Queen of England! Do you think you're so clever with this sign? Do you think I haven't seen it all in my twenty-six years in this job? Take your sign and stick it up your patient, dottore."

Baglione sat back down in his seat. He wouldn't look at the nuns. Vanessa leaned over to him and whispered that she was laughing so hard on the inside that she'd almost wet her pants. The remainder of the trip was uneventful, save for one mad dash for kottenwurst sandwiches on black bread with mustard and raw onion from the station café, in Mannheim. They arrived in Köln right on schedule.

Henri was waiting. He spotted the 1st Class carriage. From the platform Drei watched as his subjects left the train. Corrado carried both of their bags through the station and out the door to a taxi. Henri followed closely. He felt increasingly uneasy as, three minutes later, Baglione's taxi turned left on Mühlengasse, then slowed and stopped. He followed the couple as they navigated the last 100 meters on foot to the entrance of Das kleine Stapelhäuschen. Did they know that Claude and the Dreis were staying there, or was it merely an unfortunate coincidence? They registered and then squeezed into the tiny elevator with their luggage. Henri watched the indicator above the elevator doors. They were staying on two, the floor below Claude Wizman. Drei spoke to his boss from the ancient house phone.

" Henri. Where are you?"

" In the lobby. They're here."

" In Köln."

" No, I mean, yes. But here, in this hotel. On the second floor!"

" Have the desk prepare my bill. I'm leaving right now. You stay here with Léon. Find out what they're up to." In less than an hour Wizman was gone from Köln.

The following morning Baglione kissed the sleeping Vanessa Rambaudi on her cheek and set out in search of some answers. His first stop was a courtesy call at the local police headquarters. A chain smoking Polizeirat named Wolfgang Flanken had little to say about the four murders. The deaths, so far, had not caused any public outcry. Although no one said it out loud, most of the Polizei Köln were happy to say goodbye to Maxi Fleischig. As a result, the investigation moved forward slowly.

" Yes Inspector, the laboratory report confirms the poison was not Dizactin. And no Inspector, we have no suspects. The staff has all been cleared and yes, Inspector, you can make some inquiries. If it makes you feel any better."

Baglione rented an Opel Corsa and drove out of town to the hall where the poisonings took place. He spoke with several of the employees. No one remembered seeing anything out of the ordinary. The beer hall was a hangout for neo and not so neo Nazis. It was one of those places where they sang the old songs and clinked their steins to the Fuhrer. As Baglione spoke, a dozen or so grey haired men were gorging on himmel un äd mit flönz and grilled pork legs. They bore the unmistakable look of a type that most Germans wanted to forget. The burly men had close cut hair. Several wore khaki shirts and brown pants. Their loud conversations were peppered with racist comments. The last waiter that the Italian questioned shook his head and sighed.

" You know, Inspector, times are hard here. I took this job because I had to. You think I like hearing that garbage. I'm sorry, but I can't help you. I've been over this all with the police. Even that poor Jew who came here yesterday had to listen to that bullshit." He pointed towards the luncheon party with a slight nod of his head.

" You're referring to Detective Flanken?"

" I don't think he told me his name."

" Older man. A bit fat. Dressed well?"

" No. He was young. He asked me if anyone saw a stranger working that day, or someone just hanging around."

" And you answered that you hadn't."

" That's right. The guy seemed almost relieved to hear that. Strange isn't it. A policeman not wanting to find a clue."

" So he was a policeman?"

" Yes. I mean I assumed he was."

" He didn't show you any identification?"

" I..I'm not sure. There were so many police the past few days, I just..."

" Do you remember what he looked like?"

" Short, dark hair, big nose. Now don't get me wrong. I knew he was a Jew by the way he spoke German. It had nothing to do with his..."

" How does a Jew speak German?"

" It's nothing specific. You just know."

" Would you recognize the man again?"

" Of course. He had a mark on his hand, like the one on Gorbachev's head."

Later that day, over cocktails at the hotel, Baglione had little to talk about. The case was going nowhere. With each new poisoning, the Italian wines suffered enormously in the export markets. There was even some talk of an upsurge in sales of wines from France, in Italia! That, to Baglione, was totally unacceptable.

" So what did you do today, cara?"

" Oh, a little of this and a little of that. I didn't get up until noon. Corrado, you almost killed me last night. Maybe you should change your name to Tarzan."

It had been a lovely evening. A late supper at Kleinmann's. They'd had a nice crisp Markus Molitor Riesling, recommended by the old lady who ran the place, and ate much too much plump white asparagus. He'd wondered where they got it, so late in the season. It was well past two when the couple had finally tumbled into bed. For some reason, maybe it was the wine, but Baglione had not made love with such incredible passion since before he'd married Rosalba. Possibly never before in his life. This Americana had shown him some things that he'd only seen in pornographic films. The thing with the ice was incredible. Something he'd never forget.

" Corrado, you don't look so good. How long are we going to stay here?"

" I've got to meet with that detective I told you about. After that we can go. He said he'd come by the hotel. To me he seems ok. I invited him for a drink."

" And after Köln, you go back to Roma," she said laconically. A hint of a pout formed on her lower lip.

" I think that's probably right."

" That doesn't surprise me. Go back to your wife. You deserve each other."

" Vanessa. What kind of thing is that to say?"

" I say what I feel. You had no intention to stay with me. Admit it. Ugh! Men. I feel like such a jerk."

" Oh, cara. Don't start with that again. Please."

" How long do we have to wait for this German?"

" He'll be along. I've got to run out for a few minutes. Will you please be nice to him? He's not a bad fellow."

When the German detective walked into the bar, Vanessa knew that she would like him. He was somewhat portly, well groomed, dressed nicely in his Joop! jeans and Heinz Oestergaard designed uniform jacket. He had a trimmed salt and pepper beard, tortoise frame eyeglasses and most importantly for Vanessa, he had on a very good pair of shoes. Her "gay-dar" went off immediately and the shoes were the clincher.

" Good afternoon. You must be Corrado's friend. I hope I'm not interrupting." Wolfgang Flanken sat down at the table.

" No, Captain. Corrado has been telling me all about you. It is Captain, isn't it? With a C or a K?" Vanessa glanced at the gold star on his shoulder.

" Yes. It's Kapitän. With a K. But please call me Wolf.

" And you may call me Little Red Riding Hood." They spoke in English, their only common language.

" How long will you honor us Kölners with your presence, madame?"

" I'm really not sure, Wolf. Corrado is leaving tonight."

" You're not going with him?"

" The Inspector is taking the evening train. I haven't made any plans." She smiled at the German.

" A drink for you, Kapitän?"

" Thank you kindly, Miss...?"

" Missus...Rambaudi. But you may call me... Vanessa." She deliberately lowered her voice a half tone to sound like Marlene Dietrich. A bellman appeared at their table.

" Telephone for you, Kapitän."

Flanken took the call at the reception. He returned with a smile on his face.

" Apparently, your poor Corrado has a bit of a stomach problem. He said that he'll join us shortly." *Shortly* turned into an hour, and one cocktail turned into three.

" May I call you Wolfie?"

" Of course. That's what all my friends call me."

" Then I will call you Wolfie too... and then you and I will be friends. You are such a delightful man. And your boyfriend sounds divine."

" When I first was introduced to him he had a dreadful English...correction, uppercrust English accent. A total affectation. It was hilarious. I used to laugh so much. It made him very cross at first but even he could see how ridiculous it was. I'm sure you know a few English aristocrat types. So you'll understand what I'm saying."

They were really getting drunk. Baglione was nowhere in sight.

" Speaking of aristocrats, do you want to hear about my brief little somethin'-somethin' with the royals? It's a guaranteed pisser." Vanessa was way drunker than Wolfie.

" Let's have one more round. I can't wait to hear this!" The barman, slash bellman, was all over it. Two Boodles martinis arrived *tout de suite*.

" You have to promise never to tell Corrado about this."

" I promise."

" Swear to god?"

" I swear, I swear." They were laughing so loud that the barman just shook his head. They were his only customers, so no harm in having a bit of fun. Besides, it doesn't hurt to earn a few points with the police.

" OK, here it goes. Once upon a time…" She was having a difficult time sitting up straight.

" Are you alright?"

" Wolfie, I'm having soooo much fun with you. O.K., so this couple, he was Sir Geoffrey Wyck-Rissington, the 19th Earl of Chalk. Or maybe the 14th. But who gives a shit, right?

" I certainly don't," declared Wolfie, knocking back half his cocktail in one long swallow.

" The wife, Brenda, had been some kind of school teacher when they met. He was like forty-seven and she was no spring chicken herself. It was the second time around for both of them. I think the first wife died in like 1951. Anyway, she'd apparently fallen off a horse and old Geoffrey had nearly run her over. They were in some park. Brenda, I told you that was her name, right?

" Right."

" So Brenda, who was married to some Slav, maybe not Yugoslav. Anyway, he was some kind of fucking bovan... maybe Serbian...Where was I?"

" Brenda."

" Right. So she's married to this Slavic guy and apparently he gets drunk one night and takes off for good... Ok...so the royalty connection. The Ryck-Wissingtons, Wyck-Rissingtons?... they always lived in Sussex. For a long time. Very posh...indeed."

" Indeed."

" Stop interrupting me or I'll never get through this. Anyway, in like 1652, King Larry...sorry, King Charley had too much to drink, wink wink, and stayed overnight at Henfield Castle, you know, the ancestral home."

" Whose ancestral home?"

" Shut the fuck up. I'm getting to that. So three hundred years later, Brenda, her last name was like du Fuckfort or du Muckfort...du Montfort...anyway she knows a good thing when she sees it and moves right the fuck in. Did I tell you that they got married? Anyway, apparently his relatives refused to show up and her mum, who lived like in Leeds...I can't believe I remembered that."

" Vanessa, darling, is this going somewhere?"

" Absolutely. So his relatives were all busy that day."

" The wedding day."

" Wolfie stop...interrupting me...or I'll never get to the end of this."

" Sorry."

" So the Earl who was a real debaucher...is that a word?...Did I say that the first wife was a cousin to the Queen? Not important. So it was this connection, that kept old Geoffrey out of the papers. Apparently...here's where it gets good...apparently one evening, while he was still married to wife number one, a certain quote-unquote, 'unnamed gentleman', obviously you know who, was picked up by the Scottish police after he tried to mount the Canadian Ambassador's wife at a party at Bal...Bal...Balm?

" Balmoral?"

" Precisely...Balmoral Castle. That's where the Queen lives, right?"

" If you say so, Vanessa."

" Well, it turns out that old Brenda McMontfuck had the same kind of perversive, what's the word I'm lookin' for? Tastes. Same tastes that he did, even though she apparently managed to control herself around the royalers. Royalists?"

" Royals. They sound like quite the pair."

" Wolfie, you got that right. So the Earl owned a big chunk of downtown London, that old Earl #5 grabbed in like 1633."

" Wow, 1633."

" Wolfie, will you please shut the fuck up. So the way I met them is they like traveling around the world pickin' up young, good looking kids, which is what I was. So... this is great. You're not going to believe what happens next. Apparently, one day in Hong Kong, I say 'apparently' a lot, don't I?

" Go on."

" So they're touring around and he gets a big hard-on. He was big, too. Trust me on that. In a ricksha. After way too much champagne they went for a ride in Kowloon, I think. I mean I know it was champagne that they drank. That's all they ever drank. So she climbs on him someplace near TST."

" TST?"

" Tim Shat Sea - you know, where the ferry boat...is. So she decides to sit on his lap. Did I already say that?"

" I'm amazed that you can remember all this."

126

" I'm probably makin' some of it up. But it is a good story. So for thirty-five, maybe forty-five minutes they rode around Hong Kong like this. Like a pair of fucking Siamese twins...literally. And from that day on, they decided...like it was their life's mission, to fuck in public, wherever they travelled. I suppose you already know, bein' that you're a copper. I had a small run in with the law a few years ago."

" I am aware that there were some difficulties."

" Exactly. Some difficulties. I like that."

" And that's where you met these people?" Her monologue was starting to run out of steam. And where the hell was Baglione?

" Exactly. The Wyck-Rissies always 'summered.' That means they spent the entire summer...on the French Riviera.

" So that's where you met them?"

" No. I actually met them in Rome. I'm getting to that." She finished her drink and shook her head *no* in the direction of the barman, who was listening intently. "So they check into the Hassler which, by the way, in my opinion, is a shitty hotel, and they go off to dinner. OK, listen carefully now... 'cause here's where it gets good. She decides, after dinner, that she wants a gelato ball. One of those chocolate truffle thingies from Tre Scalini in...drum roll...........Piazza Navona!

" Where they find you doing charcoal portraits of the tourists."

" Did I already tell you this story?

" No, no darling. I'm just a good detective."

" Ok, then. So to make a long shorey stort...long shory short."

" They discover that you speak English..."

" I *am* an American, Wolfie."

" No disputing that, dear."

" Wolfie, don't fuck with me. Anyway, here it goes. I'm earning like, twenty bucks a day. On a good day! My frickin' room and board cost me more than that. Plus...I still owned the farm...in Italy. Then the Earl and Brenda ask me to come back to Nice with them and offer me two hundred a week to be their 'traveling companion,' which I don't have to tell you what that meant."

" I get it." Neither of them spotted Baglione lurking behind a screen that masked the entrance to the toilets.

" So we arrive back in Nice and they get me a room at a cute little hotel looking out over the harbor and then I ate my first lunch...at Café Turin...in the old town...if you ever get to Nice. Do you eat oysters? Very nice place for oysters… but the waiters suck."

" Vanessa, please."

" So...then I went off to see them, Earl and Brenda. They were staying for the whole fucking summer at The Carlton, which I gotta' say - was not too shabby. So I get there and go up to their rooms. I ring their doorbell and I wait. And I wait. All of a sudden the door swings open and there's old Geoffrey wearing these long blue boxer shorts and a pair of knee socks with the things that hold 'em up.... which I will never forget! And, get this, she's wearing the same outfit...boxers and socks with those same things! Blue. The boxers, not the socks. I don't really remember what color the socks were. I think black or brown. A dark color. But it's not important. Where was I? Nevermind. I remember… Anyway, I was fuckin' speechless. I mean, here's this little girl from Fucknuts, Michigan. Me. And all I could say was, get this..."I think I saw this cartoon in last week's New Yorker."

" I don't get it."

" Not important. So I go inside this oplient, opluent…

" Opulent."

" Opulent suite...did I already tell you this?

" Vanessa. Concentrate."

" No need to be nasty, Wolfie."

" My apologies. Please continue.

" Alright. So there we are in the suite and pretty soon things began to get strange. Not that they weren't already. But they were about to get even stranger. I did get my first taste of really good champagne - Krug '55, by the way. I'll never forget it. So she, Brenda, says to me that I should sit on the sofa. Anyhow, I tell them I'm not really comfortable and guess what she says?"

" Perhaps you'd like to take off your things?"

" Wolfie, you *are* a good detective!"

" Sorry to interrupt, my dear. But is there an end to this?"

" Yes. Here it comes. 'Vanessa,' she says to me in her snooty little English accent, "the Earl and I would like to perform a little play. You must sit back, have another sip of champagne and just enjoy yourself."

" And then?" asked a third voice. Vanessa jerked around to see Baglione standing there with a sheepish grin on his face.

" Oh, Corrado. I'm so sorry. I'm so embarrassed."

" Cara, just finish the story. I beg you. We beg you!"

" OK. If you're sure I'm not offending you. I know that you're still a little teensy weensy bit Catholic."

" And your point would be...?

" Maybe we should have another martini? Whaddya say Wolfie?"

" I think you've had enough."

" Well...Ok then. Here comes the end. You ready Wolfie? You ready, Corrado? This is gonna' be good. So I'm sitting in this huge suite at The Carlton. It was big as a house. Not his dick… the room...and for like thirty minutes, they're goin' at it, I mean, really goin' at it! And to be honest, they were pretty fuckin' athletic. I just kept reminding myself, 'Vanessa honey, you need this money.' Then he says to me in his fancy English accent, 'So, my girl, did we shock you?"

" Did they?"

" Shut up, Wolfie. So I say to them, First off, I'm not your girl, and it's not like I haven't been around. You know I used to live in New York." She paused. "And that's how I became a jewel thief."

" Did we miss something, dear?"

" Right, Wolfie. OK. So I stayed with them for a few days, and she was really mean to everybody...especially me...so I stole his Patek. Gent's Calatrava. Nice watch, actually. Beautiful watch...in an understated way.

" Vanessa. Please"

" Ok, Ok. So...then one thing led to another. I realized right away that I was very good it...at stealing jewelry, I mean...and so I did. A lot. There was this Corsican.....

" Vanessa, liebling, we get the picture. Corrado and I really have to discuss this case. You're welcome to stay."

" I don't think that's a good idea. Vanessa is done with all this nasty business. She's retired. You are retired?...Vanessa?

" Let's just say that burglary has been berry, berry good to me. Remember what's his name on Saturday Night Live? Chico, something. Right?"

" Vanessa, what are you saying?"

" I'm saying...I'm saying that slowly, slowly I brought Tenuta Rambaudi...back to life. Born again, like Jimmy Carter. I replanted the vineyards. I bought a new roof. Can you even buy a roof? I bought the Rolls – for cash. I didn't steal it...in case you were wondering. I have lots of nice clothes. Wolfie, you would die if you saw my closets. Not that I think you would wear them...I mean, you seem pretty butch. No offense. Did I tell you I support disturbing...I mean deserving young artists. Was that a Freudian slip? And...here's something I bet even you don't know, Wolfie. On my fiftieth birthday, I earned...I, little 'Vanessa the jewel thief,' earned a fucking doctorate degree in comparative cultures. From the...Univeruary of Ghent. That's in Belgium."

" I know where Ghent is, sweetie." Wolfie shook his head in total amazement.

" And that, my two friends...is the whole enchilada."

She attempted to get up but fell back into the big plush sofa. The two policemen were silent. What could they possibly say? Corrado did wonder what an enchilada was. The German detective sat up straight in his chair and addressed his colleague.

" So, tell us about your day, Inspector. We can speak in front of the lady, ja?"

" Of course. I went out to the beer hall and poked around. Not much to see though. I did eat something that gave me the shits."

" You spoke to the employees?"

" Yes. Nothing there. By the way, do you have a detective, young man, short, dark hair, has a mark on the back of his hand?"

" Let me think. No. I don't think so. I'm sure of it. Why do you ask?"

" No reason, really. There was someone out there asking questions yesterday. One of the employees thought he might have been a policeman."

The barman approached cautiously.

" What do you like to have, sir?"

Baglione winced.

" Do you have any Fernet?"

" Underberg satisfactory, sir?" Baglione nodded his approval.

" This business with the wine is causing big problems in Italy. Ja?"

" The producers are going insane. This lady has really been suffering. One of her wines killed a woman in New York. Fell right over at the dinner table. Right into her salmone. Face first." Vanessa grimaced.

" How unfortunate for the victim...And the salmon - it survived?" Wolfie chuckled to himself. "Seriously. This is obviously very damaging for your growers. We had a not so dissimilar problem in Koblenz, maybe one year ago. Some x-ray machines, which one of our German companies sells to the U.S., have been malfunctioning. The company suspected that there had been some tampering. After they left the factory. Not so different than the problems with your wines. It really hurt their business. Don't you think there are some similarities? Or am I imagining things."

" Wolfie, can I get a look at those files? I don't usually put much faith in coincidence."

" Of course. I'll copy them and send them to...where? Your office in Rome?"

" Is it possible to take them with me?"

" You mean tonight? I don't think so. Ordinarily it wouldn't be a problem. But there was a string of burglaries today. Mostly jewelry."

Baglione choked on his Underberg.

" I've got all of my staff on overtime. We think it's the work of one man. We've got to, what's the expression? Round up the usual suspects."

Baglione glared at Vanessa Rambaudi.

" Can I get them in the morning?"

" By all means. So then you aren't leaving tonight?" asked the Kapitän.

" Perhaps if I wait until tomorrow, the lady might return with me."

They both turned to look at Vanessa, who had passed out on the sofa.

Léon Drei sat in a telefonkabine at the Deutsche PTT office on the Barthelstrasse. The phone rang. Finally, his call had gone through.

" Serge here."

" It's me."

" What took you so long?" asked *The Builder*.

" I didn't want to call from there."

" Trouble?"

" I'm not sure. Henri followed the Italian out to the beer hall."

" And?"

" He spoke to four or five people. The same ones that I spoke to the other day. I'm sure he heard the same story. No one saw Olivieri. At least no one remembered seeing him."

" So what is the problem?"

" Yesterday evening, this Baglione met with a police detective called Flanken. He's Chief of Detectives in Köln."

" It's normal. No problem there."

" This morning a package was delivered to the Italian. Our man got a look at it first."

" Good work. What was in it?"

" Files... On the Gambelhauff investigation."

" Dammit. How did they make that jump?"

" This Flanken guy must have remembered the case."

" I think it's time for our man at Gambelhauff to take early retirement." Léon Drei made no comment. Another job for Jörg Bissel.

" There's something else I don't understand. The woman with Baglione. I followed her all day. She first went to another room at the Stapelhauschen. I waited down the hall. It was like she didn't want anyone to see her."

" Maybe a lover," remarked Claude.

" I don't think so. She was in there for only a minute. Let herself in and out. Then she did the same thing at another hotel across the street."

" Bizarre. What do you make of it?"

" At first I was confused. Why would a woman... she's in the wine trade by the way. Her name is Vanessa Rambaudi.

" Why do I know that name?"

" Tenuta Rambaudi wine. Chicago. Anyway, I asked myself, why was this woman going in and out of these rooms? Then in this morning's paper I saw it. A robbery. An expensive watch. Worth a lot of money. They think it was an inside job. A maid, maybe. But it matched her movements exactly."

" She's a thief? This is very strange. Too strange. I don't like this. See what you can find out about her. Where are they now?"

" Still in Köln. But he was downstairs when I left, checking on the train schedules. Henri is with them."

" I'm going back to New York tonight. Call me... And Léon, be extra smart. I have a bad feeling about this."

" Same here."

There was a sleeping car on the train and Baglione secured a private compartment. No need for the quarantine sign. Corrado checked his watch. It was five minutes after nine in the evening. Departure was scheduled at 21:11. Vanessa appeared just as the whistle blew. The Zugchef tipped his cap and helped her aboard.

" I'd just about given up on you."

" Did you think I wasn't coming?"

" I don't know what to think about you. How could you do it? I thought you were through with all that? You told me, 'Corrado, I can't go to prison. Help me'. Like an idiot I believed you!"

" Corrado. Please try to understand. It's like an addiction. I've been good for almost a year. I stayed at home. I concentrated on my wines. But yesterday...yesterday…
something happened. I can't explain it. You were out being a policeman, doing things, and I was just there. I felt so useless. It was a release. I know I was wrong."

" You have to return the watch."

" I can't."

" You still have it, don't you?"

" Not exactly."

" Oh my god. You sold it already?"

" No. I didn't sell it."

" Then where is it?"

" You have it."

" What!" Baglione could not believe what he was hearing.

" It's in your bag. I put it in with your socks."

" Porca madonna. Vanessa, I'm a policeman. Do you know what would happen if they found me with this watch? My career – my life would be over!" He leaped up and grabbed his suitcase. He was so angry that his hands were shaking. He could barely open the catches. Baglione shook his head. The case popped open. He pulled out the socks which were tied up in pairs. Just then there was a knock on the door of their compartment.

" Don't open that door," he whispered.

Someone knocked again.

" Who's there?"

" Tickets please."

" Can't you come back in a while?"

" Of course, sir" said a man's muffled voice.

" You have to give it back."

" But I don't have it. You do," she laughed.

" This is no joke. This is serious, serious business. Do you know that I could arrest you as soon as we cross into Italy?"

" Handcuffs and everything?"

" Uff! Why don't you grow up? That's it. I've had it with you. No more little tricks! No more lies!"

She reached over and kissed him. Softly at first and then with a passion. Moments after they'd finished making love the train pulled into a station. Vanessa raised the shade and looked out.

" Where are we?" he asked, gently stroking her back.

" You just asked me to turn over and grab your balls. So I did."

" Signora Rambaudi you are the most exasperating..."

" Sexy..." She offered her lips for a kiss.

" ...impossible..." He kissed her again. This time on the neck.

" ...sexy..." He flicked his tongue at her nipple.

" ...exciting woman that I have ever met in my life."

" So you forgive me?"

" I forgive you. But don't ever do that again." He laid back in bed and closed his eyes.

" Corrado."

" Si, cara."

" So...will you just look at the watch?"

" No."

" You're going to really like it. It's very you, Corrado."

" What do you mean, it's very me?" He reached for his suitcase, rooted around in it and found the watch tucked into a rolled up pair of socks. He examined it and smiled.

"I knew you'd like it."

"Mickey Mouse. Very funny, Vanessa."

"Ah, but it's not any old Mickey Mouse. It's a Gerald Genta."

"And I'm supposed to know what that means?"

"It means it's worth a lot of money."

The guard at the Ministero delle Risorse Agricole, Alimentari e Forestali on Via Sella did not feel it necessary to stand or salute as the detective walked through the door. The morning headline in **la Repubblica** was short and to the point.

BAMBONE ARRESTED IN KICKBACK SCHEME

Bambone was Minister of Agriculture, Fausto Bambone. Baglione's boss. Everyone in the building was in shock, not because of the charges, everyone knew what he was up to, but the fact that he'd been arrested at all. Tangentopoli, the Italian bribery scandal, had arrived at their doorstep. Who was next? Who would be implicated along with the boss? Baglione fumed as he read the paper. He'd heard that certain capital projects were being examined by a group of Palermo judges. But no one had asked for his help in the investigation. He finally got through to a friend in the Ministry of Justice who explained that everyone was under suspicion. However, "and you didn't hear it from me," said the man, Baglione had been given a clean bill of health. Bambone's two deputies had also been named in the probe. That meant, pretty much, that there was no one in charge at the moment. Corrado was on his own. It gave him a queasy feeling in his stomach, sort of like rowing a boat without any oars. He decided to just do his job, to ignore the scandal as if it wasn't happening. He put in a call to Köln.

"Wolfie?"

"Ja, Ja."

"It's Baglione."

" Where are you? I've been calling your office for days."

" I took a few days vacation. At Lago di Como."

" And the lady?"

" She's fine."

" Have you looked at the files I sent over?"

" Certo. I see what you mean. There are certainly similarities."

" Corrado, I think this is worth pursuing."

" I agree. Can you get someone who's familiar with this kind of medical business to draw up a list. Let's find out who benefits from this."

" Jetzt sofort, Chef. Or as you Italians say, 'subito.' Ja?"

" Si. And I'll do the same for our wines. Maybe we can find a..."

" Connection."

" Si."

" My boss thinks it's a bit far-fetched."

" Mine's too busy with his own problems. Have you heard the news?"

" About what?"

" It seems that my boss, our Minister of Agriculture has been caught, how shall I say? *Con le mani nella marmellata*."

" Even I can understand that," laughed Wolfie.

" There's a lot of that going around, eh Baglione? Be careful. It's highly contagious."

" Contagious? Si si, capisco. Contagioso."

" By the way, I went out to the beer hall. Seems the man with the mark on his hand was seen by several of the employees. One waiter thinks that he remembers the guy putting out the bottles of wine, but a few of the others said he's the guy who was asking questions."

" Either way, he's a suspect."

" Ja. A suspect. So listen, you keep in touch now. O.K.? No more sudden vacations. And give my regards to the lady."

" Capitano, grazie mille."

" Thanks for the call. Auf wiedersehen.

" Ciao, ciao ciao."

Claude Wizman also had **la Repubblica** open on his desk. He read the Italian without much problem, translating it into English for his young protégé. Although he missed the subtleties, he got the general idea.

" Brilliant," said Léon. "Divert their attention. I can't believe you could do that so fast."

" It wasn't me. It was pushed through by our man in Palermo. But it still doesn't solve our problem. This Baglione is apparently clean as a whistle. No charges filed."

" But the Ministry's in a shambles."

" Léon, don't underestimate this guy."

" So what can we do about him?"

" I think the key here is the woman."

" Did we find out any more about her?"

" It seems she has quite the story. Prostitution, some years ago. Burglary arrests in France and in Spain."

" What's her connection to this? Besides banging this policeman."

Claude grimaced. The younger man was getting a bit too comfortable with the secular world.

" I'm not sure. That break-in may have been a cover. A diversion for something else."

" I don't follow. A diversion from what?"

" Léon, I don't have an answer. And that German's also nobody's fool."

" Flanken. I agree. Jörg is keeping an eye out. We'll soon know what's going on."

" Where's Henri?"

Léon checked his watch.

" He and Ruud should be in Holland by now. The flower auctions start early in the morning - around half past six."

" And his team?"

" Already in Aalsmeer and Naaldwijk. They'll look like the usual terrorist bombings. The auctions will cease all operations after tomorrow."

" Good. What's the back story?"

" It's all set, Claude. Our newspaper in Amsterdam will break it next week. Suriname dissidents will take the credit, in exchange for some Israeli rocket launchers."

" It's o.k. with Tel Aviv?"

" You did speak to Avi, didn't you?"

Claude the Builder nodded and smiled.

" Léon, you're almost as smart as I am."

The Israeli government had agreed to ship the rockets and launchers if the splinter party of Rebbe Buchsbaum broke with the right wing and voted to limit new settlements in the occupied Golan Heights. The bill would have passed anyway, so it wasn't much of a stretch to vote yes.

" The explosions will scare the fuck out of the foreign buyers. We're almost ready to open our own auction on a new internet place called World Wide Web. Time Magazine just did a cover story. They're calling it the 'information superhighway.' I don't really understand how it works. Maybe it's just a fad?"

Wizman grimaced once more.

140

" Are we ready to pick up the slack?"

" We're good, and getting stronger, in roses, carnations and mums. The Dutch still own the tulip market. But that will change. The Turks are sucking up to Israel Aircraft for some missile guidance systems. I.A.I. can't sell them anything without our votes in the Knesset. In return, we want a stake in their tulip business. Did you know that the Ottomans started the whole tulip growing thing? Everybody thinks it was the Dutch."

" How did you manage to buy up the Colombian rose farms? I thought they were controlled by the drug lords."

" Guns for roses, my dear Léon. We shipped them arms through that rat, I forget his name, in Antigua.

" Not a rat. A Bird."

" A rat is a rat. In return for the guns we got the farms. In the long run, that business will be very successful. Everybody loves flowers."

" I guess so, Claude."

" I just want this German thing fixed and over with."

" It will be. Jörgie's like the Mounties. He always gets his man."

Baglione lay back in bed, in his boxers and canottiera, staring at Rosalba. She was in the bathroom, at the mirror, applying some cream to her mustache. It was yet another miracle product guaranteed to remove unwanted hair.

Corrado felt a little uneasy in the silk shorts. They were a gift from Vanessa Rambaudi. He'd thought about her a lot lately. He was ready to give all this up for her. Baglione looked around the shabby apartment. Rosalba was standing with her back to him, scratching the crack in her ass.

" So Corrado," she yelled from the bathroom, "what about your job, now that the Ministry's turned upside down. I'm embarrassed to show my face in the street. You know how those old women talk. 'Shame on your husband.' That's what they're saying!"

" Stai zitta, Rosalba! You're giving me heartburn."

" And you make me gonfiata!" She screamed back and let out a big noisy fart. Baglione thought about Vanessa and riding in the Rolls, making love under the stars. He made up his mind. He'd talk to Rosalba. Soon. Tell her it was over. That he wanted out of the marriage. If she wanted everything, she could have it. A few sticks of furniture, the television. What else was there? A few million lire in a joint account. He'd been hiding money from her for years. She could have the lousy bank book. He wanted Vanessa Rambaudi. But what if she didn't want him? Then what? No matter. Anything was better than this. He'd fantasized about moving to Bangkok after seeing a film about a retired cop and his sexy Thai girlfriend. He looked over at Rosalba putting color on her toenails. Pieces of toilet paper separated her fat little toes. Baglione wondered what Pippo D'Orazio saw in her. Maybe he only enjoyed plugging her because she was the boss's wife. In any event, once she was out of his life, she could do whatever the hell she pleased. Damn, she did that now, anyway. Goodbye and good riddance! Who cared what the priest would say. Goddamn hypocrites. The lot of them. He wanted his American woman. So what if she was a thief? At least she didn't rob him. Like Rosalba had for years. Robbed him of his manhood. Corrado closed his eyes and drifted off to sleep.

The phone rang putting an end to his daydream. Rosalba was still in the bathroom. He must have just dozed off. She duck walked across the room and picked up the receiver.

" Pronto... chi è?...Hold the line...Corrado, it's for you."

" Baglione, here."

" Corrado. Is that you?"

" Si. Who's speaking." It sounded like an international call.

" Baglione, it's Wolfie. I got your message. I hope I'm not calling too late. You said it was urgent."

" No, no. Hold on one minute."

He got out of bed and told his wife to hang up the phone as soon as he picked up the other extension. On the way out of the bedroom he jammed his foot on the leg of the bed. Again.

" Porca madonna bocchinara con la piorrea....!" he screamed. Rosalba crossed herself. Baglione limped into the kitchen.

" Si. I'm here. Rosalba hang up the goddamn phone." He waited until he heard the click.

" O.K. Wolfie. This is what I found out. Right after the first few poisonings, the Americans took the wines off the market. This scared the hell out of the buyers, so all of a sudden our wines are deader than Duce's nuts...pronto...pronto. Are you still there?"

" I'm listening, Inspector."

" When the orders started to dry up or get cancelled, a lot of the smaller producers were suddenly unable to meet their commitments. You know, to the bank, to the co-op."

" That's natural."

" Ah, but is it natural for one group of investors...vultures, really...to immediately start buying up a bunch of these firms? That's what we found out. At first it looked pretty ordinary. The buyers had nothing in common. But when we started to dig a little deeper we found out that they were really all one and the same. A group headed by a Brazilian, somebody named Heskel Milstein, was behind almost every purchase. Milstein also controls several wineries in Israel and lately he's been buying like crazy in France, Australia, even South Africa.

"Sounds like a smart businessman to me."

"Maybe so, but something doesn't sound..."

"Kosher," laughed Wolfie.

"Excuse me?"

"Kosher, Baglione. Something doesn't sound kosher. Isn't that what you were going to say?"

"No. I was saying that something doesn't seem right."

"Right. Not kosher. Look, just forget it. Sorry. Go ahead. Please."

"I just think that when you get your list of companies who might benefit from the bad publicity about the x-ray machines that you should look for a link to this Milstein."

"Interesting. I see where you're going with this. It'll take a few days. I'll let you know what I find. O.K.? And I'm sorry if I disturbed you."

"No, no. Thanks for returning my call. Buonanotte, Kapitän."

"Buonanotte, Corrado."

Jörg Bissel adored opera. It was the one of the first things that Claude Wizman had taken note of, many years before. The German switched off his MiniDisc player and removed the Sony in-ear style headphones he'd purchased earlier in the week. Wagner was his preferred composer and Götterdämmerung, his number one favorite. He slipped through the door of Reinhardt Von Zell's apartment while softly humming Blühenden Lebens Labendes Blut. Getting in was no problem. Bissel was as adept at picking locks as he was at slitting throats. He'd been told to make it look like an accident.

Jörg moved silently down a long hallway, pausing as the parquet floor flexed under his weight. He did not want to wake his victim. Not until he was set. Bissel had been in the apartment once before, when Von Zell was at work. The layout was familiar to him. Third door on the right was the traffic manager's bedroom. He lived alone and rarely entertained at night. Gambelhauff started the work day early. Except for the occasional two weeks in the Azores, Reinhardt was a celibate man. Von Zell preferred them young. In his milieu, fifteen was considered almost middle age. One or two dark skinned boys with big brown eyes cost him nearly as much as he earned at the factory in a month. His income was supplemented by "diverting" product from Gambelhauff's warehouse. Jörg Bissel had been a good patron, generous and reliable. For months he'd been buying a variety of goods which were under Reinhardt's control. His employer manufactured sophisticated x-ray equipment. Some said it was the among the best in the world. At first, Von Zell believed that Bissel ran a semi-legitimate buying service, occasionally delivering goods to purchasing agents for slightly less than the normal price. These *agents*, he was told, would then split the difference with Jörg, who in turn would take care of Reinhardt. At first, it all went smoothly. The traffic manager enjoyed the extra income and vacationed as often as he could. The last time, a few months before, Léon Drei was waiting for this creep to land in the Azores. He followed Reinhardt from his tourist hotel to a tacky late-night bar. He was about to approach Von Zell when a small boy crawled out from under the German's table, wiping his mouth with a paper napkin. This was more than Léon could handle. He ran for the door, desperately in need of some fresh air. For the pious young Jew, behavior like that was abhorrent. People like this deserved to be punished. Léon returned to the bar in time to see his man climbing a flight of stairs. He ran to the back of the building, found a fire escape and climbed silently up the rusty ladder. He saw a light go on above him. Cautiously he peered over the window sill and saw Reinhardt Von Zell and the boy.

The following evening he shadowed the pedophile again. This time Léon had his camera. When the German returned from his holiday, Bissel made a request. Instead of merely buying stolen goods he asked Reinhardt for something quite different. Jörg wanted to substitute some of the x-ray equipment he had brought with him, for legitimate Gambelhauff product. To be substituted and delivered through the manufacturer's regular channels.

" Absolutely not," cried Von Zell. "I won't get involved with that kind of business. It's not the way that I do things!"

" Reinhardt, leibchen, let me show you the new way that you do things."

He produced the set of photos taken in the Azores by Léon Drei.

" Where did you get these?" he demanded.

" What difference does it make. That's you with the boy, isn't it?"

The man was ashen. He shook his head.

" What do you want from me?"

" Just do as I say. Substitute my machines, actually your machines, for what you're normally shipping."

" Why are you doing this? What have you done to the..."

" Relax, Hardy. The equipment looks identical...is identical. Still wrapped up and factory fresh. I bought it from you."

" But why..."

" It's not necessary for you to know any more than this. We begin right away. If it's not too much trouble."

Trouble it would be. As soon as *The Builder* found out that the German police were looking into the Gambelhauff business, Reinhardt Von Zell was a dead man.

Bissel eased open the door to the bedroom. He could hear the manager snoring. The killer removed a pistol from his jacket pocket and placed it into the German's gaping mouth, then tugged sharply on the sleeping man's hair. His eyes opened wide. He jerked his head up, the barrel of the Vektor Z-88 (Bissel loved a bargain) scraping the roof of his target's mouth. Reinhardt started to shake.

" Easy boy. Just don't make any noise."

The pathetic pedophile nodded his head. The killer pulled out a handkerchief and shoved it in the shipping manager's mouth.

" Now get up." Von Zell got off the bed. "Unplug the TV and carry it into the bathroom." Bissel flicked on the light with a gloved left hand. "Put the TV on the edge of the tub."

His victim shook his head, no. "Put the TV on the edge of the tub." This time he followed the instructions.

" Now draw yourself a bath. Not too hot. You don't want to burn yourself."

When the bathtub was full, the assassin ordered Von Zell to take off his clothes.

" Get in. I'll tune in your favorite program."

Jörg plugged in the set and turned it on. He reached behind the bathroom door and felt around for a mop. It was just where he'd seen it before.

" Good bye, Von Zell. This is from me and all your sad young boys."

Bissel took the mop handle and shoved the television into the water. Hardy lit up like Santa Claus on Long Island lawn at Christmas. A second later the circuit breaker tripped off the power. The room turned black. The killer carefully removed the handkerchief from his victim's mouth. The body was still twitching as he let himself out of the flat.

Claude Wizman was happy to be back in New York. He walked out of C & M Computers huge underground warehouse on Maiden Lane carrying his new computer and a supply of Iomega 100mb zip disks. C & M, which stood for 'chutzpah' and 'mazel,' Yiddish for nerve and luck, was the largest electronics retailer in the United States. It was owned by a holding company called Mogen Manhattan, which in turn was owned by the real estate giant, Stein Brothers-Rifkin, one of the Solomon Companies Pty.

The Builder, Canadian by birth, considered New York his home. He lived in a converted police stable in downtown Manhattan. Pinchus Tannenbaum, his driver, waited in the beige Olds Ninety-Eight Regency, parked in a bus stop on the Broadway side of the old Customs House. Wizman crossed the street picking his way through the heavy morning traffic. Amazingly, a black Lincoln Town Car stopped and let him cross. An advertisement covering the full length of a passing bus reminded people of Barneys annual summer sale. Claude made a mental note to drop by the Madison Avenue branch. Their sweaters were some of the finest in the city. But today, he had other things on his mind. Pinchus popped the trunk and jumped out of the car when he spotted his boss.

" Here, let me take those," said the driver, reaching for the boxes in Wizman's arms.

" Thanks."

" You had a phone call. From Germany no less."

Pinchus still thought it amazing that private cars could have telephones in them. Not only that, but you could even get calls from overseas! Claude did not have to ask who called, nor whether it was important. Something was very wrong. He'd made it clear to everyone that he was not to be called in his car. It was too easy to monitor communication on these public bands. Wizman knew that if it was Léon calling, there must be a problem. A very big problem.

" Get me back to the office right away."

" One, two, six," said the driver, wheeling out into the traffic on Battery Place. He took a right on West Street and gunned the big eight cylinder Olds. They flew by slower moving cars and trucks, passed the new American Express complex, and headed uptown. Pinchus made all the lights to thirty-fourth Street.

" Not bad, huh."

" Mmm." Claude's mind was on other things.

" Holy smokes! I can't ever remember a run like that. Every light, green." Tannenbaum looked in his rearview mirror. *Claude the Builder* was deep in concentration.

Pinchus knew, from experience, when it was time to keep his mouth shut. At Fifty-eighth he turned right, drove crosstown to Fifth Avenue and pulled up in front of a pretzel vendor set up on the southeast corner. Wizman jumped out of the car.

" Hey, don't you want your packages?"

" Park the car and bring them up," he yelled over his shoulder.

" Park the car and bring them up," mimicked the ratty pretzel man.

Claude bounded into the GM Building. His office was on the thirty-ninth floor. He waited impatiently for the elevator. The doors opened and a large group of people filed out. Lunch hour traffic. He punched **39**, hoping no one else would get on. Fat chance. A half dozen others followed him in. A delivery guy, dressed in white pants, red and white striped shirt and white paper hat asked Claude to press **27**. The man was carrying a large cardboard box, stuffed with somebody's lunch. Several somebodies, from the assortment of smells wafting out from the open cardboard box. In a matter of seconds, the car reeked of vegetable soup and pastrami. Two corporate types were discussing the problem of counterfeit cosmetics as they got out on **31**. A young woman dressed in full Fed-Ex was singing a Whitney Houston tune, not so quietly to herself.

" And I.....I aye...will always love you...ooh ooh...I will always love you...ooh ooh...I will always love you."

She smiled at Claude. He did not smile back. At **39** he got off, turned right, went halfway down the beige and brown corridor and stopped at the door to

SILVAN PROPERTIES P.L.C.

He was buzzed in immediately. The receptionist had seen him on the closed circuit monitor on her desk.

" Good morning, sir," chirped his silver-haired secretary.

" Good morning, Sylvia. Any messages?" He breezed past her without waiting for the answer. She stood up and followed him along a hallway lined with windows on one side. The view was magnificent, overlooking the south end of Central Park. Wizman had the corner office. He unlocked his door by entering a five digit code on a touch sensitive keyboard. A heavy bolt tripped open. Claude's office looked like it was shopped from a Ralph Lauren home furnishings catalog. Very *goyishe*, very *waspy*, and slightly ironic. Although *The Builder* felt no obligation to explain his taste to the people he worked for. It was merely acknowledged and accepted that there was a good reason for spending this kind of money on furniture. These were legitimate business expenses. On the surface, the Boravitcher Rebbe Buchsbaum had no legitimate reason to question Claude's piety. At least that's what the rabbi told the few men he confided in. No women allowed.

The office walls were paneled in what his interior designer called 'native oak.' This particular species of wall was sourced from a particular forest in Romania. The desk had been copied from one of the French Kings Louis. The Marc Cross leather desk set was his father's, a retired banker in Montreal. Well-polished Stiffel brass was everywhere. On opposite walls were a pair of built-in bookcases lined with first editions. In the money business, appearance was important. Claude Wizman always looked for an edge. That's why this problem in Germany had him worried. Too many loose ends, too many bodies buried and now the phone call from Léon.

He glanced at his computer. A notice on the screen informed him that he'd received some electronic mail. It would have to wait. For now, he wanted to just sit and think. To reason. To resolve this crisis. And it was a crisis. At this very moment, in Germany, it would be possible to establish a link between the poisoning of Maxi Fleischig and three others to Claude's organization. If the police were smart enough. He didn't know the capabilities of this Italian, nor did he know much about Kapitän Flanken. With a bit of intuition someone could stumble onto his game plan. He tried to look on the bright side of things, not to try to fool himself, but merely to calm his nerves. The bombs had gone off as planned. The flower market in Holland was in shambles. One more year, a few more problems, and the business would come to them. Already his tulip growers were seeing an increase in orders. Just one day after the attack. And no one was killed, although a few workers were slightly injured at Aalsmeer.

Claude placed the call himself - to the number where he could reach Léon, a number known only to him and to Henri Drei. There was no answer. He glanced at his desk clock, a magnificent Cartier,14K gold,c.1940s. It was almost one. His meeting was scheduled to begin shortly. Ten minutes later, no answer again. If it was so urgent, where the hell was Léon? He should have waited by the phone for *The Builder's* call. Sylvia buzzed him. The first of the deputies had arrived. Within five minutes all the seats in his office were filled.

" Gentlemen. I see we're all here. Henri and Léon will not be joining us today. Let's begin with Florida. How are you, Allen?

" Fine sir." The heavy set man looked up from his notes.

" Tell us about things."

Allen Katz absentmindedly stroked his mustache, but it still refused to turn up on the ends. He'd finally resigned himself to waxing it, which made him look sinister, like the nasty landlords in silent movies. Tie 'em to the railroad tracks! In reality, he was a most delightful person.

" If you remember from our last meeting, the freight rates, to ship orange product north from Florida, were about to rise. As of this week past, the market prices for NFC, bulk FCOJ and even recon RTS were up about twenty percent. That increase makes our product, even landed, very competitive. We can undersell the domestic growers, at least into the East Coast markets."

" The duty-free concession helped us tremendously. Yes?"

" Yes, Claude." At these meetings, Wizman's was the only other voice allowed during these reports. Informal comments were encouraged after the last man had spoken.

Katz continued. "We can sell 'four by four,' shipped Jaffa - Port of New York, for less than Tropicana, Minute Maid, any of the biggies. And it's premium quality. I defy you to taste it and tell me it isn't as good as..."

" Allen...," interrupted *The Builder*, "you don't have to sell us." Everyone else chuckled.

" I'm sorry. I get carried away sometimes. Once a salesman, huh? Anyway, you'll see in my figures what I'm talking about." He clicked a hand-held remote tethered to a jack mounted under the front edge of Wizman's desk. The lights in the room dimmed and a slide appeared on a screen which was slowly descending from behind a polished wooden valance. It was a rear projection screen, approximately fifty inches on the diagonal. The clarity was exceptional. The first slide was a pie chart, showing the relative market shares of all the domestic orange juice producers.

" What you're looking at represents just the chilled 'recon' juice that you're used to buying in your Safeway. This is the sixteen ounce carton. Notice that we now own a twelve share of the market. That's equivalent to about twenty million quarts of product. This next slide gives you the same view, only for our sixty-four ounce."

" Allen. Excuse me. But we're kind of stretched for time. Would you mind if we skipped some of the numbers? I think that it's safe to say that you've done an impressive job."

" Don't you want to hear about our acquisitions... of the growers?

" Their business went bad. They sold low. And now, thanks to the Dreis, they have to deal with an infestation of flies. We own a significant number of groves and will add more very soon. Does that about sum it up?

" I suppose. Just one more thing. The commissioner's family wanted me to thank you all for your kind messages of condolence while they sat shiva."

The commissioner who had engineered the rate hike had been removed in Lisbon. Claude knew why. Léon and Henri and Jörg Bissel knew how. Everyone else at the table remained in the dark. His death had been reported as a heart attack. An interesting interpretation of the facts from Wizman's Portuguese coroner. 'Two in the chest' had magically morphed into one of those unfortunate myocardial infarctions that often happen to overweight American vacationers.

" Gianfranco, you're next. Please."

" Grazie. As we expected, the sales of Italian wines have sunk like a stone. All over the world. As a result, several of the biggest producers are close to bankrupt. Technically, they're about to default on their loans to Milstein's banks. Last year we encouraged them to refinance their properties. These days they have no choice. By the time, how to say this, by the time the fog lifts we will control, più o meno, eight percent of the production in the north, closer to twelve in the south."

" With the more desirable properties being in the north? Isn't that correct?" asked *The Builder.*

" Bravo. The growers in the north of Italy are generally more prosperous. We have to be patient. They have some cushion, but only a few of them can hold on forever."

" What about the government? At times they've been vocal about not letting real property transfer out of Italian hands. Is that a correct assessment, Gian?"

" The scandals, Claude, have pretty much taken all their attention. Oh, and the referendum to eliminate the Ministry of Agriculture......tutti pazzi. The whole of them."

" What's that all about? I didn't quite understand the explanation I read in the paper."

" The country is made up of regions; the Veneto, Piemonte, Friuli, eccetera. The referendum says that each of them should run their own affairs."

" I see. How does that affect us?"

" Not significantly, in the short term. It will take years to implement. In the meantime, they're running around scratching their heads."

Gianfranco Fabbri was always well-informed. His family owned several vineyards in Umbria. The Fabbris, secular Jews from Ferrara, did not approve of their son's *conversion*. He was not raised Orthodox. That came later. His *awakening*, he said, came to him over time. His parents wondered where they had gone wrong. Gianfranco was bright, committed and competent in his job, overseeing, with Moshe Segall, the operations at Kibbutz Shofar's vineyards in Israel.

" When do you think we should move to Phase 2?"

" Claude, this is really up to Heskell. To be honest, it's frustrating to me. Without more attention from his banks, we have what Italians call a *mezza sega*."

" Which is?"

" How do you say in English? Half a hand job."

" I see. Is there a problem with Milstein?"

" Not so far. He's holding a lot of paper in France. If the business there turns sour we'll pick up a bunch of good properties. Same thing in Australia and South Africa. The key is getting these producers to re-finance through Pan Pacific."

" Gianfranco, to be honest, I'm not comfortable with a move into South Africa yet. It's too unstable."

" South Africa was Milstein's idea. He asked me about the wines. I said that they had potential. But, and I want to make this very clear, I never told him to buy like he's been doing."

" I'm not suggesting that you did. He is, however, a hell of a lot smarter than we are about what's going on down there. We have no choice. We have to trust his judgment."

" Granted. It's his money. But I want it understood that..."

" You've made your point. What about the new tariffs? Dead?"

" For now. The timing was bad. We'll try again in six months. All the talk about trade wars is, like they say on TV, 'getting traction' in Washington these days. We'll just have to wait and see."

" That's not acceptable, Gianfranco. Why can't we put some pressure on them?"

" I assure you Claude. We're trying. And may I say that I don't appreciate the way you're talking to me today."

" We'll discuss it in private." Claude turned to the next man at the table. "Ruud. Give us some good news."

" You already know about Mexico. You'll find a xerox of The Times article in your folder." The Dutchman was beaming. It had been his idea to infest the Chilean apple crop as well.

" When do we see results with the melons?"

" Not for a couple of months. I'm convinced the flies will do their job."

" They better. We've invested a great deal of money at home." Oddly, Claude Wizman, a Canadian living in New York, always referred to Israel as home. "Didn't you tell us last time that the USDA was about to impose a ban?"

" That's what we heard. As far as I know, the talks are still ongoing."

" Make it happen. What about acquisitions?"

" There's the usual protectionist crap. But we've offered to share our irrigation technology with the Chileans. They won't risk a fight with Tel Aviv over some melon fields. We'll get them for a song. Especially if the crop can't be sold."

" Anything happening with your olive thing in Italy?"

" Impossible to tell now, Claude. My guy says it may take years before the trees start dying. We treated a few groves in Apulia with a bacteria. That's in the south of Italy. Just to see if it works."

" It's Puglia. Not Apulia." Fabbri was still upset. Wizman ignored his comment.

" Thank you Ruud. Good work. Dov. How about here? What's doing with the mayoral race since I've been gone?"

" Not so good. Our man can't seem to keep his mouth shut. And, on top of that, he's developed a bad case of penis envy to go along with everything else."

" What's with the hair, Dov? That thing on his head makes him look like a...I don't know what."

" If he'd just tone down the rhetoric and let the other two candidates knock each other out, he'd be a shoo-in."

" Can't his father talk some sense into him?"

" He's tried. Believe me. We've all tried."

" How do the polls look?"

" We're about ten percent."

" Going up or going down?"

" Holding steady. Let's wait and see what the riots do."

" Everything's set for September?"

" Ready to go. We'll turn up the heat in July. Crown Heights gave us a good start."

Sylvia stuck her head in the door and mouthed something to Claude. Léon was on the phone.

" Tell him to hold. Gentlemen, that should do it. To be perfectly honest, I'm not pleased with the way things are going. But I'm sure that you're not either. Perhaps when we meet in two weeks you'll have more encouraging news. Now, if you'll excuse me, I've got to take this call."

Baglione opened the package and smiled. He read the note from Vanessa a second time.

> Dearest Corrado,
>
> Just thought I'd send you a case of my lovely Arneis. I know how much you like it. Baglione, what's to become of us? I'm sorry I acted ~~like a cunt~~ improperly. I understand your position. But this leopard can't change her spots overnight. I know that my little 'indiscretion' hurt you very deeply (at least I think it did). And that's why you haven't called me. But am I really such a terrible person? I thought we had something together. Maybe I was wrong. I want to set the record straight. I'm not angry. A little hurt but not angry. Thank you for trying to help me. I know you're a good person and I'm glad that I met you. Good luck with your life.
>
> Love, Vanessa
>
> P.S: I'm putting Tenuta Rambaudi up for sale. I can't afford the upkeep and I won't steal any more to pay for it.
>
> P.P.S: sorry to write in English. I still have trouble expressing myself in Italian.

He dialed her number. It rang ten times without an answer. As soon as he put the receiver down, his phone rang.

" Pronto "

" Baglione?"

" Si "

" It's Wolfie."

" Wolfie, I was just thinking about you.

" How is the lady?"

" Funny, you should ask. I haven't spoken to her since we left Como."

" Corrado, don't let her get away. Trust me. I'm an expert in matters of the heart. In my opinion...she's mad about you. And you...you're *verrückt* about her. But that's not why I called."

" Something come up?"

"Ja. I got your list of who's buying up the Italian wineries and cross-checked it against the companies who'd benefit from the x-ray shenanigans. Does the name Heskel Milstein mean anything to you?"

" Only that he was on my list. His companies have done a lot of buying here lately."

" Corrado, what if I told you he also made my list?"

" I'd say that we're on to something."

" There's more. This Heskel Milstein is a religious Jew. He belongs to a sect called the Boravitchers. They're a fringe group, very far removed from the mainstream Orthodox Jews. Some people write them off as nuts. In my professional opinion, that would be a mistake. There's much more to them than that. They're well organized and they're rich and...they're convinced that a...not a...*the* messiah is going to show up any day now. Their old rebbe, the one they follow, is someone named Moshe Buchsbaum. This man has them believing it's him. That he's their Messiah."

" How do you know so much about these people?"

" Because I'm a good Jewish detective."

" I already knew that. So you think Milstein is behind all of this?"

" Let me finish. A few weeks ago a man fell overboard...off one of the ferries as it was docking in Bremen. He got pretty well mangled. The body was almost impossible to identify. But the forensics people got lucky. The man had a pacemaker implanted in his chest."

" And from that you were able to identify him?"

" Precisely. Corrado, are you ready for this? The man's name is Olivieri."

" He's Italian."

" Italian-American. Age fifty, last known address is Brooklyn, New York. The pacemaker had a serial number. It wasn't hard to come up with a name."

" So what does this have to do with us."

" The man lived in an area called Borough Park, in Brooklyn. Borough Park is the home of a great number of orthodox Jews including..."

" The Boravitchers."

" Exactly. So, Baglione, what do you think?"

" I'm not sure. Give me a while to digest all of this. I'll call you in a few days time. And Wolfie, bravo. Great work!"

Allen Katz was the last to leave the meeting, closing the door behind him. Claude picked up the phone.

" Léon, I'm sorry to keep you waiting. I wanted to talk in private. What's wrong?"

" The German police have identified Olivieri's body."

" What! How did that happen? I thought it was beyond..."

" I thought so too. But they did it."

" Are you sure?"

" Positive."

" Dammit to hell. They're going to tie him to us."

" For what reason? Nobody's looking at us. We've done nothing wrong."

160

" Nothing wrong, Léon? Tell me you're joking? The man used rat poison to kill four people. And then he ends up dead. If they connect him to the beer hall we're finished."

" What proof could they have? Besides when The Moshiach comes, it won't make any difference."

" And until then? You want to rot in some prison? Believe me, it will happen. No, no. We can't take these chances. We've got to erase all of Olivieri's connections to us. I'll get the word out that no one is to speak of him. No one is to admit knowing him. It has to be like he never existed."

" Can you do that? Make the community do such a thing?"

" I can't. But The Rebbe can."

" What do you want us to do?"

" Have you heard from Henri?"

" Yes. He's still in Holland."

" Have him go to Italy and watch the policeman. Find out what he's doing. Where the investigation is heading. Henri did a good job on this detective's ministry. From what I understand, the whole place in a shambles. You stay put. I want to know what that German detective, what's his name?..."

" Flanken "

" I worry about him. He's clever. See if he's got any skeletons. I don't want to turn him over to Jörg, if it can be avoided. There's been enough bad business already. And the Gambelhauff thing, it's been resolved?"

" You didn't read my eMail?"

" Not today. It's been too crazy around here."

" It's taken care of."

" Alright then, Léon. We'll speak at the end of the week. Give my best to Henri."

" Good bye Claude."

Baglione didn't bother to go home. His suitcase was packed and ready. He went straight from his office to the Stazione Termini, purchased a first class ticket to Alba, then left to have some dinner at Nazzareno, an old-fashioned place, just behind the station. The owner was a friend and he was welcomed like family. After he'd sampled almost the entire antipasti table, Mario, the padrone, brought him a classic bucatini all'amatriciana, a taste of oxtail and a gorgeous creme caramel. The train departed on schedule at 23:55. He slept in his clothes and woke up the following morning at six. At Alba, he rented a Citroen Zx from a moonlighting history teacher who didn't need to be schooled on the subject of government charge card kickbacks. Baglione pocketed his twenty-five thousand lire, stopped in the nearby barbershop for a shave, then drove directly to Tenuta Rambaudi, arriving just in time for breakfast. He knocked on the door and waited. After he knocked again, the door opened. A man of about thirty, wrapped in a silk bathrobe that revealed his hairless chest, looked him up and down.

" Can I help you?"

" Yes, I'm here to see the Signora." Baglione thought he'd also like to grab this ricchione by his ponytail and flip him across the driveway. But he didn't.

" May I tell her who's asking?"

" Yes, tell her it's the police." Baglione flashed his badge. In less than a minute he and the lady of the manor were at the door.

" Corrado. You scared Maurizio half to death. Why didn't you tell me you were coming?"

" Who is he?" snarled Baglione, pointing to the bathrobe.

" A friend."

" I can see that."

" Corrado, I don't have to explain myself to you. I don't hear from you since Como and now you come busting in here

162

demanding to know what I'm doing and who I'm with? You've got a hell of a nerve."

" Senti, babbo. The lady obviously doesn't want you here."

" Why don't you disappear before I do something crazy." Baglione gave him a quick peek at his gun, holstered under his jacket.

" Look, Vanessa, maybe I phone you later." The young Tuscan switched now to English. Perhaps this jerk wouldn't understand him.

" Don't bother. Fucking mammone!" snarled the policeman. In English.

The man turned back and went into the house, presumably to get dressed.

" Corrado, if you think you can just..."

" I love you."

" ...just waltz in here and...what did you say?"

" I love you."

" Oh, caro." She took his face between her hands and kissed him gently.

" I'm sorry for not calling. I had to work things out in my head."

" And?"

" I'm not an impulsive person. Però...Can I move in here with you?"

" But, what about your job, your..."

" My mind's made up. I'm leaving Rosalba. My future ...it's with you. If you'll have me."

" Is that a proposal?"

" Would you like it to be?"

" It's just so sudden. And it's Italy."

" This is not like some stupid soap. Vanessa, listen to me. I adore you, but I'm still a married man. You know what divorce is like in this blasted country! I'll do my best."

" What will we live on?"

" The Ministry's going to be dismantled. But technically, I don't work directly for them. I'm still Carabiniere. I can put in for a transfer. The pay is o.k. and I have lots of free time. I could help you with the business. I like wine."

" Corrado, you make it sound so simple."

" I'm a simple guy."

They heard the roar of the white Carrera CS as the friend, in a cringeworthy display of machismo, careened down the driveway leaving a trail of dust and leaves. Baglione laughed loudly. He felt on top of the world. Vanessa quickly brought him back down.

" Baglione, what about the poisonings? You've got to clear my name. I can't even sell my wines here in Italy. Forget about anywhere else."

" We're working on it. Flanken's discovered something. I tell you about it later."

" Why later?"

" I have other plans for you now."

The Polizeirat or Chefdetektiv, as he preferred to be called did not have a driver. Actually, he did. The union required it. But Wolfie Flanken had the man assigned elsewhere. He preferred to drive himself. His car was also not regulation. Instead of the standard VW Dasher, Flanken used a black BMW 735i, confiscated in a drug raid. It was against the rules, but so was a lot of what Wolfie did. His track record in solving the tough cases was justification enough for his superiors to frequently look the other way.

He was lunching at the Sun Yat Zen, a vegetarian Chinese restaurant near the Deutsche Bundesbahn building, as he did every day. The mock duck salad was one of the detective's favorites. He washed it down with a glass of beer and ordered a dish of fresh lichees. He wondered how this little place managed to have fresh ones the whole year round.

" Big mystery," said the owner. "You detective. You figure out."

The beeper on Wolfie's belt chirped out an annoying "call the office" message.

" Mr. Din, may I use the phone?" The Cambodian proprietor nodded. Flanken dialed the number.

" Richter? Ja, Flanken here."

" Can you get over to the Karl Marx Apartments right away? There's something you need to see."

" What's going on?"

" I was interviewing the people out at Gambelhauff, like you asked. One of the employees, the traffic manager, hadn't been seen for a few days, so I went to his apartment. A neighbor, with a key, let me in."

" Yes, and..."

" Dead in the bathtub. Apparently he was taking a bath with the TV on. It fell in the tub and zap-zap. Electrocuted the poor bastard. He's been in the water for three or four days. Not a pretty sight."

" I'm leaving now," said the Chefdetektiv, "It will taken me around thirty minutes to get there. Secure the place. I don't want anything touched. Not even by forensics."

The detective paid his check and grabbed the last lichee. He popped it in his mouth on the way to the car. In considerably less than half an hour he reached the Karl Marx Apartments. Once inside the lobby, a uniformed policeman saluted, then led him upstairs to the body. Flanken spotted Werner Grönemeyer, the medical examiner, in the hallway smoking the last of a Davidoff cigarette.

" Don't you know those things are bad for you? Even the expensive ones."

" Taking a bath can also be bad for you. Hello Wolfie."

" See you inside, Doktor. Freddy, how are you?"

" Gut, mein herr," replied the patrolman at the door.

" Richter?"

" In the bathroom. Watch your step. It's dark in there."

" Werner, what's it look like to you?" He'd followed Flanken into the apartment.

" *If*...and only *if* it's an accident, then I would say that cause of death was stupidity. If you're asking me, was it an accident, I can't say yes or no. That's what they pay you for."

" Thanks for the help. Can that kind of voltage kill you?"

" Considering the circumstances, yes. By the way, it's the amperes that kill you, not the voltage."

" I stand corrected, Herr Edison."

They were working with flashlights. The power had purposely not been restored.

" What's with the lights?"

" You said not to touch anything, Chef."

" Unplug the TV. Then get us some light."

" Yes sir." Alwin Richter did as he was told. In the light, Reinhardt Von Zell resembled an enormous pink raisin. The smell was like rancid butter.

" Open that little window."

" Can't, sir. It's sealed."

" Then break it out. It's disgusting in here."

The junior officer complied after checking to be sure that no one was under the window.

" That's better," said Wolfie. The room had some fresh air at last.

" What do you see, Alwin?"

" Man taking a bath, the television falls into the tub and kills him."

" That's it?"

Richter looked at his boss, warily.

" I mean, sir, I suppose that it could be a set up. We'll have to wait for the forensic report. It's possible he was killed somewhere else and dumped here."

" I don't think so. There was no sign of a struggle in here or in the other room. This guy must weigh a hundred, hundred ten kilos. The question, Richter, is not where he died - but how."

" You think he might have been murdered?"

" Look at the channel selector on the TV."

" Channel 3, sir."

" Which means what?

" Public channel. 'Kölnersport' in the morning, 'Learn a Language' at night."

" Which, this month, is what language, Alwin?"

" I don't know, sir. I'm more of a music guy."

" It's Japanese. Does he strike you as a fellow with an interest in learning Japanese?"

" Not hardly, sir."

" I agree. More the Bundesliga type. In my opinion."

" So you don't think he was watching a Japanese lesson in his bathtub?"

" When you put the circuit breaker to **ON**, Richter, what happened?

" The lights in the apartment came back."

" Precisely. So more than likely he was electrocuted at night."

" So you're saying he wasn't necessarily watching TV. The murderer, assuming there was one..."

" ...turned on the set and threw it in the tub. Very good, Richter."

" Thank you, sir."

" Chef. Look at this." Another man was working in the bathroom. "Do you see what I see?" He showed Flanken the mop.

" Looks like an ordinary mop."

" Ah, but look at the very end of the handle, where there's rubber."

" Its got spinnennetz hanging from it."

" I don't see any. Where'd they come from?"

" The TV perhaps? See if you can find where the set ordinarily stays in the apartment." Sure enough, in a corner of the living room there was a clear spot on the table, an outline of the TV. The surrounding area was covered with thick layer of grayish dust and the rest of the spiderwebs.

" Match the spinnennetz from the table with the spinnennetz on the end of the mop and we have ourselves the murder weapon. Very observant, Uwe. Good stuff."

" Ich danke ihnen. I'll have the lab boys test it."

" So then, gentlemen, we have a victim, more than likely, forced to sit in a tub of water. A TV is brought into the bathroom, turned on to whatever channel it had been set to earlier in the day, then pushed into the water with a mop handle. The questions to ask then are simple. One, who did the pushing and two, for what reason?"

168

Baglione drove the Rolls into Alba, picked up some apricot filled brioche at a bakery that looked good, grabbed **LA STAMPA** from a newsstand and returned to Tenuta Rambaudi. Vanessa had just gotten dressed when he arrived back at the house.

" Corrado, where were you? I reached over and you were gone. Don't do that to me. I like to wake up with you in my bed."

" I'll bet you say that to all the guys, and don't try and tell me that frocio with the Porsche was your nephew."

" Are you still mad about yesterday? Land on this planet. You're a married man. I'm a single woman. So, please don't tell me what's proper behavior. And for your information, he's not gay. And don't use words like that any more. O.K.?"

" I just thought..."

" Think about something else, like making the coffee or solving this case."

" You make the caffé. I'll be the detective. O.K.?"

" Si, signore. Whatever you say, sir. And Corrado…a fanabla!"

He followed Vanessa into the kitchen. It was a large, old fashioned room. The terracotta floor was in serious need of repair. The appliances were mostly from the 1970's. But it had charm and with a minimum of work and a bunch of money it could be wonderful once again. Baglione was a dedicated amateur chef. Like most Italian men he'd learned to cook at his mother's side. The ability to make a proper sugo was a rite of passage in his family. When he was young, about fifteen or sixteen, there was talk of sending him off to apprentice with his father's cousin in Potenza. But the relative had wanted too much money for the privilege of letting him work eighteen hours a day for free in his restaurant, so the deal was called off. Instead, he stayed in school. At eighteen he was drafted into the army. After training, Corrado was made a military policeman and assigned to a base near Vicenza. A logical thing for a young man to do after service is to join the Carabinieri. Eight years later, after ascending to the rank of detective, he was caught in the back seat of his unmarked police car with a prostitute. A transfer to the Ministry of Agriculture was his punishment. That was in 1980. For fourteen years he'd been assigned to a dead end job. Not that he hadn't had some success. In his first year at the ministry, in a joint operation with NAS (his counterpart at the Ministry of Health) he was handed a difficult case. It seemed that some unscrupulous rice producer in Magenta had been selling a product using someone else's name, even using identical packaging. Chicchirichí (cock-a-doodle-doo in Italian), the victim, had discovered their packaging on store shelves, filled with someone else's product. Baglione was assigned to the case. He'd gone undercover, taking a job at the firm in Magenta. He spent three weeks in the plant gathering evidence that led, eventually, to convictions. His next big case was a painful six years later, when he helped nail a group of wineries adding methanol to their inexpensive reds. This *trick* had killed half a dozen people and caused a lot of damage to the image of Italian table wines. Baglione was given a Certificate For Meritorious Service by the President of the Republic.

" Can we move out of this dump, or buy a nice car with your son of a bitch commendation?" wailed Rosalba. His answer was just as polite.

" Vai a farti fottere, you cow! For once, can't you let me take pride in my job?"

Between the two big cases, his time had been filled with inconsequential investigations. Milk tankers loaded with water, 'Italian' olive oil from Libya and many more schemes, mostly not that creative. The Italian pastime is not really Sunday football as many people believe, it's trying to scam the government. There's even an army, called the Guardia di Finanza that does nothing but look for the cheaters. You can spot them lurking outside small bars, checking to see that receipts are issued for every Campari.

" These are delicious," said Baglione, munching on a brioche.

" Did you get them at Antico Forno in Alba?"

" I don't know. Is that the small place, near the church?"

" Everything in Italy's near a church," she laughed.

" The one with the scaffolding."

" Our Lady of Bleeding Palms. You went to Panificio Parodi. Bravo. That's why they're so good. Anything in the paper?" Corrado was perusing the front page.

" Just the usual. Lega's screaming for Andriotti's hide. The Borsa's in the toilet. Terrorists bombed the two big Dutch flower auctions. Even tulips aren't safe anymore."

" Try the cheese. It's like a super Philadelphia. Spread it on these. My friend Mario just started making them."

Vanessa handed him a long, thin cracker she called *lingue di suocera*(mother-in law tongues).

" Anche il formaggio è squisito. What is it?

" Robiola. My neighbor makes it. We trade cheese for vino. Except yesterday she didn't want any of my wine. It's fucking not fair, Corrado. This is driving me crazy."

" Mmm. I love this," he said, eating the cheese straight off his knife

They ate in silence while Baglione finished the paper. He took a slice of pear from a colorful souvenir plate, then picked up the paper again.

" Listen to this." He began to read. "Dutch police are investigating...blah, blah, blah...Spokesman for the DFA, the Dutch

Flower Auctions, said yesterday, that as a result of the bombings, the daily auctions will be temporarily suspended. Its members are experiencing their first downturn in orders in this decade...Jan Van something, something...is worried that business will be permanently lost to countries like Turkey which are aggressively selling and shipping their flowers directly to the big chain stores."

" Does that mean something to you, Corrado?"

" It's possible. I need to learn everything I can about Turkish tulips. This whole thing has a very familiar ring."

" I have a friend at the Italian consulate in Malmö."

" That's in Sweden, cara."

" Geography was never one of my strong points."

" Don't worry. You have many others."

" Corrado, all you ever think about is sex."

" No. Old people think about it. I, on the other hand..."

" What about the tulips?"

" I'll get Wolfie to check it out. He must have some Turkish connection. Germany's full of Turks."

" What are you thinking?"

" I'm thinking that if a certain name pops up, we're on to something big. My whole future, our whole future could depend on it."

" There's the phone. Please don't talk too long."

Jörg Bissel said goodnight to his two superiors, who were bent over a desk looking at computer printouts.

" Alright, see you Monday," said Richter.

" Have a good weekend," replied Flanken, without looking up.

" You too, Chef."

Bissel had been a policeman for eleven years, since leaving the East. He was from Chemnitz, near Dresden and, as a teenager, had escaped from East Germany, not over the Berlin wall, but by boat, with some help from the Danes. Once inside the Jewish community in Odense he met a man named Claude Wizman. From there to Israel, then to New York and finally on to Köln. A cousin of Allen Katz had appointed him to the Köln Polizei.

" Six private companies and one state owned," said Richter, highlighting names with a marker.

" Now we take those and check them against…where's the list of stock transfers?"

" On the bottom."

" Mmm hmm," mumbled Flanken, examining the two printouts. "This one, this one and this one. That's it. Pass me the pen. Three tulip growers either sold out entirely or transferred a majority of their shares within the past two years. Get your Turkish buddy to find out who bought them."

" Check."

" Czech. No, no. Turk."

" Right. Check, you know, like check - I'll do it. Very American. Don't you watch Starsky und Hutch, Kapitän?"

New York has always been a city of neighborhoods. Italians lived on Mulberry Street, Ukrainians in the East Village, Chinese on Mott. Eighty-sixth Street was German, Hells Kitchen, mostly Irish. Even physicians; the West Seventies, psychiatrists' row; East Fifty-seventh if you're an internist. Dr. Schmuel Zipstein had offices on the ground floor of a building that was once home to Greta Garbo. The doctor shook his head. The report was conclusive. It was the second time he'd ordered the tests.

" Just tell me the truth," said Claude Wizman, without a trace of emotion.

" You've got what's called neuro-kinetic spasmosis. It's not life-threatening."

" What do I have to do?"

" Watch your diet, no red meats, no salt and no alcohol."

" Not even a brandy?"

" Look, you're a big boy Claude. If you drink, you'll keep having these attacks. Your liver is triggering something in the central nervous system. That's what's causing the pains in your arm."

" A little pain I can handle."

" One of these times it's not going to go away. It's called an engram. Think of your muscle like it's a camera. Every time it's hit with one of these 'excitements' it takes a picture. The more pictures, the more permanent the pain. Do you understand what I'm saying?"

" What's the worst case scenario?"

" Paralysis. Maybe partial, maybe complete. That's up to you."

" Curable?"

" No. It's manageable - if you'll co-operate."

" Have you seen the Rebbe lately?"

" Two weeks ago."

" How's he doing?"

" Like any ninety-three year old man. His body's shot. Thank God his mind is still sharp."

" For how long?"

" Claude, I'm a mechanic, not a fortune teller."

" You know why I'm asking."

" Claude, I give you my word. You'll be the first one I call."

174

" Not the first, Schmulie. I'm the only one who you'll call. You're clear on that?"

" Like a bell, bubula."

Wizman left the doctor's office and walked slowly west, across Fifty-seventh Street. He paused to look at the rainbow colors of the cashmere sweater display in the window of Andre Oliver, crossed the street, past Chanel and Cardin, then up Park Avenue to the Delmonico.

" Can I help you, sir?" asked the starched-cuffed Greek at the reception.

" Mr. Baum, please."

" Your name, sir?"

" Chaim Yankel. He's expecting me."

" Go right up, sir. The elevator's on your right."

Claude counted fifteen steps and entered the paneled car. The concierge put down the house phone and nodded his approval to the operator. The door closed and they ascended.

" Here we are, sir. To your left."

" Thank you. "

The hallway was carpeted down the middle. To either side was polished black marble, veined in grey. Etched glass sconces lined the corridor. At one end, a set of rosewood doors, framed in a darker wood and unmarked, opened slowly as he approached. A severe looking man of about twenty-five, dressed in a dark, single-breasted suit, white shirt and navy blue tie stood in the doorway and waited. As Wizman approached, the man moved to one side.

" Good morning, sir. Mr. Baum is in the library. I'll take you in." The younger man turned and walked down a paneled hallway. Wizman followed. The man knocked twice, turned the doorknob and entered. He waited until Claude was in the room, then left, silently closing the door behind him. Solomon Baum was looking out the window, north and east towards the Triborough Bridge.

Without turning to his visitor he began.

" Sit down, please." There were two Wassily leather and chrome chairs on Wizman's side of a massive walnut desk.

" How's Fanny?"

" Like an old lady. Thank you for asking. You know, Claude, when my father first arrived in this country he looked at the other immigrants, with their shabby clothes and tied-up suitcases, and he laughed. He was in America, where anything was possible. He spent his whole life at a worktable, piecing together ladies' fur coats for names like Lehman and Astor and Guggenheim. His whole life, Claude, bent over the skins of dead animals so that I could go to college, become a big shot lawyer and make him proud. You know what he said to me when I told him I'd made my first real money, not in a courtroom but with a piece of property? He said 'Boychik, once you figure out where you're going, don't go no place else.' You know, I never went back to the law. Fifty-two years. Buy and sell. Buy and sell. I can look out this window and say 'that one's mine,' he pointed to a nearby tower, 'and that one, and the one over there'. So tell me Claude, do you know where you're going?"

Wizman said nothing.

" I'll tell you who I see - sitting across from me. I see a yiddisher kop. A smart cookie with a genius mind for details. A real modern day Machiavelli. But someone I can trust? I'm not so sure. You tell me my son can be mayor of New York, with your help. The Rebbe sends you to me, so I believe it. The Rebbe needs money, so I give it. Now I pick up a paper and read that my son Steven has maybe ten percent of the vote, and is slipping backwards every day, and I say to myself, what's going on here? Have I been swindled? Did someone rob me of my money, or even worse, rob me of my faith? What's the answer, *Mr. Builder*? I'm listening."

Claude Wizman thought for a minute before answering.

" Solomon," he said slowly, "your son is an idiot. I came to you, when, ten years ago and asked for your help? The Rebbe doesn't make deals with goniffs like you. I do. I asked you, back then, what you wanted in return for your money and your connections. Do you remember what you said?"

" Of course I remember. I said, 'a father's greatest pleasure is to do for his children'. Steven wanted to be a politician. You assured me that if I co-operated, he would become Mayor of New York, maybe even, President of the United States. I kept my end of the bargain, Claude. What about yours?"

" We all want to see it happen. You have your reasons, we certainly have ours. But sometimes you can want so badly that you lose sight of the realities. I did everything I could to keep my end of the bargain. City Controller. I won that election for him. People said he couldn't win. But he did. Was he qualified? No. Did it matter? No. What do you want from me, Solomon? You want me to get him a special Jewish lobotomy so he'll be able to open a mouth and something intelligent will come out? I can only do what I can do."

" I gave millions to your crappy little organization!" yelled Solomon Baum. "I gave you cash, I gave you properties that are now worth what, Claude, a hundred million, two hundred? You did alright by me, you and the Rebbe. Now you've got the chutzpah to tell me it's Steven's fault. Your eyes were open, sonny boy. What you saw then is what you got now. So don't give me this crap about how my son is not qualified. He's an idiot. My son blew the deal. I will say this only once. You get him elected in November! Candidates come from behind and win all the time." He turned, finally, and faced the younger man. "Make it happen, Claude," he hissed, sitting down at last.

" Or what, Solomon? What are you gonna' do? If we fall down, you fall down. Right along side us."

The two men sat in silence. The older man closed his eyes and rubbed his forehead. He opened them and stared directly at Wizman.

" Claude, we've never discussed this before, but I think it's time some things get said. How much of this business does the Rebbe even know about?"

" You're an intelligent man, Solomon. You know how these things work. The Rebbe laid it out for me, twenty-five years ago. I do what I do. No one asks questions when they don't want to hear the answers."

" Yada, yada, yada. The end justifies the means, huh."

" An accurate assessment, Mr. Baum."

" I hope we're doing the right thing, Claude. Because if we're not, then we're no better than that mishugah down in Waco or the one with the Kool-aid or than Hitler or anyone else who tried to play God."

" Flavor-aid, Solomon."

" What the fuck did you just say?"

" It wasn't Kool-aid. It was Flavor-aid."

" **Ciao,** Pippo, it's me. What's going on down there?"

" Madonna, I'm crazy here waiting for you to call. Did you speak to that German detective? He's phoned here a half dozen times."

" Wolfie? I've been trying to call him. What else is happening?"

" Bambone is shitting his pants. The prosecutor's office came in and took all the records going back for years. I'll tell you, with Bossi and his fucking referendum and the business with Bambone, everything's come to a stop here."

" I'm surprised you could see a difference."

" Scusa?"

" Nothing, Pippo. Has Rosalba called?"

" No, but there's a raccomandata here, from a lawyer. I signed for it. Must be important. When are you coming back?"

" I'm not sure. Hold it for me, and if the German calls, tell him I'm here in..., no better still, tell him I'll call him at home."

" Ok, Capo. Ciao."

Baglione waited a few hours then called Wolfie Flanken at home.

" Hold the line please," said a man in perfect English. The Chefdetektiv took the phone.

" I hear you've been trying to get me."

" Baglione, where the hell have you been?"

" I'm in Alba."

" With the lady. I should have known. Is that where you called me from the other day?"

" Si. What did you find out?"

" I had one of my men get in touch with a friend of his at the Turkish trade bureau in Bonn. He gave us a list of the big tulip growers. We checked them for changes in ownership. Even big stock transfers."

" Going back how far?"

" Couple of years. There were three that stood out. This morning I got a full report on each of them. One of the growers was bought out by something called the Nature Conservancy of Arlington, in the U.S. They're going to turn the place back into some kind of swamp."

" Forget about that one."

" The other two seemed to be unrelated. Local investors, one in Ankara, one in Izmir. But something looked odd to me. Both deals were put together by someone named...hold on a second. I have it right here...Kiryat Balaban. We did some checking and found out that he's a Turk, working out of London, then found an address for him in the Pan Pacific Development Bank building."

" Does that mean something?"

" Pan Pacific is owned by the Mekler Group, headquarters in Geneva."

" And..."

" Mekler and Heskel Milstein are one and the same. So either it's a remarkable co-incidence that Kiryat Balaban leases space from Heskel Milstein, or the deals he brokered in Turkey are for Milstein."

" Remind me who he is, again?"

" He's the one who finances a lot of businesses for..." They said it together, "The Boravitchers."

" Wolfie, this could be what we're looking for."

" This is big, Corrado. Maybe too big for you and me."

" You think we should step aside? Let the higher-ups deal with it and take all the credit."

" Baglione, think about this. It's got to be a conspiracy. These people are trying to gain control of major industries all over the world. It's not just Italy and Germany. A lot of innocent people are getting killed. Murdered. For what? This kind of thing..."

" Could make us famous, Wolfie. Do you realize what it would mean if we, you and me, cracked this case wide open. I don't know much about your situation, but for me this could mean everything. A promotion, more money...I could.."

" It's no different for me. I'm stuck here. Don't get me wrong. I love my job. But...Do you really believe that we could do this? By ourselves?"

" Wolfie, we're good policeman. Why not us?"

" How much free rope do you have, Corrado?"

" Ha! My boss is, how do you say, in the cuffs? The ministry's about to be voted out of existence in the Camera. There is no one looking over my shoulder. As long as they don't cancel my credit cards, I can do pretty much whatever I feel like. How about you?"

" It's not so easy here. Sorry to offend you but this is Germany, not Italy."

" You're right, of course. But go ahead."

" I'm accountable to many, many people."

" Can you keep them away from this."

" I think so. As long as their fat asses are covered, they'll leave me alone. I know how to deal with them. My god, I've been at it for twenty-one years."

" You've been a policeman for twenty-one years. Me too. That's remarkable. Don't you think that's a sign? Wolfie, let's do it. Let's work together."

" Where do we go from here?"

" I don't trust anyone in Roma. Not since the shit hit the..."

" I feel the same way here. These people seem to always be one step ahead of us. We look for something and it's gone. We look for someone and they're dead. It's like my office is bugged. Maybe yours, too."

" So what now, Detective Flanken?"

" We've got to find out more about this, this group, without spooking them. Do you agree?"

" How? Where do we start?"

" Can you get two weeks vacation?"
" Are we going someplace, Wolfie?"
" Ever been to New York?"

The Polizeirat was unmarried. He wondered whether to tell
Baglione that he was gay. Maybe Vanessa had already spilled the
beans. With some Italian men, especially the ones from the south,
it could be a problem. Hell, even in Germany, in 1994, given his
position, it could be a problem. Wolfie Flanken never felt like a
woman imprisoned in a man's body. He wasn't the least bit
effeminate. Flanken simply preferred the companionship of men.
His longtime lover was an artist named Harald Helm. They shared a
small house in Hürth, a suburb on the road from Köln to Bonn. The
two men were so discreet that their private lives were known only to
a handful of others. It was all about Wolfie's position. A gay
Chefdetektiv might be seen as a security risk.

Their house was a mini Biedermeier museum. Flanken had
inherited most of the furniture from an aunt who'd been an actress.
The two men had pared it down as best they could, but it still was a
lot more than they needed. Harald's paintings, mostly large, dark
canvasses studded with broken glass (he was, after all, from Berlin)
hung from rusted chains on nearly every wall. The painter always
wore black. His complexion was the color of a frozen daiquiri. Most
thought him tiresome. However, Wolfie was amused by him and
they were deeply in love.

" I'm going to the U.S. for a few days," said the portly
policeman, attempting some sit-ups. No matter how hard he tried,
he could never do more than two. After a few aborted attempts at
three in a row, he quit and rolled over onto an intricate Chinese
carpet. He propped himself up with one arm and planted his right

182

hand on an image of a five toed dragon. The rug was also from the aunt.

" Travel bores me," said Harald, purposely leaning his head back and rolling it around to make some point - or not.

" Well, I enjoy it. For me, New York's is fascinating."

" Big cities don't interest me at all."

" Nobody's asking you to go."

" Good, because I wouldn't, even if you did ask me. It's all about my inner struggle."

" Oh Harald, take a pill."

" Everyone in New York is lost."

Flanken ignored him.

" Did you hear from the dealer in Paris?"

" I don't speak about business on the telephone. If he wants to talk to me, he'll have to come here."

" I thought he had a buyer."

" I feel like my soul is seeping out, like through a drain pipe, whenever I sell a painting. I'd really rather not bother."

" Harald, at least once a day I ask myself 'what am I doing with you?' "

" It's your punishment," he replied, "for driving too fast." A quick glance, then a very faint smile. His lips hardly moved.

" What are you saying?" laughed Wolfie.

" I'm not letting you put me in a good mood. No! Stop that!" Flanken began to tickle him.

" Stop! No, no, please...stop!"

" O.K., everybody. Big smile and...good. One more. That's it. Gorgeous!"

The photographer thought he must have said that about a million times before. But the Milsteins had big bucks to spend and not much taste. So, why not? Actually he was following his mother's advice. She said to him, more than once, 'Brian, you don't have to kiss their ass. Every once in awhile you just give it a little lick.'

The dedication of the Milstein Pavilion at New York Nose & Throat was a low key event. Heskel Milstein, the only son of a Polish Jew, wanted it that way.

" As many of you know, I'm a man of few words."

Those who really did know, just laughed at the incongruity.

" Let me start by thanking the one person most responsible for making me rich enough to afford this wonderful achievement, my darling wife, Fanny Milstein."

This time there was genuine agreement from those in attendance. She was given a standing ovation.

" As many of you already know, this lovely lady and I were married in a small, storybook shtetl in Poland called Kraków."

Several people who knew better sniggered at his description. In fact, Kraków had been home to 80,000 Jews, most of whom were resettled elsewhere when the Germans occupied the city in September of 1939.

" When my father, may he rest in peace, moved our family to Brazil, Fanny and I were still newlyweds. I remember, as if it was yesterday, seeing Copacabana beach for the first time. December the 25th, Nineteen-thirty nine. It was my father's Christmas gift to his family."

This elicited slightly more muted laughter. But not much.

" Once we settled in and found a shoykhet, it was time to get down to business. Those of you who don't know what is a shoykhet, it's a kosher butcher. Very important for a young banker to know who makes the best derma in Rio."

He paused, waiting for a laugh.

" Obviously we don't have too many derma lovers here today."

A few titters was all he could coax out of his audience.

" When Mordka Milstein, my father, opened the Banco Europeu do Brasil in the early months of 1940, he started off modestly. At least that was the way he described our first small office in the back of a furniture store. Those were the war years and many people were wary of trusting Polish Jews with their money. There was young man who worked for my father. A handsome young man, if I remember correctly." A few more laughs than the last time. Heskel was clearly not a very good public speaker.

" This young man had an idea. And this idea, to cater to the growing population of immigrants was so successful that, within a year, the bank had opened branches in Sao Paulo, Montevideo, Buenos Aires, and Santiago de Chile. At one point in the summer of 1945, it was widely rumored that Banco Europeu was the repository for almost a billion dollars in gold belonging to the Japanese royal family. I'll never tell."

Still not much reaction from this crowd.

" One of the groups that we targeted, right at the beginning, was the growing Japanese community in Brazil. In fact, it was the largest Japanese population outside the mother country. I remember vividly when a big macher from Chase Bank in New York showed up and offered to buy us out. But my father was a cagy old bird and decided to hold out for a figure so large that it was laughed at back in New York. And I can say, modestly, that it was probably the last time that anyone in the banking business laughed at Mordka Milstein."

This, unsurprisingly, got a huge reaction from the crowd.

" Have I honored my father's legacy? I think so. I hope so. Have I done well for myself and my family? Absolutely. Here's why. By the way, I hope I'm not boring you too much. And don't worry. There's coffee and cake coming. From Shlomo's, on Houston Street, no less!"

No response at all.

" Indulge an old man for a few more minutes. It's not everyday I get to spend fifty-six million dollars on a piece of property I don't even own. Now where was I?"

He looked down at his notes for the first time since he'd begun.

" Why were we so successful in South America? The answer is simple. We were one of the only ones, one of the only banks that refused to lend money in South America. Why? Because we lived there. We knew what these mamzers, who ran the countries we operated in, were like. What they were capable of. So we held off. And when those huge loans that the big banks had made started going bad, more than a few of our larger competitors combusted. Exploded! Blew up, as they say. And we were there to clean up the mess...at, I might add, very 'reasonable' rates of interest."

This time he didn't bother waiting for a reaction.

"A little bit of background, if I may. If you're old enough to remember, the 1960's and '70's was a time of great economic growth in South America. Banks all over the world were lined up waiting to lend governments as much as they wanted. All except one. Banco Europeu do Brasil refused to march in the parade. Many of these governments borrowed heavily."

Milstein paused. Embarrassingly, he'd lost his place reading from the note cards in front of him.

" Sorry. Just give me a second. I think I must have dozed off for a second."

This elicited his biggest laugh.

" Now. Where was I? Right. These governments borrowed heavily starting in the 60's. Industries did the same thing. And when it came time to pay the piper, guess what? They didn't have the gelt. That's means 'money' in Yiddish,' Mario."

Mario Cuomo, waved and acknowledged the shout-out. His opponent in the race for Governor of New York State, George Pataki, sat on the other side of the room and smiled weakly.

" For us, I'm speaking about me, things were about to get very interesting. Allow me to toot my own horn. I was acting, at the time, as unofficial adviser to a number of countries in Central and South America. The Caribbean, as well. Mexico, too. What I told these countries was this. Don't...Sign...Anything. Don't even shake hands with these goniffs from the big banks. No notes, no security pledges. Nothing. I told the leaders of these countries, not told, advised the leaders of these countries - don't give away the mule. Your people will love you for that. These banks, I won't mention any names, were so greedy, they lent them the money anyway. No security pledges. No nothing. Then, when the *shmuts* hit the fan, guess what? As the borrowers began, one by one, to default in the middle 1980's, several of these prestigious, 'my kaka don't stink,' big banks sought my help. Our family's connections in these countries were so impressive that we could command huge retainers from New York, from London, from Germany asking us to help them salvage what they could. And because of our efforts we made a fortune. Mekler Group, our little vantz of an operation, saved more foreign banks from ruin than you could ever imagine. All due to our unassailable government connections. During those years, if you can imagine, there was hardly a major bank in the world that didn't called us for help...I'm almost finished. Just keep your pants on, Solly. My friend, Mr. Baum, looks like he's ready for some rugelach."

This got a decent laugh from the Jews in the audience. He was on a roll now and into the final stretch.

" Ring. I see the light blinking on my telephone. Ring. My secretary says to me 'Mr. Milstein, the Chairman of the (giant) Pan Pacific Bank, which was in terrible shape from its bad loans in Brazil, is on line one.' I pick up the receiver and say very nicely. *'Mekler Group, How may I help you?'* "

By now, several children, as well as most of the adults, were fidgeting in their seats. A few of the kids started running around the perimeter of the room. Their parents quickly removed them from the ceremony, taking advantage of the opportunity to escape. Others in attendance tried valiantly to pay attention.

"Now the Pan Pacific Bank, at that time, was the second largest financial institution in Asia and the tenth largest bank in the world. And you know what? They were in serious trouble from the loans they'd made to Brazil, as well as loans to Peru and Argentina. All three countries had declared, with my advice, that their outstanding debts to Pan Pacific could not and would not be honored. The numbers, my friends, were staggering. I was told in that phone call, in confidence, the severity of the big bank's position. So what to do? I immediately go to work, negotiating in secret, with each of the leaders of these countries. I meet for weeks at a time with the Asians, and when it seemed that all was lost..." Heskell paused again. "I announced my solution. The Mekler Group of Geneve, Switzerland, which was where we were headquartered for a number of reasons that I won't go into..."

Another pause for a laugh that didn't come.

"... was prepared to purchase the assets of the Pan Pacific Bank. Of course we had to borrow most of the money. And where

188

did the money come from?...pause, drum roll...from a consortium of European lenders. And for collateral we used the outstanding paper from the South American loans. The kicker, and this is what made it so geshmak, the kicker was that I was able to persuade the South Americans to secure the notes with real worth. The very same countries, who I'd kept from signing away their futures, were now ready and willing to do just that for me. And by cleverly structuring the collateral, it appeared to them as if nothing terrible could happen. And, in fact, that was not so far from the truth. Only if there was a complete breakdown of the world financial order, would, could these countries be hurt."

Milstein, the repressive dictatorships, and especially the Europeans, were betting that would never happen. It was an audacious play on everyone's part, with Mekler the overall winner. Milstein was a hero to the Asians, by helping them save face. A helpful old father to the child-like Latins, and a shrewd partner to the Europeans. The Boravitchers, who'd invested heavily in Mekler, at least at that moment, were merely along for the ride.

" Ladies and gentleman, I can tell you today, with that one phone call, and a few million in lawyer's fees, we were able to swallow up Pan Pacific and step into the big leagues. And that, dear friends, is my story."

Eight years after Mekler took it over Pan Pacific, the bank was ranked nineteenth in size, worldwide. And yet, the family was one of the most private and conservative of the new mega-rich. There were no yachts or villas or airlines flying the family colors. Heskel Milstein was a devout follower of Rebbe Moshe Buchsbaum. The two men had known each other for years. Their fathers were both from the same small Polish shtetl. The Grand Rebbe's family bloodline had crossed the Milstein's about a hundred years before, when Heskel's grandmother, the daughter of a rebbe on his mother's side, married the Rebbe's uncle.

Claude Wizman sat in the small auditorium while the president of the hospital's board droned on about the generosity of the Milstein family, many of whom were in attendance. Several of the sons and sons-in-law were rebbes. They stood, in their dark suits, coats and beaver hats, on one side of the room. The women, Heskel's wife, sister-in-law and his daughter and granddaughter, sat on the other. The adjoining building was funded by the Milstein Family Circle, and built on land donated by Solomon Baum.

After a semi-respectable amount of applause, the speaker thanked everyone for coming, and the ceremony was over. Claude caught the old man's eye and the two of them walked towards a buffet table set up with coffee, Tropicana (from the carton) and Shlomo's amazing pastries.

" Congratulations, Heskel. This is quite an impressive accomplishment."

" I only wrote the check," laughed Milstein.

" I spoke with Gianfranco. He says that he needs to be buying, now that the price of vineyards in Italy is bottoming out. He told me you weren't convinced."

" That's right. I think that they'll go lower. He doesn't seem to get it. I know he's a bright boy. But I'm still smarter. And...it's my money. I understand he's nervous, but I'm not looking for more exposure, at least not there."

" He told me about South Africa. I think he's uncomfortable with what you're doing."

" Gianfranco knows wine. Period. I understand the way business is done in these farkakta countries. Especially the way it's evolving in southern Africa. The wine business down there is all about egos. Rich white men's egos. I personally know all the big players. Taking them down will win me respect from the blacks. I want to be in a position to move fast, to call in some markers, when the country opens up. Do you have any idea of the potential, of what's possible in a black South Africa? The country's not just a gold mine or a diamond mine, its a money mine. If you can manage to get in at the beginning. The vineyards I bought could produce carrot juice for all I care. It's the relationships I'm developing with the ANC that will be worth something substantial in the future. Much sooner than even you realize. And you, my boy, are one smart cookie. That's exactly the words Sol Baum used to describe you. Gianfranco, on the other hand, is a shmendrik. He thinks too small. That's not a knock, it's reality. Listen, Claude. Enough about this. You didn't come to this excruciatingly boring ceremony to talk about the wine business."

" You're right, of course. I'm worried about the Rebbe."

" He's an old man, Claude. You're talking about his health, yeah?"

" That and..."

" The succession."

" Exactly. Heskel what happens to our plans when the Rebbe dies?"

" You mean you don't believe this Moshiach bullshit? That the end is upon us. And you call yourself a pious man. Frankly, I'm shocked."

" Heskel, you don't believe that kind of talk any more than I do. Even the Rebbe doesn't believe it."

" Oh, you know that for a fact? Have you spoken to him lately?"

" Not for awhile."

" Well I have, Claude. And I'll tell you, between you and me, he's acting very strange lately."

" Maybe it's his condition."

" I don't think so. I think he's starting to take this Moshiach nonsense to heart."

" Well if he really is The Moshiach, I guess we'll know it soon enough. And if he isn't, then what?"

" I would hope that nothing would change, Claude. I have a lot at stake here."

" What about a successor?"

" If he names one, we'll deal with it."

" And if he doesn't?"

" And he's not The Moshiach? We deal with that as well."

" It was nice seeing you again, Heskel. And congratulations on today."

Vanessa insisted on buying him some new shirts.

" Corrado, I'm embarrassed to be seen with you. The collars looked like a dog chewed them up."

" You can afford to do this?" The salesman had told them the shirts were three hundred thousand lire each, almost two hundred dollars.

" I have plenty of money for shirts. I just can't afford anything bigger, like buying new equipment. If you solve this mystery and restore my name, I should be able to modernize the winery. So you see, your clothes are a good investment."

" The shirts? I don't understand."

" The shirts. You'll go to New York, looking very handsome, and some beautiful spy will fuck you and tell you all the secrets you're looking for."

" I would never..."

" Baglione, I may be a lot of things. Stupid is not one of them."

192

" How much do you know?" he asked cautiously.

" Uh, uh. A lady never gives herself away. Why don't you take me with you. I could be a lot of help."

" No thanks."

" I could also be a lot of fun."

" Oh, I bet you could. But Wolfie and I can handle it."

" Wolfie's going! That's not fair."

" I thought you knew."

" Well I didn't. But that explains everything."

" What does that mean?"

" You and your pal are going through what's called in English, a 'mid-life crisis.' You're both at that age where you think you have to do something macho to prove that you're not getting old."

" Thank you, Dottore Freud."

" I'm serious. This could be dangerous. You said yourself that people have been murdered."

" When did I say that?"

" When you were talking to Wolfie, on the telephone."

" You eavesdropped on my conversation."

" Why are you so surprised?"

" I would never do that to you."

" You had me checked out, didn't you? That was a rotten thing to do."

" That was different. You were a possible suspect in a murder investigation."

" Am I still?"

" I'll let you know."

Flanken, The Polizeirat, finished filling out the formal request, signed it and put one copy in the internal mail tray on the duty sergeant's old wooden counter. The carbon copy was left on his own desk, in full view of anyone with a roving eye. The following morning the approval came back from Personnel. Two weeks vacation, charged to his annual leave. He was entitled to more, but he'd save it for the end of the year. Flanken had stopped at the Lufthansa office to collect a handful of brochures. On the way back to his office he perused them, finally choosing the Caribbean island of St. Maarten. It was what he was looking for. There were three flights a week from Frankfurt, via Antigua. More importantly, there were good connections to the U.S. and the place had a reputation for lax immigration and customs. Somewhere he'd remembered seeing a bulletin from the German drug enforcement people, with their assessment of the island.   Flanken did not want anyone to know that he was on his way to New York. He booked one seat, Frankfurt-St. Maarten-Frankfurt. His ticket to the U.S. would be purchased for cash, once he was on the island.

" Richter, I'm leaving you in charge. I expect that you'll have enough to keep you busy. The Gambelhauff investigation remains our number one priority. See that it's handled correctly. The file was updated this morning. The forensic people confirmed the cobwebs on the mop matched the mess behind the TV."

" What did they say at...?"

" I'm getting to that. Our boy was alive when the TV went into the tub. The cause of death was definitely electrocution."

" No marks on the body?" asked his junior.

" None. Most probably, he was ordered into the water ...maybe at gunpoint. Check and see if we have anything in the files that resembles this killing. Perhaps we'll get lucky."

" Maybe you'll get lucky too, chef," he laughed. "I'll bet those island girls are really something." Richter was looking at one of the travel brochures.

194

" You never know," replied Wolfie, winking as if he cared.

" How do I find you? I mean if it's important."

" I'll call in.This is my vacation."

" I understand, sir. Shall I drive you to the airport?"

" That would be nice." Flanken wanted the man to see him get on the plane. He looked at his watch. "We'll leave at noon."

Baglione had no trouble getting his two weeks vacation. Minister of Agriculture Fausto Bambone, who had to approve it, was in jail, so Corrado just signed the man's name. He doubted that his boss would be back. Vanessa drove him to the airport in Milano in the Rolls.

" I love this car."

" It was a gift to myself, a long, long time ago."

" How much does one of these cost?"

" An extraordinary emerald necklace and matching earrings."

" You traded for this?"

" In a way. I bought it with the money I got from The Corsican. Didn't I already tell you this?"

" Where did you get the necklace? No, don't tell me!"

" Corrado, relax. It was ages ago. Besides, the theft was never reported."

" Why not?"

" How could a police chief in Marseille explain how he had a half million dollars in jewels in his house?"

" Madonna. You stole it from a cop?"

" Pretty funny, huh."

" I'd better be careful around you. There's no telling what you're capable of doing."

" Baglione, are you sure you don't want me to come? I worry about you in New York."

" Why. My English is good enough. I dress nicely, thanks to you. And besides, Wolfie will be there with me."

" Is he flying to the D.R. also?" She knew that Corrado was flying to Santo Domingo as a ruse. She assumed Flanken was doing the same."

" I didn't ask. Wolfie's had an answering machine set up in New York. He checks in every day. Just like I do."

" Corrado, do you have the number I gave you last night?"

" In my mind. Tell me about this person."

" He's an old friend. Peter scouts locations for movies. He knows his way around New York and he knows how to make things happen. Do you want me to call him for you?"

" No. If we need his help, I'll let you know."

" So you'll call me? I hate to be kept in the dark."

" Vanessa, I love you. You'll hear from me. I promise."

" Baglione...you're special to me. I haven't thought that about a man in years."

She kissed him gently on the lips after stopping the car at a toll booth. Malpensa was twenty-five minutes away.

" Vanessa, you do realize that you know nothing about me."

" And," she laughed, "you think you know everything about me."

" We've got plenty of time before we reach Malpensa. Tell me something about you that I don't already know."

They held hands. She was comfortable driving the big car.

" Alright, my sweet. Remember, Corrado. It's you who started this.

" Guilty, your grace."

She hesitated for a moment.

" I have a child, a daughter."

" Where? How old?"

" I don't know where she is or anything else about her."

" But, that's impossible. How did this happen?"

" You don't really want to hear my sad story. Besides, I'll probably cry."

Corrado sensed that she wanted to tell him everything, to let it all spill out. He wasn't sure if he should push her.

" If this is too difficult, cara, I understand."

" Corrado, I've accomplished a great deal in life. My one regret was giving up my daughter. I think about her every day. I think about her when I wake up in the morning. I think about her at night. What an awful thing I did. I robbed her of her mother."

" When did this happen?"

" In 1972. The father was a surgeon, married to his 'career.' When the baby was born he stopped taking my calls. I was disillusioned and very depressed. I even thought about suicide. I convinced myself, for the good of my child, that I had to give her up. Give her to people who could care for her. I was in a bad, bad way. And now, now I have no idea where she is."

Tears ran down her cheeks.

" Do you want me to drive?"

" No. I'll be ok. Now that I've told you."

" Is there anything else I should know? Where you were born? Where you went to school? How did you meet your Italian?"

" Alright. But I need to tell you in English. There are some things I can't translate in my head. Especially when I'm driving on the Autostrada.

" O.K., cara. Sono tutto orecchie. How do you say that in English?"

" I'm all ears. O.K. Here we go. Feel free to stop me if you get bored."

" Carissima, you may be many things. But I assure you, boring is not one of them."

" My real name is Vanessa Lynn Terry. I got my B.A. in Art in 1963 from Eastern Michigan College on a scholarship from my church. As a graduation present, my parents, who were both teachers, gave me a semester at the Sorbonne in Paris. After that, in like '64, I applied to Pratt, in New York. I studied painting and drawing at night. To support myself, I took a job at a department store called Lord & Taylor."

" Department store? I don't understand."

" A big store that sells lots of different thing. Like Rinascente or Upim.

" Ah. Un grande maggazino."

" Bravo. I got a job sketching clothes for their newspaper advertisements."

" And that's where you met your husband?"

" Not exactly. Corrado, am I telling this story or are you?

" Sorry. I won't interrupt you ever again."

" Yea, right. Anyway, I had a roommate at that time, Mary McGuire.

" Irish."

" Corrado, what did you just promise?"

" Colpa mia. Please continue."

" She...Mary, was a not very talented poet. Ever heard of Jack Kerouac. On The Road?

" Sure. I love that song. On the road again. Da da da da da."

" Uh, no. That was Canned Heat. Jack Kerouac was a writer. Anyway. Not important. As I was saying. Mary's closest brush with

198

fame was the blow job she'd supposedly given Jack Kerouac in a toilet at N.Y.U.

" NYU?"

" New York University. Mary and I fancied ourselves as beatniks. You do know what a beatnik is?

" Yes. Sure." He had no idea what she was talking about.

" Anyway, after seeing the movie Two for the See-saw ...Shirley MacLaine. Any of this ring a bell?"

" Ring a bell?"

" I knew this wasn't gonna' be easy. Girls like me who wore oversized white men's dress shirts? Black tights? And Keds. That's a beatnik outfit. Capisci?"

" Si, capisco." He really didn't understand, but knew better than to open his mouth again.

" Every evening, after classes, we took the subway up to Greenwich Village. We had an apartment downtown. Near the Brooklyn Bridge. There was a place we used to go to called the Café SINcere. SIN-cere. Get it?...No?...Never mind. Anyway, Mary would recite her 'odes to corrosive existence,' or some other bullshit, while I tapped on some bongos I borrowed from a guy whose name I can't remember. Those were the days, Corrado. We could quote Sartre at length.

" Sartre?"

She ignored him and continued.

" One day Mary announces that she's gonna' marry an oral surgeon, a dentista who lived in L.A. The apartment was in my name but I couldn't handle the rent by myself, so I moved into the YWCA on Lexington Avenue. Don't ask...not important. Not too long after I finished at Pratt, a friend of a friend took me to celebrate at a place called Max's Kansas City. Very cool. I used to go there all the time. It was at Max's that I first met Renzo... Lorenzo. But everybody called him Renzo. He preferred to be called 'Count.' Don't ask. He was handsome, fun. He introduced me to his friends. Did I mention that he was very, very rich?"

" I suspected that he might be." Corrado immediately despised him.

" At least that was the impression he gave. It turned out that he lived on a rather small monthly allowance. His father sent him to New York to ruin, I mean run, their business in America. Sorry, Freudian slip."

The Rambaudis owned a number of silk factories in northern Italy. From his headquarters near Biella, the old man controlled a respectable piece of the market. Renzo's job was to oversee the New York operation. He promptly moved the showroom from a loft on Thirty-sixth street to a suite in the Hotel Pierre. During that period, a friend introduced him to Vanessa Terry.

" Please, tell me more." He wanted to get a feel for this Renzo person. Just in case.

" He drank Chivas Regal like it was Pellegrino. To keep up with him, I used to gulp down Grasshoppers...with skim-milk no less! The bartenders at Max's kept a container on hand just for me."

" Grasshoppers. You mean cavallette? That's crazy. With milk?" He jabbed a finger in his mouth like he was going to vomit.

" It's a cocktail, silly. Not a bug." She adored him at moments like this. "Two months after we met, we were married... on a Caribbean island. In Jamaica. A month after that, Renzo's parents were killed in an avalanche."

" How awful."

" We moved back to Italy so that Renzo could run the family business. Unfortunately, he wasn't up to the challenge. Their commercialista jumped right on it and made off with most of the money."

" Made off? Non capisco."

" Ran away...with the cash. Even I could see it coming. But Renzo was in shock. The banks foreclosed. The business went into bankruptcy. And then one beautiful spring afternoon he paddled a kayak out to the center of Lago Maggiore, loaded a pearl handle Beretta 418, held it to the side of his head and made me a widow. Beautiful gun, by the way."

Tenuta Rambaudi was not just a house, it was like an entire medieval village, surrounded by some of the best vineyards in the Langhe. A staff of eight was required just to run the estate. Without any funds of her own, the young American was forced to dismiss the staff.

" Vanessa, excuse me for asking, but didn't you inherit a lot of money?"

" Renzo's father knew he'd never amount to much. The old man's will had careful instructions about what should happen to the Tenuta. Daddy had apparently set up some kind of trust, years before they were killed. The interest from it paid the taxes on the property. The big money was supposed to pass to Renzo on his sixty-fifth birthday."

" But he never made it to sixty-five." Baglione was relieved to hear that the ex-husband was permanently out of the picture.

" I inherited the house and the vineyards but not the trust. I'm sorry if I sound cinico."

" No," Corrado assured her. "I think you're just being honest. What happened after that?"

" I had to sack the staff and then the place just started to fall apart. So I closed up the main house and sold off the stables and all of the small buildings and most of the land. The fucking creditors took most of the money. I was a kid. In a foreign country. But I'll tell you, after spending four years in New York, almost a year in Paris and a few months in the north of Italy, there was no fucking way I was going back to my parent's house in Battle Creek."

Like so many others, the would-be artist, found her way to Rome. She stayed in a series of depressing hostels for the better part of a year, earning a few dollars doing portraits of the tourists in Piazza Navona.

" Are you sure you want to hear this?"

" Vanessa, I want to listen to whatever you want to tell me."

" Ok, just cut me off when you get bored."

" No, no. Really, I'm fascinated. Please go on."

" In Roma I met a Danish guy. All he did was get me started on heroin and fuck my brains out!

" Dio." Corrado had heard just about enough.

" It took all my strength to go cold turkey."

" Cold turkey?" Baglione shook his head.

" Kick the habit?" He shook his head again. "I gave up drugs - just like that." She snapped her fingers in the air. The Rolls swerved sharply on a curve. Vanessa recovered nicely. "Sorry about that."

" I think we're almost to Malpensa, cara."

" I see. Heard enough, huh. Just remember, you're the one who eavesdropped on Wolfie and me."

" Origliato? When? I never would..."

" The English couple, The Earl of Whatsis and Brenda...duh."

" Uscita!" exclaimed Baglione.

She'd almost missed the exit for the airport. After parking the car, Vanessa entered the terminal with Corrado.

" Baglione, I already miss you, and you haven't even left yet." They stood in the Alitalia line together.

" I'll be back as soon as I can."

" Will you call me?"

" Tomorrow. I promise. But it will be the last time we speak until I get back. It could be dangerous and I don't want anyone putting the two of us together."

" I understand. Give me kiss. I'm leaving before I start to cry again."

" Vanessa, please. I swear I'll be back before you know it. Why the tears?"

" Because I'm worried about you. Because I love you and I don't want anything bad to happen to you."

" Nothing's going to happen. I'm absolutely sure. Wolfie and I are going to solve this case. Then you'll get your reputation back and the wines will sell like crazy and you'll be happy. I promise. Now give me kiss and go home. Make it look good. Someone's staring at us. I recognize him, standing next to the bar."

She kissed him on each cheek, looking over his right shoulder towards the man.

" Oh my god! I see who you mean. Tall, good looking, big mustache? Baglione, I recognize him, too. Who is he? What does he want?"

" It's Magnum. "

" Excuse me?"

" You know. Magnum P.I. Red Ferrari."

" Vaffanculo! You bastard!" She laughed and punched him on his arm. "You scared me half to death."

Solomon Baum looked up from his newspaper. He instructed his driver to let him off on the corner of Houston and Allen, close by the foam store. Only in New York could such an establishment exist. Foam rubber, cut to size, at discount prices and it was open on Sundays! Even more remarkable was that it wasn't the only one. There were several others within walking distance.

The black Lincoln Town Car slowed to a crawl behind the number 15 bus on Second Avenue. It had one of those cryptically stupid John Weitz ads slapped across its rear end. 'Only in America', thought the college educated M'kambe Boku, Solomon Baum's Ethiopian Jewish driver. A junkie with a filthy rag and a squirt bottle approached, saw how big M'kambe was and changed his mind. He veered over to a white Saab with Connecticut plates. The blond man behind the wheel of the 900 reached for the wiper switch. Too late. The greasy rag was already leaving tracks across his windshield. The African nodded approval to the homeless man, who shot him a toothless smile, then eased the big car to the curb. His employer opened the door for himself.

" Pick me up in half an hour."

" Very good, Mr. B."

Another homeless man staggered over. M'kambe cracked the window and handed him a dollar bill. Solomon Baum loved this neighborhood. He was born on Rivington Street. Every Sunday morning he came down to the lower east side to buy from the few shops that remained. Russ & Daughters for lox and whitefish, Moishe's bakery and Ben's, the old-fashioned dairy. He loved their baked farmer's cheese. The two block walk to Yonah Schimmel was packed with memories of a simpler time. He'd played on these streets as a child. A meter maid was writing tickets as a couple of kids ran past her at a breakneck speed. Baum smiled to himself and entered the crumbling storefront. Yonah Schimmel was one of a kind, at least in this part of the city, though a few others like it existed in places like Brighton Beach. The shop sold fresh baked knishes in a dozen flavors, potatonik, and coffee, heated to incendiary temperatures, in a greasy microwave oven. A few tables were scattered around a dumbwaiter that delivered goods straight from the oven. The skinny woman behind the counter occasionally yelled into an intercom using words like 'kasha' and 'pletzel.' Solomon ordered a cherry cheese knish and a regular coffee, then sat down with Heskel Milstein.

" Solomon, vos machstu?"

" How am I? That's the sixty-four thousand dollar question. Thank you for coming, Heskel"

" How's the family? Your wife's feeling better?"

" Like an old lady. And Bea?"

" Fine. She's visiting her cousin Ceil in Palm Beach Gardens."

" Give her my best."

The lives and businesses of these two families, the Milsteins and the Baums, were closely intertwined. The Boravitchers could accurately be described as their "in laws." The father of the Grand Rebbe Buchsbaum and the father of Heskel Milstein were childhood friends from Łomża, a small town in northeast Poland. In fact, Heskel's grandmother had married the Rebbe's uncle making the two families practically one.

Baum, the real estate mogul took a bite of his knish.

" Good?" asked Milstein, sipping a glass of tea. "I wish I could join you."

" Still with the stomach problems? What did Zipstein say?"

" Lay off everything. What else is new?" They laughed.

" Heskel, have you spoken to Claude?"

" Briefly. At the dedication."

" I'm sorry I couldn't make it."

" You didn't miss anything. I give because I can. I'm not what you would call a humanitarian. Emis?"

" True. I'm the same way, Heskel. What did Claude have to say?"

" He's worried about the Rebbe."

" Aren't we all."

" He's says he's concerned about the Rebbe's health."

" You really mean - what do we do if it turns out that the great one's not...actually...The Moshiach?"

" Precisely."

" Look, Heskel, I don't believe that stuff anymore than you do."

" Claude said the same thing. He doesn't even think the Rebbe believes it. This whole thing got its traction from a bunch of meshuganah kids. You know as well as I do, the young ones are much more fanatical about this than we ever were."

" It's a different world. They can't make a life for themselves so they put all their energy into this nonsense."

" Solly, if they'd only have patience, Claude's grand plan, grand design, whatever, should change everything for them."

" If it works, Heskela."

" And if it doesn't?"

" That's why I wanted to talk to you. We've both got a lot invested in this thing. You more than me."

" Tell me about it."

" Let's say that the Rebbe dies, which is going to happen one of these days. Between you and me, Heskel, if he's The Moshiach, I'm Shirley Temple."

" You and I both know that."

206

" At this point, Claude's more concerned about a successor to the Rebbe."

" As he should be. But it's not his money. No, it's up to you and me. Listen, I'm as pious as the next one. But we've been a couple of times around this block. I'm sure we're both going to heaven. That's not the concern here. It's not as if 'a Boravitcher' gets a special pass. We're all one tribe, Solly. That's the important thing. This business about who's the better Jew is crazy. I supported the Rebbe because I thought he was a good person. I still do. But to say that only a Boravitcher has the keys to the kingdom is arrogance. Plain and simple. I won't be party to it any longer."

" I'm glad to hear you say that. At least you and I still have our feet on the ground."

" So what do we do about Claude?"

" Look Heskel, he's a got a brilliant mind. Maybe the most brilliant of our time. But he's a soldier. He does what he's told. We can deal with him. He drinks two hundred dollar a bottle cognac, for god's sake. No I don't worry about Claude. It's the nut cases he's got working for him that worry me.They're the crazies. The really dangerous ones."

" Let's say, hypothetically, that the Rebbe dies tomorrow. What would you do?"

" First I'd make very sure Claude understands the realities."

" I think he does."

" So do I. But let's not be naive. If the Rebbe doesn't leave a successor, Claude's going to find a way to put in one of his own. I want to be involved in that decision."

" You're right. Did you know that he threatened Schmuel Zipstein?"

" Why? For what?"

" He wants, when the time comes, for Schmulie to keep the Rebbe's death a secret."

" How can he guarantee that? Zipstein's not gonna' be there twenty-four hours a day."

" Are you aware that Claude put in two of his own this week, to be the Rebbe's companions."

" Smart move. That way he's got control…"

" I don't like it, Solly. It scares the shit out of me."

" So what do you suggest we do?"

" Number one is put a very quiet freeze on all the assets you gave the Rebbe."

" I did that months ago."

" Did you? Good. I did the same thing." Milstein tapped his head and smiled.

" Is Claude aware of that?"

" I don't think so. I did it very surreptitiously. Up to now, I've just let everything go through normally. From now on my people know to tell me in advance. Whenever anything out of the ordinary is about to happen."

" That's just what I did."

" So you and I still hold the purse strings. Heskel, that makes me feel a lot better."

" The deals are all done through Pan Pacific. There's nothing of real value in anyone else's name. Except for your things."

" Don't concern yourself. Mogen Manhattan is the owner of record on all my big properties. And Steinway owns Mogen. If I don't want something to happen, it doesn't happen."

" Solomon, I know this is difficult for you, but this business with your son…"

" I'll deal with it."

The two men silently acknowledged the obvious. It was an awkward moment.

" Are you going to finish that knish?"

" What about your stomach?"

" One bite, Solly. How much could it hurt?"

The Lufthansa DC-10-30 touched down in late afternoon at the Princess Juliana Airport in Dutch Sint Maarten. Wolfie Flanken looked out the window as the big plane slowed at the end of the runway and turned back towards the mustard yellow terminal. He'd spotted a small hotel, along the sea side of the runway that had MARY'S BOON painted on its roof. It was just the kind of place he was looking for. He was only staying the night. The line at immigration moved like it was the slow motion 'play of the day'. A surly woman in a pale blue shirt lethargically stamped his passport.

" Where are you staying?"

" I'm not sure."

" Then I can't let you through."

" I thought I'd look around first."

" No. You must have a place to stay."

" Alright then, I'm staying at Mary Boons.

" You mean Mary's Boon?" she said with a faint West Indian accent.

" Yes, that's the place."

Having fulfilled her obligations, she waved him through. He went into a prefab metal building and waited to collect his luggage. After an interminable wait the noisy belt finally started to move. His bag was among the first to appear. Flanken grabbed his old wood and canvas suitcase and slung a grey leather Bottega duffle bag on his shoulder and walked out the terminal door.

" Rental car, sir. You need a car?"

" No thank you, I want a taxi."

He found the queue and climbed into a dusty Ford Aerostar.

" Where you going, sir?"

" How about the Mary's Boon. It's open, ja?"

" Oh yes, mon. Been there forever."

" Alright then. Let's try it."

" Twelve U.S dollars. O.K.?"

" Ja. That's fine with me." He thought it was high, since he'd seen the hotel from the runway, but Flanken was not in the mood to bargain. He'd changed Deutschmarks to dollars in Frankfurt. The exchange was so good, he really didn't mind. The taxi pulled out of the airport onto a busy ring road. To his left was a Wendy's fast food franchise that looked as if it was out of business. Something called the STOP N' SHOP advertised Heineken beer for $1. At the far end of the runway, the driver turned right and they bounced along what passed as a road until they reached the front gate of Mary's Boon.

As soon as the driver stopped a pack of small brown and black dogs came bounding out of the garden. The leader was a scruffy mutt with a chopped-off tail. An older man in shorts and a good haircut ambled slowly up the path.

" Don't leave," he ordered the driver and then turned to Wolfie. "Can I help you?"

" May I have a room for tonight?"

" One night? You must be joking."

" I must leave tomorrow."

" How early?"

" I'm not sure."

" Where are you going, St. Barths?"

" No."

" On a cruise ship?"

210

" No."

" Well then, where is it that you're going?"

" New York." He was starting to think that he'd made a mistake choosing this place.

" American?"

" No, no, I'm German."

" I was referring to American Airlines. The early flight to New York."

" Look do you have a room or not?"

" No!"

" Fine then, can you suggest somewhere else?"

" The Horny Toad, just up the road. They take one-nighters."

The dogs were jumping all over Wolfie, who'd opened the sliding door on the van, licking his hands and wagging their tails. Seeing this, the hotel's proprietor had a change of heart. He grabbed Flanken's suitcase and started to carry it up the walk.

" I thought you had no rooms?"

" I've decided to make an exception after seeing your luggage."

The German detective knew that he'd found the right place.

" Aha. This case is my pride and joy. It's what they're now calling 'vintage.' I can remember when it was just called 'old.' They both laughed. "Are you busy at this time of the year?"

" Off and on." They climbed a short set of stairs. "Et voilà. Room five. Let me just turn on the fridge. If you're interested, dinner's at eight. Tonight is beef tenderloin. That's it. No options."

" That actually sounds good."

" By the way, I probably should have mentioned it before I carried this bag halfway to Saba. We do not take credit cards."

" That's not a problem. You do take dollars?"

" But of course," he half smiled. "Here's your key. When you leave the room, lock it. The beach is fabulous at this time of the day. Enjoy. Oh, one more thing. If you'd care for a drink, it's self-service. Make a page for yourself. There's a book on the bar. One slash for soda, beer and juice, two slashes for everything else."

" Thank you. May I ask your name?"

" Ashton. And yours?"

" Flanken."

" First name or last?"

" Last."

" See you later."

Claude Wizman finally got around to unpacking his brand new IBM ThinkPad 775 laptop computer. It had sat in the corner of his office for the almost a month. He was glancing through the instruction book when his private phone rang. He looked at the caller I.D. screen and immediately recognized the number.

" Hello Jörg."

" You always know it's me."

" What's going on there?"

" I thought you should know that the police are getting too close. Flanken and the Italian have tied the bombing in Holland to Milstein."

" A chorbyn! Shit. Excuse my language. How did that happen?"

" For some reason they decided to take a look at all the tulip growers in Turkey. By cross-checking the ownership records they came up with Balaban's name."

" And that led them to Milstein. I underestimated these two detectives. Jörg, something will have to be done there."

" I understand completely what you're saying."

" Do it soon."

" Flanken's gone on vacation. Very sudden, in my opinion"

" Does that make sense to you, Jörg? It doesn't to me."

" Not hardly."

" Where did he go?"

" Someplace in the Caribbean."

" Find him."

" And?"

" You know what to do."

" It will take some money, Claude."

" I'll have Léon see to it. Keep me informed."

Wizman hung up the phone and returned to the instruction manual. He turned on the computer and followed the on-screen instructions. In less than an hour he'd loaded all of the programs he needed. The active-matrix color display was better than he expected. But the real joy for him, was the speed. The 486/66 was faster, by far, than his old 386. He ran a few tests to see what the machine could do. 'Thank god,' he thought, 'for life's little pleasures. Without them I'd go out of my mind.'

To help with his English, for the trip to New York, Baglione chose a novel. This had worked in the past. He liked to read thrillers, especially Le Carré. Maybe he'd look for something by this Kerouac fellow. By the time the plane landed in Santo Domingo he'd fantasized a new persona. From here on out, he'd try thinking like a spy in one of those paperbacks. Rather than take a direct flight from the Dominican Republic to New York he decided to fly from Port au Prince. Very Bond. The long drive from the Dominican Republic to Haiti was uneventful. Even the border crossing was easy. He merely passed out some dollars to the guards on each side. Once in Port au Prince he made directly for the airport. He bought an ALM ticket to Curacao, then Continental on to New York.

It was a roundabout way of going, but it had a certain *trade craft* cache to it. Baglione was enjoying himself.

Newark Airport was empty. He breezed through it in twenty minutes.The Pakistani taxi driver asked him where he was going.

" New York City."

" Yes sir, but to where?"

" To the..." He only knew the name of one hotel. "To the Hotel Waldorf-Astoria."

Once inside the Waldorf, he fought his way past a large group of Japanese tourists. At the reception he inquired about a room.

" Of course." said the desk clerk, "We have a very nice room available. The rate is three hundred-thirty dollars plus plus."

Baglione was stunned. The clerk immediately recognized the effects of sticker shock.

" Perhaps I can suggest another accommodation."

" That's very kind of you. I didn't realize..."

" Of course, sir. It happens all the time. You might try the Paramount. I used to work there. It's just across town."

He climbed into another taxi and was deposited at the new hotel. This time he was ready. The lobby, with its space-age decor and black clad clientele was fascinating. He eyed the abundance of good looking girls. A bellman, in a Gianni Versace designed uniform, escorted him up in the elevator. When he was finally alone, he looked for a door to the rest of the room. To his utter amazement, there was none. He was standing inside a closet. At least that was the way it felt. The bed, with its renaissance tapestry headboard, took up most of the room. There were a few small pieces of furniture, of modern design, and a bathroom the size of a pizza. He looked out the window at a giant mural of a black man throwing a baseball, painted on the side of a building. Corrado looked for the phone, spotted a red high heeled shoe with a keypad attached, and dialed Wolfie's answering machine.

After it picked up, the policeman punched in a series of numbers. He was relieved to hear Flanken's voice.

" Hello, Baglione," the recorded message began, "Welcome to New York. Myself, I arrive tomorrow. Call again, after 17:00 and I'll tell you how to find me. Have some fun tonight and try not to get into too much trouble." Wolfie laughed at that one, and so did Corrado.

Baglione showered and dressed, putting on one of the shirts Vanessa had bought him and realized how much he missed her. He glanced at himself in the mirror. His dark blue silk jacket, black knit shirt, Moschino jeans and crocodile loafers (no socks), were all gifts from the signora. She must have spent a fortune on him. Never in his life had Corrado been so splendidly dressed. He took the elevator down and entered a bar off the lobby. It was crowded with noisy young people. Baglione disliked the place immediately. Everyone looked so Milanese. He found a seat at the bar. The bartender looked like he'd just stepped out of a fashion shoot.

" Good evening, sir. What would you like?"

" Something that tells me I'm in New York."

" Hmm. How 'bout an Italian Stallion? Gin and See-nar."

" I don't think so. Maybe I take a vodka."

" Stoli Crystal. I approve." Like Baglione gave a shit. He pulled a bottle from an ice bucket on the bar, chilled a martini stem and poured it right to the top, so full that it was impossible to pick up the glass.

" Where ya' from?"

" Italy."

" Me, I was an Army brat." Baglione hadn't the slightest idea what that meant. "Yeah, we lived in Texas for awhile, then

Germany, then back to the States. I'm an actor, so you know it was either here or L.A. How 'bout you? What do you do?"

Corrado was always amazed at the American fascination with other people's business.

" I am a seller of bibles, spreading the words of Jesus Christ." That usually shut them up.

" Hey, no kidding. I did that once, for a summer. Strange, you don't look like the type."

He finished his drink and paid the check. "Eight dollars, fifty! Madonna!" thought Baglione. This was like drinking in Piazza Navona, something no real Italian would be caught dead even considering. Corrado left the bar and found himself standing in front of the hotel's concierge, a pretty young woman who looked about twenty.

" Good evening, sir, how can I help you?" she bubbled.

" Si, can you recommend me a good place for eating?"

" Let me think. Do you like Mexican food?"

" I've never tried it."

" I used to work at a great place on the East side. The food's good and not expensive. I mean by New York standards."

The young woman was so enchanting that he decided to try it.

" The name of the restaurant is Zarela. I'll write it down for you...and the address."

" Perhaps, you'd care to join me?"

" I can't. I'm sorry, but we're not allowed to."

" I understand," he replied, although he didn't.

" Just tell the cab driver you want Fiftieth and Second. It's on the west side of the street between Fiftieth and Fifty-first."

" I'm sure I can find it. Grazie mille, signorina."

" De nada."

Flanken sat down to dinner at about the same time Jörg Bissel was making a reservation, Frankfurt to Sint Maarten. He'd gotten someone at Lufthansa to reveal where Wolfie had flown. Not too difficult for a member of the Polizei Köln.

" Wolf, you sit here, George you're over here, Jo Jo avec Alain, Jimmy and Colette, on the other side of Jo Jo, Nancy and Kohei down the end, by me...et voilà," the proprietor intoned as if he were a magician pulling a rabbit out of a top hat. The remaining tables were empty.

" Ah, private dining. Very intimate." A German attempt at humor, to which everyone replied in unison, "the season is over." The owner cackled at the chorus.

" You like a wine, sir?" asked the owner's French speaking partner.

" Yes, please."

" You like za red, za white or...one of each." At that, the table erupted with laughter. Apparently, like the establishment itself, this was some kind of inside joke.

" Je préfère un rouge ce soir. "

" Ah, vous parlez français. French eez ze best," crowed the tanned little Frenchman.

George, a man of about eighty, rolled his eyes at the owner. Dinner consisted of a salad to start, roast beef with cheese topped potatoes, green beans and fried onion rings. Dessert was profiteroles with chocolate sauce. Flanken ate heartily. He enjoyed the dinner as well as the company. However, it distressed the detective that his travel plans should be broadcast to the entire table. Everyone at dinner had a suggestion for where he should stay in New York. Everyone except Jo Jo, the sister of Alain, who spoke only French with her brother. Jimmy turned out to be the owner of a restaurant in Long Island, with a name that was impossible for Wolfie to say. Finally with much prompting and several bottles of wine, he was able to say "Cheek-o-lean-ohz." For that, he was given an ovation. During dinner a couple appeared at the door in hope of a meal. The owner unceremoniously denied their request. One of them, a large woman, was attired in too tight pink shorts and matching top. As she turned and left George dryly delivered his often repeated, but highly appreciated bon mot.

" She should think about going to Las Vegas." He paused. "I heard you can lose your ass there." More laughter accompanied the mortified strangers as they made their escape.

After dinner Wolfie retired to his room. He was having so much fun, he wished he could stay for the entire weekend. The restaurateur from Long Island told the proprietor, matter of factly, that in his expert opinion, the German had "cop written all over him." His companion nodded in agreement.

They don't have Mexican restaurants in Italy and Baglione had never tasted a margarita. He made up for all those years in the course of one evening. The following morning he nixed all of the classic remedies, finally locating a liquor store that sold Unicum, his old reliable cure. Two shots of the bitter brown fluid and Corrado was ready to work. He walked crosstown on Forty-second street, past the peep shows and movie houses playing kung-fu double features, past shops with windows hawking cheap switchblade knives, ending abruptly at a beautifully maintained park and the mighty main branch of The New York Public Library. The incongruity reminded him of home, where Roman treasures competed side by side with smutty video stalls.

He entered the imposing building, stopped briefly at the information desk and was directed to a bustling catalog room. There he gathered dozens of references related to Heskel Milstein and the Boravitcher organization. Baglione spent the rest of the day absorbing this vast amount of information. He made photocopies to show to his German colleague. There was an interesting piece in The New York Times from a year before. The article mentioned one Solomon Baum. A real estate mogul with connections to Rebbe Buchsbaum had a son who had aspirations to be mayor of New York City. The Rebbe had issued a strong endorsement. Baglione also copied a NEWSWEEK report about power brokers in the Israeli government's endless string of fragile coalitions. The Boravitchers were often mentioned by the magazine's Jerusalem correspondent. Even though he found nothing incriminating, he believed that at some point Wolfie would be glad that he'd done the research. The fact that the two detectives were no closer to tying the Boravitchers to the wine murders, the x-ray machines or the Amsterdam tulip explosion made this trip to New York crucial. A trip that had better produce some results. As of now, Flanken and Baglione were each out more than a thousand dollars of their own money, not even counting their forfeited vacation days.

At five o'clock Corrado gathered up his notes and left in search of a phone. He found an outdoor booth at Forty-second and Fifth. It was out of order, as were the ones at Forty-sixth and Forty-seventh streets. He ducked into a fast food place. He was confused by their sign.

ROY ROGERS – DEL TACO — NATHAN'S FAMOUS

They did have a pay phone that worked. He dialed the number, punched in the code and was greeted with a cheerful voice.

" Baglione, welcome to the Big Apple! Wolfie Flanken here. Fit as a fiddle and ready to go. I'm at the Howard Johnson's hotel on Eighth Avenue. Can we meet for a drink about six? I suggest, in honor of your Italian heritage, that we try the Harry's Bar in the Netherlands Hotel at Fifty-ninth Plaza. See you soon!"

Corrado thought the German sounded absolutely buoyant. Perhaps he had some good news. Back out on Fifth Avenue, Baglione walked north heading uptown. He had an hour to kill and looked forward to seeing the famous Rockefeller Center.

" Excuse me," said the small, bearded man, in a porkpie hat. "Ya'Jush?"

" Mi scusi?"

" Lay tefillin?"

" I'm sorry, I don't understand what you're saying."

" You speak English?"

" Si."

" Good. I'm asking if you're Jewish."

" No, I'm not."

" Have a nice day anyway."

The man was standing in front of a large caravan, or 'RV' as the American's call it. Painted on its side was a sign that read:

✡ MITZVAH MOBILE ✡   A SERVICE TO G✡D
COMMUNITY ALLIANCE OF BORAVITCHER ORGANIZATIONS, Inc.(CABO)
BOROUGH PARK, BROOKLYN, NEW YORK U.S.A

The policeman almost cried out with joy. Here was a man asking total strangers to come inside their caravan. For what, he didn't know. But what difference did it make? This was a chance to get face to face with their target. He couldn't wait to tell Wolfie.

" Pardon," he said to the man, "are you here every day?"

" Monday through Thursday. I'm thinkin' mister, maybe you are Jush?"

" No, no. But I have friend who is."

The man looked somewhat puzzled as Corrado danced up the street, his feet barely touching the ground.

The police building looked brand new. Jörg Bissel went in and introduced himself to the officer at the front desk. He showed the West Indian his credentials, stolen from an Interpol official killed in Köln, eighteen months before. Jörg was the first policeman on the scene. He had swiftly pocketed the dead man's I.D. The photograph looked vaguely like Bissel. He'd known that someday it would come in handy.

" How can I help you, Lieutenant Becker?

" I'm looking for a man who arrived here on the island, Saturday last." The German spoke passable English.

" You'll need to go to Immigration. It's on the Back Street. But it's closed now. They're open tomorrow morning at eight"

" It's only half past one in the afternoon. How can they be closed for the day?"

" The hours are eight to twelve in the morning, Monday to Saturday, sir."

" But surely there is someone there. It's very important."

He finished his sentence just as the officer turned and walked away, leaving Bissel alone and frustrated. Later that day the German checked into Reese's Guesthouse, a rundown hotel just down the street from the Korps Politzie Van De Nederlandse Antillen/Immigratie.

The following morning he paid a visit to the department. After he'd waited nearly half an hour, a surly island woman informed him that the records he'd asked for were still at Princess Juliana Airport. Bissel found a taxi and arrived there at half past eleven.

" The office is closed until two."

" But you do have those records?"

" Oh yes, they're stacked in that room over there." The clerk pointed at a dingy closet piled to the ceiling with forms.

" The entries from Saturday should be near the top, ja?"

" I couldn't tell you, sir."

" I mean, don't you keep them in some order."

" I just told you, sir! I don't know the answer. You'll have to come back after two."

Bissel ate an ice cream, read the local paper and browsed the airport shops. At two o'clock he returned. The same clerk now allowed him into the open closet he'd seen earlier. She was reading a day old New York Post, most likely appropriated off an arriving aircraft. Her lunch was spread out on the table.

" Why couldn't you have let me in here earlier?"

" Look, sir, I'm not allowed to admit anyone during our lunch hour. It's against the regulations. If you have a complaint don't tell it to me." She went back to her pork chop and rice, spitting slivers of bone into her hand. It took Bissel almost two hours to find what he needed. He matched both pieces of Wolfie Flanken's immigration card. The large top piece, for arrivals, indicated where he was staying. The smaller detached card for departure did not show the detective's next destination, but it did give the date Flanken had left the island. A few minutes later another taxi dropped him off at Mary's Boon. A man in khaki shorts glared at Jörg as the German came up the walk. The pack of dogs barked incessantly then left Bissel to deal with the owner.

" Yes. Can I help you?"

" I hope so. I'm looking for a friend who arrived here Saturday last. Do you remember a Mr. Flanken?"

" Vaguely. He was only here for the night."

" Did he, by chance, mention where he was going next?"

" He said nothing and I made no reply. You'll have to excuse me, I'm rather busy." Bissel watched the man, followed by his pack of dogs, disappear into a dark hotel room with a television set

222

flickering somewhere inside. The voice of a CNN talking head reached all the way back to his taxi.

American Airlines proved to have much more stringent policies about disclosing information than did the Netherlands Antilles police. The airline's station manager was unimpressed with the German's credentials. Finally, after a lot of head shaking, he surrendered the information. A Mr. Flanken had left Sint Maarten on Monday morning, ticketed to New York's JFK on flight 633 via San Juan.

Claude picked absentmindedly at the cuff of his silk and cotton sweater. The sweater was already losing its shape, after just one wearing. *The Builder* made up his mind to return it to the toney Soho shop where he'd purchased it. For six hundred dollars, he expected better than this. Sylvia interrupted him with a call from a Mr. Becker.

" Jörg, what's up?"

" Flanken's in New York."

" Are you sure?"

" He's been there since yesterday. I confirmed it with the airline."

" Any idea where he's staying."

" None. I was hoping one of your people could help me."

" What do you need?"

" Have someone check the hotels. So far, he's using his real name."

" That's a lot of hotels."

" Concentrate on the less expensive places. Our department won't pay more than two hundred marks."

" A hundred and fourteen dollars."

" If you say so, Claude. How did you do calculate so fast?"

" I eat a lot of fish. By the way, that doesn't buy much of a hotel in New York. Where are you now?"

" At the airport in Sint Maarten. I'll be there tonight."

" What time do you get in? I'll have someone meet you."

" No, no. I'd rather be on my own, especially with Flanken nosing around."

" He may be with the Italian."

" What's your man say in Rome?"

" This Baglione's also taken two weeks vacation."

" So he could be anywhere. Jesus, Claude, you may be correct. They could be in New York together."

" Jörg, we need to find out how much they know… and fast."

" You want Flanken alive, ja? I'll do the best that I can. But first we have to find him."

" I'll get Léon on it today."

" Good. When should I call you?"

" No more than a day. You know Léon."

The detective from Köln was waiting for him as Baglione entered the Cipriani bar. They sat at a table near the rear. A waiter was there before he'd even sat down.

" Do you speak Italian?"

" No. I'm sorry, sir."

" Do you have a good spumante?"

" Just a moment. I'll find out."

" Wolfie, have I got a surprise for you."

" I'm fine. Thanks for asking. And you?"

" Sorry. It's just that when I was walking up the Quintesima, I mean the Fifth Avenue, I..."

The waiter returned to the table.

" Excuse me, sir. We have Franciacorta and Fontanafredda."

" Which Franciacorta? No, no, never mind. I'll buy a glass. Wolfie what are you drinking?"

" I take the same, ja."

They waited for their wine, then resumed the conversation.

" So. Commissario. What's this incredible news?"

" The Boravitchers have a caravan set up not more than ten streets from here."

" It's actually twelve."

" You know about it?"

" I saw you talking to them."

" You what? You were watching me? Mannaggia! I don't believe this!"

" Baglione, I knew you'd go to the library. You're a very thorough detective. I followed you to see if you had any company."

" And did I?"

" Not that I could tell."

" What about you? Maybe I should be doing some watching."

" Nobody knows that I'm here."

" That's not true. Vanessa..."

" You told her?"

" Wolfie, she's o.k."

" Famous last words. You can write that on my grave marker."

" Look. She and I..."

" Hey, I'm sorry. But there's a lot at stake, my friend. Including our lives. You forget that these people have already killed..."

" You're right, of course, but Wolfie, you need to understand that I love her and she loves me. At least I think that she does."

" O.K. O.K. What did you find at the library?"

" I mostly looked for things about the Boravitchers.

" So what did you learn?"

" Let me find my notes."

" Take your time. Let's have another spumante. This one's not bad."

Baglione pulled a yellow legal pad out of his man bag.

" O.K." He began to read from his notes. "Allora. The Boravitchers are an ultra-orthodox Jewish...blah blah...one hundred and thirty years old. Founded in Poland...blah blah...went to Russia, and finally blossomed...blossomed?

" I think it means flowered."

" Si...flowered in New York. The leader is a descendent of...not sure how to pronounce this...Yehudah Buchsbaum... nineteenth century scholar...blah blah... pronounced himself the first in a line of Grand Rebbes...

" You don't mean the Lubavitchers, do you? We have many living in Germany."

" No, no...Listen to this...The group is often confused with another movement, the much larger and more powerful *Lubavitchers*, headquartered on Eastern Parkway, Brooklyn.

" So they're a completely separate group."

The German was scribbling into a black moleskine notebook.

" Exactly. Here's something interesting." Baglione referred back to his legal pad. "According to an article I read, there are some similarities...some rivalries...but for the most part the members of each sect keep to themselves..."

" Go on, Baglione. This is good." The Italian continued to read from his notes. "The Boravitchers have a strong political presence in Israel."

" Just as I suspected."

" Don't you mean *we*, Kapitän?"

" Sorry. What else did you learn?

" I found this in The New York Times from last year."
He pulled out a photocopy for Wolfie to look at.

" What's *this*, Corrado?"

" It's about a real estate big shot named Solomon
Baum. According to this, Baum has very strong connections to
Rebbe Buchsbaum. I also found *una montagna*, sorry, I mean a
mountain of information on Heskel Milstein. I photocopied
everything. Most of it is pretty dull. There's a lot of financial stuff
that I don't really understand."

When he was finished, Flanken pulled a newspaper clipping out
of his pocket. It was a picture from The New York Daily News
identifying New York City Comptroller Steven Baum, Heskel
Milstein, and Councilman Dov Tolchin cutting a ribbon to open the
Milstein Pavilion at New York Nose & Throat.

" Wolfie, we know there's a connection between the
Boravitchers and Milstein and now this Solomon Baum. The one
with the son who's running for mayor."

" Who's Tolchin?"

" I don't know. It just says Councilman Dov Tolchin. I'll do
some more checking tomorrow.

" What about Olivieri? By the way, am I pronouncing that
correctly?"

" Si, si. Perfect. If we can tie Olivieri's death to the
Boravitchers...Wolfie, you think you could get yourself inside that
caravan?"

" I was thinking the same thing. Tomorrow, I'm going to take
a walk on Fifth Avenue. Maybe see what's inside it."

" Are you much of a Jew?"

" What kind of question is that? A Jew is a Jew. There's no
'much' involved. I'm circumcised...and I speak Yiddish. These

yeshiva bochers want a promise or two from me, no problem. By the way, where are we eating tonight?"

" You like Mexican food?"

Léon Drei did not wait until morning to begin his search for the German detective. He supposed that it would be easier to deal with a night desk clerk, who had little or nothing to do, than with someone on the busy day shift. He was correct. Armed with a list of moderately priced midtown hotels and an envelope full of fifty dollar bills, (tens and twenties got you no respect), he began his exploration. Drei had to assume that Flanken was using a fictitious name. That's what he, himself, would have done. Jörg Bissel had supplied a recent photo of Wolfie, taken from the police department's personnel files in Köln. Léon started to canvas from Eleventh Avenue going east. It was almost a miracle but on the seventh try he hit pay dirt.

" Have you seen this man?"

" I see a lot of people."

" Do you recognize *this* man?" Drei showed a fifty dollar bill honoring Ulysses S. Grant to the clerk.

" Could be that he's here." The man eyed the bill.

" Could be or is?" Léon slid him the fifty.

" You just missed him. Him and another guy."

" What's the other guy look like?"

" I'm not really sure."

" Maybe this will help you remember." Another U.S. Grant changed hands.

" Five feet-seven, maybe five-eight, gray around the edges, sharp dresser. Had on a beautiful pair of crocodile loafers. Italian most probably."

" How do you know he was Italian?"

228

" Not him, the shoes. I used to work in the shoe department at Saks. 'Til I got downsized and ended up in this shit hole. Take your shoes for example. Size nine...nine and a half. Corfam and leather. Probably set you back sixty maybe seventy bucks. Shoe Town or..."

" I'm impressed. How about a name for the one who's staying here."

" Let me look. Room 1022, Mr. Schmitz."

" You said they just went out?"

" About an hour ago. They came in together. The other one waited for him here in the lobby while Mr. Schmitz went upstairs."

" You don't know where they were going, do you?"

" Hey gimme a break. Does it say INFORMATION over my head?"

" When he's ready to check out, I'd appreciate you give me a call."

Léon handed him a yellow piece of paper with a 718 number written in pencil and another fifty dollar bill. He walked out of the Howard Johnson's, turned right and stopped at a pay phone on the corner. It ate his quarter and did nothing else. The phone just next to it had no dial tone. At Fifty-sixth street, outside a McDonald's, he finally got through to *The Builder*.

" Who's speaking?" Claude didn't recognize the caller I.D.

" It's me. I found him."

" Léon, you never cease to amaze me."

" Thanks, but this was pure luck. He's at the Howard Johnson's on Eighth Avenue, registered under the name Schmitz."

" Is he there now?"

" No, he went out an hour ago. That's not all, Claude. I think Baglione was with him."

" How do you know?"

" From the way the desk clerk described him. It's the same guy that Henri saw in Köln."

" At the hotel. I remember. Listen, you stay there until Flanken comes back. I don't want to lose him now. Jörg just got into town."

" Claude, you're not thinking of..."

" Do we really have a choice?"

" I don't like this."

" You think I do?"

" If The Rebbe..."

" Enough, Léon! I'll take care of The Rebbe."

Drei did not like the sound of that.

" You're making me uneasy, Claude. Have you spoken to Henri today?"

" No. Why do you ask?"

" When I left the house, the Rebbe was flat on his back."

" Zipstein was there?"

" This morning. He said it was nothing."

" I'll give Henri a call. Please keep me posted. And Léon, thank you. That was really brilliant work."

Zarela Martinez served the best Mexican food in New York. When the concierge at the Paramount sent Baglione to her for dinner, she knew what she was doing. The previous night he'd dined there alone. The food was wonderfully different, the drinks were terrific and Zarela was a gracious host. Corrado decided on the spot, that Wolfie must try this place. Neither of the men knew anything about Mexican food. But what they ate was delicious. The burrito and refried bean crowd did not eat like this. This was top of the line.

Baglione was recognized as soon as they walked in the door. The owner was vivacious in her "bet you wish you could fuck me" strapless, señorita dress. All that was missing was the rose in her teeth. She greeted Corrado as if she were genuinely glad he'd returned. Wolfie thought she was great, as well. They were given a table near the bar, reserved for friends of the house. Two margaritas magically appeared. The cocktail was 'fabelhaft' according to Flanken, who fancied himself an expert taster. She explained that the secret was in the tequila.

" Would you like some help with the menu?"

" Zarela, it all sounds so divine." She smiled at the German and wished them both a pleasant dinner.

" So Baglione, how did you find this place?"

" A girl that I know told me all about it."

" You already know a girl? You just got here."

" Let's just say she was interested in me. What shall we eat?"

" First, Corrado, let's toast. To luck and to friendship."

" Cin Cin "

" L'chaim!"

They each took a sip. The warm tortilla chips were gone in minutes. With two kinds of salsa, one red and one green, it was easy to finish the basket. They ordered tamales and oysters and something called chilaquiles, which turned out to be a bowl of melted cheese. They feasted on tuna with mole and duck breast with pumpkin and several more margaritas. A trio, dressed in mariachi drag, sang *Cielito Lindo* accompanied by Baglione and Wolfie. By the time dessert was offered they were thoroughly drunk.

" Hey Flanken, look who just came in."

" What are you saying?"

" At the bar. I bet you'd like some of that."

A man and woman, looking like fashion models, were ordering drinks.

" He is quite something. And just my type."

" Are my ears hearing what I think I'm hearing?"

" Are you serious, Baglione? I'm gay. Homosexual. Remember? Köln. At the bar with Vanessa."

" Madonna! I thought you liked boys...as friends. Not that way. Wolfie how...?"

" I have a few good answers for that."

" Minchia. Who would have ever believed..."

" Look, Baglione. That's it. I can't believe you're so naive. If we're going to be working together you'll have to get used to the fact..."

" Si, now I understand what you're saying. But..."

" No but, Corrado. I've been a policeman for exactly as long as you have. Remember? If I didn't do my job well..."

" O.K. I don't mention it again." Baglione made a gesture, as if he was zipping his lips shut.

" That's not what I want. I want you to believe that I'm every bit the macho policeman that you are. Someday your life might just depend on me."

" Alright, alright."

The two sat in awkward silence. The same musicians, now arranged on a steep staircase that led to the upstairs dining room, played *Coo Coo Roo Coo Coo Paloma.*

" Are you o.k. Baglione?"

" I'll be fine tomorrow. Wolfie, you must understand. I'm Cattolico. From a Catholic country and a Catholic family. Maybe someday there will be a Pope who…"

*S*OUVLAKI PALACE is open twenty-four hours a day, selling sandwiches, cold drinks from a wheezing glass doored fridge, cigarettes and lottery tickets. That item, incidentally, generated more profit for the owners than all the others combined. In fact, The Palace had something of a reputation as *the* place to play, having generated three winning tickets of over a million dollars each. Léon Drei sat at the counter munching on a whole wheat pita wrapped around some very tired falafel. The greasy front window afforded him an excellent view of the Howard Johnson's Motor Lodge. At one in the morning the Palace was jumping. Midwestern tourists sat side by side with hookers in satin hot pants. Next to Léon sat the Olsens from Fairfax, Minnesota. Or perhaps they were Junior and Mrs. Coleman, in town for a Rotary Club convention. Invariably, they would be staying at the HoJo's, or perhaps, The Milford Plaza. Mrs. Olsen couldn't take her eyes off a lanky pimp in a purple fur coat and matching fedora. In the doorway, an exhausted transvestite stood chewing on a blue and white plastic straw. The counterman eyed him suspiciously while explaining to Junior Coleman what all came with the "gyro deluxe." A table of older women was laughing about something.

" I wouldn't give Jesus Christ my resale number!" They all thought that was the funniest thing they'd ever heard. Léon Drei didn't get the joke.

At about ten past one Wolfie Flanken miraculously made it through the hotel's front door, executing a perfect 'I'm not drunk' turn towards the elevators. Léon got up, paid his check quickly, crossed the busy street and walked casually into the lobby. He saw the German detective waiting for the elevator. Flanken entered it and went up to ten. Drei waited for a short time to make sure Wolfie was in for the evening, then looked around for a pay phone, changed his mind and left. He walked uptown, stopped at a phone booth on Fifty-fourth, lost a quarter, tried again at Fifty-fifth, before finally hitting a working one in front of the same McDonald's he'd stopped at earlier at Eighth and Fifty-sixth.

" It's me. I just tucked him in. He was pretty drunk."

" Go home. Get some sleep. I want you back there by seven."

Claude knew that Léon would be there at six. He loved the dedication and work ethic of those two boys. Wizman, a former Israeli commando himself, had wisely sent the brothers Drei to the Israeli Army when they were barely out of their teens.

" Have you heard from Jörg?"

" He called an hour ago."

" Where is he staying, Claude?"

" The Marriott Marquis."

" In Times Square?"

" Uh huh."

" Good. That's close to Flanken."

" He wants you to call him."

" What name is he using?"

" Gerhardt Putz."

" How does he dream up these names?"

" You know Jörg. Listen, boychik. He wants to end it tomorrow."

" Tomorrow? How can he..."

" We have no other option. The three of you need to make it happen."

" Henri, too? Who's going to stay with The Rebbe?"

" I will. Call Jörgie now and tell him yes. He's waiting."

Baglione passed by the Speedy Print shop on 44th Street to pick up his new business cards. He'd ordered them one day before and marveled at the service...until he saw the finished product. He'd thought he'd instructed them to use the sample of his government issued *biglietto da visita* and to add 'SPECIAL BRANCH' under his name. The stoner behind the counter did include the *special branch* b.s. to the card but somehow the policeman's name had been changed as well. When Corrado asked for his money back the marijuana addled teenager pointed, laconically, to a large NO CASH REFUNDS sign on the wall behind the counter. So his new cards now reflected all the changes.

my name is Baglione (CARABINIERI)

INVESTIGATORE - SPECIAL BRANCH

MINISTERO DELLE RISORSE AGRICOLE, ALIMENTARI E FORESTALI   ROMA, ITALIA

The Paramount's lounge was jammed when Baglione walked in the door. Michael, the barman spotted him and waved. He pointed to a lone empty stool at the far end of the bar.

" Stoli crystal, straight up?"

" I don't think so. Unicum, if you have it."

The bartender looked confused.

" What I need is a digestivo. How about a Fernet or a Branca Menta?"

Although he sometimes ordered one to freshen his breath, this time he need something to settle his stomach. Too much Mexican food for the Italian detective.

" Is that the same as Fernet-Branca?"

" That's fine...with one piece of ice, please."

He sipped the old-fashioned bitter, which has the dubious distinction of having been Hitler's favorite drink. Out of the corner of his eye he spotted a young woman seated to his left. The blond, in her red leather skirt and black sweater, was pretty, but in Corrado's professional opinion she had an unappealing hard edge.

" Is that good?"

" Would you like to try one?"

" No thanks, I think I'll stick to manhattans."

" Do you need another one?"

" Sure, why not. You're Italian, right?"

" How could you tell?"

" It's your accent. She smiled. "I'm Stacy."

" Hi, Stacy. I'm Corrado."

" That's an interesting name. What does it mean?"

" I never thought about that. It just means Corrado. Like Stacy."

" Ah, but Stacy means good company, a nice evening. You get the picture?"

" I'm starting to." 'She's working,' he thought, 'with the barman. That's how I got a seat.'

" So maybe you'd like a date, Corrado?"

" That's possible."

" You're not a cop, are you?"

" Why do you ask?"

" Habit, I guess. Corrado, you do understand that I get paid for my time."

" No. Really? You mean you're a...?"

" You got it, baby."

" Mamma mia. I thought you liked me."

Léon Drei walked quickly down Broadway to Times Square. He entered the Marriott Marquis and headed towards a row of public phones. He dialed the number, printed on a book of matches that he'd picked up at the reception, and asked to be connected to Mr. Putz.

" Ja."

" Mister Putz. Good evening."

" Where are you?"

" Close. You wanted to meet."

" Ja."

" The Amtrak waiting room at Penn Station. Half an hour."

Jörg Bissel got in a taxi in front of the Marriott Marquis. The Nigerian driver, spotting an opportunity, turned a three dollar ride into five by taking Broadway rather than Seventh. He came across Thirty-first, then back up Eighth Avenue. To add insult to injury he made his passenger walk from the Post Office side of the street. Léon Drei was waiting under the departures board. He spotted Bissel climbing the steps, up from the L.I.R.R platforms. To anyone watching, they looked like two strangers cursing the 02:55, NJ Transit to New Brunswick, now posted for 03:30.

" Jörg, how are you?"

" Tired. Let's get this over with."

" I'm listening." The two men did not really like each other. Neither of the Drei brothers approved of the German's behavior. It was one thing to kill someone, it was another thing to enjoy it. He did, begrudgingly, admit that Bissel was very good at his job.

" Claude told you that we need to deal with the German tomorrow?"

" Yes, Jörg. He told me."

" Did he tell you that I'll need you and Henri."

" Yes, Jörg. He told me."

" Fuck you, Léon. Pay attention. This is how it's going to work. I can't get near Flanken. He'd notice me right off. You'll have to do it."

" I'm listening."

" I've left a briefcase at the Marriott's cloakroom, lower level. The claim ticket's in your pocket. Don't bother to look."

Léon wondered how he had done that. It was typical Bissel. Totally unnecessary, but nevertheless, skillfully done.

"The case is fitted with a spring loaded syringe. You'll dress like a Hasid. Wait for him at his hotel. When Flanken's in the lobby get up next to him with the scuffed end facing forward. Squeeze the handle and jab. The hydrogen cyanide works very fast. He'll drop almost immediately."

" How very German of you, Jörg."

" Küss mein arsch, Léon. I don't need your..."

" And how, may I ask, do we cart him away? Call the bellman?"

" You will identify yourself as his friend. Tell the hotel people that he's had these attacks before and that he's an orthodox Jew. They won't question that. Have them call the Eretz Yisrael Volunteer Ambulance. You'll produce the number. Everybody's seen them around the city. This will not draw any attention. Henri and I will answer the call and dispose of the body."

Drei had to admit that the plan was sound although the thought of it disgusted him.

238

" **No,** operator, the country code is five-nine-nine-five...Sint Maarten...No, the Netherlands Antilles...No,no. Not the Netherlands. It's in the Caribbean...the Caribbean...S-I-N-T...new word...M-A-A-R-T-E-N...that's impossible. I have the number in front of me. It's country code five-nine-nine-five. The telephone number is five-five-four-two-three...Thank you." After another minute had passed, he was finally connected....."Hello...Is this the Mary's Boon?...Mr. Small?...Hello, this is Wolfie Flanken, remember me?...Ja, ja. I'm fine, and you?...Good. I hope I didn't wake you...I was wondering if you had room for me towards the end of the month?...Just a few days, I'm afraid...excellent... Really? When was that?...Do you remember what he looked like?...No, of course you wouldn't...Well, thank you. I look forward to it...Good-bye."

The detective hung up the phone and sat for a minute. He picked it up again, got an outside line and called Baglione's hotel.

" Corrado, it's me."

" What time is it?"

" Half after seven. Are you awake?"

" I am now."

" We have a problem."

" What's wrong."

" Someone followed me to Sint Maarten."

" How do you know?"

" It doesn't matter. If they're that clever they could easily find me here."

" You're right. What do you think we should do?"

" I want you to follow me today. See if I have company."

" Give me an hour. I'll be down in the lobby when you come out. Actually, give me two hours. There's something I need to finish."

" What am I supposed to do in this room for two hours?

Baglione smiled at his new friend, Stacy. He wondered if she worked the day shift as well.

" Watch TV, Wolfie."

" That's a great idea." His laugh had a nervous edge. "Halb zehn. Half past nine. I'm downstairs."

Baglione hunted through his wallet for Peter Shield's phone number. The person Vanessa had told him to call. Corrado remembered that he had something to do with the movies.

He reached him at his apartment. Yes, he did have a friend in the costume rental business and of course he would call him. For Vanessa, he would do anything. A half hour later, after a second helping of Stacy, Baglione was in a taxi headed for Queens.

Adams-Cook was New York's largest costume company. Anton Fuchs was expecting him. In less than an hour Baglione was transformed into an Indian businessman. The policeman, coming from the south of Italy, was naturally dark-skinned. He did regret the loss of his mustache. He shaved under his nose for the first time in years. The head of men's costumes found him a beige knee length jacket, trousers tight on his calves and brown slip-on shoes. Fuchs wrapped a turban around Baglione's head, transforming him into a Sikh. In New York, these days, he'd blend right in.

The Rebbe's house was a large, two story brick, built in the early 1930's. He'd lived there with his wife, Rivka, for forty- eight years until her death in 1986. Since that awful day, when she'd been struck by a Mister Softee truck on The Grand Concourse while visiting her sister, the Rebbe had lived alone. In Moscow for a visit, near the end of Gorbachev's rule, he suffered the first of a series of strokes. It was then that Claude Wizman began to manage the Grand Rebbe Buchsbaum's life. He installed a pair of palace guards, a cook and Dr. Schmuel Zipstein.

The Doctor was a very competent physician. In his private life - perhaps a bit odd. Zipstein enjoyed shaving women, more specifically, he got off on removing their most southerly growth. Claude Wizman first heard about this strange predilection from a girl of sixteen, whom he'd recruited some years before. She'd been brought to his attention by her parents who were college mates of *The Builder*, as well as second generation followers of The Grand Rebbe Buchsbaum. It seems that the girl, to the horror of her extremely pious parents, was what the guidance counselors at Sheepshead Bay High School called "sexually focussed." It was common practice among the Boravitchers in the 1970's to send their male offspring to Yeshiva, while girls were enrolled in the public schools. Fruma Veytz had dosed the backfield of the Pirate's varsity squad with a nasty STD. Shortly thereafter, the girl was taken to an Orthodox doctor, the internist Schmuel Zipstein, who insisted on removing her pubic hair on the first visit to his office. She reported this strange behavior to her parents, who turned to their old friend Claude for advice. It was common knowledge among the Boravitchers that Wizman had successfully and discreetly dealt with an assortment of unsavory situations that not so occasionally cropped up within the close- knit community. Upon hearing the details, *The Builder* began his usual methodical examination of the facts. Here was a young woman who did things that, though repugnant, were quite useful to the movement. As he suspected, she had no reservations about sexually compromising both enemies and allies of Wizman. Thanks to her, he now had the goods on Rebbe Buchsbaum's private physician. At about the same time, Claude's machinations on behalf of the Boravitchers were slowly being supplanted in his mind with his own less religious ambitions. The actions of Claude *The Builder,* the devoted soldier, were starting to clash with the objectives of Claude, the six hundred dollar sweater collector. When the Rebbe first asked for a long-term proposal to strengthen the movement, his devoted young follower thought only of eternal salvation. The Rebbe represented all that was good. To help in this cause was an affirmation of the glories of God on this planet. It was not all that dissimilar to the fervent beliefs of the various Islamic jihadis. But power inevitably corrupts and *The Builder* was hooked. He began to believe that he alone had the capacity to control the destinies of nations. It was simply too overwhelming a temptation for his Machiavellian mind.

" You know," said the Rebbe, speaking slowly from his bed, "I never, in all the years, interfered with what you were doing. I made a pact with you twenty-five years ago, that as long as you allowed God's teachings to guide you I'd never question your faith or your methods. I know that many, many of the things that you did were necessary. But lately, Claude, lately you've gone too far. You've brought shame upon this house."

" I'm sorry that you feel that way, Rebbe. The world is a different place than it was twenty-five years ago."

" Which is precisely why God has asked me to act in his place. It's upon us, my boy. The Talmud explains it very clearly. The war in the Gulf was predicted a thousand years ago. Harmony and peace, meyn ahzes ponim…"

" You call me impudent! How dare you say that to me. I've devoted my whole life to you...

" Harmony and peace is not just for Jews but for all mankind. It is a gift that only a just God can give."

" What gives you the right to sit in judgment over me. You're a crazy old fool. You're not who you think you are. Who I thought you were! So don't lecture me. You knew damned well what I was doing. You made me do your dirty work and now I'm damaged goods. Now I'm the bad guy. Screw you, Rebbe. I'm over this.

242

You're not the Moshiach. You're just another human being. Like the rest of us."

" You're wrong! He talks to me, Claude. His gift...will be given through me. I am *The Moshiach*."

" So, then what happens to me, Rebbe? What about my plans?"

" A mentsh tracht und Gott lacht. A person plans, Claude, and God laughs. Your job will be finished sooner than you realize. It's time for you to take a rest. To take comfort now. Celebrate the glory of HaShem...Rofeh Cholim - healer of the sick...Yotsehr 'Or - fashioner of light...Zokef kefufim - straightener of the bent..."

" What do you mean, finished? You think I'm a fool. A nishtikeit?

" You're not a nobody, Claude. It's just that I understand you too well."

" Do you Rebbe? I devoted my life to you. I'm not that horrible person that you think I am. But that's exactly what I'm hearing from you, Rebbe!"

" Oh but you are that person, mister Builder. A volf farlirt zayne hor, ober nit zayn natur. A wolf, Claude, may lose his hair, but not his nature. Give an old man some credit. I never believed in your promises. Or in you. And now, it doesn't matter."

" So you'll just wake up one day and announce that The Moshiach has arrived? Make a puff of smoke and pronounce yourself 'Prince of the People.' Here to deliver us out of our misery? Don't make me laugh! A ritch in kop, Rebbe. You're crazy in the head. You're not the Moshiach. You're a bitter old man who knows he's going to die soon and can't do anything about it!"

Wizman very rarely lost his temper. However, this time he felt like he was in danger of losing control.

" It is written, Claude. Daniel, the prophet tells us this. He speaks of a time of great trouble, when Moishe shall arise and our people shall be delivered." The old Rebbe's voice was weak but clear, like a lightning bolt shrouded in dense fog.

He continued. "Daniel tells us that many who sleep in the dust of the earth shall awake. Some to everlasting life and some, Claude, to shame and everlasting contempt."

Wizman's heart was pounding. He'd thought this through so many times in his head that it was no spur of the moment decision. He avoided eye contact with old man, looked around the room for anything that appeared out of the ordinary, then picked up a spare pillow that someone had left on the bed and held it fast to the Rebbe's face. Stealing the life from his body. There was no struggle.

" Time to sleep, old man, roll yourself in your precious dust of the earth. Awake if you can. I dare you. You old fool. I really did believe in you. Those first years. They were magic. What a sucker I was. I let you do this to me."

Claude checked for vital signs. When he was sufficiently convinced that the Rebbe was dead, he picked up the phone and dialed Schmuel Zipstein.

By 10:00 a.m., Baglione was back in the city. He stopped, bought a copy of the INDIA TRIBUNE from a newsstand watched over, as almost every one was, by two bearded Pakistanis. They stared at Baglione as if he was a cartoon character. The Italian hoped that he'd be more successful in fooling everyone else. Once inside the Howard Johnson's, Corrado took a seat on a couch near the car rental counter. Maybe that's why they called the place a "motor lodge." He glanced at his day old newspaper, published in Chicago for the Indian community across the United States.

244

The hotel lobby was pretty quiet. A group of school kids with their chaperones took up one end of the room. Across from Baglione a husband and wife sporting shoulder bags that said **suissetours+** examined a Gray Line sightseeing brochure. Seated near to the policeman were a mother and baby engaged in some sort of postnatal bonding. The woman kept saying something that sounded like "moo or boo." Italians, in general, love babies. He smiled and made believe that he gave a shit. What did catch his eye was an orthodox Jew with a briefcase. Something about the man wasn't right. Baglione continued to watch him from behind his newspaper. He then realized just what it was that had caught his attention. A few minutes before, the man had scratched his forehead, under the brim of the black beaver hat. When he'd done so, the curls at the ears had lifted up to reveal a small diamond in his pierced left lobe. The curls were fake. Baglione wasn't the only person in costume. He now saw that the man had a decidedly military bearing. Tall, perfect posture, manicured nails, well-polished shoes, this was no Hasid. The briefcase was brand new except for a scuff at one end. When the man approached Flanken, who'd emerged from an otherwise empty elevator, Corrado leapt into action. He reached his partner before the aggressor could react. Baglione gave Flanken a big Bollywood style hug, kissed him on both cheeks and hustled the German out the front door of the hotel.

" Don't look back," he whispered, as they walked out into the daylight. "There's a guy dressed like a...how do you say?...ebreo ortodosso, but I swear that's not what he is."

" I'm not surprised," answered Flanken. "These people are very good."

" Let's get that taxi!" They climbed into 1Y694, a yellow Chevy Caprice. The driver's hack license read M. GJELOSH GEGA.

" Vai. Go now. Take us to….. anyplace!"

" Irving Place, hokay misters." With their destination settled, the Albanian tripped the meter and roared off into the traffic. Léon Drei was left in the dust scratching his synthetic payess.

" Baglione, would you mind telling me what the hell is going on?"

" The guy, the one dressed like a Jew...I watched him look right at you when you came out of the elevator."

" Jesus Christ, how did they find me, and where did you get those clothes?"

" Wolfie, it's time to ask for some help."

" Ask who? Your office? My office? Corrado, we don't know the good guys from the bad guys. No, this investigation belongs to us. You and me. That's it. No help from the outside."

" Are you positive that there's no one we can trust?"

" I can't think of anybody." Baglione started to laugh. "You should have seen the expression on your face when I ran up and hugged you."

Flanken smiled nervously. The tension was still thick in the yellow taxi. Even Gjelosh Gega felt it.

" Wolfie, how about something to eat?"

" Good idea. I'm starved. Getting kidnapped by Mahatma Gandhi always makes me hungry."

" Me too," cried Gjelosh.

" Pasta?" The Italian needed a fix.

" Oh boy," chirped Gega," I'm also spaghetti meatballs man! I take you downtown. Mulberry Street. No extra charge. You now my new friends."

246

At six feet-seven, skinny and pale as a ghost, Schmuel Zipstein looked more like an undertaker than a respected New York physician. He arrived at the Rebbe's house in Brooklyn in an olive green Jeep Wagoneer. The doctor did not like the sound of *The Builder's* voice when he'd summoned him to the scene. In the Rebbe's sunken face, Zipstein's worst fears were confirmed. Schmuel knew a dead man when he saw one and the Rebbe was absolutely 100% guaranteed dead. Wizman waited for Zipstein's pronouncement.

" The Rebbe is gone."

" Are you sure?"

" Don't pull my chain here, you know very well that he's dead. He was dead when you called me, wasn't he Claude?"

" I had my suspicions."

" What do you want from me? You didn't get me all the way out here to tell you something you already know."

" Schmuel, is this any way to behave? We have a tragedy of immense proportions here."

" Claude, I beg you. Don't make me do it."

" I'm afraid I don't understand you. Make you do what?"

" You want me to sign his death certificate. Don't you, you son of a bitch?"

" He is dead. So what's the problem, Schmulie?"

" You bastard! You killed him. I can see it in your face."

" As long as no one can see it in your face. The Rebbe certainly isn't talking."

" What kind of monster are you? Don't you realize what you've done?"

" I've insured my future, Doctor. How about, we discuss yours for a minute?"

Gega parked the taxi on Broome Street, in a red zone, directly under one of former mayor Ed Koch's signature signs.

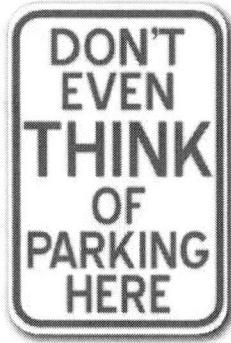

A sign that first appeared in the early 1980's and could only exist in New York. They turned the corner onto Mulberry Street, Little Italy's main drag, then ducked into an inviting place called Renato Due. The proprietor welcomed them, immediately offered a bottle of Mastroberardino Lacryma Rosso, and relieved them of the burden of ordering from a menu. Clearly, thought Salvatore Spadaro, the restaurant's owner, these tourists are going to need help with my nice Italian food. He almost fainted when the Indian in the party began to speak in a dialect common to Naples, fifteen minutes from his own hometown..

" No, it's impossible. You sound like you lived there all of your life. How could that be? Giovanna, vieni qui! Where you from?

" Cetara."

" No way. I mean you look..."

Salvatore shook his head in Baglione's direction.

" E la moglie? Napulitana, anche?" asked the detective, glancing at the woman in the open kitchen who surely had to be the wife.

" Scampia."

" Peggio." They both laughed. Napoli was bad enough. But
Scampia. That place was even worse.

" Giovanna, ma cche staje faccen'? O ppane?" Salvatore
shouted a well worn expression at his wife. He asked what was
taking her so long. "Hai fame, guagliù?"

" Hungry? We're starving." Baglione lapsed back into
English.

" You leave it to me. Giovanna...Giovanna. Che palle!"

In short order they were rewarded with a beautiful assortment of
vegetables to start, roasted peppers with anchovies and garlic,
zucchini with mint and garlic, green beans with garlic, carrots with
garlic, cucina 'Nnapulitana'. They ate spiedini (fried mozzarella
sandwiches with a lemon and anchovy sauce) and perfect mussels
with, no surprise, tomato and parsley and garlic.

" You like this food?" Flanken was starting to relax.

" Oh yes, Mister Woofy. Is soup of my remember." A
statement which obviously meant something to Gega.

The proprietor returned to the table carrying a huge platter and
three empty plates.

" Special pasta for special people."

And it was. The penne rigate was sauced with two kinds of
cheese, a touch of tomato and a generous amount of fresh
asparagus tips, cooked briefly to bring out their nutty flavor.

" Ach du meine güte! That's not what I was expecting,"
exclaimed the German.

" What do you think? I'm gonna' bring you spaghetti with
tomato sauce."

" O spaghett' ca' pummarola 'ncoppa." Baglione was also
enjoying this immensely.

" You gonna' make me cry, the way you speak."

Salvatore was waving both hands in the air and laughing. He gave them a few minutes to eat their pasta and then returned to the table.

" Allora. What do you like next? Some chicken? Maybe some shrimps?

" Gega, you decide?" The two detectives were having as much fun feeding their new friend as they were stuffing their own faces with Giovanna's fabulous food.

" Chicken and shrimps, why the hell we don't!"

" I don't even wanna' ask who's this guy." Their host was clearly enjoying himself.

" O furastère. Albanese"

" Sul serio?"

" I told him you were a foreigner, Gega."

" Ogne strunzo tene 'o fummo suio." Salvatore slapped the Albanian on the shoulders with both hands.

" I'm not going to translate that one. You really need to be from *Napule* to understand what he is saying."

The chicken was 'scarpariello style', which Baglione assured the table was clearly an American invention. Nevertheless it was great. The chunks of chicken were first deep-fried then sauteed with olive oil and garlic. Sausage was added next and the whole thing was doused with red vinegar that sizzled when it hit the pan. The shrimps were simmered with tomato and garlic and finished with a shot of anisette. Bottle number two of the light red wine was opened and poured for the trio, with a glass for the proprietor as well.

" Dolce, signore, you like some dessert?"

" No more," said the German.

" Basta," agreed the Italian.

" Sure, sure! Dessert!" exclaimed Gjelosh, spraying the table with the last bits of shrimp in his mouth.

A silver tray laden with quartered, ice cream filled chocolate balls, buried in cannoli cream and topped with a mountain of berries arrived at the table. Gega ate most of the platter. Strong coffee, in glasses, with a shot of Nocillo di Sorrento mercifully ended the meal. Thanks and good-byes took some time. The staff all came out of the kitchen. The three happy diners stumbled back to Gjelosh's yellow Chevy Caprice.

" Where we go now, good friends of Gega?"

" Just drive, we'll let you know." Flanken had the beginnings of a plan crystallizing in his head. Their driver headed west on Broome, took a right on Centre Street and headed uptown.

" Corrado, the guy in the Howard Johnson's, do you think he knew that we picked him out?"

" I was thinking that myself. When I came over to you, he backed off. It's possible that he was just being careful."

" So he's probably still waiting..."

" Si. At the hotel. Most likely, it's going to be somebody else."

" Suppose you go in looking drunk. You think they might follow you up to your room?"

" If the idea was to kill me, I think that they might try again."

" Why don't I slip into your room. Then you come staggering into the lobby and lure him into our trap."

" He'd spot you in minute, in that outfit you're wearing."

" É vero. Gega, can you take us to Queens? I need to change my clothes."

" I can do. Sure. You know where to get there?"

" I'll find the address. Give me a minute. I remember that you can see it from a bridge."

" Bridge I can find! You betcha."

He jerked the wheel to the right, cutting across the heavy traffic on Lafayette, hoping to turn right onto Houston. With just a little more luck he would have missed the U.P.S. truck and been on his way crosstown to the FDR. The unmistakeable sound of metal on metal was followed by an anguished groan from the front seat of the taxi. Gjelosh jerked to a halt in a bus stop. By the time he opened the glove box and pulled out his papers, the U.P.S. man was on him.

" Are you fuckin high? Look what you did to my truck. You know how much fuckin trouble this is gonna make? Get the fuck outta the cab!"

The man was about to rip Gega's door off when a foot cop appeared on the scene.

" This fuckin' moron shoots across three lanes and clips my fuckin' bumper. You can see for yourself. This prick is a fuckin menace! Fuckin camel jockeys. I'd like to know the idiot that gives out licenses to these people?"

" Sir," the cop began, "please stand on the sidewalk."

" Gimme a fuckin' break! Next thing, you gonna tell me it's my fault?"

" I'm not saying it's anyone's fault. Just stand over there."

" Why the fuck should..."

" NOW!"

The delivery driver reluctantly followed the instructions. The young patrolman peered into the back of the taxi.

" Everybody o.k. in there?"

" We're fine," answered Flanken.

" Please step out of the cab."

Baglione and Flanken complied. The rookie cop then turned his attention to Gega.

" Hack license and FS-1."

252

Gjelosh was already waiting with his documents.

" What hopping me now?" he queried the policeman.

" What hopping you is you exchange your info with the U.P.S. guy, then get out of here."

" He crazy man."

" I'll make sure he's calmed down. After that, I don't wanna hear any more. O.K?"

" Hokay." Gega looked warily at the other driver.

The patrolman pointed his finger and gestured for the U.P.S. man to approach him. When he sauntered over, the cop held up a hand.

" I don't wanna' hear no yelling. I don't wanna' see no punchin'. I only wanna' see you exchangin' what you need to. Then I wanna' see you disappear. Am I makin' myself clear?"

" You mean you ain't arrestin' this bohunk? Look what he did to my truck!"

" Did you not just hear what I said?"

" This fuckin' hajji..."

" Did you hear what I just said?"

" You ain't gonna..."

" DID - YOU - HEAR - WHAT - I - SAID!"

" I heard ya. I heard ya."

" Fine. Then do it!"

The policeman was getting a bit hot under the collar himself. He'd been talking to a dynamite babe in a white mini-dress when the collision occurred up the street. He could see from where he was standing now, that she'd already taken a powder. Gega, who was clearly to blame, stood there looking like he was the victim.

" How bout you, cabbie? You understand me?"

" What hoppin' now? Who pay my car?"

" I'm gonna look at my watch and god help youse both if you ain't gone from here in five minutes. Capeesh?"

Baglione stepped forward.

" Ah, parla Italiano."

" Now you got somethin' to say?"

" You speak Italian. I'm Italian. I just thought..."

The officer looked at Corrado's costume.

" Is this a fuckin' clown show? Am I at the fuckin' circus? Listen to me. I do not need this. You have no injuries. You are not the driver. So stay the fuck outta this. O.K!"

" Hey, officer. This guy's been drinkin'. I can smell it! How come you don't give him a test?" The U.P.S. man still refused to give it up.

" Fucking brown shirt," muttered Baglione, to Flanken who stood there smiling.

" You got somethin' to say, Swami?" The delivery man was now standing face to face with Baglione.

" THAT'S IT! WE'RE DONE! YOU TWO, BACK IN THE TAXI. YOU - BACK IN THE TRUCK. YOU, CABBIE - GET THIS PIECE A' SHIT OUTTA HERE. NOW!"

" Wadda'bout his insurance?"

" You wanna' talk to a judge? No problem. You're about one second away, buddy!"

The U.P.S. man looked at his fender, admitted to himself that the damage was probably not worth reporting, then climbed back in the truck. As a final gesture he gave the finger to everyone watching.

" Make you hoppy, you do dot? Deeknose sheet!" screamed Gjelosh, to the departing back of the truck.

" Hokay boys. Now we go Queens!"

Gega took a hammer from under the front seat and pounded his bumper back into place. Once the repair was completed, he

254

gunned the engine and roared off into the rush hour traffic, barely missing another taxi. By the time they got crossed the 59th Street Bridge and found Adams-Cook it was nearly a quarter to five.

Anton Fuchs was on the phone when the three walked into his office. He motioned for them to sit. Baglione and Wolfie pulled up chairs, Gega searched out the bathroom. The huge old building was crammed full of costumes from every show in creation. Fuchs was apparently working on something medieval at the moment. His room was loaded with suits of armor. Gjelosh returned from his piss and suddenly felt the need to try some on.

" Yoo hoo, look me now, mister. You maybe got this in 38 short?"

The costumer, still on the phone, turned to Baglione and pointed at the Albanian with a "what the fuck is going on here?" expression. He finished his call, then shook hands with Corrado and Wolfie.

" How did it go? Did they like it?" Baglione had told him he was playing a joke on some friends.

" They couldn't believe it. Is it possible to try something else? And I insist on paying this time."

" Not to worry, sweetie. You can see we've got plenty to choose from. By the way, how do you know Peter?"

" He's a friend of..."

" Vanessa. I forgot that he told me. Is she back in New York? She's such a hoot."

" I didn't realize you knew her."

" Vanessa. I used to do some things for her. She was here in eighty-eight or eighty-nine. Somewhere around there. Say hello from me when you see her."

Baglione was about to ask why she'd needed his help, but decided that he really didn't want to know. He also decided to call her that evening.

" So what do you want to be tonight?"

" Non lo so. I don't know, Anton. What are my choices?"

Léon Drei phoned *The Builder* every half hour from eleven in the morning to five-thirty that afternoon until he reached him.

" Claude, finally. I've been calling you all day. We missed him this morning."

" What happened?"

" There was somebody waiting for him in the lobby. They were out the door before I could..."

" The Italian?"

" No, no, an Indian or a Paki. Did you speak with Jörg? He must be going crazy."

" Not yet. I just got back here. Listen to me, Léon. Something...terrible has happened." Claude took a breath.
" The Rebbe is dead."

" Oh, no!"

" He passed away this morning. The doctor and I were with him. Thank God he went quickly. There was no pain. He just closed his eyes and..."

" What about...?"

" He didn't say anything. Not a word. Zipstein even tried to revive him. But nothing."

There was a long pause, while Léon Drei absorbed the news.

" Claude, how can we tell if The Rebbe is..."

" Forget that nonsense. He told Shmuel yesterday, in the morning, that he never really believed he was The Moshiach. I think he knew he was dying. Léon, it's over. Until they sit down and choose a new Grand Rebbe, it's up to us to keep things together."

" When is the funeral?"

" Day after tomorrow. They need time to make the arrangements. It's going out on the satellite, like Chanukah last year. Besides Israel, the broadcast is going to Paris and London, even Moscow, if Yeltsin gives his o.k. The Rebbes are all arriving tomorrow. Léon, where are you now?"

" I changed clothes right after the German left the hotel. I'm back in the lobby now."

" Do you think he suspected anything this morning."

" I'm not a hundred percent sure, but he didn't act like he felt threatened. There was no reason for him to..."

" Good. When Jörg calls, I'll tell him to meet you there."

" Tell him he needs to be extra careful. If Flanken spots him we're through."

" Spots Bissel? Not a chance. Don't worry. He'll think of another way to grab Flanken."

" Claude, should we be doing this so soon after..."

" Léon, our work did not end with the Rebbe's death. It's more important than ever."

" I'll say a prayer."

" Say one for me, too."

Gjelosh Gega dropped a heavily bandaged man about a block from the Howard Johnson's. He looked, to all the pedestrians on Fifty-first Street, like someone who'd been burned in a fire. His hands were scarred and still a bit red, thanks to some convincing theatrical make-up. His face was wrapped in layers of sterile gauze. Baglione felt like a mummy. In the elevator, several hotel guests gave him sympathetic glances as he ascended to the 8th floor, two below Wolfie's. He took the stairs the rest of the way up. Once he was safely alone, in a stairwell near Flanken's door, he removed the bandages, got rid of the Mets jacket and emerged as a room service waiter. Thankfully, the cart he had left there earlier was still at the end of the hallway. The policeman looked at his watch. His colleague should have just entered the lobby. The German detective would seem to be very drunk. They hoped someone would follow him up.

Flanken, his shirt tail hanging and a long string of toilet paper tucked into the top of his trousers at the rear, looked the part. He veered drunkenly through the lobby. Jörg Bissel came out of the hotel's newsstand and rang for the other elevator. He'd waited long enough for Wolfie to disappear into the first one.

The Chefdetektiv exited the elevator on the 10th floor, nodded to the room service waiter, then staggered towards his room. He fell to one knee as if trying to unlock his door. Baglione stood at the opposite end of the hallway. The other elevator arrived and when the doors opened he pushed his cart towards it, as if he'd been waiting a long time. Bissel stepped out. Corrado got in right as the doors were closing. He hit the open button with no time to spare. In the corridor, Wolfie had rolled his head back. The attacker lunged at his target just as Baglione came up from the rear. One zap from his stun gun, and Jörgie was down for the count. Flanken quickly unlocked his door. They dragged the assailant inside and shoved some Temazepam down his throat. Baglione always had a supply of the tablets in his travel kit. He knew from personal experience that they really worked. The detective often had trouble sleeping and had taken them many times before.

" Jesus Christ, it's Jörg Bissel!"

" You know him?"

" He's one of my men! The miserable bastard! Is he dead? I see blood."

" It's not blood." I think he peed in his pants."

258

Baglione was on an adrenaline high. He'd never used a Taser before. In fact he'd never used any weapon in the line of duty. The criminals he'd caught selling bogus Nutella rarely put up a struggle. Flanken had purchased the stun gun in a shop on Dutch Sint Maarten.

" What's he doing here, Wolfie?"

" Donnerwetter! Wau. Somebody must have sent him to kill me!"

" So he's the one who was following you."

" It makes sense. Bissel knew I was going on vacation. I made sure to leave a few travel folders on my desk. You know, to make it look real."

" You've got to wonder about your department, Detective."

" I want, very much, to believe that he's the only sour apple. You can understand that this is a great shock."

" Come on, you said yourself that something was rotten."

" Baglione, you sound like you're enjoying this."

The German was very perceptive. Baglione was enjoying this. Finally, he was acting like a real detective, not a glorified meat inspector. But he did understand how his colleague was feeling. Not able to trust those around you. That was a frightening thing for a cop.

" Is there anyone in Köln that you can trust?

" Richter...If he's dirty, I'm really fucked. No, I'd bet anything that he's straight."

" You'd trust him with your life?"

" Yes. I think so. I know so." Flanken nodded his head.

It was strange. Until now, Baglione had deferred to Flanken. This business with Bissel had really shaken the German.

" Wolfie, get to your man and have him check out this one completely; who his friends are, where he lives, his background. You know what to ask for."

" I'll call him now." Flanken looked at his watch. "He should be at home. Corrado, what if there are more of them downstairs? If he doesn't come down, or call them, they'll know that something is wrong."

" We can't keep him here forever. The maid will be in first thing tomorrow. I say we move him tonight."

" Any idea how?"

Corrado thought for a moment.

" Call the Albanese. He has a car."

" And I suppose we just roll him out to the taxi on the room service cart? Right through the lobby? Are you crazy? Besides, where would we take him?"

" I wonder what Bond would do?"

" Baglione, for heaven's sake! This isn't a fucking movie."

" That's it!"

" What's it?"

" We'll roll him out. I'll tell Gega to find a wheelchair."

Solomon Baum picked up his phone and dialed Heskel Milstein's private number.

" It's me."

" I was just getting ready to call you."

" I'm sure you were. You were doing the same thing I was. Did you freeze everything?"

" The son-of-a-bitch beat me to the Cayman account. It was the only one left he could sign on."

" How much did he get?"

" Not quite two million."

260

Solomon Baum had to laugh.

" That'll put a cramp in his style. I wish I'd seen his face when he discovered the piggy bank was empty."

" Two million isn't exactly empty."

" No, but he still needs us. Who's he going to turn to besides you and me?

" Solly, he's not going to like taking orders. Claude's accustomed to calling the shots.

" Then he'd better get used to it fast. He's a bright boy, but the world doesn't spin around him."

" You're going to the funeral. Yes?"

" Of course. You want to ride with me? It'll give us a chance to talk to Steven. Maybe he'll listen to you."

" Solly, I know it's painful for you and Fanny. But he needs to be told."

" Not so easy for a father. If Steven knew that I bought him every single election, I'd lose him. Look, I know he's no Einstein, but Heskel, he's my son. I love him...no matter what. Let him go on thinking he's Mario Cuomo. If he loses this election, I'll find him something here, with me. He's got some crazy idea to put up a huge building on Fifth Avenue - with his goddamn name in gold."

" Look, my friend, you do what you think is right. You know, whatever it is, I'll back you up."

" So who do you put your money on. Who's the next Grand Rebbe?"

" It sounds to me like you're looking for another wager. You don't remember I beat the pants off of you when the Pope picked, what's his name, Donald O'Connor to replace Cooke."

" Solly, the Cardinal's name is John O'Connor. Donald O'Connor is a song and dance man."

" And a pretty good one, too. So Heskela, who would you choose? Who's the next Grand Rebbe?"

" **Claude.** It's me."

" Léon, everything alright? What's happening?"

" Bissel followed him up to his room."

" And?"

" He never came back down."

" Maybe he went out another way."

" I don't think so. He was very specific. It was supposed to look like a robbery gone wrong. Like in France. Claude, I have a bad feeling about this. He specifically told me to wait for him in the lobby."

" Damn it. Get out of there now. I can't afford to lose you. Léon, I don't need this tsores."

" Alright. I'll phone you later. This can't be happening."

" Just keep your cool. Jörg is as good as there is. I'm sure we'll hear from him soon."

It was after seven when the severely burned man in the Mets jacket, bandages back in place, left the Howard Johnson's and headed downtown to Macy's. The ad in the paper said that the store closed at nine. He glanced quickly around the hotel lobby looking at faces. He knew that Bissel probably had help somewhere nearby. No one stood out. He walked to the street, turned left and strolled at a sightseer's pace in the direction of Herald Square. By the time he reached Macy's, Baglione was confident that he hadn't been followed. He shopped quickly, buying the items he needed to disguise the unconscious German.

He stopped to call Gjelosh Gega. Fortunately, the Albanian was home with his mother. He asked him to find a wheelchair and deliver it to the Howard Johnson's. The cabbie needed little convincing. Baglione's stomach growled. He realized that he hadn't eaten. He stopped at a Sabrett cart parked across from Madison Square Garden.

" One würstel, please."

" One what? What you want?"

" One panino."

" Mustard-relish or mustard-onions?"

" Si, o.k." Baglione hardly understand a word of the man's broken English, so the frankfurter was delivered with mustard and onions, the way almost everyone ordered them.

" Drink?"

" I take a caffé."

The man looked at him as if he'd just stepped out of a spacecraft."

" No coffee. Only Yoo-Hoo and Coke. I also got water."

" O.K. "

" The man extracted a dripping yellow can from an icy well in the cart. He shook it, reached for a straw and handed it to Baglione, who by this time had already smeared red-orange onions on his carefully wrapped sterile bandage. It looked like blood and pus had been seeping out from an open wound in his chin.

" Two-twenty-five."

Corrado paid him, then pulled up the tab on the can. He plunged the straw into the watery brown liquid. It tasted strange. Very strange. Fascinated, he examined the can. It read 'Yogi says, It's me-hee for Yoo-Hoo'." Now he was thoroughly confused. Baglione finished his "chocolate flavored energy drink," threw the can and the napkin in an overflowing metal trash bin and walked back uptown clutching his two Macy's shopping bags.

The lobby of the HoJo's looked normal. Nothing out of place. He went up to Wolfie's room, tapped out their pre-arranged knock and waited for Flanken to open up.

" Baglione?"

" No, it's the Queen of Fucking England."

The Chefdetektiv unbolted the door and let him in.

" You don't look anything like her."

" Let's hope that he does," pointing at Bissel.

The Italian unpacked the bags. He'd bought an extra large size cotton dress, one size fits all panty hose, a pair of cheap men's running shoes and a large floppy hat that said 'diva' on the brim. At a shop down the street from the big department store, he'd purchased a wig made of something white. On the corner next to the hot dog cart, he'd bought some rhinestone shades from a skinny Senegalese peddler. Their captive's eyes opened briefly so they shoved another Temazepam into his mouth and forced him to swallow. Once they had him dressed, the two detectives stepped back to admire their work. Bissel looked like just another drugged-out drag queen. When Gega arrived with the wheelchair he stared, wide-eyed at this incredible apparition.

" I recognize. I recognize! Ho boy! She, she Benjii Hills!" The Albanian driver could not believe his good luck. A famous celebrity was going to ride in his taxi.

" I wish I got camera. My nënë she love Benjii Hills!"

" Gega, what are you talking about?"

" Mr. Woofy. Benjii Hills. You don't know Benjii Hills?" The man was shouting and pointing at Bissel.

" Look, Gega, whatever it is that's getting you so verrückt will just have to wait. We need to get him into that wheelchair. You're going to take him down. Corrado give me a hand." Flanken was clearly back in charge. They dumped Bissel into the chair.

" Gega, where did you leave the taxi?"

" In front. Like limo. I do good, Mr. Woofy?"

" Wunderbar, Gega. Remind me later and I'll give you a *hundekuchen.* Now listen carefully to me. You're going to take him down in the elevator, then out the main entrance to the car. Can you handle that yourself."

" Sure. Then where I gotta take him, NBC Tonight Show? You think we can have ticket? My mother, she no bee-leeve this! When you give to me this cookie?"

" Gega, do you think your momma would like to...?"

" Meet Benjii...you kidding?"

" Why don't we stop by her house. Where does she live?"

" Coney Island. With me! Hey you serious, right? You sure he's ok? He don't look so hot."

" He's just tired. That's why we needed the wheelchair."

Baglione looked on. He shook his head wondering if he was dreaming. The sight of the two men pushing the drugged German out of the Wolfie's room and into the hallway snapped him back.

" Gega, get him in the taxi, then drive around the block, once. We'll be waiting outside the hotel.

" You betcha!" The elevator arrived. Gjela and Flanken wheeled Bissel into it. The German detective punched **L** for lobby and stepped out. The doors closed and the stranger-than-strange pair of them disappeared. Wolfie turned to Corrado and, relieved for the moment, managed a smile.

The Grand Rebbe's funeral was part ritual, part performance. The Brooklyn synagogue was packed with his followers from around the world. Rebbes from Paris, Montreal, Los Angeles, London and Moscow. There were even two Rebbes from Buenos Aires. Those who couldn't squeeze into the building stood outside. A hundred thousand more watched on closed circuit TV in cities around the world. A large television control room was parked at the curb, its roof top dish bounced the funeral service off a satellite leased for the afternoon. Near the front of the synagogue, in a section reserved for men, sat Solomon Baum, Heskel Milstein, New York City Comptroller Steven Baum, Mayor Dinkins and Senator Alphonse D'Amato. Even Ron Kuby, the flamboyant attorney who represented some of the most notorious Arab terrorists was there, wearing a blue and white yarmulke with *ARM THE UNEMPLOYED* embroidered around its edge, and former mayor Ed Koch, and his buddy, Herman Badillo, the perennial candidate who'd just announced that he too, would be running for mayor. Behind them was the entire (male) New York Congressional delegation, the Borough President of Brooklyn, Phil Caruso of the PBA, Phil Donahue, the talk show host, and a NY State Troopers Police Surgeon, aka…Schmuel Zipstein. Claude Wizman and the Dreis sat two rows back.

Gittel Mandelbaum, Rebbe from Los Angeles conducted the service in Yiddish. He was relieved by Rebbe Ziv Tevelowitz (who'd flown in from his vacation home, north of Puerto Vallarta) when emotion made it impossible for Mandelbaum to continue. The room was filled with hundreds of men. Bearded, bowing, and praying.

" The place looks like a Z.Z Top cover band convention." Phil Caruso hardly ever minced his words. Donahue chuckled to himself and shook his head in mock disbelief.

While the majority of the congregation prayed and/or politicked, a couple of whispered exchanges were taking place. In the front row Milstein and Solomon Baum faced forward while they chatted.

" Solly, have you noticed that Claude can't look us in the face?"

" Maybe he's too overcome with grief."

266

" Sure, like pigs have wings, you should excuse the expression in a shul."

" Who are the two little pishers he's with? They keep staring over at us."

" I've never seen them before. I bet it's the two who Claude put with the Rebbe. I'll tell you, the one on the right looks like he eats his Wheaties."

" Heskel, you think our *Builder's* trying to send us a message?"

" I'm shivering in my boots. How about you, Sol?"

" Never underestimate a desperate man. And believe me, we've backed Claude into a corner."

" He's a talented boy. I genuinely admire his work. There should be some way to keep him happy. To tell you the truth, I'd hate to lose him."

" I don't see him coming around. All of this 'we can rule the world nonsense' makes me uncomfortable. I think it's time to dump him."

" Solly, he's not the type who goes quietly. He got almost two million from the Cayman account, but believe me, it's not nearly enough to shut him up."

" That fancy shmancy office must cost an arm and a leg."

" He says it gives him cred-i-bility." Heskel enunciated the word with undisguised displeasure

" I won't tell you what it gives me. How long do you think this thing will go on? I have to get back to the city."

" You're not going to the cemetery, Solly?"

" Ahh, I suppose I should. It might be a good time to talk to Steven."

" You're sure about pulling the plug? I know how hard it must be."

" It's my own fault. I let Claude talk me into believing that Steven could be mayor. What a shmuck I am."

" You're a father and a father wants the best for his only son."

" I don't like being blackmailed. If...if by some miracle Steven were to get elected, Claude would be forever yanking my chain. I don't need this. I'm seventy-six years old. Why should I let myself be manipulated by a mamzer like him?"

" I agree. Today we tell Steven. He won't like it, but in the long run I think it's best."

" Thank you, Heskel. You're a good friend. The best I ever had. And as far as I'm concerned, with regards to Claude, just let him try and make us trouble."

Two rows back, a second whispered conversation was becoming animated.

" This isn't right. Not at the Rebbe's funeral."

The Builder ignored Henri Drei.

" Don't tell *me* what's right! Jörg couldn't have just disappeared. How can you be so stupid? It's not like him to be outmaneuvered. He's too good for that to happen."

" Claude, we went up to the room. Trust me, everyone was gone."

" Léon, you really think they snatched Bissel?"

" What else could it be."

" Jesus Christ, Léon!" Henri exclaimed, much too loudly. Two rows forward, Donahue turned around. Then the Borough President of Brooklyn, clearly annoyed, turned around. They both stared at *The Builder*.

" Léon, I will not let this thing fall apart. Twenty-five years of my life. No! I will not let that happen. And those two old bastards there, just waiting to pick me to pieces." Wizman pointed at Solomon Baum and Heskel Milstein.

" I want that woman. The one the Italian's always running around with. I want her brought to me asap. Léon, I'm sure you know where to find her. We need to deal with this shit before it gets too out of hand."

" Claude, please, not at the Rebbe's funeral."

" Henri, you think that the dearly departed honestly gives a good goddamn about what we're saying? It's his big day. A Hallmark Hall of Fame production. Grand Rebbe Buchsbaum's Funeral, brought to you in gorgeous living color. By satellite, for God's sake. Grow up, Henri. This whole stage show is bullshit! Honestly, I can't take anymore. I'm leaving." He got up from his seat. "Are you two coming or not?"

The Gegas lived upstairs in a narrow two story house, a block off the beach in Coney Island. The ground floor was rented by Mrs. Zelma - Reader and Advisor and her extended family. Gjelosh's elderly mother hadn't been out of the house in three years. It wasn't that she couldn't manage the stairs, she simply chose not to. Her son, who leased his own taxi had provided her with a 21 inch RCA color TV, "with remote control" as Mrs. G. was quick to point out to her friends. She clicked it on at 7:00 a.m. and she clicked it off just as the eleven o'clock news turned into the Leno show. Nënë was especially fond of Al Roker, Channel Four's rotund weatherman. By midnight she was asleep. At various times of the day she interrupted her TV viewing to prepare meals for Gjelosh and herself. There were no other family members living in the United States, although she'd heard that there might be some cousins in Canada.

Gega wheeled the taxi into the driveway next to the house. It was illuminated by Mrs. Zelma's neon sign. She was apparently available at all hours for those desperate souls in need of a midnight reading. By the time they'd reached Coney Island, Bissel had rejoined the living. They'd bound and gagged him once they were clear of the Brooklyn Battery Tunnel. At the rear of the house were steps leading down to the basement. Gega Controlled Territory. No trespassing allowed.

Gjelosh was the first one down. He found the switch and flipped on the dim yellow bug light, the single source of illumination in a room that was knotty pine at the near end and cement block at the rear. An ancient oil burning furnace sat directly in the middle, dividing the space in half. In the finished part a convertible couch stood open, naked without its mattress. On top of the rusting metal frame lay a sheet of half-inch plywood covered with Gega's treasure trove of antique barbed wire fencing. There were at least a hundred pieces, each one trimmed to exactly eighteen inches.

" These my babies," he announced, proudly showing off the collection to his two new friends. "Great. Yes?"

There was no reply from Flanken or Baglione. Only what could be described as utter amazement.

" This here, from Brazeel. This here, from Poland, but best is from America. Look, this from U.S. Navy. Very special. I go last year to museum. You know museum, right? La Croze Wheeze-konzin. Birth town of barb wire. Look my picture."

He grabbed a magazine called **BARB WIRE COLLECTOR** easily flipped open to a page entitled 'Prickly Pairs,' and sure enough there was a smiling Gega holding up a display board, with mama looking on, a somewhat bemused expression on her face.

Once again the thought crossed Baglione's mind that he must be fast asleep and dreaming. But how could it be a dream? It would be impossible to dream this stuff up.

" Gega, this is all very interesting, but we need to be left alone." Flanken pointed to their prisoner. Somewhere between the Howard Johnson's and Nathan's Famous in Coney Island, it became obvious to the driver that this was not Benny Hill. Bissel was not the famous TV performer after all. He took it well enough, lamenting only the fact that his nënë would be disappointed.

Wolfie sat the East German down on a chair next to a four inch galvanized drain pipe, tied his arms back and secured them with duct tape through a bend in the pipe. His ankles were held together by a piece of clothesline and then fastened to the front legs of the chair. Once this was accomplishing he removed the gag from Bissel's mouth. Their prisoner was surprisingly calm.

" Jörg, ich würde sagen... du bist erledigt. I don't have to tell you...you're fucked."

Flanken knew that the man spoke excellent English. Wolfie used it now so that Baglione could follow the conversation.

" I have nothing to say to you."

" Why are you in New York?"

" I have nothing to say."

" Jörgie, be reasonable. You won't gain a thing by being stubborn. If you cooperate I can try to help you."

" Go to hell."

" Who do you work for?" demanded Baglione.

" Piss off!"

" Jörg, that's no way to speak to this man. He's one of us. A colleague. You are still, technically, a policeman. Ja?" No answer. "I suppose that you no longer feel any...any, what's the word in English, camaraderie? I can understand your position."

" Look, Corrado" he said, turning back to his partner, "I don't think that our friend here is in the right frame of mind at the moment. I suggest we leave him here for a while. Let him think things over. Gega can see to his needs. Perhaps he's interested in learning more about barbed wire. You remember this stuff from your formative years in Dresden? Am I right, Jörgie? What do you think? You want to pass some time down here?"

Vanessa Rambaudi spent the morning in Alba. She shopped for groceries at the Super Gulliver, for vegetables at the open air market and for pasta at a small place that she liked, near the Duomo. Lunch would be at La Vecchia Collina. They still served her lovely Arneis after others had banished it from their wine lists. Vanessa ate alone. Gnocchi verde sauced with a decadent spoonful of Castelmagno cream. She knew how much Corrado would enjoy this pasta. She also thought about him as she picked over the remains of the quaglia nella sfoglia, the tiny bird wrapped snugly in grape leaves. She recalled their last day together in bed, his arm around her, his breath gently caressing her hair. Saying *no* to the panna cotta, she ordering instead, a simple poached pear. As Vanessa got older, her firm, well-toned body was increasingly harder to maintain. She hoped that Baglione wouldn't notice the couple of extra pounds.

After lunch, she strolled for a while, stopping to chat with some friends. They were artists, one of whom Vanessa really admired. His paintings were bright and naively old fashioned, almost Haitian in style. She often displayed them in winter, down in her dark and dreary cantina, to give some lift to the chilly surroundings. Another artist, Bregje, a stringy Belgian whom she knew from her time in Ghent, remarked that Vanessa was not looking well. "Fuck her," she said out loud, driving back to Cornegliano, stopping the Rolls to put down the top. That always cheered her up. By the time Vanessa reached home, she was back to a decent state of mind. Someone was stopped near the gate to her driveway, changing a tire.

" Hai bisogno di aiuto? Can I be of some help? Do you want to make a call from my house?."

Léon Drei smiled and pointed his gun at the woman.

" That's very nice of you to offer. I have to be in New York quite early tomorrow. Perhaps you can drive me to the airport. Fortunately I have a plane standing by. Who knows, you might even end up coming with me."

Léon Drei had always been an overachiever. His brother, Henri, was constantly reminded of that. 'Why can't you be more like your brother?' they would say. Their mother had married young (and rather badly), to an Israeli transplant from France who traded in rough diamonds. Her father, an Orthodox Rebbe, was not pleased. When the couple moved to New York with their two young sons and the husband took up with a shikse from Rockaway Beach, old Rebbe Fehrman felt the need to intervene. He flew in from Paris, snatched the two little boys and hid them in upstate New York. The Boravitcher community in Utica was small and tightly knit. No one would dare speak out about the circumstances that had brought them the two young children. For three years they fed them and educated them in the manner prescribed by the ultra-orthodox sect. When they were ten and twelve, Claude Wizman came to town in search of bright young minds. He had been solidifying his position in the movement for several years. At first, Grand Rebbe Buchsbaum startled Claude with his vision of the future.

" My boy," said the Rebbe, "God has spoken to me and directed me to work miracles in his name."

" What kind of miracles, Rebbe?"

" Through me, we build for tomorrow. When the Moshiach comes, the world must be ready for change. And in this day and age that means money and power as well as unyielding devotion to the laws of God. The laws of God, Claude, not the rules set forth by man. We must prepare the world for the time when he will come. I'm going to charge *you* with that enormous responsibility. Plan ahead, do what you must, but do it well. The necessary funds will be put at your disposal. Choose from our young men those whom you feel are capable and worthy to accomplish this work. And Claude, listen to me carefully." He paused for effect. "I trust you. You needn't get me involved. Indeed, I cannot be involved. Do I make myself clear?"

There it was. The message that Wizman had waited years to receive. One of the first things he did was to take control of the lives of Léon and Henri Drei. He schooled them, raised them, and when they came of age he sent them to the Army of Israel to learn the business of war. There, they prayed twice a day, and learned about an eye for an eye and that the end often justified the means. Right and wrong turned upside down.

Vanessa drove the Rolls, following her captor's instructions. At a farm outside the small city of Alessandria they transferred to an Opel estate wagon. She was tied, gagged and blindfolded. From the warmth of the late afternoon sun on her cheek, she deduced that they were headed south. After half an hour, as darkness fell, they arrived at their destination. A small grass airfield. She had no idea that she was in Novi Ligure until the Piper Malibu took off, her blindfold was removed, and she was able to steal a glance at a large billboard as they began their climb out.

" Surely we're not flying to New York in this thing?"

Her captor did not answer. And for her trouble, the gag was put back in her mouth. Hours later they landed somewhere semi-tropical. She could see that from the palms that dotted the landscape. Once on the ground she could hear a faint Spanish melody. She'd lost track of time. 'Where am I?' She asked herself. 'An island, maybe? Somewhere close to Italy. Probably Spain.'

Vanessa was correct. It was Son Bonet on the island of Mallorca

" Let's go."

The man barked a few commands in English to the two men standing outside. One was the pilot of the Piper; the other she couldn't see. They walked across a short stretch of asphalt where a Gulfstream II was parked and waiting. The second man appeared, climbed aboard and reached for her arm as she walked up the metal stairs. He disappeared into the cockpit without uttering a word. There were only two passenger seats, forward in the cabin. The rest of the space was devoted to cargo. Although the aircraft was empty, a sharp odor permeated the air. It was familiar to the woman. She knew that she'd smelled it before. 'Of course,' she thought to herself. 'It's freshly cut marijuana.' She remembered the distinct aroma from a six month vacation in Jamaica, almost twenty years before. The French police had been looking for her in connection with a daring daylight robbery of a house in Cap Ferrat. The Caribbean seemed like a good place to disappear.

Léon had given careful thought to this latest assignment. He had a commodity, the woman, to bring into the United States. She had no papers and was there against her will. The plane would have to set down somewhere without customs or immigration getting in the way. Who was better at that than anyone? Drug smugglers. He made a few discreet inquiries and was introduced to a former Navy pilot who regularly flew cocaine and marijuana up to the U.S. from Panama. This pilot knew how to avoid coastal radar, which airports were lax in their document checking and where he could purchase supplies en-route. Once he left Europe and reached the familiar Caribbean airways, it was clear sailing into the U.S. The jet had a range of about 3600 nautical miles. He flew first to the Azores, re-fueled, and then west and south to Bermuda and on to the Leeward Islands. They stopped again for fuel in the Turks and Caicos. From there it was a piece of cake. He regularly picked his way through the Caribbean and up the Atlantic coast. They landed just outside Princeton, New Jersey, using all of the 3500 foot runway. The flight plan he'd filed showed Hilton Head direct to Somerset County. It was the exact reverse of the trip going over, which Léon insisted on making. The pilot was talented, well paid and very accommodating. He watched the ambulance pull up to the side of the plane. What his customer did with the woman was not really any business of his.

   Jörg Bissel looked around the filthy room with the eyes of a professional. Where the average person might see an old dictionary, Bissel saw a bludgeon. Where there appeared to be a pile of old bed sheets and a bottle of paint remover he saw a molotov cocktail. Then he spotted something that got his full attention. In the faint light, the German could make out two electric meters, two switch boxes and above, two sets of wires leading up through the ceiling. Perhaps there were other tenants in this building. What better way to get their attention? Cause a power outage. If he could stand up and make his way across the room, he could easily short out one of the boxes. His problem was the duct tape around his wrists, his arms looped around the enormous old drain pipe, tethering him to it. A cloth stuffed in his mouth and tied firmly around his head made breathing very difficult. His years of training helped sharpened his concentration. The possibility to cause some trouble was giving him hope. There was no easy way to free himself. What to do? Just then, the creaky old furnace kicked over and came to life. Bissel could see the gas flame under the boiler. When Wolfie Flanken had tied his legs to the chair, Jörg noticed that the chair seemed a bit wobbly. The young German tensed his legs and pushed up and out. He heard the left leg of the chair start to crack. It broke smoothly off at the seat, dropping Bissel to one knee. He put pressure on the other chair leg and slid his ankles down. At least now he had his lower body free. With his feet, he pulled the pile of sheets and the can of paint remover closer to him. His arms were bound together behind him. There was nothing much he could do about that. His only chance was to get someone to come down the stairs and release him. If he could somehow get a fire started, attract some attention, he might have a chance to escape. Carefully, he worked the can between his feet. The top appeared to be rusted shut. Time to try something else. He maneuvered the can under the heel of one of his shoes, used the other foot to hold the side of the can, then pushed down with all his body weight. The container flattened slightly and began to leak. He quickly shoved one of the sheets close to the can, to soak up the fluid. When it was sufficiently wet with the flammable liquid he eased it towards the furnace. Bissel hoped that the burner would not kick off before he could position the sheet, all the while formulating a plan. In the event that somebody came down for a look. There was also the possibility that the whole basement would go up in flames and he would be burned alive for his efforts. But either way he was a dead man, so why not try. He got the edge of the sheet under the old iron grate of the furnace and watched as the very tip began to burn. After just a few seconds the entire sheet caught fire and started sending flames up towards the ceiling. As he leaned in, the rag in his mouth caught fire. The pain was excruciating. After a minute, two at the most, he heard movement and screams from above. The cellar door flew open and a woman came running down the stairs. She was wearing a long flowered skirt which made it difficult for her to negotiate the narrow steps. When she reached the third step from the bottom her shoe caught the hem of her skirt, which sent her sprawling. The material ripped cleanly, leaving her in a sitting position, her thick legs spread wide with a pair of enormous bright red underpants catching the light from the fire. She pulled herself up and stared with amazement at the man duct taped to the galvanized drain pipe. By this time the sheet was about burned out. It had not ignited anything else. The woman, jewelry and scarves still intact, gaped at the German as she gathered the remains of her skirt around her..

" Dumnezeule!" She crossed herself and yanked the smoldering cloth from Bissels mouth.

" Please, please help me." He could hardly speak. His lips were badly burned. That crazy man...brought me here...to rape me." 'Not bad,' thought Bissel, for a spur of the moment remark.

" Dumnezeule!" she repeated, crossing herself one more time and stepping away.

" Please, will you untie me before he comes back?"

" Sheka. I always knew he was crazy. One time I saw him naked...naked as the day he was born, standing in front of the furnace...beating himself with a tree branch. Can you imagine?"

" Please...My hands?"

The woman moved cautiously towards him, then realized her skirt was slipping off again. She grabbed for the fabric and wrapped it back around her plump lower body, fastening it with a quick tug and a swirl. Then she examined the thick wrapping that bound him to the drainpipe, found the remains of what had once been a curved linoleum knife, and deftly cut the tape from the German's wrists. He

278

did not stop to thank her. Bissel ran like hell up the stairs and out the side door of the house. Mrs. Zelma, Reader and Advisor, was left in the basement to sort it all out.

Solomon Baum sat at his massive George II mahogany pedestal desk, leaned back in the button-tufted leather banker's chair, clasped his hands together and rested them on his stomach. Heskel Milstein looked carefully at the boy, trying to discern if their young visitor was playing straight or if this was part of something orchestrated by *The Builder*.

" Mr. Milstein, I swear I knew nothing about it. I was as shocked as you were when the Rebbe passed away. But I'm telling you. It was no accident. I realized it at the funeral. You should hear how he spoke. And I'll tell you, you should both be careful. He's crazy."

" Henri, why come to us now, with this?"

" Mr. Baum, this is wrong. I realize that it looks bad for me and Léon. But what we did we did for him. For the Rebbe. Not for Claude. From the very beginning, when we were kids, we were told that our work was for the good of us all. I still believe it. We did things that, on the surface, seemed wrong. But the way Claude explained it, the way he justified it, we believed him. He even once had the Rebbe talk to us. Rebbe Buchsbaum, may he rest in peace, told us that whatever Claude asked of me and my brother, it was for the good of the movement. How could we not have believed?"

" These *things* that you did, Henri, tell us about them."

" Mr. Milstein we did terrible, awful things. We ruined people's lives. We poisoned crops and blew up buildings. We took a life..." The boy shook his head slowly. It seemed like he was about to cry.

" You killed, Henri? Who did you kill?" Henri Drei, related the entire series of events that had transpired in the past few years. Baum remained outwardly calm. However, his old friend Heskel could see that he was near panic.

" Solomon, I think this young man needs a little time to compose himself. Henri, why don't you go outside, into the garden for a while? A little fresh air will feel good. Come on now. I'll walk you down there. Solly, I'll be back in a minute."

Heskel Milstein escorted the boy out of the office and down a flight of stairs to the building's interior garden. Baum's private retreat. He carefully locked the heavy french doors behind him and began his climb. From the office window above, they could observe the young man. The early twentieth century cast bronze doorway by H.H. Martyn, had once graced the main post office in London. They were Henri Drei's only way out of the garden. It was time for caution. Even more caution than usual. Heskel sat down across from his friend.

" So, what do you think?"

" Heskel, it doesn't do any good to beat ourselves up over something we had no part in."

" Ah, but we did. We put up our own funds. We legitimized everything."

" And........ we made a great deal of money. It's true. Heskela, our hands are not the cleanest. Look at what I tried to do for my son. You think if he got elected, that things would be better? Not on your life. Claude would have him jumping through hoops. Let's be honest. We've both done things over the years that were, shall we say, questionable. But murder...no! I never killed anyone. I - never - killed - anyone." He slowly removed his eyeglasses and leaned towards Millstein. "How about you, my old friend? Did you ever commit a murder? Use your own hands? Did you even ever think about it? I doubt it. To take a human life. To put your hands around someone's neck and squeeze. To pull a trigger on a gun and watch someone bleed to death. No. But Claude...the boy came right out and accused him. Pointed a finger. Wizman killed the Rebbe. That's exactly what he said. My god, what if that's true?"

" True? Why would Henri lie to us? If it ever got out, we'd be ruined. We're too involved in all this. It would be the end. Period. For all of us. Not just me. Not just you. Think about our families?"

" So how do we contain it?"

" You really mean, what do we do about Claude?"

" If he can be...removed, then we've still got a chance."

" Solly, what are you saying?"

" I'm saying that we're in a fight for our lives. That anything goes at this point."

" And that would be..."

" Eliminate Claude. It's the only way out."

" Solomon, I hear what you're saying, but I can't believe it."

" Don't act like you're so shocked. Remember...you and me...and a certain 'Mr. White?' Ring any bells, my friend? Or is that something you've managed to erase from your memory? Do I need to remind you what a shittern mogn Hoffa was. That miserable grober. It was him or us."

" And you're personally going to do it, Solly? How? With a pistol, or maybe you'll use a knife or...or "

" Or it will be used on us. You think Claude would hesitate to kill us both? We may be useful to him now. But not for very much longer. I can assure you of that. No Heskel, I propose that we use Henri and Léon. If Léon's thinking like his brother. They can do the job. You heard it yourself. They've done it before."

" I have to think about this, Solly. I'm not sure I'm capable. Maybe Claude will come around."

" Az di bobe volt gehat beytsim volt zi geven mayn zeyde!
" Which means?"
" Which means...if my grandmother had testicles she would be my grandfather."

Baglione spent the entire day at the Forbes Magazine archives on lower Fifth Avenue, pouring over every article they'd published on Heskel Milstein, Pan Pacific Bank, and its owner, The Mekler Group. He sort of knew that anyone computer savvy could have accomplished this in a couple of hours.

" Have you ever done this before?" asked the young intern, a prep-school boy who looked no more than sixteen, in his perfectly ironed, crisp white Turnbull & Asser shirt, skinny blue tie and chino pants.

" You're a very observant fellow. I'm not exactly sure what to do."

" Is this the first time you've ever used a computer, sir?"

" No, no. It's just that my eyes are not what they once were. The page is so small."

" You're trying to read the thumbnails," laughed the boy. " I can't even read those and my eyes are 20-20."

" So why bother..."

" Uh, ever heard of double-click? You know, click, click and they open up."

" Double click?"

The young guy just shook his head and showed Baglione how to enlarge the pages. With this bit of information, Corrado was now able to read about Mekler's far-flung deals, buying and selling property in South Africa, gobbling up medical equipment manufacturers in Europe, vineyards all over the world and most interestingly, to the Italian investigator, the deals involving Solomon

Baum. It was Baum's connection to the Boravitchers that had attracted the detective's attention at the beginning of the investigation. It appeared to Baglione that a lot of the businesses controlled by Milstein and Baum were dominated by these ultra-religious Jews. Not so unusual in itself. Were the two men philanthropic in the extreme, did they offer employment to any Boravitcher in need of a job or was there something else? Something more complicated or more...he couldn't quite put his finger on it. By the end of the day, Baglione had constructed a chart that depicted as much of the activities of Milstein as the public record afforded. Several of the articles spoke of the speculative nature of his acquisitions. Acquisitions made either just before or just after a major shift in the markets they operated in. Several apparently caused by freak occurrences like the poisonings of Italian wines and the fruit fly infestation in Chile. Even the explosions in Holland, at the giant auction houses, were followed by heavy purchases in other flower producing countries. In almost every instance there was a mention of one or more of Milstein's enterprises 'assessing' the situation. Baglione concluded that, either the man was a genius with a crystal ball, or he had access to inside information. The Baum connection proved equally interesting. Through his huge real estate holdings, Baum's reach extended into many other businesses. If you wanted to sell fruits and vegetables at the wholesale level in New York, Ellis Island Enterprises would rent you a space in the enormous Bronx Terminal Market. No lease, no business. Ellis was one hundred percent owned by Petseleh Properties, a Solomon Baum company. If you rented space in a Solomon Baum building, of which there were hundreds throughout the United States, the painters and plumbers and cleaning supplies had to be sourced from approved vendors who were, not coincidentally, controlled by Baum. Need a huge, prime space in a dozen cities across the U.S.A. for electronics retailing or a giant supermarket, there was only one landlord to talk to. Even industrial powerhouses like GM and Boeing needed rights of way and easements through properties owned by Baum. One time, in the state of Texas, the Air Force was informed that in order for the government of The United States of America to land a top secret aircraft at a private field near Brownsville, it needed permission from its owner, Worthington-Fitz Ryan Industries, a division of King Solomon LLC. The scope of his enterprises made even the Mafia drool. Time and again, he was approached by organized crime. Each time they were rebuffed. So many times that they finally just gave it up.

Baglione was discovering how to use the computer to cross reference all these facts. He found three-way deals with surprising partners, odd ties to foreign governments and several references to Rebbe Buchsbaum. The Rebbe urging his followers in Israel's parliament to vote one way or another on a Milstein project. The Rebbe endorsing Steven Baum for Mayor of New York City despite his outrageous support for the Mullahs in Iran. A New York Times article speculated that his endorsement of the Iranian government just might be in exchange for concessions granted to subsidiaries of the Pan Pacific Bank to operate in the Islamic Middle East.

The problem, thought Baglione, was that all of it appeared to be perfectly legal. To bring down this house of cards, they needed some direct evidence of criminality. Tie a murder or an explosion to Milstein or Baum or the Boravitchers and you had a chance. Without a positive, verifiable link, the idea of yet another 'Jewish conspiracy' would die in a matter of days.

"As it should," Flanken was quick to point out. The German-Jewish detective had insisted from the beginning on extreme caution, when they had first uncovered their evidence. He stressed

284

often and loudly to Baglione, that they must never paint this as a picture of anything more than greed on the part of a small number of Ultra-Orthodox Jews. Even that would surely be enough to reinforce the worn out anti-semitic thinking throughout the world. Flanken was particularly sensitive to this kind of caricature.

The Italian detective was halfway through an account, in the current issue of Forbes, about the impending bankruptcy of a German manufacturer of a certain line of heart and blood pressure monitors, after disclosure of quality control problems in some equipment they'd sent to England. An Israeli company had, miraculously, stepped in and offered their own replacements shortly after the news was made public.

" Sir, I'm sorry but it's five minutes to five. We're just about to close."

Baglione looked up from the computer terminal to see a good looking blond with rimless glasses, dressed in a tight white skirt and blue blazer.

" I'm sorry. I was involved with my work."

" I could see that," she laughed. Corrado thought she might like to go for a drink. He certainly would!

" Excuse me, signorina, but since it's the end of the day, would you..."

" I'd love to, but the convent serves dinner at six. If I'm late, it's double vespers for me. You wouldn't want that to happen, would you sweetie?"

Corrado spoke English well enough to get the message. He gathered up his papers, including the printouts he'd made of everything he'd found. Baglione hoped that Flanken had come up with something more concrete, more 'sale-able' in a court of law.

Indeed, Wolfie was trying. They'd concluded that the death of Johnnie Olivieri, the floater who was found in the harbor in Bremen, was a lead that needed to be pursued. If he was involved, as Flanken suspected, in the death of Maxi Fleischig and the other old Nazis who were poisoned, tying Olivieri to the Boravitchers would be a significant break in the case.

Earlier that morning, the German detective strolled down Fifth Avenue to the parked Mitzvah Mobile. He walked slowly enough so that the two young men who were working the street had plenty of time to spot him.

" Ya'Jush?" asked one of them, as the German paused for a moment to look.

" I am."

" Lay tefillin?"

" I used to. Not for a very long time." The man was referring to the Orthodox practice of wrapping a religious symbol around the forearm before beginning to pray.

" If you don't remember how, come inside. We'll show you."

" I...I don't think so. I'm in a little bit of a hurry."

" Five minutes. What could it hurt?" The man sensed that he had a live one.

" No really. I'm late for an appointment. I'd like to, but..."

" So come back when you're through. We'll still be here."

" No, I can't. I'm on my way to Brooklyn."

" Brooklyn. Even better. We have a shul in Borough Park. You can go there instead. Come in. Please. I'll give you the directions." Wolfie hesitated. "Come on. I'm not going to bite you."

They walked towards the big Winnebago. It's right side door swung open, as if by remote control. The young man reached in, grabbed a pamphlet and handed it to Flanken.

" This explains some things about being a Jew. A real Jew. A serious, pious Jew."

" I try to keep kosher back home."

" You do! That's wonderful. It's a good start." The two men shared a laugh. The young missionary was delighted to find such a fellow.

" Here's the address. What's your name? I'll have to call ahead. It's not so easy to get in there. You know...," he lowered his voice. "...there's a lot of problems with the shvartzes in the neighborhood. You go if you can. Good luck to you and God bless. What's your name, again?"

Wolfie was caught off guard for a second.

" Uh..." He looked up at a sign in a health food restaurant window.

" Burger. Tuvya Burger. I'm German."

" Gey gezunderheit, Berger!"

In a building in lower Manhattan the phone rang on Claude Wizman's desk. Once, twice, then a third time. He did not recognize the caller ID. On the fourth ring *The Builder* picked it up. He was weary and depressed. His elaborate plans were in danger of unraveling. It was frustrating for him to know that he was smarter than almost everyone, yet still unable to put things completely right. The situation was spinning out of his control. This was an unfamiliar circumstance for someone who was used to being out in front of things. Milstein had frozen all of the assets, except for the million-nine he was able to grab in a hurry, by wiring the funds out of The Caymans just ahead of the old man's orders.

" Yes."

" Claude, it's me."

" Jorg? I can barely hear you. Where are you? What happened?"

" My lips are badly burned. I can hardly speak. First, they got me with a fucking Taser. Can you believe it? I had him Claude, I had Flanken. Then the lights went out. Next thing I know I'm in a basement in Brooklyn. That's where the fire started.

" What fire?"

" I doesn't really matter now. Just bring me up to date, Claude. What's going on?"

" I'll tell you when you get here. Where are you now?

" Close."

" Be careful, Jörgie."

" Listen. I did my best. I'm sorry about what happened. Don't worry. I'll take care of these bastards."

" I know you will." It was this dark side of Bissel that appealed to *The Builder*. This was a man you don't turn your back on.

" I can be there in ten minutes."

" Good. This is what I want you to do. Stay downstairs until Léon arrives with the woman. We can't afford any more screw-ups. Vishtez?"

" What woman?"

" The Italian."

" You've got her here?" Bissel snickered. "That's perfect."

She would lead them to Flanken and the other one. The taser attack was still fresh in the German's mind. Revenge was something to be savored. Like the last raisinette in the box.

The trip into Manhattan by private ambulance took two hours and twenty-five minutes. The traffic was unusually bad as they approached the Holland Tunnel. Léon Drei hardly spoke, even though Vanessa tried several times to start up a conversation. She was scared, although fear was something she'd learned to deal with, as a professional thief. But this was different. The penalty here wasn't a short stretch in prison. It was, most probably, her life. Someone had gone to great expense to bring her here. She wondered who it could be, and how it affected Corrado. She worried so much about him. He was a policeman but he had little experience in dealing with really bad guys, and this one, her captor, was that and more. Vanessa always relied on her instincts.

She was on her back, strapped to the gurney, but could still turn her head. The New York skyline was not far away. After about twenty minutes, the ambulance crawled through the tunnel into lower Manhattan. They were approaching their destination. Not more than a few blocks from the exit on Hudson. She could barely make out the names on the street signs. **CANAL** and then **RENWICK**. The neighborhood was dark at this hour. Then she was gagged and blindfolded once more. The driver pulled up to a loft building, stopped and got out, then rang for the freight elevator. It arrived soundlessly. This was a building that had seen some renovation.

The ride up was short. Perhaps two or three floors at most. The large double doors opened and Vanessa was wheeled into a small entryway that smelled faintly of incense. Her blindfold and gag were removed. A slatted, cherry wood door stood between a pair of rough timber benches. The floor was tiled in slate. Léon Drei signaled to the driver, who removed the constraints from the stretcher. Vanessa sat up for the first time in hours.

" You can stand now." She did, somewhat shakily.

" Inside, through the door, then turn left."

The enormous loft was set on two levels. A rock garden constructed with shiny black stones outlined with larger rough cut blocks defined a portion of the main floor. She could hear running water, like a brook, behind a rustic wooden fence. It had to be a recording, she decided. This was no place for a stream. She followed another slate path to a short set of heavy wooden stairs. A room, with walls fashioned from rice paper, was illuminated from the inside. The space was beautifully finished. Under other circumstances, Vanessa would have been pleased to be there. Léon gestured to her to slide open the shoji screen at the head of the stairs. She did and then took two steps forward.

" That will be all, Léon. Stay close, in case I need you."

' Stay close, in case I need you.' Drei had traveled ten thousand miles in two days, had just executed a textbook perfect kidnapping, and this was how he was spoken to. Like he was some kind of man servant. This was really pissing him off. He'd been feeling disillusioned. Betrayed. For quite some time. Henri felt the same way. Ever since they'd learned of the Rebbe's death.

Drei slid the door closed behind the woman. In the dim light she could just make out the form of a man, lighting a pipe. Her eyes adjusted quickly. She was now able to see him, dark complexioned with a salt and pepper beard. He wore a cardigan sweater. Expensive. Probably Missoni. It had that distinctive pattern that made Missoni sweaters so easy to identify. The aroma from his pipe was not at all unpleasant. The only jarring note in the room was the light from a notebook computer on a rough cut stone shelf behind the man. The colors on the screen were vivid. She'd never seen a display like this before. He noticed her looking at it, then reached over and closed the lid. Claude Wizman rose from the tatami and crossed over to where Vanessa was standing.

" Please remove your shoes." She hesitated. "I assure you that you won't be harmed. It protects the mats and shows respect for the person who crafted them."

There was an edge to his voice that made her shiver. Nevertheless, she followed his instruction. The woven straw mats felt good under her feet. Feet still swollen from the long journey across the Atlantic.

" Please sit down. Would you like some tea? It's twig tea. Kukicha. Quite special, actually. I have a friend who sends it to me from Tokyo."

" Yes, thank you." She really wanted a vodka. But it made no sense to offend her captor.

" I'm sure you're wondering why you're here." She chose not to speak. "Have you spoken to your boyfriend lately?"

" He's not my boyfriend." Vanessa wondered why she'd said that. Instinct, probably. It wasn't the first time in her life that she'd been in a tight spot. Her mind drifted, to a house outside Nice, where she'd been caught by a burly security man as she rifled through an ebony and walnut art deco desk. Apparently the place wasn't exactly empty on the night she chose. In the cavernous basement, a meeting was taking place. The participants included several members of the Marseille underworld. She was much younger at the time, and quite innocent looking. Vanessa was taken to the owner of the house. He coldly informed her that it would be his pleasure to pass her among his houseguests. For six terrifying hours she sat in wait. But she hadn't been harmed. The boss decided she deserved some credit for her daring. Honor among thieves, she thought at the time. But this was different. She was brought here at great expense from very far away. Whatever they wanted of her, it wouldn't end as pleasantly as that night outside Nice. She was certain of that.

" Not your boyfriend? I think otherwise."

" Think what you like. He caught me doing something I shouldn't have been doing. My choice was to play along with him or go to jail. I picked the least unpleasant of my options. Fucking him every so often beats the hell out of a prison stretch."

" Ah, yes. Your unsavory background. I am familiar with your history. Does he love you?"

" I'm not certain. Probably so." She smiled at *The Builder*. This performance was for him.

" Do you know how to find him?"

" So this is why I'm here. Sorry but I can't help you." That was not completely true. If she really tried, she could get through to him one way or another. She was terrified of what would happen if these people got their hands on Corrado.

" That's really too bad. Because without him, we have no reason to keep you entertained."

' Entertained,' thought Vanessa, was another way of saying 'alive.'

" What do you want with Corrado? He's a nobody. A second class jerk with a badge."

" Ah, but he's managed to stick his paw in the honey. He and that other hungry bear, Flanken. You've met the man, I'm sure."

" I don't believe so."

" Let me refresh your memory. Köln, Das kleine Stapelhauschen. Drinks in that wretched room they call a bar. You and the German drank martinis. Boodles wasn't it? I believe your Italian had stomach problems. Unicum, one ice cube.

" I'm impressed, Mr...?"

" So how do we find these two? Any ideas, Miss Terry? Forgive me. I meant to say Signora Rambaudi."

That really scared her. How did he know so much about her? Miss Terry! She hadn't been called that in years.

" I'm afraid I can't help you, even if I wanted to. Which I don't. Seriously, if you killed him, and I think that's your intention, it would let me off the hook."

Wizman was not sure whether or not to believe her. She was a career criminal. That was indisputable. Maybe she really was telling the truth. He tried another approach.

" Vanessa, I can call you Vanessa?"

" By all means...?"

" I'm Claude. I suppose it doesn't make any difference if you know my name. I'm afraid that one way or the other, we're going to have to...there's really no delicate way to put it."

" Why kill me? I told you I can't help you. What more could you want from me?"

" Apparently, very little. O.K. then. You leave me no choice." He picked up a telephone and spoke softly into the mouthpiece. "Léon, has Jörg come up yet?...Good. Send him in please."

In a few seconds the shoji panel slid open and Jörg Bissel padded barefoot into the room. Vanessa shuddered. She knew that something bad was about to happen.

" My colleague here is apparently quite upset with your friends. Isn't that true, Jörg?" The man turned his head slowly and fixed his eyes on Vanessa. "I'm afraid that this woman is of no value to us. Please remove her from here. Be gentle...Or not. Whatever suits your mood."

" Look, Claude, or whatever your name is..." Bissel took a step towards her. "I'd love to help you out, here. But, honestly, I just don't know how to find him. Maybe I have something else we could trade for."

" Hardly. Sex without love? I've never understood the currency. Maybe it's my strong religious convictions. You do know, actually you probably don't, but I'm an observant Jew. I find it difficult to cultivate a meaningful relationship with the opposite sex. A whore like you? I don't think so. So what else have you got to trade?"

" Don't flatter yourself. As far as I'm concerned, sucking a cock is just like any other clause in a contract. If it suits my purposes, I suck it."

Wizman didn't flinch, but, to be honest, he wasn't used to talk like that from a woman. From anyone. He'd lived his life, for the most part, faithful to his religious beliefs. But things had changed. Dramatically. Since he'd smothered the Rebbe. He tried not to show his displeasure at her directness. But he was a pragmatist. So he held his nose and jumped into the water.

" Fucked anyone interesting lately, Vanessa?"

" This sounds like the beginning of a negotiation. Am I reading you right, honey?"

" Who else are you fucking?" he almost whispered.

" Limo drivers, doctors, you know. Whatever it takes?"

" Politicians?"

" One or two."

" Tell me more."

Vanessa decided to go for broke. She had nothing to lose at this point and she was betting on her own skills to pull her through.

" Well, right now I'm sleeping with the creep who was just elected Prime Minister of Italy. Somehow, he managed to convince the Italian voters that he's got clean hands. That's very important for a politician in Italy these days. I can tell you for sure that those clean hands have been all over me."

" This politician, isn't he married?"

" He's an Italian, sweetie. Married in the church. Married to the church."

" Actually, that's relevant only to nuns and priests."

" Whatever. This one's got three kids and a devoted wife." Vanessa had to laugh. She wasn't making this up as she went along. It was all true.

" And his associates. Know any of them?"

" One or two. You have to understand something about Italy. The north is much too rich and much too strong to let just anyone be elected Prime Minister. This "Forza" as they call it, has already shoved aside most of the old crooks. It's just a matter of time before the new ones get their hands in everything."

Claude's mind raced. The Boravitchers had major holdings in Italy. A Prime Minister there, in Wizman's pocket, might just be the thing he needed to thwart Milstein and Baum. Milstein would plotz if he heard that Claude was pulling the strings in Rome. To hell with that idiot son of Solomon Baum's. New York City was small potatoes compared with having control of a rich, powerful European country. Those alter kockers who'd just cut him off… especially with the Rebbe out of the picture, would be begging him to take their money. The thought was too delicious for words. And, if this whore was telling the truth…

" **First** time in a gypsy cab?"

Wolfie was confused. This black man with his gold tooth and African kufi hat did not look at all like the European gypsies he encountered on a daily basis in Köln. He'd learned in a multicultural seminar to use Romani or Roma in place of *gypsy.*

" Ja, first time in a *gypsy*."

" Well don't worry. I'm a serious family man. I got more values than Crazy Eddie. Not like some of these stick-up mo'fuggahs they got driving these days. Know what I'm sayin'?"

" I can imagine," replied his passenger. Even though he had no idea what a *crazy eddie* is...or was.

" I mean, like I was usin' a car service the other evening, with my wife, and I say to this nigga', 'we wanna' go to Manhattan. How much you gonna' charge me?' And he turn around and say to me, 'I don't go to Manhattan.' Fuckin' money-makin' Manhattan and this nigga' don't wanna' go there? I said, sheeet, let me get my ass into another cab. I tell him 'stop the fuckin' car, jim.' And this nigga' got the nerve to say to me, 'three dollars.' I said, three dollars. What the fuck for? He look me right in my motha'fuckin' eye and he say, 'for wastin' his time.' I look at my wife and start laughin' and the next thing I know, this motha' got a gun, and I mean a big fuckin' gun, stuck in my face. So, right away I figure… this dude is crazy. Let me give him his three dollars and get the fuck outta' there. You understand what I'm sayin'? Anyways, that's the kind of crazy mo'fuggahs they got behind the wheel these days. Gangsta mo'fuggahs. I mean it's hard enough makin' a livin' at this, without mixed up mo'fuggahs, like this one, chasing John Public back into the motha'fuckin' subway. I mean, isn't that why we're out here? So people don't have to take the trains at night. Mo'fuggah gonna' charge me three dollars for wastin' his time. Shit, like he got somethin' better to do. Damn!"

Wolfie was mesmerized. This was like watching a film. He flashed on the black director who did all those extraordinary movies. The one who made MALCOLM X. He thought about his boyfriend Harald, who loved American films. Wolfie missed him and their house in Hürth. He would call Harald that evening.

" You sure you wanna' be let out around here? Ain't nothin' but poor black folks and a bunch of them curly locks Jews. You know, the ones that was fightin' with the young'uns last year. I don't understand it. These people got serious coin and they live in a shithole neighborhood like this? It don't make sense. If I was rich like they is, I'd be doin' the duff. Get my family the fuck outta' here in a mo'fugghin' hurry. Understand what I'm sayin'?"

" This is good for me, ja. Stop here, please."

The driver looked at the Boravitcher headquarters building, looked at Flanken and realized his faux pas.

" Look, no offense. I mean, I didn't realize that you…Hey, you really one of them?"

" Those mother-fuckers? Hell no!" replied Wolfie, trying to keep a straight face. " I mean, you askin' me that seriously, Jim?"

The driver was silent for a few seconds, then he and the German both began to laugh.

" Hey, you o.k. for a old, fat white man."

" Thanks. How much?"

" Gimme three dollars."

" For wasting your time? Where's the gun?"

" You really wanna' see it?"

" Just joking." Flanken handed the man a five and jumped out.

" You take care of yourself. Watch your back in this neighborhood. You hear me?"

" I hear you, and thanks."

" Thank you."

The man drove away swiftly, leaving Köln's Chefdetektiv on the sidewalk. Flanken approached the iron gate. There was an intercom encased in a heavy metal box. A sign in several languages directed callers to ring for assistance.

" Yes. Can I help you?" Wolfie looked for the video camera and spotted it just above his head.

" My name is Berger. I spoke to someone this morning. On the street in Manhattan."

" Just a moment." After a short wait he heard the latch release, which allowed him to enter. "Please close the gate behind you."

The detective did as he was asked, then walked slowly towards the front door. He was met there by two men, dressed in black. They wore long coats, knickers, black stockings, black shoes and black fedoras, turned smartly down at the brim. Each had peyess, the long curls of hair that fell out of the hats at their ears. Flanken guessed that they were both around twenty years old.

" Please empty your pockets into the tray, then walk through."

Wolfie complied immediately. The security check was similar to those found at airports and lately, at most public buildings in Germany. He glanced at the manufacturer's name. This set-up was first class and very expensive.

" May we see some identification please?"

" I'm sorry. I don't have anything with me."

The German had purposely left his identification back at the hotel. He suspected that there would be some kind of check when he got to Brooklyn.

" No identification. Why aren't you carrying a wallet?" asked the taller of the two men.

" I was afraid to - in this neighborhood."

The other man nodded, as if in agreement.

" Very well. Follow me."

298

He was led through the huge old mansion to a staircase at the rear. Another man, dressed similarly, but with an enormous black beaver hat, was waiting at the foot of the stairs.

" Please." The man gestured towards the stairs. He followed Flanken up.

" Where are you from, Mista' Berger?"

" I'm German."

" Jiddischer sprecher?

" Ja." It was true enough. His grandparents spoke only Yiddish in their house, and it was close enough to German for Wolfie to fake his way through.

" Why are you here?"

For a moment, the detective felt somewhat concerned. He quickly realized that the question was non-threatening.

" I was brought up pious, but to be honest, I've moved away from it in the past twenty years."

" A familiar story, Mista' Berger. Now you're thinking maybe you should come home. What do you know about us, about the Boravitcher movement?"

" Just what I've seen on the TV and read. You seem able to live in the real world, without...without having to be part of the...the, you know what I'm trying to say."

" Very perceptive. You want, like they say, to have your cake and eat some too. You want that God should see you as a religious man, but you still want your car and your fancy house...How about a family? You have a family, Berger?"

Wolfie thought about Harald and smiled.

" Yes, thank God. I have a very nice wife and...and five gorgeous children."

" Kaynahorah, Berger. Any sons?"

" All boys. The five of them." That ought to whet his appetite, thought Flanken.

" Me, got tsu danken, I have three...and a lovely daughter. Every family should have one."

Wolf replied with a Yiddish expression he remembered from his grandfather.

" A pish un a fortz iz vi a khasene un a klezmer!" which loosely translated meant something like 'a pee without a fart is like a wedding without a band.'

" You're a funny guy, Mista' Berger. Now, what can we do for you? You live here in New York or no?"

" No, I live in Germany, in Würzburg. Do you know it?"

" I've never been to your country, although when you think about it, it can't really be called your country, either. Can it Mista' Berger?"

" I'm not sure I agree with you."

" Es gefelt mir, Berger. I like a good challenge. All part of my job," laughed the man. "Now I'm going to show you why you're a man without a country. I know that you stopped at the mitzvah tank this morning. Most people don't, by the way. Sometimes I wonder if it's worth the effort."

" I know someone, an Italian Jew, who's involved in your movement."

" Here in Brooklyn?"

" Uh huh."

" Who's that?"

" His name is Johnnie Olivieri." Flanken watched carefully, for any kind of reaction. He detected a slight twitch in one eye. At least he thought he saw something at the mention of Olivieri's name.

" I don't believe I know him. There are many, many of us here in Borough Park. Shall we go into the study. There are some scriptures I'd like you to look at."

The man led Wolfie along a balcony overlooking the first floor entry, then through an arched wooden door. The room appeared to be a kind of library, with bookshelves lining the walls and a cluster of five or six small cubicles, each one with a plain wooden desk and a reading lamp. There were two young men in the room, each seated at a desk, each one deep into some kind of manuscript that looked old to the German detective.

" Take a seat, Berger. By the way, do you read Yiddish as well as you speak it?"

" I'm not sure. It's been a long time."

" And Hebrew?"

" Not at all. I mean I can read some things..."

" But you can't understand what you're reading."

" Exactly."

" Not to worry. Let me get you something in German."

He returned with a large tome, somewhat dusty, entitled WIE WEIT, or 'which way' in English.

" This was written in the middle of the last century, by a Jewish scholar in Mannheim. His name was Fritz Kobus. Do you know of him?"

" No. I don't."

" Sit for a while and look at what he's written. I think you'll find it amazing. Kobus had an unbelievable gift for seeing into the future. Kind of like Rebbe Buchsbaum, he should rest in peace."

" I saw on the TV that the Rebbe died recently. Who will replace him?"

" The Rebbe can never be...*replaced*!" He spit out the word as if Flanken had insulted the man's name.

" I'm sorry. I just meant..."

" No, no, I should apologize. It's been a difficult time here, these past few weeks. Read on, my friend. I'll be back to see you shortly."

The man reappeared in half an hour.

" Mr. Berger, you are no longer welcome here."

" What's wrong?" The German sensed that his charade was over

" There's no Berger in Würzburg with five sons. So what's your real game, mista'?"

" I can explain."

" We know who you are, Detective Flanken. Please leave now."

" Who's Johnnie Olivieri?"

" Leave now or you will regret it. Or rather, your Harald will regret it."

The spacious Park Avenue office was quiet most weekends. On this rainy morning, four men sat in the executive suite, eating breakfast. Solomon Baum had insisted on it. It was a ritual with him. Sundays meant bagels and lox and everything that went with it. There was herring in cream sauce, sable and whitefish, sliced tomato, red onion and baked farmer cheese in three flavors. The blueberry was his favorite. And cream cheese with scallions. The bagels, bialys and bulkas and the seven layer cake were all from Shlomo's, the Houston Street bakery part-owned by a cousin of Baum's wife.

" Try the whitefish, Henri, it's delicious."

" I'm not a big eater, Mr. Baum."

" Nonsense. Today, you make an exception. I bet they didn't feed you like this in the army. Am I right, Léon?"

302

" Not like this at all."

The older brother was making himself an enormous sandwich of lox, vegetable cream cheese and sliced red onion, on a ten inch long bulka (which is really a bialy shaped like a torpedo).

" Heskell, you eat like a bird." Their host pointed to the single slice of smoked sable that Milstein was picking at with his fork. He'd succeeded in cutting away the orange edges, which Baum considered to be the tastiest part of the fish.

" Gib zich a traisel, Solly. Can't we just get down to business?"

" Shoyn genug, Heskela! I don't know how Fanny still to puts up with you...after all these years." He was referring to Milstein's wife. A woman of infinite patience. They'd married in Poland, shortly before the family emigrated to Brazil.

Although the banker was not a spiritual leader, he was a benefactor and an active member of the Boravitchers' council of financial advisors. When Rebbe Buchsbaum introduced a young man named Claude Wizman to Milstein, he was immediately impressed with his intelligence and dedication to the movement. The Grand Rebbe made known his vision of the future and how the banker could help. Wizman was charged with the responsibility of making it happen.

The Builder was a brilliant strategist. His master plan was a work of art. Start small, concentrate on a few industries with growth potential, tap the resources of the burgeoning State of Israel and cultivate not only crops but contacts, everywhere in the world. The two hundred thousand Boravitchers, spread out among a dozen countries, were educated, motivated, and with the financial backing of the Milsteins and others like Solomon Baum, disposed to make reality of Rebbe Buchsbaum's visions.

The turning point for Wizman and the movement coincided with the quantum leap that the Milsteins took in 1986, the year the Mekler Group acquired Pan Pacific Bank. Now, Rebbe Buchsbaum had the funds and the connections that he needed.

" **Wolfie**, it's me."

" Baglione, where have you been. I've been trying to reach you for hours."

" I was going over everything I found at the library. Not a library, exactly. I don't know the word in English for archivio."

" Archives. You were there all night?"

" Not all night. But very late. I didn't finish until the early morning." By 'finish' he really meant 'with Stacy.' The hooker he'd met a few days before at the Paramount. She was back for round number two.

" You need to stay in touch with me, Corrado. We have big problems."

" Big problems?"

" Bissel's gone."

" Porca troia! Where is he?"

" I don't know. Apparently he started a fire in Gega's basement. The fortune teller went down there to see what was happening and I guess she freed him."

" Where the hell was the Albanian?"

" That's not important now. The problem is Bissel."

" Wolfie, that stronzo scares the shit out of me."

" Me too. He's capable of anything."

" You said big problems. Is there something else I should know?"

" The Boravitchers are on to us."

" Cazzo. How do you know?"

" They threatened my friend. They threatened Harald. By name."

" **Miss Terry**, or rather Signora Rambaudi, I need you to return to Italy and do me a favor."

" And why would I want to do that, Claude?

" Very simply, if you don't I will have your daughter sent to a very dangerous, very bad place." Vanessa was stunned. For the first time, since she could remember, she was speechless.

" Excellent. I see that I now have your full attention. That's a good first step."

" How do you...what do you know...?

" About your daughter? I know that if you don't follow my instructions she will find herself in Libya. In the hands of a certain very nasty General with a taste for young white...paraplegics."

" Paraplegic? Tell me what you know about my daughter?"

" Don't worry, Vanessa. She's a perfectly healthy, physically fit and very beautiful young lady. It would be a shame to see her lose a leg. Or an arm, because her whore of a mother decided not to co-operate."

" You bastard. You miserable piece of shit. If you dare..."

"...Oh, spare me the drama. You will return to Italy and do what I say. If you really have a 'relationship' with this *Cavaliere*, as they call him..."

" It's what he calls himself."

" And you, how shall I say this, manage to compromise this person who will soon be the next Prime Minister of Italy, your daughter will be released unharmed.

" Fuck you!"

" Wrong answer. Now, I want you to think very carefully. Do we or do we not have an understanding?"

The white rental car crossed Batchelor Avenue and pulled off Route 37 into a Getty gas station in Toms River. Claude Wizman rarely drove himself. Today was an exception. He parked the car to the right of the office and opened the rear passenger door on the driver's side of the Oldsmobile Eighty-Eight. The car was equipped with something Avis called a **GPS NAVIGATION SYSTEM**. It worked flawlessly. He'd make sure that Pinchus had one installed, the next time they purchased a car. He retrieved his Martin Greenfield worsted wool suit jacket, neatly folded on the rear seat, put it on and entered the office.

" Mr. White please."

The attendant gave Claude a long look.

" Who's asking?"

" I'm Mr. Riddle. I spoke with him this morning."

" Just a minute."

The man punched in a number on a pay phone that hung on the wall next to a Pirelli calendar featuring a scantily clad Kate Moss with her back turned towards the camera.

" Somebody named Riddle is here to see Mr. White… o.k…In there."

He gestured toward a door that said **NO ADMITTANCE**.

" Thank you." Wizman opened the door and was surprised to see an elegant wood paneled anteroom. An older woman, fresh from the tanning parlor, was seated at a desk.

" Mr. Riddle, please go in. Mr. White is expecting you."

Claude turned the heavy, polished brass knob and entered. The first thing that caught his eye was the young man standing behind a glass and chrome library table, empty except for a large crystal sculpture of a panther about to leap in Wizman's direction. Then he heard a low growl and saw the real thing, black, on a short silver

306

chain. The glistening beast was fastened tightly to the wall on the visitor's right.

"Don't worry about Chaka, Mr. Riddle. She's already eaten."

"Abundantly, I hope." The visitor was still digesting the fact that he'd entered this bizarre tableau through a gas station. "Thank you for seeing me."

"When you phoned this morning I wasn't sure that you were for real. I'm Anthony White."

He extended his arm and offered a powerful handshake. The elegantly dressed young man had the appearance of a bodybuilder - in a three piece Berluti suit. *The Builder* admired the distinctive French tailoring.

"Sorry, Mr. White. I was expecting someone a bit older."

"My father. People often make the mistake. I can assure you, Mr. Riddle, that you and I can discuss whatever it is that brought you here. My pop is happily retired and enjoying the weather, and his horses, in Florida."

The younger 'Mr. White' represented the first generation in the family to attend university. His law degree was from Georgetown. 'Mr. Riddle' and 'Mr. White' sat adjacent to each other. On the opposite side of the room from Chaka.

"How can I help you?"

"I'm here today to make you two proposals. One that will allow you to fill several closets with the same quality of clothing that you're wearing and second that will afford your father a jail free rest of his life "

Wizman knew from experience that the prices for bespoke suits from Berluti were astronomical.

"My closets are already full, Mr. Riddle. My father's well being, however, is of paramount importance to me. So please, let's get to the point.

The Builder was now convinced that this was a man not to be taken lightly.

" Very well, Mr. White."

Claude quickly realized that he'd need to demonstrate, convincingly, that his swinging dick was significantly longer than Mr. White's.

" Sonny boy, I suggest you pay careful attention to what I'm about to tell you."

" Go ahead. I'm listening."

" Excellent, Mr. White. You should know that I'm in possession of a recording, made recently, that implicates your father in the murder of Jimmy Hoffa." 'Chew on that you little shit,' thought Wizman.

The younger man hesitated, for just a moment, before speaking.

" My compliments. You now have my full attention. Nice touch with the name, by the way." He was referring to the Teamster's president whose full name was James Riddle Hoffa. "So what can I do for you, Mr. Riddle?"

" After you verify the tape, which I assure you is genuine, you'll reveal to me, the precise location of Hoffa's body. In return, your father's involvement will remain a secret."

" How do I know you won't use the tape anyway?"

" Mr. White, I have enough complications in my life. I don't need you added to the list.

Baglione finished the last few bites of his lunch. He was almost out of money. New York was not a cheap place to be. Especially if you are an Italian policeman on 'vacation.' He was having a hard time adjusting to the local pizza. First of all, it was served by the slice. It had much too much in the way of topping and it was meant to be eaten with the hands. It also had its advantages. It was cheap. It was available everywhere, at all hours of the day and night, and it was filling. Two slices and a small **7 Up** cost him three dollars. Less, if he skipped the drink. Corrado walked dejectedly back to The Paramount. He was contemplating a move to a cheaper place, even an apartment, when he was handed a letter by the desk clerk, addressed to him at the hotel. He immediately recognized the handwriting.

Carissimo,

I hope this letter finds you and you are o.k. Since you warned me, on the way to Malpensa, that it was too dangerous for us to communicate, I asked my friend Peter if you'd contacted him when you got to New York. He didn't know where you were staying and suggested I ask Anton. So I called him. Anton told me he thought you said something about the Paramount to a taxi driver who was with you and some German. I assume it was Wolfie. Please give him my best.

Corrado, you know I'm no good at small talk. So I'll get right to the point. I can't see you anymore. I've fallen in love with someone else. Someone very rich, who has promised to take care of me and my daughter. Yes! He found her for me. Please don't hate me for this. I know it's the right thing to do - for all of us.

Be very careful, my sweet. I have a bad feeling about these people you are investigating. And Corrado, please try to understand and remember the good times we shared. I'm giving up Tenuta Rambaudi and starting a new life with my daughter. I beg you not to try and find me.

ti amo sempre - V

The *late* Claude Wizman, he should rest in peace, sat in the First Class lounge at Toronto Pearson Airport waiting to board his flight to Karachi. He'd chosen PIA for one very simple reason. Their security procedures were among the weakest of all the international airlines. He was able to board the 747 using a Chilean passport issued in the name of Serge Souverein. One of many passports provided to him by Artur Bubin, the master document forger in Asuncion. A man whose services he'd relied on for many years. Once in Karachi, it was a short three and a half hour flight to Dhaka, Bangladesh. Jörg Bissel was waiting for him when his plane landed at Zia International Airport.

" Claude, it's good to see you."

" Serge, for now."

" Sorry. Serge it is."

" Don't get too used to it. Once you've done your job, I'll be forever known as...what's my name, again?"

" Leland Sorker, if I recall correctly."

" Right. Spelled with an 'o.' Apparently, this Sorker is quite the recluse. Extremely wealthy, money in a series of numbered accounts in Switzerland and elsewhere. Lives alone in a big house out in the Chittagong hills. English mother, deceased. Bangladeshi father, also deceased. Lived here all of his life. No friends and very few acquaintances. Made his money the old fashioned way."

" Inherited it?"

" Precisely, Jörg. I see you've done your homework. With a bit of reconstructive surgery, which I'm not looking forward to, the new and improved Mr. Sorker will say good-bye to this hellhole and divide his time between London and New York. Of course, that's assuming you do your part."

Chefdetektiv Flanken stroked the head of Harald Helm and reached for his glass of wine.

" Of course I love you. Why else would I put in my papers and retire to this lovely countryside?"

" Sorry, Wolf. This is not where I want to spend the rest of my life. It's so boring here. There isn't even a word for it."

" So what would you have us do? You hate big cities. You hate the country. You hate travelling. And you despise rich people."

" And poor people. And especially, middle-class people… like you."

" So now you hate me, too?" The soon to be ex- policeman flicked his tongue in his longtime lover's ear. The slightly younger man pulled away.

" Igitt! I hate you so much." They laughed together, as Flanken headed towards the kitchen to prepare dinner.

Baglione, alone and running out of money, left New York shortly after his German colleague was ordered back to Köln by his bosses and told to terminate his investigation of the Boravitchers. The BKA, Germany's equivalent to the FBI, would now be jointly running the investigation with the Americans. Flanken was so upset he swore to Corrado that he would be submitting his retirement papers asap.

" Pippo, I'm back."

" Capo. I'm surprised to hear your voice."

" I noticed you didn't say 'happy' or 'pleased' to hear my voice."

" You saw the raccomandata?"

" You mean the one on my desk? Right where you left it. How could I miss it? When I called you from Alba you told me that a raccomandata had arrived. You neglected to mention that Rosalba was divorcing me and you were moving in with her."

" I thought it best to not say anything. You were on a case."

" Speaking of which, what is this shit about SISDE taking over my investigation. I don't trust those bastards to blow me without taking a bite. Cretini!"

" They swarmed in here like a bunch of fucking ultras." Italy had its own nasty equivalent to the football hooligans in the U.K. and elsewhere.

" What were they looking for, Pippo?"

" Anything to do with the poisoned wines and all the other stuff you were looking into. They took everything."

" Cazzo di merda!" Calling someone a dick-faced piece of shit always made Corrado feel like a twelve year old. "Who's in charge now? I read that Bambone's under house arrest."

" His number two's been around here a few times."

" Moscatelli! He couldn't find his ass with a road map and a steamshovel. I tell you, Pippo, I'm putting in my papers today. You can have this porca madosca of a job and my puttana of a wife, as well. I'm done. Finito!"

On the fifth of September 1995, Rahul Veena, the U.S. Attorney for the Southern District of New York, indicted the Community Alliance of Boravitcher Organizations, Inc. (CABO) and Claude Raymonde Wizman, Léon Mojze Drei, Sami Henri Drei, Allen Gary Katz, Ruud Lodewijk Kluytmans and Gianfranco Fabbri on 137 counts of racketeering conspiracy, securities fraud, mail fraud, and wire fraud using the Federal Racketeer Influenced and Corrupt Organization Act(RICO). Not surprisingly, Heskel Milstein and Solomon Baum were not mentioned in the indictment. Persons of their wealth and influence rarely are.

One week prior to the indictments, two men lost their lives in a light plane crash just outside of Aspen, Colorado. The bodies of the former Navy pilot and his passenger were charred beyond recognition. *The Builder* was ultimately identified by comparing the dental records of Claude Wizman, who'd chartered the Beechcraft A36 Bonanza, to x-rays kept, for some unexplained reason, in Shmuel Zipstein's office.

In late September 1995, an individual resembling the *late* Claude Wizman successfully ~~blackmailed~~ convinced Heskel Milstein and Solomon Baum to fund his new operation by merely mentioning to them, the fact that he'd visited with a certain Mr. White. Junior had revealed, in confidence, an interesting sidenote to the mystery disappearance of Jimmy Hoffa.

Although Baum and Milstein were never charged by U.S. Attorney Rahul Veena with a crime, the Boravitchers had been disgraced. Mainstream media with their 24/7 news cycle soon turned them into yesterday's headline. With the Grand Rebbe's refusal to name a successor, and the evidence and blame for the diabolical master plan cleverly dropped on the head of a dead man, *The Builder's* prescient bugging of Milstein's office had paid off in spades.

Milstein, Baum and a certain Mr. White, retired in Florida, were clearly responsible for the disappearance of Jimmy Hoffa. That was a powerful piece of information to have in one's possession. Information that threatened to destroy the Mekler Group, whose headquarters in Geneva, Switzerland sat atop the Teamster's remains.

and then, in...

2010

Paul Curatone, the Republican candidate for Governor of New York, smiled and accepted the warm round of applause from the Orthodox Jewish leaders gathered to hear him speak. In his address, Curatone promised to veto any legislation that permitted gay marriage and boasted of the fact that he would not march in New York City's Gay Pride parade.

At the edge of the room, Leland Sorker applauded along with the rest of the men, mostly Hasidic, in attendance. Sorker, according to his publicist, personally loathed this kind of hateful rhetoric. However, he was satisfied knowing that this patsy of a candidate, Curatone, was continuing to inflict damage to his own campaign. His bid for the Governor's office was tanking in every poll taken within the past two weeks. By election day he would be safely behind by 15 or 20 percentage points. On the other hand, his opponent was a man who listened well. Listened to Leland Sorker, as did the three term mayor of New York City, Steven Baum. As did Livio Falanghini, the three time Prime Minister of Italy; as did

Bertrand de Chassy, the embattled President of France. One month before, these two European leaders made a dramatic announcement. They would take their countries out of the eurozone and if pressured to do so, out of the European Union. This had an immediate effect on the value of the euro and anyone selling the currency short stood to make a staggering amount of money.

Eighteen years prior, on September 17,1992, Claude Wizman had begun an in depth study of the master currency trader George Soros. Soros had bet 10 billion dollars against the U.K. Pound the previous day and won. It was now Sorker's turn. He, like his *alter ego,* had meticulously laid the groundwork over four decades and now, at the age of 64, he had achieved his dream. This *Bangladeshi,* Sorker, a mysterious recluse, who some said was merely fronting for an unnamed Saudi prince, held sway over much of the financial world. Was it a co-incidence that Soros was the exact same age as Leland Sorker when he broke the Bank of England?

At 6:00 a.m., Celestine, one of the island ladies that Wolfie Flanken had "inherited" when he purchased Mary's Boon, knocked on the door to the room that the two owners of the hotel kept for themselves. It was a place to relax, shower and watch CNN in the off hours. The hours before breakfast and after dinner. Wolfie was lying on the bed enjoying the coolness of the early morning. Harald Helm, his companion of twenty-two years, preferred the beach. He'd recently returned to painting after a brief time-out, following their move from Germany to Sint Maarten. The island was divided in two. The Dutch side held little interest for Harald. He preferred the chic French towns and villages and the restaurants, bars and beaches. Wolfie just shrugged and mixed up another batch of cosmos.

" Mister Wolf, policeman here to see you."

" Tell him I'll be there in a minute."

" Good good, Mister Wolf." Celestine returned to the officer who often flirted with her at the supermarket. Her enormous butt was a source of pride and greatly admired by the local fellas.

" Inspector Carty, you're up early today. Or is this just the end of your evening?"

Wolfie liked this man and felt he was one of the few professionals among the local police.

" When town is asleep, thief is on the prowl."

" So true. When I was on the job in Germany, I preferred to work at night. The bad guys were much easier to find in the dark."

" Do you miss it? Is that what this is about?"

Wolfie laughed. It was true that he sometimes wished that he was still a detective. He noticed things. It was his nature. And he'd noticed something that he wanted to share with this very capable policeman.

" Cyril, I'm wondering about the security precautions for this summit meeting they're having on the French side. These VIP's are going to land right at my door."

He gestured towards the entrance to the hotel which faced the airport. The single runway was no more than 20 meters from Wolfie's front gate.

" Would it not be easy for someone to stand right there with a rocket launcher and blow the shit out of any plane that was taxiing by? They go so slowly past here, even I could hit a 747...and I'm an old man with terrible eyesight."

" Wolfie, something tells me that you could still handle yourself pretty well. But, I see what you're saying."

" Especially on this island. No offence, but you can't control the guns and whatever else comes in here. It's an acknowledged fact. I could bring anything I want in my luggage or send cargo through the port. I could sail a boat here and swim ashore with a goddamn bazooka if I wanted to."

" So you think someone might set up in your parking lot and take aim at one of these big shots? A big shot for a big shot," roared Cyril Carty.

" I'm serious. You're going to have the President of the United States here in two days time along with our German Chancellor. Even the Chinese are coming. I read in the paper that the President of France is due to land right after Mrs. Merkel. Come on Cyril. I'm here all day, every day and I haven't spotted one single security team from any of these countries. Not a single person here to make sure this perimeter is secure. And believe me, I can recognize these people very easily. I know a good many of them personally. It's a disgrace."

" So what do you suggest I do? Call the U.S. Secret Service and the KGB and tell them how to do their jobs?"

" It's SVR now, not KGB."

" We have an expression here, my friend. Make sure your brains are engaged before you put your mouth in motion. I assure you, these people have things under control. They been here for weeks already. Sure enough."

" O.K. Cyril, it's your island. I only thought..."

" So you want to help me? That's fine. I accept your offer. You know..."

" I know. You have an expression here."

They both laughed. The two men shook hands and agreed to have lunch the following day. Kapitän Wolfgang Flanken, retired Chefdetektiv, felt invigorated. He wasn't sure why he was doing this but it felt good to him.

Baglione waited for the water to warm before stepping into the terracotta tiled shower. In the intense heat of the morning he looked forward to the slightly less than body temperature trickle to drip over his tired body. Last night's "girlfriend" had just left the one room studio apartment that he leased in Bangkok Noi. The Chao Phraya river, alive with long-tail boats, river taxis and tugs pulling their strings of enormous barges loaded down with sand and coal, never failed to charm the retired policeman. After Vanessa had dumped him for a rich guy and his divorce from Rosalba was final, Corrado put in his retirement papers, secured his pension and set out on a trip to Southeast Asia that changed his life forever. He'd never been anywhere like this. Neither the chaotic south of Italy where he'd grown up, nor Roma where he'd worked for his entire adult life had prepared him for the tumultuous multi-ringed circus that was Bangkok. He hadn't come for the sex tourism that his colleagues had ribbed him about, although he did avail himself on occasion. He'd come to forget, to try and put his sad life in Italy behind him. The retired policeman's mobile phone vibrated and came to life. His ringtone always made him smile.

"o bella ciao, bella ciao, bella ciao ciao ciao."
He recognized the country code. It was Wolfie Flanken, calling from Sint Maarten.

" Wolfie, what a nice surprise,"

" Baglione, how soon can you get here?"

One day earlier, at the start of the G8 summit meeting in St. Martin, Kapitän Wolfgang Flanken(retired), wearing the four-pointed Golden Star, presented to him by the German government, in his lapel, stood next to Cyril Carty. They were two rows behind Bertrand de Chassy and Barack Obama.

Unbelievably, he'd spotted someone who made him shudder. Badly scarred face, dark glasses, but unmistakable - it was Jörg Bissel. He was standing to one side of an elegantly dressed older gentleman, with a salt and pepper beard. An unlit pipe between his lips. This man looked supremely confident in a pale salmon, Loro Piana summer weight sweater. After the Euro had crashed, Leland Sorker and his forty-one billion dollar fortune, was front page news. Wolfie recognized him from the TV and it all began to make sense. Sorker, "king of the currency markets," and the fourth wealthiest person in the world, just below Warren Buffet and well above a pair of Indian industrialists, was truly a man of mystery. To the retired Chefdetektiv it was now obvious. This Sorker was, in fact, Claude Wizman. Neither Baglione nor Flanken had been allowed to pursue their investigations. The brain behind the Machiavellian scheme to control the most powerful force in the universe, the food chain, was standing directly in front of him. He might be Leland Sorker to everyone else. To Flanken and Baglione, he was the man who got away with murder.

MESSIAH END NOTES

esteemed readers ... this group of notes, anecdotes, and thoughts is not, I repeat, not a wiki. The various *'pedias, 'hows, 'travels, 'leaks,* etc. do a fine job of explaining things and I urge you to consult them for more relevant information. The following are merely musings on various mentions in my book. Read them at your leisure and enjoy them for what they are.

Cortese ... this grape, local to the Alto Monferrato, is a favorite. In fact, it's my go-to white for many reasons. It's easy drinking, refreshing and cheap. It's made in a few different styles. They're all delicious. Actually, there are a few crappy examples. But they're even cheaper and none of them will give you a headache. Cortese, in purezza(100% cortese) is the exact same grape that makes a much better known wine called Gavi. Same grape, same terroir, same everything. Except the price! In fact, I have friends whose vineyards are, literally, just across a country lane from Gavi producers but they cannot call their wines Gavi for bullshit reasons that I won't go into here. There are also blends with sauvignon or chardonnay that can be fabulous. My daily drinker is one of them. It's called *Bionda* and is made by my buds at Gaggino winery, three minutes from my house in Ovada.

Arneis ... this grape, from over near Alba, is getting some good play these days. It's usually delicious (if the winemaker doesn't go overboard with oak) and is a vino autoctono – which means that it's native to the area. VALDINERA is a good small producer that I've known for years.

Ca' del Bosco Brut ... expensive pinonero(pinot noir) sparkler from Franciacorta - well made and makes a *bella figura*(a good impression) when you show up at a dinner party carrying a cold one. BTW – always show up with a chilled bottle. It makes it difficult for your host to squirrel it away for another occasion!

Mascarello '82 ... a legendary Barolo from an old master. He's passed but I'll always remember him fondly for the *vaffanculo* he gave to the Barolo modernists in the 80's and 90's. One label read No Barrique(french oak barrels), No Berlusconi(oy vey).

Gavi ... alright – I admit it's a great white(wine-not shark) from my area in Italy. But please don't forget *little* ~~bimbo~~ *cortese!* Anybody see the 1927 film, Chang? On second thought- disregard the stupid reference.

cardo from the Monferrato ... this celery shaped thing looks like something you'd find in a dumpster behind a fruit and vegetable market. However, it's really wonderful to eat with bagna cauda and the best ones come from Gobbi, near Nizza Monferrato.

poulet de Bresse ... not a bad little chicken. For some reason, these birds are sold *gift-wrapped* in upscale markets in Italy at Christmas time with the head, feet and feathers still attached - with a stupid bow tied around their necks!

Punt e Mes ... a classic Piemontese vermouth and the first sexy aperitivo(aperitif) that I started my drinking career with back in the day. I thought it was so much cooler than ordering a Campari. Just a younger me - acting like a shmuck. Campari is equally fab – and made just a 25 minute ride from Ovada in Novi Ligure. However, if you really want to wow your geeky friends, search for a new vermouth made in Silvano d'Orba (10 minutes away) by Distilleria Gualco.

green lentils from Puy(lentilles du Puy) ... amazing stuff. Find these and cook them. A bit more expensive – but they're still just fucking lentils. You won't need to stick-up a liquor store to afford them!

Comté Fort Saint-Antoine from the Jura ... forget about supermarket Gruyere, forget about Emmenthal, forget about Jarlsberg, forget about swiss cheese. This puppy puts the shizzle in my dizzle. Props, Dogg.

Boutignane Corbières ... totally delicious red from the much sneered at Languedoc-Roussillon region of southern France. When you've lived and worked in Asia for as long as I have, recognizing the good, cheap French plonk on the chalkboard becomes all important.

Quiberons ... oysters from Atlantic Brittany

Cancales ... oysters from Brittany, as well. Cancale calls itself "the oyster capital of Brittany" which must come as a shock to the people of Belon. Speaking of shellfish, we once ate a creature identified as a *violet* in the lovely French city of Sete. Let me put it this way. It was not a pleasant experience. The American Thanksgiving dinner at our friendìs house in Barbaste the following day was one long race to the loo. Or maybe it was the kilo of Roquefort we consumed in Roquefort on the way to turkey day!

Pineau d'Aunis ... I'm not a wine snob. I'm a wine lover. This grape, unrelated to Pinot, is flyin' way under the radar – even if Eric Asimov crowed about it in The New York Times. Drink it to enjoy – not to get drunk. It's a low-alcohol surpriser from the Loire Valley and should satisfy any wine geek on your guest list.

Crottin de Chavignol and a Sainte-Maure de Touraine ... God, you gotta' love France! Rule #1-eat cheese when you're drinking wine. Rule#2-find a reputable cheese monger and frequent it often. The people behind the counter will always steer you in the right direction. Like these two cheeses from the Loire. We're fortunate, in Ovada, to have the Bottega del Formagg e del Salam(cheese and cured meats) - a true national treasure of a shop.

Louis Métaireau '91 Sèvre-et-Maine ... this family-run winery defines the category. Yes, it's delicious with shellfish. Yes, it's delicious with shellfish. Yes ... have I made myself clear?

Porcini and ovoli nostrani ... wild mushroom season(autumn) in Ovada is total madness. It dominates the conversation, appears on every menu, clogs the forests with hunters carrying *cestini* (wicker baskets) and pretty much causes a free for all when the first ones appear in the outdoor markets. Porcini are the alpha males, but ovoli ... ovoli are the true royalty. Orange in color, they're best eaten raw, sliced and drizzled with good olive oil and a pinch of salt and pepper. I'll occasionally give them a spritz of Riviera or Amalfi lemon if there's one in the house.

Balestrino ... a beautiful olive growing town near Savona - waay waay up in the mountains overlooking the Italian Riviera. There's a guy named Ronco who does all things olive. The brand is Lotus ... and the *madonna of something* has been spotted over 125 times in this lovely village!

Silvano d'Orba ... the next hill town from Ovada, it has a castle, a some decent bars and two outstanding makers of grappa(Barile and Gualco). Worth a stop at either. Careful if you're driving. The Carabinieri will not be amused! You've been warned.

Cantine del Gavi ... a nice place to have a meal in a just okay town. If you want old school ambiance come to Ovada. If you love to drink Gavi wines, it's worth a visit. It's why we first came to this part of Italy.

Gancia, Cuvée del Fondatore ... this is a legendary wine I used to like a lot. Something's happened to it. Maybe it's just me, but it tastes different than it used to. Perhaps it's due to the Gancia family selling the business to Russians.

Muscat Lo Triolet ... a nice easy drinker from Val D'Aosta. Not sweet, as are many of its cousins, it's dry and austere just like the Valdostani – an interesting mountain people who remain stubbornly independent from the rest of Italy. Not such a bad idea given the dismal politicians we seem to elect over and over again. Hey, talkin' about you, Silvio.

Ovada ... I'm from New York, work all over the world and live in Ovada. Although many of the locals don't see it, it's a great unpolished, thousand year old jewel. Its centro storico(historic center) has barely changed in all those years. People tell me that it's because the Ovadese are really cheap ... so everything remains the same. Even the little graffiti that's around is old. And many of the residents are old. And the ruling party is old. They've been around in one form or another since the end of the second world war. Ex-commies in Gucci loafers. We love everything about it and hope you do too!

lardo from Biella ... oh lardo, we love you for so many reasons. You are delicious, thinly sliced, and eaten with a piece of bread. You melt beautifully when topping a foccaccino(puffed pizza dough) straight from the wood oven. But most importantly, we adore you because you are 100% pig fat and it's so much fun to serve it to Americans and then tell them what they're eating.

Tagliolo ... a lovely castle town, overlooking Ovada. It's noted for its wines and for agnolotti(ravioli's elegant cousin from a few kilometers over) splashed with a glass of dolcetto. The castle, property of the family of the Marchese di Tagliolo (our dear friend Luca), is breathtakingly beautiful.

Barbera ... Piemonte's original red wine(first cultivated in the 700's). I confess. It's my numero uno fave wine in the world. It's made in many styles(from light, fruity and slightly sparkling to thick, oaked and highly alcoholic). The Godfather of good Barbera was Giacamo Bologna. His family continues the tradition. There are several great producers from around my 'hood. I'm a lucky guy. Hunt for one you like. They're readily available . My top choice locals are in the €5-10 range.

Dolcetto ... the grape that made Ovada famous. Not actually famous, yet. But on the way to gaining the recognition that it deserves. I owned a restaurant for many years in the U.S. The kitchen was Piemontese / Liguria with a wine list consisting of 250 labels - limited to Piemonte ... and maybe a champagne or two. We had two pages of dolcetti alone! Even though my staff was well versed and really enjoyed the wines, it was a tough sale. Why? For Americans, dolcetto was confused with dolce (like dolce vita), dulce (like dulce de leche) or dulcet (like dulcet tones). In other words, people thought it was sweet. When, in fact, the word *dolcetto* derives from the dialect word "dusset," which are rolling hills. The grape thrives in Ovada for a few reasons. The first, and most important, is that we can't plant nebbiolo and make barolo or barbaresco. It's against the rules. So we use our best vineyard sites for dolcetto ... rather than in the neighboring Langhe which plants the big money vines in the choicest plots. Secondly, our terroir is fantastic for the dolcetto grape. In 2008, the local producers obtained the coveted DOCG (**D**enominazione di **O**rigine **C**ontrollato e **G**arantita) and created a new classificationfor the grape, named simply *Ovada DOCG*. Italy, being Italy, this garantita(guarantee) assures the consumer that not only is it what it's supposed to be by law ... it *really is* what it's supposed to be! Aah, Italia. BTW, there are many, many other wines in Piemonte made from dolcetto. Except for Dogliani (also DOCG) they're sometimes unexciting - but relatively cheap and very drinkable.

Carpeneto and its castle ... this is another of the charming hill towns that surround Ovada. There are 12 – each with a castle. This is unique in all of Europe and has led to the Monferrato being designated a UNESCO world heritage site. There are some really good wines being made in Carpeneto, as well. All of these towns are under the Ovada DOCG umbrella.

Furmagetta ... a Piemontese dialect word most probably derived from the word *formaggio*(cheese). It's eaten very fresh, comes in many varieties and appears at table various times throughout the day. The most famous is *robiola di Roccaverano*, a combination of unpasturized sheep's milk and/or goat's milk or cow's milk which is made near Acqui Terme in the Alto Monferrato region of Piemonte. A particular version that it most wonderful is 100% goat and made by Benedetta Rebora at Cascina dell'Isadora just outside Ovada.

passito ... dislike sweet wines? These babies will change your mindset. Not to be confused with dessert wines like Brachetto or Moscato, *passiti* are specially selected grapes, dried for several months and then slowly and gently pressed to produce a concentrated, sweet, grapey-honey elixir that will entice you from the first sip. In the Alto Monferrato, small producers abound. I think the best are from Scaglione in Loazzolo.

brioche, more like a croissant ... breakfast is not really a serious meal in Italy. A bread or pastry and coffee is about it. Maybe a ciggy or two(grazie davehagerman). And a brioche is not really a brioche – like in France. Mon dieu, le scandale! It's more like a crappy frozen croissant – unless you're eating them in Torino or in the south of Italy – where they're called *cornetti* or in Sicilia where they're split and filled with gelato. A fucking gelato sandwich – for breakfast. God, you gotta' love Italy.

Pasticceria Zoccola Alessandria ... this *old school* pasticceria is famous for their cannoli. They are a whole other thing than the cannoli you're probably thinking about. Those are from the south. These are from the very properly northern province of Alessandria. Zoccola has been around since 1806. The pastry is a small, crispy, cream filled *bomba atomica*. Your first bite will be one to remember. Try all the flavors. Pick up an assortment and ring my doorbell. Grazie.

Delamain Tres Venerable ... if you're like me, you've lied so many times about how much you enjoy scotch, bourbon and the like. Cognac, Armagnac, Calvados ... they all taste nasty. Some less than others. Or perhaps you think I'm an idiot. My wife loves them all and sometimes does think I'm an idiot. So there. I've proved my point. BTW, this one is pretty good.

Mastroberardino Lacryma Rosso ... actually, Lacryma Christi del Vesuvio Rosso DOC. Aside from the whole *tears of Christ* thing, it's a delicious red wine (piedirosso is the grape) from the volcanic soils of Mount Vesuvius. A classic example from southern Italy, its importer in the U.S. (talkin' about you, Winebow) recommends it with spaghetti and meatballs. You can't get more Italo-Americano than that!

Nocillo di Sorrento ... Italians really like liquors made from nuts. Maybe because their grandparents always made them at home. This one is made from walnuts, is extremely aromatic(and alcoholic) and is drunk in celebration of San Giovanni Battista at the end of June.

Sabrett cart ... dirty water hot dogs, anyone? Classic New York street food – before there was "*streetfood.*" I always ordered two with everything (not to be confused with a Dalai Lama dog – which is one with everything) and sat on a park bench enjoying them – more often than not, after smokin' a spliff. Wash it down with a Yoo-hoo. Priceless.

Kukicha ... my dear friend Kohei Katsura once brought us this tea from Japan. It's unique in that it's made not only from tea leaves but also from the stems and twigs of the plant. Said to be ideal for a macrobiotic diet. But don't hold that against it. It tastes amazing.

bagels & lox/sable & whitefish/baked farmer cheese/bialys & bulkas ... I'm not going to waste your time here. If you're old school New York Jewish, you know what I'm talking about. If you're not – please go to Russ & Daughters when you're in the 'hood or check out their website. And please don't give me that whiny "I'm from L.A." or I'm from Montreal" yadda, yadda. Sorry to offend you.

MESSIAH GLOSSARY

Jackie Baker It was Jaki Byard, a multi/instrumentalist, composer arranger and educator that Axel was referring to. He'd played with Eric Dolphy, Charles Mingus and many other noted jazz artists, and recorded 35 albums as a leader. Byard's death in early 1999, from a gunshot wound, remains an unsolved homicide.

Hai fame? Are you hungry? (Italian)

Sempre Always (Italian)

salmone affumicato smoked salmon (Italian)

feca a curious slang spoken along the Rio Plata in Argentina and Uruguay that scrambles syllables for no apparent reason. Thus *café(coffee)* becomes *feca* just to fuck with us!

maricon derogatory term for *homosexual* (Spanish)

Dispénseme Excuse me? (Spanish)

scimmia ape (Italian)

Moshiach Messiah (Hebrew)

MITH in 1986, several people died from drinking inexpensive wines from Piemonte that had been adulterated with methyl alcohol (MITH).

d.b. dead body

Rebbe rabbi (Yiddish)

Porca miseria! Literally, *miserable pig* ... but used colloquially as an all purpose exclamation of disgust or surprise. Variations that you will encounter in this book include *porca troia* (pig whore), *porca eva* (Eve, like Adam & Eve), the dreaded *porca madonna* (the virgin Mary is a pig) and *porco zio,* which twists the meaning even further by substituting zio (uncle) for dio (god).

stronzi assholes (Italian)

Dio cantante! Like the porca/porca exclamations cited previously, Italians use the word *dio* (god) in a colorful series of expletives like *dio cane* (god is a dog). Some think it a sin so they bend the rules a bit by substituting *dio cantante* (god is a singer)*, porca disco, porca madosca, porca* maremma (a seaside area in Toscana – say what?), dio *caro,* dio *bono* and dozens of others. Up until 1999 many of these were prosecutable as public blasphemies.

Union Cooperative de Viticulteurs Muscadet a French wine growers cooperative for the Muscadet grape

boychik term of endearment for young man (Yiddish)

Porco zio! Yet another *porco*

Vaffanculo fuck you (Italian)

buongustaio a gourmet (Italian)

Buongiorno, capo Good morning, boss (Italian)

Speriamo let's hope (Italian)

Give you the horns, capo one of the worst affronts to an Italian's manhood is to refer to him as *cornuto* by extending the index and pinkie fingers straight up (the horns). It means that your wife is fucking everyone ... but you!

Parigi Paris (Italian)

Biglietto, signore Ticket, sir

capotreno head conductor

Mi dispiace I'm sorry

fratello bro' (Italian)

Vabbè short for "va bene" - means o.k. (Italian)

Cretino cretin (Italian)

ICRF **I**spettorato **C**entrale **R**epressions **F**rodi ... Italian sub-agency for food & wine fraud and quality control

Ministero delle Risorse Agricole, Alimentari e Forestali Department of Agriculture, Food / Wine and Forests

Paris, Gare de Lyon Lyon Train Station, Paris (French)

Quattrocento Italians refer to each century in an interesting way. *Quattrocento,* literally, *four hundred*, is actually the 1400's ... which everyone else knows is the 15th Century ... Aah Italia! (Italian)

Terrone a person of the earth (or dirt farmer) is a derogatory term for someone from the south of Italy ... kind of like a *redneck.*

vip obvious meaning but pronounced *veep* in italian

payess uncut sideburns of orthodox Jewish men and boys

farkakte crazy or screwed up (Yiddish)

k'vetsh whine or complain (Yiddish)

schvartzes demeaning term for black people (Yiddish)

Buonasera. Sono Baglione Good evening. I'm Baglione

Puis-je vous acheter une bière, mon oncle? Can I buy you a beer, uncle?

GAAT General **A**greement on **T**ariffs and **T**rade was a multilateral agreement signed in by 23 countries in 1947 under the auspices of the United Nations. It was essentially replaced by the **W**orld **T**rade **O**rganization in 1994.

kibbutz agricultural, "live on the land," collective communities in Israel

meshuval a kosher wine that has been pasturized

kashrut the formalized set of Jewish religious dietary laws (rules)

Knesset Israel's parliament

saucisson thick, dry-cured sausage (French)

rillettes prepared meat or fish, heavily salted and slowly cooked in fat

Fiamme Gialle Italy financial police force...aka Guardia di Finanza

spumantino small glass of spumante...a *not sweet* sparkling wine

senti listen up (Italian)

Belin In the dialect of Genova (Genoa), it's one of dozens of slang words in Italian for penis. Mostly used to exclaim "what the fuck!" (Zeneise dialect)

puttana prostitute (Italian)

Gazzetta dello Sport Italy's daily sports newspaper

Grazie per niente ... Niente, grazie Thanks for nothing ... an exchange of fuck you's (Italian)

Buongiorno. Posso mangiare? Good day. Can I eat? (Italian)

Poi? Anything more? (Italian)

Secondo literally, *second plate*...not to be confused with the American, *main course* (Italian)

Strepitoso extraordinary ... when referring to food (Italian)

Molto gentile very kind of you (Italian)

Fiumicino Rome's International Airport ... also called *Leonardo da Vinci*

Boh' a very Italian exclamation which, in this context, means *I don't know*

citta city (Italian)

tabaccaio old fashioned name for a place that sold tobacco(and salt and various kinds of stamps ... both postal and bureaucratic). Lottery tickets have replaced the salt, but the rest remains pretty much as it once was.

Braccia corte literally *short arms* ... but really refers to someone who is cheap – someone whose hands don't reach their pockets

produttori producers of ... (Italian)

Dimmi tell me (Italian)

parcheggio parking spot

multa a penalty, a fine

centro center of town (Italian)

polenta cake also called *polenta di ovada...a* sweet dessert resembling a mound of polenta, it's covered in cornmeal and filled with chocolate cream

Fame hungry (Italian)

Bianco o nero? Used in the Monferrato areas of Piemonte, it's a colloquial way of saying white *or red wine* (Italian)

Gran bel culo, eh? Great ass, no? (Italian)

Si. Vero. Yes, it's true

Primo literally, *first course* ... when referring to a meal. It follows *antipasto* and precedes *secondo*

Fatto in casa a dish made at home ... or in a restaurant (Italian)

Funghi freschi fresh picked mushrooms ... almost always wild (Italian) Kindle

Certo certainly (Italian)

e portami un bicchiere and bring me a glass (Italian)

Oy a veytik chaz meir! a catastrophe (Yiddish)

Vishtayz? Do you understand (Yiddish)

disastro disaster (Italian)

Strada dei Vini a designated tourist route for wine lovers

titolare owner of a business (Italian)

tuttofare a worker who does a little of everything ... a handyman

Va bene O.K. Fine

clima climate (Italian)

Deliziosi, these acciughe Delicious, these anchovies ... floured and fried, in this case (Italian)

Squisito exquisite (Italian)

guardaroba a piece of furniture often called a *wardrobe* (Italian)

Egregio Commissario, a formal way of beginning a note or letter ... like remarkable *sir* ... in this case, "honorable police official" (Italian)

grazie e cari saluti thanks and best regards(Italian)

Talmud the central text of Judaism (Hebrew)

Grand Rebbe the leader of a Hasidic(ultra-orthodox Jewish) dynasty (Yiddish)

macchiato *stained* coffee ... an espresso with a drop of foamed milk (Italian)

Figurati think nothing of it (Italian)

Poverino poor little person (Italian)

Odense a small city in Denmark with a Jewish population that suffered during the Nazi occupation.

bigliette da visita business card or calling card (Italian)

L.I.R.R. **L**ong **I**sland **R**ail **R**oad

Küss mein Arsch Kiss my ass! (German)

Eretz Yisrael Volunteer Ambulance an emergency ambulance service that is pointedly respectful of the religious and cultural needs of Orthodox Jewish communities

Mister Softee iconic forerunner of street food trucks ... serving frozen custard

meyn ahzes ponim my impudent fellow ... a derogatory term (Yiddish)

HaShem the act of thanking god (Hebrew)

ebreo ortodosso orthodox Jew (Italian)

Don't pull my chain here colloquial way of saying "don't try to fool me"

Giovanna, vieni qui! Giovanna, come here! (Italian)

Cetara a picturesque fishing village in the province of Salerno, Italy

E la moglie? Napulitana, anche? And your wife? Also from Naples? (Napolitano dialect)

Scampia a troubled suburb of Napoli (Naples)

Peggio worse

ma cche staje faccen'? O ppane? Literally, *what are you doing, making bread?* It really means, *what's taking you so long? (Napolitano dialect)*

guagliù? anyone? (Napolitano dialect)

Che palle! What balls! (Italian)

cucina 'Nnapulitana' Naples style food (Napolitano dialect)

Ach du meine Güte! Good grief! (German)

O furastère. Albanese a foreigner ... Albanian (Napolitano dialect)

Sul serio? seriously (Italian)

Ogne strunzo tene 'o fummo suio literally, every asshole releases its own smoke (Napolitano dialect)

Napule Naples (Napolitano diallect)

hajji generally derogatory term for Arabs used by members of the U.S. military

Temazepam drug used for treating anxiety ... also a strong sleep aid

Donnerwetter! Wau. Well, I'll be damned! (German)

Mario Cuomo popular three term governor of New York State

tsores trouble (Yiddish)

würstel uncured sausage or hotdog (Italian)

verrückt crazy / insane (German)

Hundekuchen dog biscuit (German)

PBA Patrolmen's **B**enevolent **A**ssociation ... labor union representing New York City police officers

shul synagogue (Hebrew)

little pishers little *squirts* ... nobodies (Yiddish)

shmuck literally, a penis ... in reality, a dickhead

mamzer a bastard ... an untrustworthy person (Yiddish)

Jörg, ich würde sagen ... du bist erledigt. I would say you're done (German)

quaglia quail (Italian)

shikse derogatory term for non-Jewish girl or woman (Yiddish)

Dumnezeule! My goodness! (Romany)

Sheka shit (Romany)

shittern mogn literally, a loose bowel movement (Yiddish)

Hoffa Jimmy Hoffa was a powerful, American labor leader, who mysteriously disappeared in 1975

grober coarse, uncouth person (Yiddish)

a chorbyn - a shit! (Yiddish)

Ya'Jush? Are you Jewish?

shvartzes derogatory term for black people (Yiddish)

Gey gezunderheit In good health (Yiddish)

Vishtez? Understand? (Yiddish)

alter kockers derogatory term for *old men* (Yiddish)

Jiddischer Sprecher? Do you speak Yiddish? (Yiddish)

Kaynahorah literally, *the evil eye.* Saying *it* protects a person from *it.* (Yiddish)

Me, got tsu danken Thanks to god (German)

Made in the USA
San Bernardino, CA
17 October 2017